SAMANTHA SHREVES

Journey of the Heart: The way we break, The way we heal

For the ones who never said it out loud.
For the quiet survivors, the ones who smile through the ache,
the ones who thought they had to carry it alone.
For every soul that's cracked but still standing,
every heart searching for peace,
every voice learning to believe it deserves to be heard—
this is for you.
And to the One who saw us in our shadows and stayed,
who writes mercy into the mess,
who makes broken things whole again—
Jesus, this story is Yours.

Contents

Content Disclaimer

This book contains sensitive themes that may be distressing to some readers. While fictional, the story engages with real-world issues related to trauma, mental health, emotional abuse, and spiritual exploration. It is intended to bring awareness, foster empathy, and offer a message of hope and healing.

Throughout the narrative, readers may encounter emotionally intense scenes and subject matter, including but not limited to:

- Mental health struggles
- Emotional, Physical, and Psychological Trauma
- Questions of identity, faith, and personal healing
- Depictions of strong emotional breakdowns and recovery

This story is written with care and intentionality, with the goal of providing insight, not harm. Reader discretion is advised.

Recommended for mature teen and adult audiences. If you or someone you know is experiencing emotional distress or trauma, please consider seeking support from a trusted individual or licensed professional. You are not alone. There is help, and there is hope.

Map

Arts Building

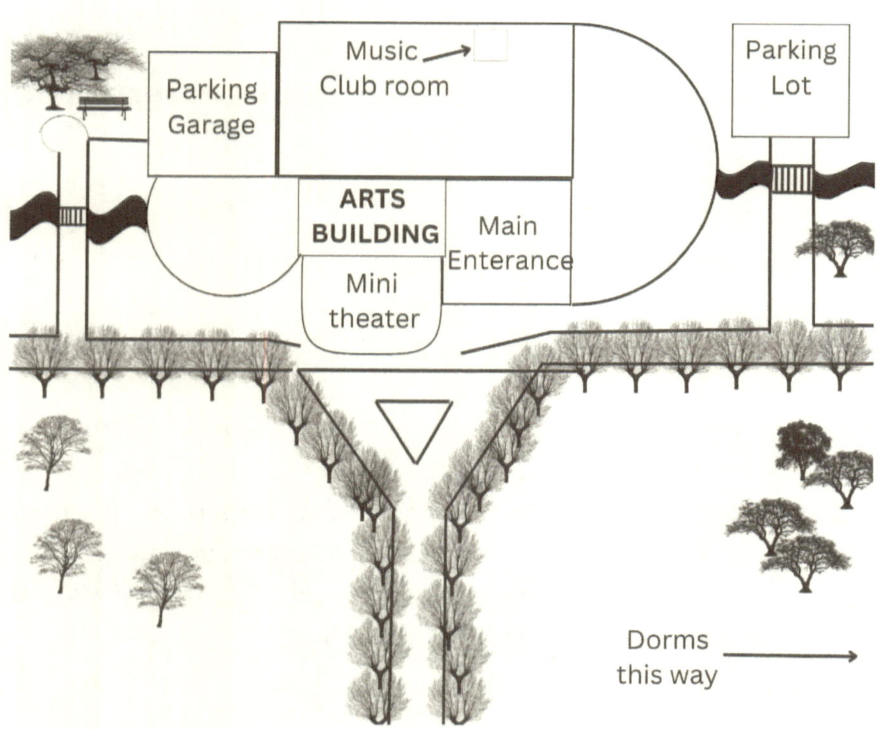

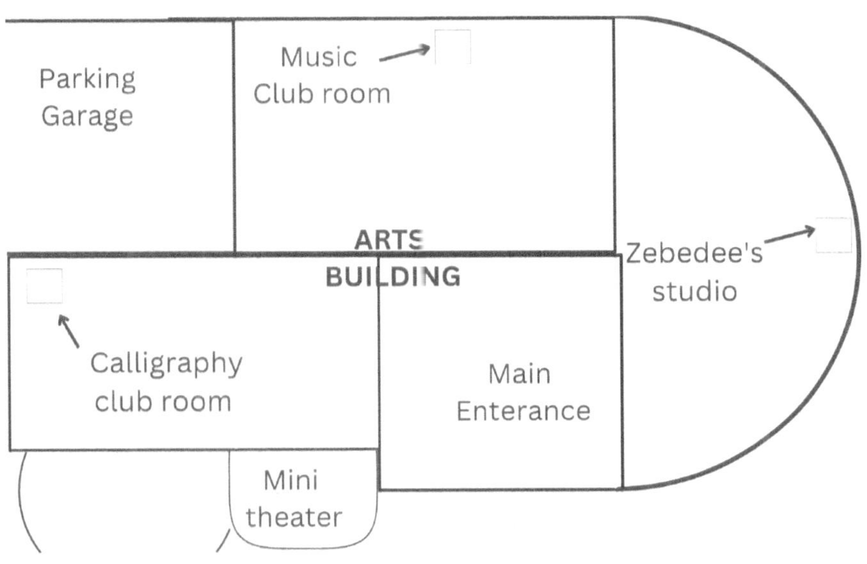

Parking Garage
Music Club room
ARTS BUILDING
Zebedee's studio
Calligraphy club room
Main Enterance
Mini theater

Music Club
Arts Building
Arts Parking Lot
Parking Garage
Main Entrance
Mini Theater
West Parking Lot
East Parking Lot
Dorms →

Dorms

Dorm parking
SCB parking
Dorm parking
Female Dorm building
Shared common building (SCB)
Male Dorm building

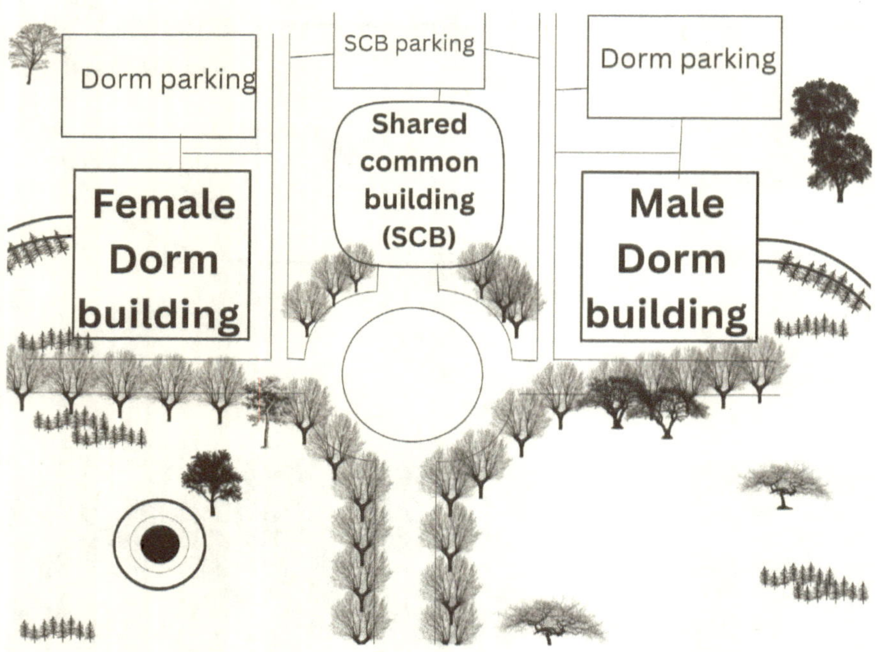

SCB Parking
Shared Common Building
(SCB)
Female Dorm Building
Male Dorm Building
Dorm Parking
Dorm Parking
Dorm Parking
Dorm Parking

SCB Parking
Shared Common Building
SCB)
Female Dorm Building
Male Dorm Building
Dorm Parking
Dorm Parking
Dorm Parking
Dorm Parking

INTRO: *Amerei*

Amerei never meant to stand out. But somehow, without trying, she became part of something unforgettable.

Her first year at university was a whirlwind of awkward hellos, midnight snacks, and unexpected friendships. She came in quietly, more of an observer than a participant, but life had other plans.

She ended up rooming with Mita who wore sarcasm like armor and had more layers than a psychology textbook, but somehow, they clicked. Then came Odessa, sharp-tongued, stunning, and wildly confident. Leaving Andromeda, all precision and ambition, and could probably organize the stars if given the time.

They weren't supposed to work as a friend group. But they did.

It wasn't all perfect. The semester turned upside down when Reed, one of their first friends, got caught in a freak accident that left everyone shaken. Amerei stayed close, helping where she could, being the quiet, supportive kind; that was her thing. She didn't speak loudly, but when she was there, you felt it.

And somewhere between the chaos and coffee-fueled cramming sessions, she met Merrick Hughes.

Tall, composed, way too good looking for someone who knew how to fix a spreadsheet and charm an entire student council room. He wasn't just smart; he was calm, steady, and kind. The kind of person who didn't just notice people… he remembered them.

He noticed her.

He remembered *her.*

And maybe that was the most unexpected thing of all.

Amerei didn't plan to fall for someone. But then again, she hadn't planned for most of the things that made her first year unforgettable.

Chapter 1: Not the Loud Type

Amerei

Amerei still remembered the way the air smelled that day: freshly cut grass, fast food, and too much excitement packed into their side of campus.

Her first day at university had been… loud.

Not in volume, although yes, people were shouting and moving like caffeine-fueled ants, but she was talking about loudness in feeling. Everything felt like a lot. The buildings were big, the crowd was bigger, and her suitcase wheel kept squeaking like it was protesting as much as she was.

She wasn't used to crowds. Or chaos. Or too many introductions.

So naturally, when she was in her dorm, packing up her room and met the cool, sarcastic girl with the layered personality and unreadable eyes, Mita she panicked and made a joke about having tea parties with herself.

Not her best moment.

But Mita had laughed.

And that had been the first quiet crack in the wall she kept around herself.

Then came the others: Odessa with her high heels and sharper wit; Andromeda, who looked like she didn't breathe unless it was scheduled in her planner; and Reed, who showed up one day with messy hair and sunshine in his voice.

Somehow, they all stuck.

Amerei hadn't expected to find friends, especially so soon in the semester, because when she planted her feet on the soil of this institution for the first time, she came with the mindset to survive, not thrive. Thriving was for the people who had it all together, and Amerei wouldn't even dare to mention the characteristic and herself in an autobiography. Her plan to endure until graduation was to keep her head down, get good grades, and maybe, just maybe, learn how to be a little braver, but that wasn't high on the list of accomplishments.

But by the end of that first week, she'd learned three things:

1. College showers here had better water pressure than she expected.
2. Mita was the kind of friend who saw through your silences.
3. And Merrick Hughes existed.
4. (Which was… unfair, honestly. But she was not complaining.)

Looking back now, it was easy to laugh at how tightly she clung to her "introvert plan." No parties. No drama. No falling for anyone with cheekbones that could slice through paper.

Yeah.

That aged well.

Chapter 2: Something Like Full Circle

Amerei

Second year didn't feel as scary as the first.

Not anymore.

Amerei tugged her cardigan over her shoulders and glanced at herself in the mirror. Soft sage green, oversized just enough to feel like comfort. Paired with wide leg jeans and her usual low-rise sneakers. Hair half up, half down, her hair had grown a lot since her first year, when she had gotten a fresh chop. To her, at the time, her hair was supposed to symbolize a fresh start at college. With some simple gold studs in her ears, it was just her, no try hard energy, no pretending to be louder than she was.

She'd spent a year figuring out how to live in her skin in this new environment. Though it still didn't fit perfectly, it was better.

"You almost ready?" Mita's voice called from her room across the way, the door widely open, showing where she was digging for her boots like they were hiding on purpose.

"Yup," Amerei said, grabbing her cross-body bag and slipping her phone inside.

Mita stepped out a second later, pulling on a denim jacket over a fitted black top, her favorite heeled ankle boots giving her a few extra inches of height. Her high-waisted jeans that brought the entire outfit together. Her hair was tied back loosely, with a few strands falling out.

"You look cute," Amerei said, grinning.

Mita gave a mock twirl. "I try. Ready to go vibe with the coma king?"

They both winced at the dark joke, but it was Mita's way of coping, and Amerei got that.

Reed had been in a coma for nine months now. Nine months of visits, Mita's prayers, hopeful updates, and too many days that felt exactly the same. They all came when they could, but life happened. Summer had stretched long and lovely. Amerei had spent it mostly with Merrick, late-night drives, quiet brunches, mornings spent reading on park benches.

He'd graduated in May, but the student council had asked him back to help run the annual welcome events.

Mr. Perfect Boyfriend: Textbook 101. Still hers.

And today, the group had agreed to visit Reed together for the first time since summer break.

They met up just outside the front entrance of the hospital.

Odessa was already there, leaning against the stone wall, tapping through her phone with one hand and holding an iced coffee in the other. She wore wide-leg tailored pants in burnt orange, a cropped blazer over a silky tank top, and sleek heels. Her sunglasses sat on top of her head like a crown.

Next to her stood Andromeda, a med student but looking like a walking ad for "function meets fashion." She wore black cigarette pants, a neatly pressed button-down tucked in, and white sneakers so clean they looked brand-new; they most likely were. Her hair was in a tight bun, and a planner peeked from the tote on her arm.

"Look who finally showed up," Odessa teased as Mita and Amerei walked over.

"We like to make an entrance," Mita shot back, giving her a playful bump with her shoulder.

"Of what? Fashionably forgettable," Odessa said, sipping her coffee.

Andromeda rolled her eyes. "Can we go in before you two start a passive-aggressive showdown?"

They checked in, took the elevator up to the third floor, and walked quietly down the corridor. The moment always hit different at the door to Reed's room.

Inside, the familiar beeping and sterile white walls greeted them. Reed laid there just as he had all those months: peaceful, still, a little too quiet for someone who used to talk with his hands and laugh like the world was light.

They each grab a space to settle down on: Odessa grabbed for a chair, crossing her legs, and leaned against the back of it. Andromeda grabs one as well, sitting upright with her hands folded in her lap, while Mita flopped sideways into a recliner near the window, leaving Amerei to pull her chair close to the side of Reed's bed.

"Hey, Reed," she whispered gently, her fingers brushing gently over his wrist, before taking his hands in hers. "We're back."

There was a long pause, the kind that used to feel heavy, but now was the expected reply from him.

Then Odessa broke it.

"So," she chimed, glancing around. "Should we catch him up? Or should we talk trash and assume he's secretly listening?"

"Doctor says he can probably hear us," Mita added. "And if he is, I suspect he would be silently judging."

And just like that, the vibe shifted.

They started filling Reed in on what classes they were taking, how Odessa was already networking like she was about to host a TED Talk, how Andromeda almost made a TA cry during a lab critique, and how Mita had joined the music society "by accident" and was now somehow treasurer of the club.

"And me?" Amerei said. "Still the same. And Merrick and I are still a thing."

Mita grinned. "Still the hottest couple on campus. Technically off-campus now, but still."

Odessa raised an eyebrow. "You're literally dating a spreadsheet with cheekbones."

"Don't be jealous just because your type is 'emotionally unavailable guy with a guitar.'" Amerei teased.

Andromeda snorted, actually snorted, which made all of them burst out laughing.

After the laughter settled, Mita leaned forward, a soft expression on her face. "Remember the freshman welcome event? When we were all painfully new and pretending we weren't scared?"

"Oh my gosh," Odessa groaned. "The treasure hunt."

Andromeda smiled, barely. "You and Dessa were on the same as Reed, right? "

"Yep," Mita replied popping her 'p'. "Our dream team. Until we got lost in the library for like, an hour."

Amerei grinned. "We were in the other group. Me, Andromeda and Zyran, that one guy who acted like everything bored him."

"He did have great sarcasm," Odessa remarked. "Terrible sense of direction, though."

"And then Rune showed up," Amerei added. "Gave his poetic speech about how the real prize was the journey."

Andromeda rolled her eyes. "Which was code for: I forgot where I hid the next clue."

"But he wasn't wrong," Mita muttered softly. "It really was the journey."

They all went quiet for a beat, letting that sink in.

Mita glanced at Reed's face; it was still pale but had a bit more colour in his cheeks since she last saw him. "You should've seen yourself, dude. You were in full 'let's go' mode. Solving clues like Sherlock Holmes."

"We should play the 'What Would Reed Say' game," Odessa said suddenly. "It's only fair we let him roast us through our imaginations."

They were confused at her suggestion, so Odessa explained it to them.

They laughed again at the stupidity but the humor in it, nodding and a few 'sures' they agreed.

"What would Reed say about Mita being treasurer now?" Andromeda asked.

Mita answered instantly. "He'd say, 'God help us all.'"

"What would Reed say about Andromeda finally being in a group project and not taking over everything?" Odessa added, sitting up in her chair

Andromeda smirked. "He'd say, 'Are you okay? Blink twice if you're being blackmailed.'"

They kept going like that, teasing, laughing, remembering.

And even though Reed didn't respond, even though his breathing stayed slow and steady, there was something about the way the room shifted after they settled in. Like he was awake, and really there with them, soaking in all the drama.

Amerei leaned her head against the side of his bed, smiling to herself.

They had come a long way.

And the journey wasn't over yet.

Later That Afternoon

Amerei's phone buzzed quietly in her lap.

Merrick: *Dinner date? Got something planned. Say yes.*

She smiled as her heart did that soft flip it always did when his name popped up.

Mita, who'd been quietly scrolling on her own phone in the recliner beside her, raised a brow as Amerei moved onto the recliner bench beside her. "Is that textbook 101?" Mita prompted.

Amerei nodded, showing her the message.

Mita read it, then smirked. "Look at him. Mr. Spontaneous."

Odessa came over, leaning her head against Amerei's to get a peek at the message, "Dinner date, huh? You're not gonna say no, are you?"

"I wasn't going to," Amerei laughed, already typing a response.

Amerei: *Yes.*

"But I feel bad leaving you guys early. Is it okay if I dip out in a bit?" she asked, glancing between them. "I know we just got back to campus, but Merrick's got something planned and—"

"Girl, we already said yes, go," Odessa waved her off. "I think we're about to wrap up, and we're probably going to crash the moment we get back anyway."

Andromeda nodded. "We've been here all day. This was good. Reed would want us to still live our lives."

"Exactly," Mita added, nudging her. They ended up staying for a few more hours, talking softly, watching the sun melt into the sky through the hospital window. Reed never stirred. But they didn't expect him to; they knew being there, for him, around him was enough.

When it was time to head out, they all lingered at the back entrance of the hospital.

"Tell Merrick he's not allowed to set the boyfriend bar so high; some of us can't find Prince Philip," Odessa retorted, giving Amerei a mock glare.

"Have fun, love," Andromeda added, brushing a strand of hair behind her ear. "And text us when you arrive and when you get back."

"Yeah," Odessa said, pulling her blazer tighter around her. "Go fall deeper in love or whatever."

They hugged and split off; they split into two, going their own way down the hospital entrance. Amerei stayed near the exit like Merrick asked, watching the sky shift to a soft, amber dusk, while the others went to the parking lot to their car to head back to campus.

Ten minutes later, she heard it before she saw it; the smooth, low rumbling of an engine of a machine she knew belonged to *him*.

A **black Mercedes-Benz S-Class** rolled up to the curb: sleek, polished, and quiet like wealth didn't need to announce itself. The windows were tinted, but the moment it stopped, the passenger door popped open like it knew who it was waiting for.

She laughed under her breath. "Of course, he would," she murmured

Merrick stepped out from the driver's side, in a crisp button-down and rolled-up sleeves, his dark hair just slightly messy like he hadn't meant to be that good-looking. But of course, he was.

"You're late," she commented as she slid into the car with him closing it behind her.

He rounded back to the driver's seat, grinning as he slipped in. "Fashion-ably. You would've missed this beautiful sunset otherwise."

She turned in her seat to look at him. "Excuses," she taunted before continuing, "How was your day?"

"Long," he said, pulling away from the curb. "Meetings, freshman chaos, two event schedule changes, and one minor existential crisis when the banner order came in with the wrong logo."

She laughed. "That's what happens in the student council life."

"You?" he asked, glancing at her before returning his focus on the road

"We spent the whole day with Reed," she said, voice softer now. "It was… nice. We talked to him. Played a game where we guessed what he'd say to roast us. It was actually felt.. great to do that, it made it feel like he was a part of the conversation."

Merrick glanced at her, reaching over the console to squeeze her hand. "I'm glad."

She looked out the window as they turned onto a quieter road. "So… what's this date plan of yours?"

"You'll see."

An Hour Later

They were no longer in the middle of the city.

Merrick had driven out to the edge of town, where a quiet greenhouse café sat tucked behind a row of trees. It wasn't flashy, but it was hidden. Intimate. Glass walls that stretched from floor to ceiling, and even the roof was glass, permitting them a view of the night sky clearly, fairy lights that ran along the top of the wall and the bottom of the roof all around the establishment, with hanging plants that gave the whole place a whimsical kind of privacy. Only a few other tables were filled, soft instrumental music playing under the hum of conversation.

He had reserved the back corner, secluded, with a view of the small indoor koi pond and candlelight on the table that flickered like it was dancing just for them.

Merrick pulled Amerei's seat, allowing her to sit down, and robotically did so, too stunned by how calm the place felt and the atmosphere to pay attention. "This is beautiful," she breathed

"I thought you'd like something… quiet and different," he said, before taking his seat across from her.

"And totally not over the top," she teased, even as her heart softened again.

"Okay, maybe a *little* over the top," he quipped, a mischievous grin slid across his lips.

They laughed, shared pasta and flatbread, and tiny desserts on matching plates. They started to talk about their lives, how things can change so quickly and feel so different since the last school year.

He listened as she told him about her new classes, how Mita might be on her way to taking over the student Music club, and how Odessa was still thriving on her ability to walk into any room like she owned it.

He told her about the council's plans for the freshman mixer, how someone accidentally ordered glow-in-the-dark flyers for a formal event, and how a new freshman asked him if he was single within five minutes of walking into his office.

She raised a brow, amused. "And what did you say?"

He leaned closer, eyes warm. "Told her I'm very, very taken."

That made Amerei giggle.

By the end of the night, her shoes were off under the table and she was laughing more than talking. They stayed until the lights dimmed and the soft clinking of plates of workers slowly closing for the day became background noise.

When they finally walked out into the warm night air, Merrick slipped his hand into hers.

"You always know what I need," Amerei said, looking up at him

He smiled down at her. "That's kind of my job."

"No," she affirmed, shaking her head. "It's not. But you still do it anyway."

He pressed a kiss to her temple, then whispered just low enough for only her to hear:

"I love you, Amerei. and I want you to have everything you want for."

She smiled, resting her head against his arm as they walked to the car.

"I know. I love you too."

INTRO: Andromeda

Andromeda didn't come to university to play games. She came to win.

Top of her class. Planner color-coded down to the hour. She had her future mapped out with surgical precision and no intention of letting distractions reroute her.

At least, that was the plan.

People had opinions about her. Too intense. Too focused. Too much. She didn't mind. In fact, she liked it. There was comfort in control, in knowing who you were and where you were going.

But somewhere between the flashcard marathons and lab reports, the perfect rhythm started to slip.

She ended up orbiting a group she never expected to care about. Mita, the unexpectedly digital marketing major with eyes that saw more than she let on. Odessa, a walking hurricane of beauty and confidence. And then… Amerei. The roommate of Mita, soft-spoken, tea-drinking, and book-loving. Andromeda had dismissed her at first. But quiet people had layers, and Amerei, oddly enough, was the one she felt safest around.

It wasn't that Andromeda didn't want connection. She just didn't trust it. People came and went.

Plans stayed.

Still, somewhere along the way, the late-night talks, the shared silences, the eye rolls exchanged in class… it started to mean something.

She hadn't planned for that either. But maybe not everything in life could be charted.

Perhaps the parts that mattered most were the ones that didn't fit the plan.

Chapter 3: The Quiet Between Pages

Andromeda

Her first year was one long, uninterrupted breath held tight between lectures, labs, and exam dates she could still recite from memory.

There were no "lazy Saturdays" or "late-night dorm chats" on her schedule. Just whiteboard formulas, half-finished flashcards, and enough caffeine to keep a city running. If her professors asked for excellence, she gave them near-perfection. That's who she was.

But even perfectionists get tired. *Right?*

She just didn't say it out loud.

If she did have free time, it was usually spent with her friends, half-because she loved them, half-because she needed to remember she was a person outside of med school. Odessa's dramatics, Mita's dry wit, Amerei's quiet loyalty… those were the things that grounded her, reminded her she wasn't just a walking GPA.

Mita came to the forefront of her thoughts just then.

At some point during that first year after Reed's accident and then again in the second semester after her trip with her boyfriend, Rune, Andromeda had watched her dim.

No warning. No meltdown. Just little things that someone who wasn't close to her wouldn't pick up on: Less sarcasm. More silence in conversation. Eyes that used to sparkle now had a subtle distance in them.

Andromeda wasn't the emotional expert in their group; Odessa had that title locked in, but even she could tell something wasn't right.

She worried, but she gave Mita space. People like Mita didn't take well to being hovered over. And Andromeda didn't know the right words to offer anyway.

Now, second year had rolled around, and Mita was back.

Laughing again. Glowing, even. It was weird, but not in a bad way. Just unexpected, like a puzzle piece you thought was lost turning up under the couch.

Andromeda didn't ask what changed. She was just glad her friend was okay.

As for her?

Second year med school was… not lighter. Not yet.

But maybe, hopefully, this year could be different. Even just a little. She still planned her weeks in color-coded blocks. Still kept a master to-do list on her wall. Still carried a highlighter in her back pocket like it was part of her anatomy.

But she also had a playlist of songs she liked that had nothing to do with studying.

And a favorite coffee order that had too much sugar.

And, occasionally, leave space in her planner that said *"free"* and meant it.

As she walked through campus, the early September breeze threaded through her loose braid as she made her way towards the science building. A part of her hoped this year wouldn't just be about surviving the schedule.

For all that, she hopes it could be about finding what life looked like in the in-between.

Chapter 4: Something Like Rest

Andromeda

They stayed longer than planned at the hospital.

None of them said it out loud, but none of them really wanted to leave. Not when the room felt so full. Not when laughter floated between memories like a lifeline. Not when Reed, even in his silence, still felt like part of the conversation.

When they finally peeled themselves away, after sending Amerei on her date, they headed out.

They stood in the parking lot for a few minutes after parting with her at the entrance, stretching, yawning, lingering.

The sun was on its way down, casting everything in the kind of golden haze that made even the chipped pavement look beautiful.

Andromeda leaned against her car, watching the others with a small smile.

"Feels weird to say this," Odessa said, twirling her car keys, "but that was actually kind of… fun?"

"Reed would've roasted you just for saying that," Mita retorted, grinning.

"Which makes it all the more," Odessa replied with a smirk, leaning against her car.

Everyone was silent for a moment, all of them looking at the sunset, taking in the scene and the reason why everyone was here, recollecting their reality.

"We're really back, huh?" Mita lamented, tucking a few strands of hair behind her ear as the wind picked up.

"Don't remind me," Andromeda muttered, though her voice was light.

They all laughed, that soft, familiar sound of girls coming home to each other.

After their impromptu non-verbal humanistic therapy, Odessa slid into her sleek Cadillac Celestiq and pulled away with a wave, heading back to her off-campus apartment. Andromeda and Mita piled into Andromeda's car, a new, tidy Chevrolet Suburban SUV that ran like a dream and had personality, which was exactly how she liked it.

The drive back to campus was filled with light chatter: guesses about Amerei's date, Odessa's new internship, Mita's offhand comments about needing to do laundry or else recycle outfits from last year.

Andromeda didn't talk much, but she didn't need to. She just liked listening, and Mita loved talking. Letting the voices fill the space, she relaxed in the comfort of her friend's presence as she drove them back to campus.

She dropped Mita off at the dorm building entrance, letting her think she was going to park before heading up to her room, but she watched Mita disappear inside the elevator, as the building's first floor was mainly glass, allowing a clear view of the floor, before turning back onto the road.

She should've gone straight to her own dorm. Her bed was waiting. Her planner was waiting.

But she wasn't ready.

She took a left instead of a right and drove toward the edge of town, past quiet neighborhoods and corner stores she never visited, until she reached the small park that overlooked the lac de souvenirs.

It was still full of people, families with ice cream, couples on benches, and joggers looping the path, but it was peaceful. The kind of place that made silence feel safe.

Andromeda pulled into a space beneath a tree, turned off the engine, and reclined her seat.

The sunset was folding into the sky in pinks and golds and the kind of soft orange that made her wish she believed in poetry. She locked the doors, let her head rest against the cushion of the headrest, and just… breathed.

No schedule. No flashcards. No expectations.

Just a moment of no responsibilities.

She didn't mean to fall asleep.

But the quiet was warm, the evening air just cool enough, and for once, her mind wasn't racing with equations or outcomes.

So she closed her eyes. Just for a second.

And let herself rest.

Chapter 5: Beneath the Surface

Andromeda

Lying down, sleeping, in a room lit only by the moon, between the warmth of comfortable sheets, which were a stark contrast to the air outside that whooshed against the glass of her window, Meda laid in a fetal position trying to contain every ounce of warmth she could. The heater was broken and needed repair about 4 hours ago, but neither mother nor father could find someone to fix it before tomorrow morning.

It was quiet except for the wind outside, but for some reason, the atmosphere was not peaceful.

This was the kind of quiet that presses down like a warning.

There was a shirt. A faded blue shirt with a tree printed on the center. Almost invisible in the dark of the night. But her eyes were sharp back then.

Sharp like a wolf leading a pack, surviving in the dark.

She couldn't move; she tried, but to no avail. *This was a weird nightmare*

However, what was more important was that something, no, someone, was holding her down, pressing down on her, using their weight as an advantage against her.

Without warning, wet breath smeared across her neck.

Something hard pressed against her leg, unmistakably real.

Her arms were pinned above her head, wrists aching beneath the harsh, tight grip.

"Stop… please." The words came out tiny. Fragile.

A whisper, a prayer for help from something she didn't know exactly what yet, but she knew she needed it.

"Please—"

A hand clamped over her mouth just as her scream tried to break free.

The dream didn't last long.

But the memory did.

Outside her dream in her car, in the very real world, Andromeda twisted sharply in her seat. Her body jerked, her breath caught in her throat, her lungs trying to grasp for air as much as they could. Her face was wet with tears as if they were trying to stain the memories onto her skin, regardless of the fact that her thoughts were already soiled by the memories.

"Stop," she whispered, the word caught somewhere between the dream and the present. "Please…"

Not able to bear it any longer, she woke up.

Gasping. Shaking in cold sweat. Her chest rising as though she'd just surfaced from deep waters.

She stared out through the windshield. The moon was now high in the sky. Silver light spread over the park like frost. The voices of loud chatter with the gentle fold of laughter and footsteps of passersby all sound amplified in the dark of night as the city was now at bed. She reminded herself that she was in her car, the doors were locked, and if she kept the memory of the man in the faded blue shirt distant, muffled, she would be safe in her own skin.

Safe.

She blinked.

This was her car. Her seat. The place she'd parked earlier, trying to avoid the pressure of returning to her perfectly curated dorm room. She was okay.

She. Was. Okay.

But the tears didn't care.

They came again, fast, falling in hot, silent streams down her cheeks, and for a moment, she let them. Dropping her head in her hands, she folded into herself and wept.

It was not just for the dream.

But for the fact that it still followed her.

She hadn't dreamed of *that* in months.

Perhaps the summer trip back home had stirred it up. Maybe it was seeing Reed today, so still, so helpless, that triggered something buried.

Or maybe trauma didn't need a reason. It just… remembered.

After continuous effort to get her breathing somewhat normal, she wiped her face with the sleeve of her jacket and pushed the start button. Her headlights flicked on, slicing through the evening.

She pulled away from the park in silence.

By the time she reached the dorm, everything felt cold again. Tidy. Controlled.

Just how she needed it to be.

Her room was empty. By design.

She didn't want a roommate. In fact, she insisted on that.

She couldn't risk someone hearing her cry out in the night.

Wouldn't want there to be hushed gossip about the girl who thinks she is better than everyone else, tosses and screams in her sleep.

Couldn't let anyone see the cracks beneath her carefully constructed poise.

So she lived alone. Slept alone.

Carried herself with elegance, wore grace like armor.

It wasn't a lie.

It was just… only part of the truth.

Here, away from home, away from the past. She could be someone else.

Someone who didn't wake up drenched in memory.

Someone who had a plan, a future, and a name professors respected.

But on nights like this, she remembered.

And remembering hurt.

Chapter 6: New Rhythms

Amerei

The date ended the way all perfect evenings should, slowly and sweetly, like the last page of a favorite book.

Merrick pulled up in front of her dorm, headlights casting soft shadows across the building's front steps. Inside the car, everything felt still. Like the night had stretched itself out for just the two of them.

"Thanks for tonight, I needed this," Amerei said softly, leaning against her seat with a smile she didn't even try to hide, reminiscing on the night's previous events.

"Thank *you* for saying yes," Merrick replied, reaching across the console to brush his fingers gently along her wrist. "With the days I've had leading up to today, I definitely needed to recharge, and you always have this way of making everything feel better." He paused, bringing his hands up to cradle her face. She responded to his touch, leaning into it. "So I might have been the one who needed this more than you; in fact, I might even say I craved this." He finished, never breaking eye contact.

Amerei inclined her head; he followed suit, leaning in to her, as she was eager to have him close but was sad that it was the mark of the end of their night.

The kiss was not rushed, as they both wanted to linger longer but didn't want to impose on the other. The embrace was not heavy either; it wasn't demanding that they continue any further. The kiss was an intentional expression of their gratitude for each other.

She smiled into it, fingers lightly brushing the collar of his shirt before pulling back.

"I should go," she said, though her body didn't quite agree yet.

"Go on, before I convince you to break dorm rules," he teased, opening her door for her.

She stepped out, pausing to look back one last time. "Don't stay up too late planning world domination with the student council."

"No promises," he said, giving her a lazy grin before pulling away.

She watched his taillights disappear before turning toward the building, feeling warm from the inside out.

Inside the dorm, the living room lights were low. Mita sat cross-legged on the couch, blanket wrapped around her shoulders, half-focused on some show playing low on the TV.

"You're back," she said without looking away from the screen. "Did he feed you or just look at you lovingly all night?" Amerei didn't miss the hint of a smile behind her roommate's sarcastic comment.

Amerei grinned, kicking off her shoes. "Both. He's multi-talented."

Mita chuckled. "Of course he is."

"I'm gonna shower," Amerei said, already grabbing her towel.

"Cool. I'll still be here when you get out."

After her shower, Amerei came back in fresh pajamas, hair towel-dried, and sat beside Mita with a contented sigh before she began.

"Okay, so… there were fairy lights. Actual fairy lights."

"No way."

"And a koi pond."

"Amerei. Stop. You're making me raise my standards."

They spent the rest of the night talking and reliving Amerei's date before they headed to bed.

The next morning, the campus was already alive by the time Amerei stepped out of her building.

Her first class of the semester: Financial Analytics.

Which basically meant brain fog with a hint of panic.

Everyone moved like they were late. Freshmen stared at maps on their phones, clutching iced coffees and bumping into upperclassmen who were too sleep-deprived to care.

'Like, guys, it's the first day of school.'

Amerei moved with quiet confidence now, compared to her first year. She knew where she was going. Mostly.

Some new students stopped *her*, of all people, for directions. She helped when she could, but honestly, to say the campus was huge was an understatement, and she mostly knew her little corner of it: the dorm, classes, the library, and Merrick's old haunts.

That was it.

She walked into class and found a seat near the back. Familiar faces greeted her with nods and polite smiles. She smiled back, not wanting to be rude. These were her classmates, sure, people she partnered with for group projects previously. They'd text, meet, and finish the work.

Then she'd delete their number.

It wasn't personal. It just… wasn't necessary to fill her phone with the contacts of people she will never communicate with outside class, especially if their majors were different. Plus, it was a waste of phone storage.

She had her friends. Real ones. The kind you didn't need icebreakers for.

Still, she was kind. Always respectful. She could have small talk about the weather, midterms, whatever. She wasn't cold, just reserved.

And now, a sophomore, she was getting used to her own rhythm.

This was not new. Not overwhelming. Just moving forward in her life.

It was the weekend when she rolled out of bed early to get ready for the day's event, slipping on the clean, navy blue shirt that read **VOLUNTEER** in bold white letters across the front and back. Her hair was in a ponytail, soft strands tucked behind her ears. She added a pair of jeans and her most reliable sneakers, nothing flashy.

Merrick had already texted her that he was at the quad setting up with the team. He was probably stressing out, overmanaging, and triple-checking everything. That's how he was whenever he was in full-on *event mode.*

She smiled just thinking about it. He was so adorable when he got stressed

And maybe that's why she volunteered, just for setup, though. To help her overly dedicated, low-key, adorable boyfriend keep his sanity.

Besides, she and the girls had plans that night.

And nothing, not even being a volunteer, was going to mess with that.

Chapter 7: A Night to Breathe

Amerei

After hours of helping set up booths, sorting flyers, and dodging last-minute panic from student council members, Amerei finally stepped back and took in the scene.

The welcome event was in full swing.

Departments had their info tables decked out with banners and balloons. The arts club booth already had students sketching portraits, the med tent was passing out branded hand sanitizer to passersby, and the refreshment station was stacked with enough mini water bottles and cookies to feed a stadium. It was a job well done.

She turned and caught sight of Merrick across the quad, clipboard in hand, still troubleshooting, and was probably three steps ahead of everyone else, looking like he was running a small country.

She walked up to him, brushing her knuckles softly against his arm, catching his attention

"Everything looks amazing. You did great," she said, trying to reassure him.

He looked at her with that tired, proud smile that always made her heart catch in her throat.

"Couldn't have done it without you," he said, switching his clipboard to his other hand to allow space for him to pull Amerei to his side before placing a kiss atop her head, sighing into her hairline.

"Yes, you could've," she teased, looking up at him before removing a strand of hair sticking to his forehead. "But I'm glad I was here to help anyway."

She enveloped him in a hug as she whispered, "I'm heading out now. Girls' night."

Understanding her perfectly, he nodded, placing another kiss on her temple before being beckoned by the maintenance team. "Have fun. Text when you're home."

"Always and I will," she shouted as she retreated in the direction of her dorm.

Back at the dorm, she changed into something cuter: high-waisted denim shorts, a soft plum tank top, and her favorite necklace. Her hair was pulled into a cute side braid, allowing strands to frame her face. Normally, Mita would be off at her Christian club or Friday nights, but all clubs had booths at the event today, so there were no meetings today.

Mita was in ripped jeans, an oversized button-up shirt tucked at the front, and chunky sneakers. Her hair was pulled into a high ponytail, gold hoops glinting under the light as they waited outside for Andromeda to drive around and pick them up.

"She's five minutes late," Mita said, scrolling on her phone.

"She's always five minutes late," Amerei replied, sipping the iced tea she had just gotten from the cafeteria.

As if on cue, her sleek suburban pulled around to the entrance of the building.

"There she is," Amerei smiled, already heading toward it ahead of Mita.

Andromeda rolled down the window, looking effortlessly put together. Black slacks that match well with her tucked-in satin blouse with hair in a low dual twist, accessorized with minimalist earrings, as though she could go from bowling alley to business dinner without missing a beat.

"Get in, losers," she said with a rare smirk.

They met Odessa at the bowling alley, already waiting by the check-in counter, dressed to *not* blend in. A dark emerald body-con dress under an oversized denim jacket, statement earrings, and boots that clicked when she walked.

"You look like you're about to host a pop-up shop," Mita said, looking Odessa up and down.

"I always dress for the life I want, not the life I have," Odessa replied, flipping her hair as if she wished to emphasize her point.

They signed up for two lanes, Amerei and Mita versus Andromeda and Odessa. It was mostly chaos. Mita had no form but somehow kept getting strikes. Odessa bowled like it was a competition, and Andromeda treated each throw like a physics experiment. Amerei mostly giggled between sips of soda and tried her best not to let herself or the ball fall over the line.

Between frames, they joked about what kind of chaos the student council had planned for this year's freshmen icebreaker. The treasure hunt from last year had been iconic.

"I still can't believe Rune gave that weird speech about the prize being the journey," Amerei said.

"As Mita said before," Andromeda added, "he wasn't wrong." They went back and forth on the subject before calling it quits.

After bowling, they hit a late-night movie. They had no specific preference tonight; they just wanted something dumb and funny, perfect for the end of a long week and the start of another long one and many more to come. No overthinking. Just laughter and popcorn and leaning on each other in that soft way friends do when the night starts to wear them down.

Back parking lot of the movie theaters. They all piled into Andromeda's car as no one was ready to say goodbye just yet.

They sat in the parking lot, music low, windows slightly cracked as the midnight air wrapped around them.

They played **21 Questions**, told embarrassing stories, made up a ridiculous fairytale involving a cursed espresso machine and a professor with a secret identity. Odessa documented the night on video, snapping candids, capturing the joy in real time.

None of them said it, but they all felt it:

Next week, life would get serious all over again.

Deadlines. Labs. Group projects

And no one would have time to just *be*.

So tonight?

They gave themselves permission to laugh too loud and stay out too late.

When they finally drove back to campus, Andromeda dropped off Amerei and Mita at the dorm entrance, told them to go on ahead, and went to park the car.

They walked up quietly, shoes in hand, up the stairs of the entrance. Both were exhausted with the kind of tiredness that came from a day that was full and satisfying.

When they entered their dorm room, Amerei headed toward the kitchen, then her room, but paused when she passed Mita's door.

It was open, just a sliver.

And inside, she heard Mita's voice.

Soft. Passionate. Pouring out in a way Amerei hadn't heard since before summer break.

She'd heard it before, back at the beginning of their first year, when they were still figuring each other out. Then it faded. Mita had grown quiet, distant.

But now?

Now her voice carried peace. Power. Like she wasn't just saying words, but knew she was being heard.

Amerei didn't understand it. Didn't need to. She wasn't sure what she believed, or if she even believed in anything 'supernatural.'

But hearing Mita's prayer…

Somehow calmed something in her.

She left her own door open and climbed into bed, letting the distant murmur of praise float through the air like a lullaby.

She wasn't sure when sleep came.
Only that when it did, it came softly.
And for the first time in a while,
She slept well.

Chapter 8: Counterfeit Peace

Andromeda Pov

I was exhausted but not tired.

Which sounds contradictory, I know. But if you live like this long enough, it starts making perfect sense.

It's the kind of exhaustion that refuses to grant the pleasure of slumber. The kind that settles into your bones while your mind keeps moving anyway.

Loud.

Relentless.

I took my pills—two small tablets from the bottle I once promised myself I wouldn't need again.

Antidepressants.

Anti-anxiety medication.

My chemical armor.

I'd stopped taking them for a while because I really was doing better.

But going home always ruins that progress…. It always stirs things up.

It drags old memories back to the surface too quickly and too sharply, until suddenly I'm drowning in things I thought I'd already survived.

And now here I was again, back on medication, trying to figure out where the line existed between functioning and merely surviving.

Sleep never came, so I studied instead.
That was always my fallback.
When in doubt: read, memorize, solve.
If I built enough new neural pathways, maybe eventually they'd over-power the ones still
screaming from the past.

My weeks blurred together after that.
Classes.
Labs.
Tests.
Study.
Repeat.
People love saying things like "take it one day at a time" or "make every day count."
But when nightmares start feeling more vivid than your actual life, those phrases stop meaning much.
Life stops feeling like something you experience.
It becomes something you ~~survive~~ endure.

It happened again during one of my labs.
A male classmate leaned closer to whisper something near my ear.
Too close.
Too warm.
And suddenly I wasn't in the lab anymore.
I was back there.
Back in that moonlit room.
Pinned down.
The faded blue shirt blurred in the darkness.
The burn against my thigh from rough fabric scraping my skin.
I remembered thinking something stupid in the middle of it all:

My legs are too small to matter.
I was too young.
But apparently still old enough to damage.
Convenient enough to become a victim.
And honestly?
Who would've believed me anyway?
I was the girl constantly climbing hills and throwing myself down grassy slopes with my cousins while my parents handled business calls indoors.
Always scraped up.
Always rough-and-tumble.
~~No one questions bruises when you're already expected to fall.~~

Even now, seeing someone with that same build—a tall frame, broad shoulders, faded blue
shirt—makes my body lock up before my brain can catch up.

It feels like being twelve again.
Afraid of shadows in broad daylight.
Today was worse than usual.
On my way across the quad, I walked straight into a student demonstration.
Too much noise.
Too many voices.
Too much stimulation pressing against my skull all at once.

Students crowded together holding signs about violence awareness, women's rights, and
autonomy while angry voices echoed beneath the afternoon heat.
Someone nearby mentioned the movement had been started by *her*.

The girl who ran when it happened
Mita told me that part.

Said Reed stepped in to protect her from an obviously abusive boyfriend, got stabbed for it, and she panicked and fled while he bled out on the floor.

Maybe she was terrified.

Maybe the blood sent her into shock.

Maybe she's blood-phobic or whatever.

I don't know and I don't care about her excuses.

But if someone risks their life for you, bleeds out for you… For crying out loud, *acknowledge it.* You could at least say *thank you.* You could visit him at the hospital if nothing else.

I don't hate that girl for being afraid.

But I also don't like her.

Because she *let* someone else carry the weight of her choices and never looked back.

I know it sounds bitter,

but…hey, life is bitter.

As I said, I don't hate her…

Not really.

She's just another girl with a family more interested in optics than honesty.

Her parents, massive donors to the school, poured money into Reed's hospital bills. Covered the costs. In other words, "bought concern," and as usual, the press ate it up.

But according to Reed's family, they never visited. Never showed their faces at the hospital.

Not once.

Not even a card or an apology.

All that "concern" was for the public. So they could be the kind of parents who *looked* like they cared.

But they are actually people who played the role of responsible benefactors while their daughter ran from the boy who bled for her and a boy who made that someone bleed in the first place.

It hits too close to home, honestly.
My parents aren't mega-donors to this school, but they are very affluent.
Image-first people.
Old money, new rules.
Reputation-first money.
My siblings? All successful. High-paying jobs, name-brand lives. We were the perfect family on paper.
The funny thing is, we don't live on paper, now do we?
In reality, we, *my family,* live in silence. Perfection polished to distraction.

But as I said, it's not that I hate the girl.
Maybe she really was another victim trying to survive inside her own counterfeit happily-ever-after.
And maybe that girl was trapped in something similar to me.
I get that.
I just hated that Reed suffered because of it.

I turned up the volume in my headphones and kept walking.
The quad had become unbearable—chanting, clapping, shouting bouncing from every direction until it felt like my skin couldn't breathe properly.
I didn't want conversation.
Didn't want sympathy.
Didn't even want eye contact.
I just wanted quiet.

By the time I reached my dorm, exhaustion finally crashed into me.
I collapsed face-first onto my mattress fully dressed, my bag still hanging halfway off my
shoulder while my shoes kicked somewhere across the room.
Lights off.
Door locked.

Headphones still on.
I don't know how long I lay there.
But I know I didn't cry.
That part's gone. I don't cry anymore.
I just lie still and hope that sleep comes before the memories do.

Chapter 9: The Edge of Listening

Andromeda Pov

Weeks passed like spring in the mountains: fast, cold, and just a little bit heavy.

Midterms came, and with them, the kind of stress that made even my planner look nervous. I'd just finished my last test for the day, handed it in with a silent prayer that I'd survive grading, and stepped outside, relieved to breathe in air that didn't smell like disinfectant and pencils.

The protest was still happening.

They hadn't moved. Not really. Same signs, same chants, same faces. It wasn't as loud today, more like a low, pulsing hum in the background of campus life. Some students ignored them. Some cheered. Others rolled their eyes.

I just sat.

There was a bench under a tree, shaded and half-cracked from years of college kids carving initials into it. I sat down without really thinking. The kind of sitting you do when you're not ready to go anywhere yet, even if you don't know why.

I was staring at the dirt patch beside my shoes, watching a trail of ants carry crumbs that didn't belong to them back to their territory, trying to clear my mind that was fuzzy. Still wired from the test, still too loud inside to relax.

Then a voice broke through the static.

"It's a lot, right?"

I blinked. Turned.

A girl sat beside me. Had been sitting beside me, apparently. She wore an oversized hoodie and wide-legged jeans. Hair braided back. Calm face. Clear voice.

She looked at me, not like she was waiting for a response. Just… acknowledging me.

I didn't answer.

She didn't seem offended. indicated by the fact that she kept talking. Why do people do that?

"They're trying to make women's voices be heard, you know," she said, nodding toward the group across the quad. "Sometimes we're heard but not helped. And sometimes? We're not even heard."

I stayed quiet.

She didn't. *Ugggh, Lord help me!*

"No one really listens when a woman says she was harassed for wearing 'too little' as they would say. But they are not only about that, the group is about something so much bigger. This is also about kids, too you know; victims have no age range, everyone knows that. So we also want kids who have been assaulted to have somewhere to go and get help when their family is not doing anything to help, or if the abuser is family. We want a place for people like that. Somewhere to go when home is the problem."

That made my heart stutter.

Still, I didn't let it show.

She leaned back slightly, her gaze remaining on the scene ahead of us. "Some people think that because humans are animals, it gives them an excuse to act like one. But we're not wild animals. We know right from wrong. Men need to be taught to keep their hands to themselves, and to be held accountable when they don't act like an intelligent, civilized species."

I didn't speak.

But I nodded, *she had a point.*

She caught it. A faint smile masked her lips. "Well, " she said, getting up, before turning to me, "it was nice to meet you." Then walked away.

I watched her go. Didn't say anything. But something in me shifted. I'd thought this was just another rich-girl club trying to help the less fortunate to show how 'kind' they are. Another protest bought by a family trying to save face. But maybe… it wasn't.

The next day, and the days that followed, I passed by the group like always. But I didn't keep my head straight and drowned them out with my music. I just… noticed them more each time. Actually listening to the words of their chanting and shouts.

And then one afternoon, something was different.

They had a booth. Which, to my recollection, was never there before, and my memory is impeccable; trust me, I would know.

There was a table with a banner in bold black lettering that read:

"Why should we submit to men? Why submit to our abusers?"

The question hit like a rock to the chest.

I don't know what made me walk over.

Curiosity? Resentment? Or is it desperation? Maybe all three.

But one thing was for sure, though: the girl behind the table smiled when I stepped into her FOV. She had a clipboard, a stack of flyers, and eyes that didn't flinch.

"Hey," she said. "Wanna learn more about us?" *she sounded like a robot.*

I crossed my arms. "What exactly is this?" I said, as I was not about to sign myself into something I had inadequate info about, to regret it later.

"We're part of a support initiative on campus," she said. "We partner with off-campus shelters and counselors. For survivors of abuse, harassment, and assault, anyone who's been through it or knows someone who has. We help them find help."

I raised an eyebrow. "Shelters?"

"Yeah. Safe housing. Crisis hotlines. Group therapy, if you want it. Or just someone to talk to. You don't have to report anything. Just show up."

That… piqued my interest.

She handed me a small, folded flyer. "We're also hosting a group meeting next week. It's less about politics, more about healing. You're welcome to join us. No pressure."

I opened my mouth to thank her—

And that's when I saw her.

The *bench girl*.

Same calm face. Same hoodie. Same presence, I guess?.

She noticed me too and smiled as she headed in my direction.

"Hey," she said when she stood in front of me. "Didn't expect to see you again." I nodded, not sure what to reply, so I said what made sense. "Yeah. Me neither." She gestured to the clipboard. "Wanna write your name down? For the meeting?"

I hesitated.

Then, for reasons I still don't totally understand, I said,

"Yeah. Sure."

And I wrote it. First name only.

Andromeda.

Just Andromeda.

Chapter 10: Bare Rooms and Cracked Windows

Andromeda Pov

Midterms were over. The kind of "over" that doesn't feel like freedom, just an empty space where panic used to live, and memory didn't, but now it was reversed.

I was in my room, half-dressed in a sweater I didn't remember putting on, staring at my phone. The club meeting was tonight.

I wasn't sure if I was going.

I'd said maybe. That safe little '*maybe*'. The kind of '*maybe*' people say to get out of committing to something. It had worked… until now. Now it was here, and the clock kept ticking, and I kept scrolling through nothing, pretending I didn't already know I was going. Gaslighting at its peak. I don't know if it was considered gaslighting or gatekeeping, really.

After about an hour of internal debate and pacing like a ghost in my dorm, I grabbed an outfit. High-waisted black trousers, paired with a cream turtleneck, and my hair in a double-braided low bun. I kept the makeup simple, natural, just enough to look composed.

Clean. Controlled.

Walking to the meeting, I almost turned around twice. But I didn't.

That's progress.

When I arrived, they were still setting up. The lights were low lamps in the corners with soft lights along the walls as well. The space was intimate. Personal. Too personal, perhaps.

I wondered if coming was a mistake.

Then I heard that familiar voice behind me.

"Hey. You came."

I turned slightly. It was ^{Bench Girl,} with her calm, composed demeanor, again, like she was always exactly where she needed to be.

"Yeah," I said. Short. Not cold, just blunt.

"I'm glad," she smiled, stepping beside me. "Come on, I'll show you where to sit."

She ushered me to a circle of chairs already set up. No stage. No spotlights. Just people. One of the counselors, I assumed, greeted me with a polite nod.

The girl, whose name I still didn't know, explained everything as we sat.

"So, usually we open the floor to some of the older members," she said, tucking her legs beneath her seat. "They'd share their stories and maybe a few tips. It's kind of like… gentle guidance to help newcomers feel comfortable speaking, and when they do, it, in turn, helps the counselors better help, guide, and advise them. There's no pressure to speak if they don't want to; it's up to them. We've all been there, and the last thing we want is for them to feel *forced* into doing something."

so coercion… I thought

I nodded, still not speaking. Because I didn't have to, and I'll exercise that right for the rest of the night when best suited. She wasn't going to 'coerce' me into doing *anything*.

"There's always a counselor here, in case anything gets heavy. Sometimes activists join us. But it's not all trauma bonding, you know, we do snacks, games, dance-offs. It's chill."

So you spill your guts and deflect… sigh, but if it was helping people, then so be it. I would stick around and see if it would do the same for me.

So I stayed.

Why not? The lights were nice. The chairs were comfy. The people seemed real. Let's not judge too hastily now.

When the meeting started, the room grew quieter. Someone passed around snacks. The counselor spoke briefly, opening the night before one of the older members stood up, I am guessing. She looked like someone who should've been on a student magazine cover: flawless skin, perfect hair, an outfit that could double as a fashion shoot.

She started talking about her story.

"I was thirteen," she said, voice steady but soft. "It started with 'you're pretty' and ended with him in my bedroom after school one day. He was a family friend. I told my parents, and you know what they told me after I told them that their daughter was taken advantage of sexually? They told me to be careful not to 'tempt him again.'"

Silence.

*OK, but where is the sexual violence in that, where does 'hate all men' come in? Her parents were just very disagreeable, that's it. They both were consensual, well, then again, maybe 'in her bed' meant he raped her, but based on her account, the guy **did** groom her. But that story was kind of vague, not saying spill your guts, but then again, that's what we are here for. How can newcomers be brave enough to talk about scars that ran so deep when older members barely scratch the surface of their own stories?*

Then I was proven wrong, well 50/50, the other stories were vague but not as the first girl's which is understandable for newcomers

Another voice rang through the gathering, this one from a girl with nervous hands and perfect eyeliner. *Definitely a newcomer,* I thought.

"My ex used to follow me. Even after I blocked him. Showed up where I worked. One night I left my shift and he was parked next to my car. I laughed it off… until he started sending pictures of me getting into my apartment."

She laughed it off? girl? Then again, I would have thought I was overreacting if I saw a car similar to my ex's next to mine too, and thought 'was I still thinking about him' and gaslight myself saying wasn't over him but pics of her going into her apartment....... is wild?

A girl near me kept picking at her sleeve and bouncing her leg. She looked like she was trying to hold herself in place.

"I was eight," she whispered. "My cousin. No one believed me."

Another voice.

"He wasn't even someone I knew. Just a guy on the train. Cornered me. Touched me. And I stood there. Frozen. Like it wasn't even happening."

There were pit stains. Nail biting. Eyes wide with that glassy kind of fear that never really leaves. But they shared their heart.

They said their names. Or didn't.

They told their stories. Or hinted.

And me?

I sat there with my mouth shut.

Because I'm new.

And I know what that word means.

People always wonder why someone would come to a club like this and not speak. Like silence equals dishonesty. Or weakness. But it doesn't. Sometimes silence is a survival tactic.

I had my reasons. I don't owe them my story.

After the sharing circle, the energy shifted. Music played low. People smiled. Ate cookies. Laughed too loudly. It felt like exhaling after a storm.

The ^{bench girl}, still calm, still soft, found her way back to me after chatting it up with the others in the club.

"I'm Reize, by the way, I just realized I hadn't told you my name," she said, offering her hand.

I didn't take it. Just nodded. "Andromeda."

Not that I needed her to know my name. I just... gave it.

Reize kept talking. About the group. The games. The stories. "It's wild, isn't it?" she said, gesturing toward the others. "They don't *look* like survivors. But I guess… who does?"

I raised an eyebrow. "No one wears abuse printed on their forehead."

Reize paused. Like she hadn't expected me to respond like that. Then she smiled again, masking her genuine reaction. "True."

But something about the way she talked, how she watched people, how she kept one eye on everyone in the room like she was checking for cracks, it made me wonder.

Was she amazed at how far people had come? Or bitter that they had? Was she proud to support, or just sticking close to the wreckage so she didn't have to look at her own?

I couldn't tell.

But something about her rubbed me sideways. Not in a loud way. Call it… intuition.

After a while, she got pulled into another conversation. which I obviously did not object to.

I stayed until the dance-off. It was dumb and awkward and fun.

Then I left, just before the last activity wrapped up. That way, no one could follow up or ask if I was "coming back next time."

I needed space to decide that for myself.

Walking back to the dorm, I saw her.

Mita.

She was across the quad, cackling with two guys, shoulders shaking, eyes crinkled, full-on belly laughter that made her light up like a firefly.

They were walking in sync. Comfortable. Effortless.

I didn't want to just walk by my friend and say nothing; that would be rude so I slowed down, maintaining a bit of distance between the group and me. Trying not to eavesdrop, okay, maybe a little, but I couldn't just join in; that would be weird and rude, so I hung back and watched.

I think this is what people call 'people watching

Their dynamic was smooth: Jokes tossed back and forth. The guy from the treasure hunt event, and from what I remember, he was dry sarcasm in human form. Ethan, I remember him from first year, was smiling like he was eating up every word from the other guy's mouth, and Mita, right in the middle, glowing as she belonged.

It was strange because I wasn't envious of her happiness and ease around men as I would normally be for others; rather, I was happy for my friend to have that connection with these guys. To have friends, men who could make her laugh so hard that her stomach hurt. To tease her, to be trusted by her.

All the men I knew were scums of the earth, but I digress

I couldn't hear every word they said, but I heard enough. One joke had me biting back a laugh. Another one caught me off guard. Eventually, I stepped forward towards them because it would be weird if she or one of the guys heard me or turned to see me just lagging like a creep, just as I did, Mita turned and saw me.

"Meda?" she called, voice warm in the cool night.

Meda. Huh. First time hearing that one.

"Yeah," I said, walking closer toward them.

"Come here," she said, waving.

I joined them.

"Hey," Ethan said. "Andromeda, right? We had math together last year?"

"Yeah. Good to see you again."

Zyran chimed in. "We were on the same team during the treasure hunt, remember? I'm Zyran."

"Oh. Yeah. Didn't know your name then."

They started back up with the jokes; we were all cackling with heads thrown back as we walked toward the dorm building. The vibe was light and easy.

They talked about their Christian club. About the teaching that night, so I didn't say much. First of all, I wasn't there. And second, I'm not exactly a believer in all that. But they were a great group of people, the three of them. Better than where I'd just been, honestly.

It gave me a mini revelation.

You don't always need to be surrounded by people with the same wounds to feel light, like a weight was taken off your shoulders.

Sometimes healing means being around joy. Around laughter. Around people who don't ask for your pain but give you space to breathe.

When we got to the building, the guys headed off to their dorms. Mita and I walked to the elevator.

She glanced over. "How was your night?"

"Went to a club for women rights and abuse," I said. "It was… interesting. Heavy. But not terrible."

She nodded. "Good. Glad you went to something other than classes."

"And you?" I said, trying to deflect from her brutally honest observation, "We had a lesson from Philippians 4. Really good one."

"What's it about?"

"Peace. Joy. Gratitude. It's about choosing your mindset, focusing on what's true, noble, and right. Even when life is a mess," she said, casting her gaze at her feet.

Ain't that a fact, maybe I should have gone to her club instead of whatever the heck I went to tonight.

I didn't say anything, kinda dismissing the thought.

"You should come sometime," Mita said as the elevator dinged.

"Maybe," I replied. "One day."

She smiled. "No pressure."

She walked me to my door before saying goodnight.

Inside, I peeled off my clothes and took a hot shower. I stood there under the water long enough to feel real again. Then I stepped out, wrapped in a towel, breathing in steam and silence.

I checked my schedule.

Memorized the top three things I needed to do tomorrow.

Took my pills.

Crawled into bed.

And hoped, just for tonight, that sleep would come easy.

Chapter 11: Flyers and Freedom

Amerei POV

Midterms had left me somewhere between brain-dead and emotionally dehydrated.

Financial Analytics? Barely survived. Managerial Accounting? I don't even remember writing half that paper. I'd lived off caffeine and academic panic for two weeks straight, and all I wanted now, more than world peace, more than clarity on my group project rubric, was my bed.

Just me, my pillow, and a sleep so deep I might legally be considered in a coma.

I was halfway across the quad, earbuds in, playlist mellow, on a direct path back to the dorms when I caught sight of them.

Banners.

Big, bold, and very much still standing: the women's rights protest group. They'd been out there for weeks now, marching, chanting, handing out pamphlets, holding up signs. Passionate, loud, and committed. I respected it, I did.

But right now?

I wasn't in the mood for a movement. I was in the mood for melatonin and a nap.

So I kept walking.

Or tried to.

I was a few steps from making a clean escape when someone stepped into my peripheral vision and waved a flyer so close to my face I could read it backward.

"Hey!" the guy said, bright smile and all. "You should come to our Calligraphy Club! Make friends, have fun, create beautiful things with your fellow students!"

He held out the flyer like it was a golden ticket.

And I, against all odds, actually paused.

Calligraphy?

Okay, that was… kind of cute.

I took the flyer. "You actually write? With, like, those fancy pens?"

"Yup," he grinned. "We're Old school. No iPads allowed. We meet once a week, we share snacks, and everyone's chill. And most importantly, there is no pressure to be a good writer. You just come to relax and create."

Huh.

I looked down at the flyer again. A little doodled ink feather in the corner. Handmade. Something about it made me smile.

"Well," I said, folding the paper neatly in half. "You had me at snacks and low expectations."

He laughed. "That's our brand."

After a few more questions, and maybe even promising to stop by next Thursday, I continued my walk back to the dorm.

But I wasn't walking anymore. I was skipping. Or close to it. Same difference.

The wind was soft. The sun peaked through the clouds. The world suddenly felt… light.

It was the first time in weeks I felt like my life didn't revolve around deadlines or Google Docs with passive-aggressive group chat messages.

Life was looking up.

Back in the dorm, the silence welcomed me like a hug.

Mita wasn't back yet.

I tossed my bag into the corner of my room with the kind of dramatic flair that only comes from academic survival. I stripped off my clothes, dragged myself to the bathroom, and turned on the shower. Warm water rained down like grace.

I let it wash over me: midterms, stress, social fatigue, all of it.

Gone. Down the drain.

By the time I stepped out, wrapped in my fluffy robe, hair up in a towel, my entire body sighed.

I didn't bother putting on anything elaborate. Just soft cotton pajamas and fuzzy socks—the kind that feel like walking on baby clouds.

It was still mid-day, but who cared? The blinds were half-closed, casting stripes of afternoon light across the room. I climbed into bed, pulled the covers up to my chest, and opened my laptop.

I clicked *We Are Bears,* comfort food for the soul, and curled up with my stuffed giraffe that no one but Mita knew I still slept with.

As grizzly panda and Ice met each other for the first time on the train tracks as babies, I smiled to myself.

Midterms were over.

Life was okay.

And for once, I didn't feel the need to be productive. Or profound. Or even particularly deep in anything.

I was cozy.

And I was waiting for Mita to come home.

Chapter 12: Fruits and Flashbacks

Amerei POV

I didn't leave my bed for hours after my We Are Bears binge. My body refused.

But eventually, the door creaked open.

The dorm immediately smelled like popcorn and fabric softener. Mita had just returned with a bowl of buttery goodness, her oversized bartz tee half-tucked into joggers like always.

She walked in with her bag falling off her arm, her bun messy, and her eyes half-alive. She looked how I felt earlier today, worn out but finally free.

I sat up. "Midterms have officially murdered us."

She dropped her bag and face-planted onto my bed. "Rest in peace, brain cells."

I tossed her a pillow. "How'd your last exam go?"

She groaned into the mattress. "Digital marketing theory is just made-up words in confident fonts."

I laughed, taken aback by her creativity in describing her course. "Still think you passed?" I asked.

"I don't even care anymore. If I passed, praise Jesus. If I didn't, sanctify my summer."

I rolled my eyes. "You're so dramatic."

"You're just saying that because you didn't have a project where the rubric was literally longer than the textbook."

We stared at each other for a beat before our laughter burst through the silence.

It felt *so* good to finally sit and not be racing a deadline or have a group chat blowing up with last-minute edits. I leaned back against the headboard, pulling my knees up.

We shared war stories, code for class problems, group project trauma, etc., late nights, caffeine-fueled breakdowns, awkward group partners who disappeared for half the project, then magically returned like they invented the PowerPoint. According to Mita, the music club had to go on pause for her because of her schedule, and even her attendance at Christian club meetings had been less frequent for a bit.

"I haven't touched the piano in weeks," she said, tugging at the sleeve of her shirt, her expression wistful as if her thought had reverted to the distant memories of her playing on the piano. "I miss it."

"Same, I hadn't touched any books other than academic ones in weeks," I lamented, laying my head on my knees. "I haven't had time for anything except survival."

She turned to face me, finally a little more present. "But we made it."

"Barely," I grinned.

Then silence.

A thoughtful kind of pause. Not uncomfortable. Just… natural, soaking up all we had gone through and still made it out.

I tilted my head. "Hey, I've been meaning to ask."

Mita looked up.

"What happened with Rune?"

She froze, looking caught off guard.

"Oh," she said, sitting up straighter. "Yeah… we broke up."

"I kinda figured," I murmured, looking down at my toes, wiggling them. "You stopped mentioning him. And since he graduated, I thought it was either because you broke up or because of the distance. But may I ask when it happened?"

"A little before we went off for summer break."

I nodded, pausing to process what she just said,

"And you're just now telling me? Girl—why?" I exclaimed, finally understanding what she said.

She hugged the pillow to her chest. "Because it was a spiritual heart attack."

I tilted my head. "That sounds dramatic even for you."

"No, Ame." She looked at me then, eyes now glossing over and wet.

No, crap. I might have messed up. It's always me and my big mouth.

"We had sex."

And I knew I sat there, looking at her deadpan for 8 seconds while my half-dead brain loaded.

I sat up straighter. "Y-you—what?" I said, trying to contain my shock, and failed miserably.

"I know," she whispered. "I know. I was always the one who said '**no sex before marriage**.'" She sighed, before she continued, "I believed that still do. But after the trip, things blurred. The first time was… confusing. The second time felt better. And the third time, well, I stopped counting."

I couldn't speak. I genuinely couldn't. Mita?

"I told myself it was okay because we were going to get married one day, well, that's what he said," she stated. "He said he wanted it, marriage. Promised it even. But that's not the point, is it?"

She went to her room, leaving me stunned for a moment with the whole proposal thing, then came back with her Bible in hand and flipped through pages with practiced fingers, stopping somewhere she called Matthew 7.

"***By their fruit you will recognize them… A good tree cannot bear bad fruit.***'" Mita took a deep breath and leaned back against the pillows, legs crisscrossed. "Okay. So, Rune told me he was a Christian. Like, early on. Said he believed in Jesus, loved God, showed up at the Christian club time after time, and all that. And I didn't question it at first. But after a while, his words and actions weren't lining up. And neither were mine, we're being honest."

I waited, I waited patiently for the tea.

"He was saying one thing with his mouth," she explained, her eye still focused on the bible in her lap, "but not living it with his life. And I don't mean he was some horrible person. I just mean, his fruit didn't match his words."

"Fruit?" I said not really getting the fruit thing, and how plants and someone adds up together

She nodded, finally looking up at me. "Yeah. In the Bible, there's this passage. *Matthew 7:15–20.* It talks about how you can tell what kind of person someone really is by their fruit, which fruit here means their actions, their character. Like how an apple tree produces apples, not pears, and how a pear tree gives pears, not apples. Similarly, a good tree produces good fruit, and a bad tree produces bad fruit."

I blinked, kinda getting what she is saying. "Okay… wow. That's actually kind of deep."

She nodded. "It hit me hard. Rune *said* he followed Jesus. But the way he spoke, what he did, what he prioritized… it didn't reflect that. He wasn't growing. Or changing nor was showing any signs of" she paused, taking a breath, "and honestly… neither was I, when I was with him."

I frowned. "You think you're a bad Christian because you had sex?" I summarized, trying to confirm my thoughts.

"It's not just the act. It's what the act revealed," she said honestly

"And I knew I couldn't stay in a relationship where I was constantly battling temptation and actively losing the battle, pretending it was fine," she said, flipping through her bible again.

I just watched her, curious now

"Matthew 5:27-30 talks about how even looking at someone with lust is like committing adultery in your heart. And if something causes you to sin, you should cut it off. Drastic? Yes. But the point is, God takes our purity seriously. And I want to honor that. Even if he, meaning Rune, doesn't. "

She paused, tucking a few loose strands of her hair back into her bun.

"Jesus said if your right eye causes you to stumble, gouge it out. If your right hand causes you to sin, cut it off. It's hyperbole, but it simply means if anything or someone influences or brings you to a place where you're tempted to sin, cut it or them off, which is saying take sin seriously and have nothing to do with it or people who cause you to fall into it. I didn't do that; I made excuses. I compromised truth for comfort. Obedience for affection."

She went quiet for a second.

Then added, "*Galatians 4:15–13* also hit me. Paul's talking to the Galatians, at the time asking where their joy went. He's saying, '***What happened to your love for truth? Your joy in the Gospel? Don't let people lead you astray just because they seem good on the outside.***' That was Rune for me. Sweet. Charming. But spiritually… he was a distraction. '***Have I now become your enemy by telling you the truth?***' That verse kept echoing in my spirit. I had to ask myself, was *I* leading Rune toward Christ or away from Him? And was *he* leading me to Christ or away from him"

Dang. That hit deep, even for me.

"I didn't feel close to God afterward," she said, her voice cracking a bit, "I couldn't pray. I couldn't worship. It felt like He went silent on me. I begged for forgiveness, but it was like my prayers were hitting concrete."

I swallowed hard. "But… He forgives, right? That's what *you* kept telling us."

"Yes," she said, flipping to another page. "***But because of His great love for us, God, who is rich in mercy, made us alive with Christ… even when we were dead in transgressions.***" she said out loud before glancing at me. "I wasn't just guilty, I was spiritually dead. But God didn't leave me there, he never did. I was the one who walked away because of my own guilt and shame but He called *me* back."

I nodded slowly. "And Rune?" I prompted.

She bit her lip. "He didn't fight me on the breakup. No anger, no sadness. Just… acceptance. And that kind of scared me, too." She chuckled, "I thought maybe he never planned to fight for purity with me. Maybe he just didn't care."

She closed the Bible, her eyes still damp, but I could see fierce determination burning inside of them.

I processed all that we had discussed, more than I expected to. This fruit thing is kinda legit, I was also impressed with Mita's knowledge regarding stuff like this.

"You really studied all this, huh?" I asked, finally stretching out my legs.

She nodded. "Yeah. I had to. My heart was confused, and I needed clarity. God gave it to me through His word."

I sat with that for a moment. And even though I'm agnostic, even though I'm still not sure what I believe about God or the Bible or salvation and that mess, I couldn't lie.

That made *sense*.

We sat in silence for a long while, and I looked at her. Really looked.

This was the same girl who used to cry silently while writing in her journal, thinking I couldn't hear her. The one who stopped smiling for a season. I know now why. The one who would disappear behind locked doors after class and avoid eye contact with everyone, even me, at some point

Now?

She was glowing. Clear. She is someone who'd been through a storm and actually *made it out*.

And if that peace, this bright, wise version of Mita, was because of her Jesus?

I wasn't going to argue.

"You're... different," I said finally. "You're not all gloomy like before. You seem brighter."

She smiled. "Because I finally let go. I surrendered. God wasn't punishing me. He's restoring me."

I didn't know what to say to that, so I said the only thing I truly meant.

"Well, I'm proud of you. I really am. I may not understand all of this Jesus stuff, but... you? You're glowing, you're happy, Mita. I'm proud of you," I said softly.

She looked at me, surprised. "Yeah?"

"Yeah. You did what was right for *you*. You didn't fold just because it was easier to stay where you were. That takes guts."

"Thanks, Ame." Mita smiled, "That means a lot."

I shrugged. "As long as you're happy… I'm good."

"I'm more than happy," she said. "I'm free."

We let that sit between us a moment.

Then she reached for my laptop and flipped it open. "We are bears?"

I grinned. "Obviously."

We slipped under the covers, side by side, wrapped in soft blankets and watching our favorite cartoon characters, making a mess of everything. Watching HSM for the fifth time this year. She passed me tissues during the sad parts.

We laughed too loud. Cried a little harder than expected. Quoted lines like we'd written the script.

And for once,

The world didn't feel so complicated.

It was just us in this moment.

And the quiet comfort of knowing we were still growing, together, but in our own ways.

I didn't mind hearing her whisper prayers under her breath during the credits.

They didn't make me feel weird in a bad way.

They made me feel… safe.

Chapter 13: Ink and Irony

Amerei Pov

The week was speeding by like someone accidentally hit fast-forward. Classes. Projects. More classes. Group chats were 90% chaos and 10% actual productivity. I was grappling through the semester like a rookie soldier in a platoon, but barely.

But when Thursday came. I was *ready*.

I slipped on my oversized cardigan, cropped cream top, and wide-leg jeans. Soft, cozy, but still cute. Tied my hair up with a ribbon because, well, aesthetics. Then I snapped a quick mirror selfie and captioned it:

"Heading to a new club I might be joining."

and sent it straight to Merrick.

He was busier than usual these days, taking on new roles at his dad's company. Suit meetings. Strategic planning. Things with the word "leverage" in them. But I knew he'd see the picture eventually.

When I arrived at the Calligraphy Club's meeting room, my jaw actually dropped.

It looked like time had stopped somewhere around the mid-19th century. Velvet-draped windows. Antique desks with inkwell slots. Candles (electric, obviously) flickering on the sills. There was a globe in the corner for *no reason*, and I loved it.

This was it. This was my little pocket of peace.

Everyone seemed to know each other, their conversations easy and warm like a small community that had already claimed one another. I felt a tiny flutter of nerves until I heard—

"YOU!!"

I whipped around, startled by the sudden volume.

There, standing not too far off from me, was the guy who handed me the flyer that day after midterms, bounding toward me like he'd just spotted a long-lost friend at an airport.

"You came!" he beamed, reaching his hand out.

"Wouldn't miss it for the world." I grinned, shaking his outstretched hand.

"I'm Kazuya, by the way," he said finally offering his name like a secret. "We're starting soon, so you'll get the gist of how things run. But what are your first impressions?"

"It's cute," I said, glancing around. "Very… Regencycore meets scholarly Pinterest."

"I *know*, right? It's got that cozy-but-sophisticated vibe," he blurted out.

It did, in fact, have that vibe.

I smiled to myself, thinking how much this would fit Andromeda's whole aesthetic. Honestly, she could pass for a duchess. Or a viscountess in her next life. Something with land and strong opinions back in those times.

I couldn't resist. Snapped a pic of the room and sent it to the girls' group chat.

Me: *"Pretty sure I've wandered into Duchess Andromeda's study."*

The replies rolled in:

Mita: *"I can see it. Please address her as 'Her Grace' moving forward."*

Odessa: *"Tell her I demand an invitation to her next soirée."*

Andromeda: *"Her Grace is currently unavailable. She's attending to her estate."*

I laughed under my breath, just as a sharp, authoritative voice echoed across the room.

"Okay, students, time to begin."

I turned to see a man standing at the front of the room, put together so precisely it felt like a crime. His hair was *immaculate;* not a strand dared defy gravity. His outfit? Neutral-toned, pressed to perfection. The vibe screamed 'novelist in an Austen adaptation.'

"Students, find your desks," he continued. "Place all devices on vibrate and slide them under your bench. If it is an emergency, you may take your call or text outside. Otherwise, no phones, iPads, or laptops. We work with our minds and hands, not machines."

A few students chuckled softly.

"I am Baltasar Reyes, founder of this club. For newcomers, make yourselves at home, but not too much."

Even his name sounded aristocratic.

"We are not simply here to improve penmanship," he went on. "We are here to learn the power of individuality through lettering. Not in paragraphs. Not in essays. But in every letter you craft. Each curve of the ink says something about who you are."

Honestly? That was kind of beautiful. I'm digging this, very genteel.

"Tonight, we begin with English. Then we'll transition to French calligraphy. Same letters, new rhythm."

He gestured toward us before continuing. "Now, take up the pen on your table. Begin tracing the guide sheet. Then add your own style to it."

I picked up the pen.

And my, may I say, it was a thing of beauty: a metal nib, an elegant black body, and just enough weight to feel intentional, like I was writing with purpose to the Viscount of Catinbor. I snapped a quick POV photo beneath my desk and sent it to Merrick with a

"Wish you were here. You'd love this."

Then put the phone away, just like I was told.

Next to me, Kazuya leaned in. "Nice, right?"

"Yup," I whispered, smiling, still admiring the pen.

The rest of the evening blurred in the best way possible. The soft scrape of nibs against paper. The smell of ink. The quiet pride of seeing my loops and lines take on life. Sure, I was supposed to be tracing, but I added my own flair as instructed. Some letters dipped lower, others flicked upward like they were dancing.

I was creating something. Just for me.

By the time we wrapped up, I felt light. Joyful. Like, I'd just spent two hours *seeing another world that was not exposed to everyone, and* even if I never said a word, this place captivated me in a way unknown to myself.

I took out my phone to snap a pic of my finished piece.

Caught Kazuya accidentally in the background, looking hilariously focused.

He noticed. "Wait—no! I wasn't camera-ready!"

I laughed as he straightened up and struck a better pose, holding up his sheet and throwing a peace sign in the background of this other photo, which I hadn't planned on taking.

We took another photo—me, him, ink-stained hands, messy curls, and all.

He gave me his number. "Send me that, will you?"

"Sure," I said, sending it to him immediately.

Excuse me to slip out of the room to the restroom to get the excess ink off my hand before returning to my table.

"You're coming again next week? We're doing French calligraphy. It's beautiful. Well, from what I saw on Pinterest."

I nodded, slipping my phone into my bag after gathering my stuff. "I will."

The walk back to the dorm was crisp. The air tonight was different, or was it because I had a great evening? But for some reason, it made me feel like something new was beginning.

Just as I reached the dorm steps, Merrick finally replied.

Merrick: *"Cute. Hope you had fun. Sorry for the late reply. Meeting ran long."*

Then, a minute later—

Merrick: *"ADORABLE. That pic is frame-worthy."*

I giggled, typing:

Me: *"You free?"*

He replied almost instantly.

Merrick: *"I am now."*

I hit video call.

He answered with his signature smile. "Look at my little artist. You look like you've just walked out of a Jane Austen film."

"I basically did," I said. "It was perfect. You'd love it."

We talked all the way to my room about his day and about mine. He asked when I was free because he wanted to plan another date.

We made cringy kissy faces at each other. Spoke in terrible accents. I laughed until my cheeks hurt, and I ended the call before opening my dorm door.

And as I walked through the door, toeing off my shoes, I thought—

Maybe this year won't just be books and group texts and waiting for everyone to be free.

Maybe I have something just for me now, too.

Chapter 14: One of Those Fridays

Amerei POv

I woke up with a single thought:

I'm **going to see Merrick today**

No classes, no deadlines were on my mind; I couldn't push off the thought of seeing Merrick now. I had two lectures scheduled, but… it was Friday. Midterms were over last week, and the burnout was still very real. My brain had earned a vacation, even if it was only for a day.

Besides… I miss him.

Last night during our video call, he'd mentioned he was mostly free today. just one long meeting in the morning, and the rest of the day he had to himself. And since he was now stepping into the family company, these "free" days were rare. So I decided to be spontaneous.

I picked out an outfit he'd like, cute but cozy: a cropped cable-knit sweater in mocha brown, high-waisted jeans, and my favorite white sneakers. Just enough makeup to feel fresh but not effortful. I spritzed a little of my vanilla and sandalwood perfume, *just a little,* and fluffed out my curls in the mirror before snapping a selfie.

Me: *Skipping class. Headed to see Mr. Corporate. Pray for me if his dad shows up at his house.*

The group chat lit up instantly:

Odessa: *WEAK. I'd skip too, tbh.*

Mita: *Girl, sigh, I can't with you. But also, have fun and be careful.*
Andromeda: *Just don't forget college exists.*
Me: *It's Friday. School doesn't count on Fridays.*

I went to the dorm's parking lot and started my car to head over to Merrick's.

When I rolled up to the gated entrance to Merrick's place, well, his *family's* estate, the same weird feeling crept up on me. *We are really in two different worlds.*

The life he lived… it was so different from mine.

Every time I came here, I was reminded. Long iron gates. Guard stations. A literal fountain in the front yard up ahead of this long, winding driveway. It was like stepping into a movie where everyone casually owns art pieces worth more than my tuition. Not claiming I'm poor or anything; quite the opposite, actually, but this was a whole higher level of the wealthy.

Cain, the gate guard, spotted me and smiled. "Afternoon, Miss Amerei."

"Hi, Cain." I waved from the car window. No ID check, no nothing. He just buzzed me in and gestured for me to head in.

As I walked up the stairway entrance toward the house after handing my car over to a valet to park it in the underground garage, I caught myself wondering, again, what it must be like to grow up like this. To know money like this. To have entire *teams* looking after you.

When I stepped inside, Cain, who had driven behind me up the driveway, closed the door after me and disappeared down the hall.

And just like that, I was alone.

No Merrick. Just me, the big marble foyer, and way too many chandeliers for a house of one person.

I walked into the living room and flopped onto the couch like it was mine. Which, to be fair, I'd been on often enough that it felt like it.

I texted Merrick:

Me: *Hey love, how's the day?*
Merrick: *Just got out of the meeting. Heading home now.*
I grinned but didn't reply. I pulled up his location instead, *because yes,*

we shared trackers. Okay, technically it was *my* idea, but he went along with it. He never really used it, though, said he didn't bring his phone into meetings. Blah blah something about always leaving it in his office.

I watched his dot slowly get closer to home.

When he finally pulled up, and I heard the keypad making a beeping noise at the front door, echoing throughout the house. I ducked behind the couch, heart fluttering with anticipation. I heard him walk into the living room, sighing like the day had dragged him and it wasn't even noon.

He tossed his keys on the side table, I heard him shrug off his blazer, and before landing on the couch with a groan.

Then he flicked on the TV and started browsing through movies.

Which was weird.

Merrick wasn't a movie guy. That was *my* thing.

Then—

"So… are you gonna come out from behind the couch, or am I supposed to pretend I can't smell your perfume from the door?"

I *cackled.*

I smacked his arm as I popped up. "I didn't wear a lot!"

He side-eyed me. "You've been here all day; it's everywhere."

"Wait, how would you even know that?"

"Because no one's allowed past the gate without my permission."

My eyes widened. "But Cain let me in the moment he saw me!"

Merrick smirked. "Sweetheart, I *sent* Cain to meet you."

My jaw dropped. "That fast? But how? You said you don't keep your phone on you!" I argued.

"I didn't lie," he said, stretching smugly into the couch, looking up at me. "I don't *personally* carry it in meetings. But I've got people who update me on things that happen at home or alerts on my phone that I have listed as important, and your location is one of them. I *own* the company now. If something important happens, the meeting pauses until I say otherwise."

I stared at him, borderline speechless. "Okay, Mr. 'I got all the power.' Move over. You're man-spreading and taking up the whole couch."

"You act like you don't *like* when I man-spread," he teased, pulling me down into a kiss.

I melted a little, okay, a lot.

"Welcome home," I whispered.

"You know," he said, brushing his nose against mine, "I could get used to this."

"What?" I said. "Are you asking me to move in?" I joked.

He stared at me, saying nothing

I blinked, pushing away slightly. "Wait… you're serious?"

He looked at me a little *too* seriously. Like the kind of serious that made me a little nervous.

"Babe, stop looking at me like that," I said, half-laughing. "It's creepy. And are you actually serious?"

"Yeah," he affirmed, tone shifting. "But I know you wouldn't be okay with that right now. You've got school. I can wait. But God, Ame, I miss you," he confessed. "Like, *miss* you. Now that I've graduated, it's like our worlds run on opposite clocks."

He ran a finger along my arm before leaning down, kissing the side of my neck, trailing up until he met my lips again.

We were mid-makeout when he suddenly pulled away.

"Wait. Didn't you have class today?"

"Huh?" I blinked, dazed.

"Two classes today. It's on the schedule you sent me"

"Oh…" I smiled sheepishly. "Yeah. I just… didn't feel like going. And I missed you."

He leaned his forehead against mine. "I get it. But school's important too, you know."

"I know," I said, running a hand through his hair. "I'm not dropping out. Just taking a Friday."

He mumbled something incoherent before he stood up and stretched. "I'm heading to the kitchen. You want anything?"

"June plum juice, please," I said in a singsong voice.

"Coming right *up*," he said, mocking my tone with a wink.

I giggled, grabbed the blanket from the armrest, and curled up on the couch. I queued up a movie, one of our favorites, and waited for him to return, juice in hand.

As the intro music started and the room filled with the smell of dinner slowly being prepared in the distant kitchen, I smiled to myself.

Maybe this wasn't how I *should* be spending my Friday.

But this?

This was exactly where I wanted to be.

Chapter 15: Glass Ceilings and Gentle Hands

Amerei Pov

We were already halfway through another movie. Some indie drama I'd picked because the trailer said it would make me cry, and I needed that. It centered around a single mom and her son. Nothing flashy, just honest storytelling. Her sacrifices. Her protection. Her fierce love wrapped in gentle hands.

Merrick had his arm around me, his hand absentmindedly stroking my curls, and I didn't realize I'd been watching the screen in silence until I heard his voice.

"You know…" he said softly, "I know you've been curious. But you never asked about my mom."

I turned to him, a little caught off guard. "Yeah, I didn't want to overstep."

He looked down at me, brushing hair away from my face. "You can ask me anything, Ame."

So I did. "What was she like?"

He stared at the screen for a moment, then back at me.

"My mom died when I was about eight. I don't remember everything, but I remember she loved to cook. Bake. I can still smell the vanilla she used to add to pancakes. One thing about her, she wasn't just domestic. She was… brilliant."

I stayed quiet to let him unfold his own story.

"She and my dad built the company from scratch. Back when they were broke college grads with nothing but matching ambition and one desk they took turns using. She was the vision. He was the executioner. They made it work."

He exhaled slowly, his voice softer now.

"When she got sick, my dad also deteriorated; it was fast, the progression of her disease that is." He paused, entangling his fingers between mine as if he was seeking strength from our contact. "We knew this was something we wouldn't recover from, but what Dad didn't know was… she'd already made plans. Business plans. Backup structures. Contingency portfolios. It was all hidden away until the night she passed."

My heart clenched. "She planned for her absence?"

"She planned *ahead* for all of us," he affirmed. "Those are the plans that made the company what it is now. Not just my dad's effort, but hers. Quietly, behind the scenes."

I rested my head on his chest, trying to provide some sort of comfort. He was being vulnerable, and I didn't want to interrupt.

"Dad says I'm like her," he added. "Business-minded. Strategic. But he's a firm believer in earning your place. Even though I'm the only kid, I still had to *prove* myself."

"You've definitely done that," I murmured.

"You know how people say to me that I'm a 'nepo baby' like it's an insult?" He smiled bitterly. "That doesn't exist in our house. Not in this family. You earn your way to the top, or you don't get there."

He shifted slightly, arms tightening around me.

"In high school and college, I worked every part-time role the company offered: mailroom, finance intern, and HR shadowing. While still being on the student council. While still being a TA for math. While pulling my GPA high enough to earn merit scholarships so Dad couldn't say I got help I didn't earn."

"That's… a lot, Merrick," I whispered, not being able to fathom what he had to go through.

He nodded. "It was. But it helped. Balancing all that taught me what no lecture ever could. It made learning the company easier, not easy but *manageable*. Nothing pulls you like being a student, a leader, and a tutor all at once."

He pressed a kiss to the top of my head, smiling into my hair.

I pulled back slightly, resting my chin on his shoulder with a grin. "Am I dating Wonder Man or Superman? I can't choose."

He laughed quietly. "I'll take either. But just so you know, Wonder Man doesn't exist. Only Wonder Woman."

I swatted his chest playfully. "Hey, anything is possible in the nation of the imagination."

We giggled together, listened to each stories and caught up with each other on our lives while the movie was still playing in the background, but neither of us was really watching anymore.

"I'm proud of you," I whispered.

He looked at me then, really looked. The kind of gaze that says *thank you* without words. He didn't need to say it.

At some point, I must've dozed off. Still wrapped in the warmth of his arms, surrounded by pillows and soft blankets. The weight of midterms, expectations, and everything else I'd been carrying for the past few weeks... gone.

I was somewhere between dreams and reality when I felt something gentle, warm, but unfamiliar in a sleepy sort of way.

That's when I felt it.

Something repetitive. Gentle, but definitely real. Like a slow rhythm brushing against my hip.

A breath. Warm and close.

Then. A hand… traveling.

I stirred a little, slowly cracking my eyes open.

The room was dim. The TV had gone to the home screen, screensaver flickering like city lights.

And Merrick was still next to me, no, he was straddling me

—his hand…

Trailing down my side, fingers slipping beneath the edge of my shirt.

I blinked, heart skipping, not in fear, not even in discomfort.

It made me shiver, not in fear, but surprise. The kind that creeps in when you're still wrapped in sleep and suddenly aware that someone else is fully awake.

"Merrick…" I mumbled, voice tangled with sleep.

He paused for half a second, like he'd been caught doing something halfway between innocent and selfish.

"You're awake?" he asked, barely above a whisper.

"Kind of," I breathed.

"I didn't mean to wake you," he said quietly. "I just…"

His lips grazed my collarbone. "We don't get moments like this often. And I… missed you."

I didn't answer right away.

Because I didn't know what to say.

It was strange, being touched while not fully present; it was a little jarring. A little tender but, at the same time, a little complicated.

But this wasn't a stranger. It was Merrick. The guy who knew my go-to boba order and how I like my socks folded. The one who'd stayed on FaceTime when I cried through finals last semester. The one whose silence was never empty.

So I let myself breathe in the closeness. The familiarity. The weight of someone I loved.

And I didn't pull away.

Later, when the room was still again, he wrapped his arms around me tighter and pressed his face into my neck.

"Stay the weekend?" he asked, voice low.

I blinked slowly, still hazy.

"I didn't bring clothes," I murmured.

"Wear mine," he said instantly, brushing hair from my face. "Or I can order some for you. Whatever you want."

I smiled against his chest. "I'll wear yours."

He looked down at me, one brow raised. "So… is that a yes to staying over?"

I smirked sleepily. "Are you continuing this or do I?"

He let out a soft laugh and leaned in to kiss me again, arms pulling me closer like he was trying to memorize the shape of me.

And even though a small voice in the back of my head questioned the way it all started…

I didn't say anything.

Not because I didn't care.

But because sometimes it's ok to let moments like these slide when time feels borrowed, because life is too fast, and love is rare, and the person I care about is always busy building empires.

Chapter 16: Trenches and Hallways

Andromeda POV

Friday was like every other day.

I went to class. Sat in the second row. Took notes like a machine. Listened, nodded, participated. Pretended.

Then I came home and did what I've been doing more than breathing lately, studied.

And studied.

And studied.

Because when your brain's wired to relive memories you never asked for, silence becomes your enemy. Stillness becomes a threat. So you fill it. With noise. With facts. With theorems and textbooks and color-coded sticky notes.

Because if you can keep your mind busy enough, maybe it won't eat you alive.

But in my case, it still does.

The night at the support group was supposed to help. Guess what? It didn't. If anything, it made things worse. The stories I heard echoed in my head like ghost recordings. And then there were the visuals: blue shirts, trees, shadows. It's like my memory decided to host a rerun marathon of the worst episodes of my life.

I see a tree? I see the faint print on that faded shirt.

I walk to class? I remember his hand, the pressure, the breath.

So, I took my meds, again. Knowing they weren't really helping. I'm not saying they don't work. I'm just saying they haven't worked lately. They're supposed to numb the anxiety, slow the panic.

But it still finds me.

So, I kept studying.

Because when the walls close in, the best I can do is try to bury myself under facts.

By the time Saturday hit, I hadn't left my room except for water and painkillers. My vision was going blurry from staring too long at the screen, and my head throbbed with the kind of ache that can't be solved with Tylenol alone.

Odessa was off-campus this weekend. Mita had music club. And Amerei? Living her rom-com life with Lover Boy Merrick and shamelessly rubbing it in our faces with pictures and memes in the group chat.

I should've been annoyed.

But I was just... tired.

Eventually, I got up, downed some pills, grabbed my hoodie, and decided to leave the dorm. I didn't even know where I was going until my feet took me halfway across campus.

I just needed to breathe.

And maybe... to find Mita.

I'd never been to the music building before. It was tucked off near the east quad, where the grass was always greener, and the air felt richer, if that's possible. I walked slowly, doing my best to avoid trees, not that you *can* on this campus. They're everywhere. But I kept my eyes low. Focused on the pavement. On the signs.

I almost got lost twice.

But eventually, I found it:

"MUSIC CLUB ROOM" was written in elegant gold letters above a pair of tall double doors. I walked in like I owned the place, because confidence covers everything, including disorientation, and immediately spotted her or heard her.

Trenches by Tauren Wells

Mita was at the piano.

No one else in the room, no chatter or noise to distract from the melody she created. Just her, lost in the keys.

I stopped at the threshold and remained there and just… listened. Absorbing the air of the song.

It was soft. Gentle. Deep without being dramatic. Like the music itself was exhaling.

The notes flowed like water, smooth and layered, wrapping the room in something unspoken. And for the first time in days, I didn't feel haunted. I just felt… present. I soaked in every second like it was salve for my soul. Then, when she finally lifted her hands from the keys, I clapped softly.

She spun around.

"Meda?" she blinked. "What are you doing here?"

"Looking for you," I said, shrugging. "I needed to get out of the dorm, so I came to find you."

"Awwww, did you miss me?" she teased.

"Yes, actually. Can I sit?"

"Yeah, come here," she said, patting the space beside her on the bench.

I joined her, dropping my bag at my feet.

"I can play the viola," I said out of nowhere. "But not the piano."

Mita stared at me. "You can play an instrument? And you never told me?!"

"You never asked," I smirked. "I was actually thinking of learning viola," she added.

"It's good to learn," I said. "But for me, it wasn't a choice. My parents love showing off their kids' talents." I sighed, "I was in music school by the time I could read. And I had to ace regular school, music lessons, taekwondo, and jujutsu. I wanted to take up boxing, but apparently that's 'too vulgar for girls'. The Double standards, am I right?"

Mita's eyes were wide. "I didn't know any of that."

I shrugged. "Well, yeah, of course you wouldn't. I don't talk about my family."

"None of us really do," she said after a pause. "It's weird, isn't it? We're close, but we barely know each other's pasts."

"Maybe because those pasts are closets full of skeletons we've chosen not to open," I replied. "But hey, I'm down to hang out even if that means letting some skeletons out to party."

"Next sleepover," Mita said immediately. "It's happening."

"Sure. But hey, what was that song you were playing earlier?"

She smiled. "Trenches by Tauren Wells. How was it? Was it great?"

I blinked. "That was… wow. It was better than great."

"Thanks," she said softly. "I love it too."

"Why that song?"

She leaned back slightly, looking at the keys like they held her memories.

"It's about how we sometimes think we have it all together and we can do it without much, if any, help from God," she chuckled, more like at herself. "But we learned the hard way, yet God didn't wait for us to be completely defeated to help. It's both the realization that the Lord already fought our battles on the cross long before we were born, and also that God is active, present help in trouble," she remarked before turning fully toward me.

"It reminds me that the Great, Mighty, Majestic, all-powerful God came down and became a man and was ridiculed, spat on, mocked, and murdered by his own creation inorder to save them. To know that there is no depth that he wouldn't go to save those he loves, and he loves everyone. I feel like that's my whole story with God, I have placed myself in places and positions allowing things and people to access me in a way I was already warned, **will harm me** but I thought I knew better, that I knew what I was doing, which resulted in me having my own share of warfare I could have avoided because of my action, basically *consequences of my own actions* and despite me **blatantly** putting my self in that, in those situations, he still came and rescue me form my own self." she explained, smiling so brightly, confusing me a bit.

"People always say that *"you are your biggest enemy"* but you will never understand that until you are stand there with a knife in your back and knife in your stomach with another knife plunged in you neck and knife if your leg topped off with the deepest wound; a knife in your heart only to turn to look the culprit in their eyes while you feel like you're taking your last breath only to see yourself looking back at you, is one of the most sickening awakening and betrayal ever known to mankind, but, my God, the Lord swoops in and remove all the knives and put the salve of "**GRACE**" on each wound and tells you *'its ok'* and to come to him, into his arms for the embrace of a lifetime is to most healing thing ever. So that's why," she said, her eyes and hands still animated after that long explanation. She continued,

"It's a really long answer to your question, but I wanted you to understand how much it meant to me."

"No, that's completely fine, it makes sense since you explained it in such detail," I replied, wanting to ensure she doesn't feel like she over-shared when it was I who asked such a probing question in the first place.

I thought about her answer to my question, relishing how mature it was, and let that sit for a while.

I didn't comment on anything else, and I don't believe I needed to.

Not long after, more students started trickling in, the club members. Mita turned to me with a smile and a whisper.

"Hey, I'm gonna run to the bathroom before we start. Don't let them touch my keyboard."

I saluted. "Yes, ma'am."

She laughed and disappeared out the door, leaving me with the soft buzz of music nerds filing in and tuning their instruments.

I leaned back into a stretch, looking around, still enjoying the strange comfort this room brought me. It felt more like a home than my actual house. No pressure. No politics. Just music and people trying their best.

After a minute or two, I got up, deciding to explore a little while I waited think Mita was overreacting with the keyboard.

During my walk, I strolled down an unfamiliar hallway, taking in the scenery.

Then something, *something* caught my eye.

A door, just slightly open.

A room I hadn't noticed before.

And whatever was inside made my breath hitch.

The light inside was golden. Warm. Dim but purposeful.

And sitting at the center of the room was—

No.

Wait.

Was that…?

Chapter 17: Paint, Presence, and the Softness of Sound

Andromeda

She hadn't meant to wander.

But after Mita darted off to the bathroom and the music club began to buzz with what she guesses is its usual pre-meeting energy, the hallway suddenly felt like a safer place to breathe.

Quieter.

So she went for a walk.

There were rooms on either side of this particular corridor, some with half-open doors, some closed completely. She didn't think anything of it… until she passed the one that was open just a sliver too wide. Something caught her eye. Not noise, not movement.

Color.

She stopped mid-step. Turned.

And froze.

Inside, resting like royalty on a massive easel, was a canvas.

No, not just a canvas.

A **masterpiece**.

A swirl of tones that danced and faded into each other: blues, burgundies, cream, and hints of deep gold. Colors that didn't just blend; they breathed.

And in the center of it all stood a woman.

Draped in 17th-century couture, her posture graceful, her hair pulled into something too perfect to be practical. She looked like she belonged in a royal portrait gallery. Every detail, the fall of her sleeves, the hint of lace under the cuffs, and the muted shimmer of her skirts, felt designed with obsession.

But then you noticed the **squares**.

Drawn across her body, like windows revealing a second version beneath.

One showed her watery eyes. Another, the bruises under her gloves. The perfect hem lifted just enough to expose a faint scar on her ankle. Her beauty remained intact, but the painting **dared** you to look deeper.

It was beautiful.

Painfully so.

A shadow moved in her peripheral vision.

Andromeda blinked as a guy stepped into view, standing between her and the canvas. Paint-streaked apron. Splashes of pigment on his forearms. Curls slightly flattened by headphones hanging around his neck.

He began brushing something over the painting, clear and glossy. A sealant.

She didn't mean to step forward.

But she did.

Drawn in like a moth to candlelight.

He must've heard her. He turned around, startled just slightly, then smiled, that kind of soft, crooked smile only really **certain** people have.

"Oh," he said, blinking. "Didn't know we had an audience."

For a second, Andromeda wasn't sure if he was talking to her or the painting.

She didn't answer.

She didn't have to.

"You like the painting that much?" He asked again; this time, he was definitely talking to her.

She nodded. "It's... well done."

He tilted his head, amused. "Thank you. You don't have to stay all the way out there, you know."

So she stepped forward. Calm. Measured. Like she was walking into a gallery, not some random artist's personal space.

He moved out of the way as she approached so she could get a complete view of the canvas.

"I think you found an admirer," he said; this time, he was most definitely speaking to the painting.

Andromeda glanced at him sideways, eyebrows raised.

"I know it looks weird," he hurriedly remarked. "Talking to a canvas like it's a person. But I always do. I don't paint still life. I paint moments. People. Emotions. They're real. They deserve to be spoken to."

She folded her arms. "At first, yeah. I thought it was weird. But you don't need to explain. It speaks for itself."

Her voice was flat. Unapologetic.

He blinked, his smile stretching wider across his face, still looking at his work as if he were still taking in the chef-d'oeuvre.

"You really like her, don't you?" he said, turning to look at Andromeda once again.

"I do," she replied instantaneously, their eyes meeting as if they were evaluating the genuineness shown in each other's gaze.

Something shifted in his eyes. Not surprise, something closer to respect.

"I'm Zebedee, Zeb" he said, holding out his hand.

She took it, briefly.

"Andromeda."

He nodded, like the name meant something.

Then she stepped back, already recalibrating her exit.

"Well, I've got to go, Zebedee. I'll see you… when I do." She said her words trailing off as she turned to make her way to the door, trying to escape from this uncomfortable situation she had placed herself in.

"It's Zeb," he called after her.

She smirked at his confidence. "We're not close enough for nicknames."

"You're by the music room, right?" he asked casually.

Her body tensed. Just slightly as she reached the threshold.

She looked over her at him; she didn't show emotions on her face, but she still asked,

"And how would you know that?" Not accusatory. Not alarmed. But cautious, she already had wild scenarios spinning in her head.

He held both hands up in defense, paintbrush still between two fingers, sensing where this would go if he didn't explain himself. "It's not how it sounds. I swear. I was here earlier working on another piece. I took a walk to stretch. I heard music. I saw you talking to another girl in the club room. That's all."

He looked… nervous. Like he wasn't used to explaining himself.

Andromeda watched him for a beat, searching for any sign of deception in his body language, before giving a slight nod.

"Well, then. That's that," she said. "See you around, Zebedee."

He grinned, finally dropping his hands. "It's still Zeb."

She didn't answer as she stepped out in the corridor that brought her there.

Back in the music room, Mita had returned, cheeks flushed and smiling like she always did when surrounded by music and warmth. Andromeda slid beside her, quieter than usual.

"Rune had taught me how to play the piano, you know," Mita said. "But I've never tried viola," she repeated from earlier, hinting towards her interest in learning to play the instrument, and Andromeda picked up on the hint.

"Wanna learn?" Andromeda asked.

"Seriously?"

"Yeah."

So she went and grabbed one from the corner of the room and began instructing her.

Starting with how to hold the bow, how to position her wrist, and how not to crush the strings. It was awkward and clumsy, and Mita nearly knocked over a music stand trying to get the posture right.

They laughed so hard it felt like a purge to Andromeda with everything going on lately.

"You're a good teacher," Mita said, half-winded from laughter.

"You're a determined student."

"Next week, you're learning piano."

"Deal."

Andromeda hadn't laughed like that in months. She didn't even realize how much her shoulders usually ached from tension until they didn't.

After club, they walked back to the dorms together.

When they reached the dorms, she stood in front of the elevator, hesitant.

Then pulled out her phone and sent Amerei a DM.

Me: *Hey. Mind if I crash with Mita tonight? Just... not in the mood to sleep alone.*

Amerei: *Totally fine. I'm not even home lol. Stay as long as you want.*

That night, she curled up on Mita's bed in the spare comforter, wearing one of her oversize tees. They put on crime documentaries and barely blinked for hours, whispering sarcastic commentary and theorizing wildly before each episode ended.

They fell asleep sometime after 3 a.m.

Andromeda opened her eyes to the dark sometime later and stared at the ceiling.

"I kind of wish I had a roommate," she whispered.

Mita didn't answer; of course, she was still asleep.

Andromeda smiled faintly. She knew she couldn't have one as it was already set that way, but it would be nice to have a friend in the next room.

Closing her eyes once more, she hoped her memories wouldn't intrude on her dreams tonight. However, she oddly felt that sleep might be more restful this time, possibly because in this room, on this night, this version of her life where healing seemed more attainable.

Chapter 18: Ink, Laughter, and A Little Bit of Chaos

Amerei POV

The weekend had ended faster than it started.

I walked back into the dorm Sunday evening to find Mita in full cleanup mode, vacuum in hand, gospel playing low in the background, and the scent of citrus cleaner hanging in the air.

"You just missed Andromeda," Mita called over her shoulder when she saw me.

I dropped my bag with a groan. "Oh snap, I wanted to see my munchkin."

"She said the same thing about you. Well, not the munchkin part." Mita shot me a look before asking, "How was the weekend with Merrick?"

"It was good." I stretched, cracking my neck. "Finally got time to just… be. No assignments. No

interruptions. Just us."

Mita paused her vacuuming and smiled faintly. "Good. You deserved that. So, since you enjoyed

yourself all weekend, ready for the week ahead?"

"Nooo," I whined, throwing myself face-down onto the freshly cleaned couch.

"Hey!" Mita snapped, swatting my leg with the vacuum nozzle. "Sulking is fine, but not on the couch I just cleaned."

I groaned louder but rolled off dramatically onto the carpet like I was dying in a soap opera.

Monday hit like a truck. Life snapped back into its usual rhythm: lectures, projects, group presentations, and awkward small talk with people I only planned to speak to until the final grade came in.

What kept me sane?

My girls. Their random memes and their chaotic group chat updates.

Mita's late-night prayers that I definitely didn't eavesdrop on.

And my calligraphy club. Or more specifically—**Kazuya.**

Kaz.

My partner-in-crime.

My ink-stained brother-from-another-mother.

It was wild how fast we clicked. He got me. Like, *really* got me. And not in a complicated way like Merrick, whom I love, but in an "I can throw ink on you, and we'll still walk home laughing" kind of way.

That Thursday, we sat in our usual spots, Kaz already doodling along the edge of his tracing

sheet before the meeting even started.

At the front of the room, our club founder, the forever regal Baltasar Reyes, cleared his throat dramatically,

"Students, tonight, instead of French calligraphy, we'll be exploring Japanese calligraphy: precision, grace, and discipline."

I lit up immediately. "Yesss. Finally."

Kaz glanced at me. "You seem way too excited about this."

"Dude, I love everything Japanese. Anime, food, music, culture—you name it."

"Yeah, yeah. Weeb alert." He rolled his eyes. "I'm half Japanese, and even I'm not this excited."

I gasped. "Neutrality? That's treason."

"I said *half*-Japanese. That gives me half the right to be 'meh.'"

I elbowed him, nearly knocking the ink well over.

Kaz immediately retaliated by ruffling my curls, fully aware of how long it took me to tame them this morning because I'd complained about it earlier.

"Hey! My curls, Kaz!" I smacked his arm. "Do you know how much leave-in conditioner I used today?"

He laughed. "Can't help it. They look like springy clouds."

"Our banter's gonna get us banned one day," I muttered as another older club member shot us a disapproving look.

To be fair, we deserved it.

We spent most sessions sneaking ink smudges onto each other's aprons, wrists, or foreheads whenever Baltasar got too invested in one of his dramatic speeches.

"Stop wasting the ink!" he'd complain at least once every meeting.

Honestly, I understood the *apron rule* now.

Calligraphy club sounded classy until Kaz started finger-painting kanji onto your elbow.

By the end of the session, we were both covered in ink stains again.

Naturally, that meant selfies and posting them on our social media.

Kaz threw an arm around my shoulder while I held up my brush dramatically like some

victorious warrior.

We both commented under the post,

Me: *"Ink Masters 🖊️📜"*

Kaz: *"Calligraphy but make it chaos"*

Me: "We seriously need that on shirts."

The laughter still lingered between us as we stepped outside into the cool night air. Campus had gone quiet, washed in soft lamplight, with only the occasional skateboarder passing through.

As usual, Kaz walked me back to the dorm.

Somewhere along the path, I sent Merrick a quick text:

"Club's finished, heading back ❤"

When I looked up again, Kaz had slowed his pace and drifted a few steps ahead, hands tucked into his hoodie pockets to give me privacy.

He was honestly too considerate for his own good sometimes.

So naturally, I sprinted forward and jumped onto his back.

"Giddy up, horsey!" Kaz nearly lost his balance. "Erei! What the heck—OW. This is animal abuse."

I burst out laughing, tightening my grip around his shoulders. "Kaz, horses don't talk. Move faster."

He groaned dramatically but took off anyway.

We raced across campus like complete idiots while he made exaggerated horse noises and I laughed hard enough that my stomach hurt.

"I regret every decision that led me here," he complained.

"You should. Your gallop sucks."

"Your jokes suck."

"Your face sucks."

By the time we reached the dorm building, we were both breathless from laughing.

Kaz lowered me back onto my feet gently, and we stood near the entrance catching our breath.

"Okay," he said carefully. "One last thing."

I narrowed my eyes at him. "Don't."

His grin widened. "La Lick."

I shrieked and bolted for the dorm entrance.. He chased after me, trying to get a hit at me before I could disappear.

"Not today!" I shouted from behind the door to the girls' dorm entrance, having the security guard look at us weirdly.

"Cheater!" He shouted from the other side of the rotating doors.

"Later, Kaz!"

"Bye, Erei!"

By the time I made it upstairs, I was exhausted but still buzzing with leftover adrenaline. I flopped onto my bed and sent Merrick one last text.

Me: *"Goodnight ❤ ✎"*

Then I curled beneath my blanket with dried ink still staining my arms, a smile still stuck to my face, thinking that maybe life didn't need to be perfect to still be good.

Chapter 19: Strings and Keys

Andromeda

The next weekend came quietly.

Andromeda met up with Mita early Saturday morning, both girls armed with coffee cups and brownies. The campus was still sleepy as they crossed the quad, sunlight cutting between the trees. Andromeda hated that the shape of tree branches made her think of *him*, but she blinked it away, not wanting to ruin a day that had barely started.

"Ready to make me a pianist?" Andromeda asked.

"As ready as you'll ever be," Mita smirked, nudging her shoulder.

They entered the music building; it was quiet, as expected this early in the morning. The soft creak of the door, the icy fingers of the cool air danced across wherever our skin was exposed, and the faint hum of the floor heater below their feet made the day start with a cozy, slow start.

Mita led the way to the grand piano in the corner where they sat last week.

"Alright. Sit." Mita patted the bench beside her eagerly.

"You're bossy when you're infront a piano," Andromeda said, humor lacing her voice as she sat by Mita.

"Only because Rune was," Mita replied, her voice turning soft. "He taught me how to slow down. Not just with my hands, but my thoughts too. Watch."

Mita began to play a simple scale. Her fingers moved slowly, deliberately. It was as though Andromeda could see the notes float into the air off the physical keys, wrapping themselves together before encircling Mita.

"See this?" She took Andromeda's fingers gently and laid them on the keys. "You don't press down with your whole hand. It's like… whispering with your fingers."

"That sounds unnecessarily poetic," Andromeda muttered, but let her guide her hand anyway.

"It *is* poetic. It's supposed to sound like feeling," Mita said. "Rune always told me, 'Music doesn't start from the keys, it starts from your chest.'"

Mita leaned in and showed her how to relax her shoulders, how to feel the natural rhythm, how not to rush transitions, exactly how Rune had once calmed her trembling fingers when she was too anxious to play.

The rest of the morning blurred into chords, shared laughter, and little triumphs. Andromeda managed to play a basic melody, then messed it up, then nailed it again.

"I'll admit it," Andromeda said as she wiped her brow. "This… is fun."

"Told you." Mita grinned, proud of her friend's achievement and herself for being able to help her friend. "Next week, you teach me viola again; let's do alternate teaching sessions. Deal?"

"Deal."

By the time evening rolled around, the other music club members had started trickling in, filling the space with scattered melodies and chatter once again. The club president introduced the night's topic, "History of Global Music Chords," a fast-paced but fascinating presentation.

Andromeda, surprisingly, was completely into it.

She glanced over at Mita and whispered, "Now you get why I love this."

Mita nodded before adding, "More than you know."

But partway through, something made her look toward the door, and there he was.

Zebedee.

Standing like he didn't know how doorways worked, arms crossed and waving like an idiot when their eyes met.

She muttered, "I'll be back," and slipped away headlong toward the door.

She walked right past him, not breaking stride, before stopping ahead of him and turning to face him. Crossing her arms against her chest, she looked up at him. "Stalking doesn't suit you, Zebedee."

"It's Zeb," he corrected, running to catch up to her. "And I'm not stalking. I just had a feeling you'd be here."

"So… stalking," she said, overly pronounced, like a teacher correcting a toddler.

"Come on," he groaned, trailing beside her as she continued walking down the hall. "I was nearby. I thought you might be there. That's all."

"You sound like a walking red flag."

"Hey, I was being friendly, and I *barely* waved," he said with a crooked smile, like it could get him out of this.

They stopped outside the bathroom.

"This is the ladies' room," she said, narrowing her eyes. "You wanna come in?" She was mocking him; she knew he wouldn't dare, but she really wanted to ruffle his feathers a little for some incoherent reason.

Zeb threw up his hands. "I'm not *that* bold."

She went in, holding in the laugh threatening to break free.

When she came back out, she half-expected him to still be there, lurking, trying to be funny. But he wasn't. And she hated that she was kind of disheartened that he wasn't.

She walked back to the music room, ignoring the flicker of disappointment in her chest. She didn't like men. Not really. Reed was the exception, and he was in a hospital bed. The rest were noise. Vermin. Chaos. Unreliable.

But…

Zeb wasn't horrible.

The night continued, and Mita kept her promise, letting Andromeda take the lead for once. They played, they learned, they laughed. And for once, she didn't feel like she was trying to forget something. She was just… here in this moment.

After the club had ended, they walked back together.

Andromeda paused on Mita's floor, not ready to head upstairs. "I think I'll crash in your room tonight, again?" she asked Mita as casually as she could.

"Sure. You okay?" Mita asked gently.

"I'm just not ready to be alone," Andromeda replied, her voice low but even.

That night, they curled up on Mita's bed with snacks and crime documentaries, this time with Amerei joining them, whispering comments and laughing until their eyes stung.

At one point, Andromeda turned to Mita, "You know, I think I finally get why you love music. It's like a type of outlet while being an expression," she randomly said.

Mita smiled. "Yeah. It's like prayer without words. You know, my mom told me that music is another form of worship to God."

They continued chatting about the allure of music and its hidden treasures, ignoring the documentary playing in the background. That night, beneath the gentle glow of the screen and surrounded by a pile of blankets, Andromeda didn't feel haunted. She simply felt… human once more.

Chapter 20: The Edge of the Semester

Andromeda POV

The weeks leading up to finals were nothing short of a dumpster fire.

A beautifully academic, meticulously scheduled, utterly exhausting dumpster fire.

I had mock exams, presentations, lab submissions, case studies, two oral tests, and a capstone outline due. There were days when I stared at my screen and couldn't remember if I was working on pathophysiology or bioethics or if I was just hallucinating an entire thesis in my head.

Even the air on campus was heavy.

Like the trees were studying too. Like the sky had forgotten how to exhale.

Everyone was frantic. There was this dull background noise of stressed students crying in library corners, study groups turning into debate clubs, and professors giving that ever-condescending "you've had all semester" speech.

Please. As if we hadn't *also* had fifteen other things to juggle.

Mita looked just as wrecked as I felt. We saw each other in passing, blurry hellos in the kitchen when I stayed over, and brief updates over burnt toast. She didn't make it to the music room either. And I knew, if *Mita* was missing out on the music club, things were bad.

We were all just trying to survive.

And I was back to chasing perfection. Not because anyone told me to, because that's just how I'm wired.

Near-perfect was my thing.

It wasn't healthy. It wasn't sustainable. But it was me.

I hadn't seen Zeb since that night in the music hallway. Not even in passing.

And I told myself I was fine with that.

He probably had his own finals, his own life. He was a whole artist; he could disappear into a canvas for weeks and still come out with a smile and a paintbrush between his teeth.

Not that I cared.

I didn't have time to care.

But sometimes, when I'd leave a lecture hall and pass the art building, which was out of my regular route, might I add, my eyes would linger on the entrance. And I hated myself for it.

The truth?

I wasn't scared of him.

I was scared of what he represented: the possibility that not all guys were monsters. That some could smile without smirking. That some didn't want anything from me. That someone could *see me* and not try to *take* me.

I didn't know if Zeb was that kind of guy. But he hadn't earned my suspicion yet. Which was strange.

Because most people did by now.

You wanna know the one relief in the chaos?

My notes.

All that over-studying I did throughout the semester? The cramming sessions that blurred my vision and sent me into panic spirals?

They came in clutch now.

While other students were just now trying to catch up, I was reviewing. I already had my color-coded diagrams, my flashcards, my chapter highlights. I wasn't cruising, but I wasn't drowning either.

And that felt good.

Like… maybe all that breakdown wasn't useless after all.

And then, one night, it hit me.

I hadn't taken my meds in over a week.

Not because I forgot.

Because I *chose* not to.

I'd tapered down first. Gradually. The withdrawal was brutal. I had cold sweats one night so bad I thought I had a fever. My heart raced at random. Sleep came in jolts instead of hours. I cried at a TV commercial once and then couldn't remember why.

But now?

I could breathe again.

Not clearly. Not fully. But better.

I wasn't recommending it to anyone. My therapist would definitely disapprove. But for me, the meds had become a wall. They kept the storm out, sure, but they also blocked the light.

I needed to feel again. Even the bad stuff. Otherwise, I'd forget what healing even looked like.

The nightmares had dulled. Not vanished. But dulled.

The trees didn't haunt me like they used to. I could walk past them now without freezing. I could see the bark, not just the shadows. I even noticed how some of them bloomed in pink, small, delicate flowers, climbing their limbs.

That had to mean something.

One afternoon, I sat by the window in the campus café, reviewing hematology flashcards, sipping an overpriced chai latte, overhearing a loud group of students nearby who were arguing over case study answers. I tried my best and ignored them, thinking that it would be hopeless and leaving would be a better option.

Instead, I caught myself watching the wind outside. The way it moved through the leaves. The way the sunlight filtered through the glass, warm but indirect.

For a moment, I smiled to myself.

Not because something was funny.

Because I was still here.

Still pushing.

Still showing up, even if only for myself.

I wasn't ready to say I was healed.

I wasn't even ready to say I was okay.

But I was present.

And I'm ok with that, it's progress.

That night, I got back to Mita and Amerei's dorm, pulled off my coat, and found Mita half-asleep on the floor with a marketing textbook on her stomach.

"Are you dead or just dreaming of metrics?" I asked.

Her eyes opened, one at a time. "Both," she muttered, drool sliding down the corner of her mouth.

I sat beside her, the carpet cool under my legs.

"We're gonna get through this," I told her.

She mumbled something I think was "I know," then rolled onto her side and kept reading.

We didn't talk much after that, didn't need to, because in the quiet?

I wasn't drowning anymore.

And maybe, when finals were over...

Maybe I'd go back to the music room.

Maybe Zeb would be there.

Maybe not.

But for now, I had flashcards, coffee, and breath in my lungs.

That was more than I had last semester.

And I'd take it.

Chapter 21: Crunch Time and Colored Tabs

Amerei POV

Finals week.

I didn't cry.

Okay, I *almost* cried. Twice. But those don't count unless actual tears hit the cheek. Near-cries are just… blinking aggressively; that's the best I can describe it.

As an aspiring financial analyst, in a finance major, the weeks leading up to finals were a slow-burn descent into madness. Excel spreadsheets, case studies, market simulations, group presentations where two people pulled the weight of five. It was chaos.

Productivity felt like a mood swing. One minute, I was a Master of Finance. Next, I was lying on the floor, eating cold takeout, questioning my entire academic journey and wondering if I could make a living selling clay earrings on Etsy.

The worst part?

I barely had time to call Merrick.

We texted. Quick check-ins. Sweet "good luck, babe" and "I'm proud of You". And he understood. He really did. But that didn't stop the ache in my chest when my phone would light up with his name and I'd swipe it away with a "can't talk now."

Still, he never complained. He'd just send me motivational videos, gifs of animated kittens studying, and the occasional order of boba to my dorm without saying anything. Just a text:

Merrick: *"Your brain deserves a treat."*

And honestly? He was right.

Somehow, in the middle of the academic jungle, I still made it to Calligraphy Club.

Every Thursday, I dragged my sleep-deprived body across campus just to write letters I wouldn't use and splash ink on Kaz.

Correction: **he** splashed ink on me first. I retaliated. And now, it's basically tradition.

Kazuya, Kaz, as I now call him, was still my favorite unintentional stress relief. Even when we didn't see each other at the club, we'd text random things just to annoy each other.

Me: *How does it feel knowing your "A"s look like deranged shrimp?*

Kaz: *Like art, Erei. Ever heard of abstract expressionism?*

Me: *You express nonsense.*

We passed each other on campus more often than we realized. Once in the dining hall line, we both pretended not to see each other. We even did that thing where you walk toward someone and try to pass without acknowledging them, only to end up walking side by side for a few awkward steps.

"Don't trip on your shoelace," he said one time without looking at me.

"They're velcro, Kaz," I shot back.

"You're velcro."

"What does that even mean?!" I'd snapped

Back at the dorm, it was a different kind of battlefield.

Andromeda had decided to stay with us during finals. Not permanently, just enough to survive the academic storm. And I couldn't lie... I was grateful for her company.

Seeing her color-coded binders and insane highlighter game did something to me. The organization? The tabs? The precision?

It made me, *me,* actually care.

I started color-coding. I wasn't an expert, but I tried my best. I even bought new pens. I caught myself re-writing notes just because hers looked prettier.

"Wow," Andromeda said one night. "Peer pressure finally got to you."

"This isn't peer pressure," I said. "This is aesthetic inspiration."

She raised an eyebrow. "Call it what you want, copycat."

"You're lucky I like you." I shot back

Mita, meanwhile, was also on the floor surrounded by flashcards and sticky notes.

"Why is there a sticky note in the *fridge?*" I asked one day.

She shrugged. "It's where I keep snacks. Why not revise while getting a snack too?"

Fair point.

We had this routine now.

- Wake up.
- Groan.
- Make caffeine.
- Study.
- Get distracted.
- Complain.
- Repeat.

Sometimes we'd play soft music. Sometimes, just the low hum of our laptop fans and the scratch of pens.

At night, we took turns venting.

"My group partner ghosted me two hours before our presentation," Mita grumbled.

"I submitted the wrong version of my mock exam," Andromeda muttered.

"My spreadsheet crashed and deleted everything," I whispered into my ramen like it had the power to listen.

And then we'd all fall silent again, in the kind of exhausted solidarity that only academic death can bring.

But there was beauty in the chaos.

Beauty in the little things.

Mita's spontaneous dance breaks. Andromeda's sarcastic commentary that made us laugh-snort in the middle of study sessions. The smell of instant noodles and chai lattes blending in weirdly comforting ways.

We may not have had our lives together, but at least we weren't falling apart alone.

One night, just before finals week officially began, I sat by the window with a notebook on my lap. Mita was asleep. Andromeda was cross-legged on the bed, flipping through flashcards with the cold efficiency of a trained assassin.

"I don't know how you do it," I said.

"Do what?" She asked, still focusing on her cards

"Stay so… precise. So calm. Even when things are crashing." I muttered, playing with the edge of the pages of my notes

She paused. Her face softened just a little before letting out a slight chuckle.

"I don't stay calm," she said. "I just make it *look* like I do."

We both went quiet for a while.

Then I whispered, "I'm glad you're here," knowing I shouldn't probe any longer.

She didn't answer.

But she didn't have to.

I texted Kaz that night.

Me: *Hey, if I fail finals, I'm blaming you and your bad handwriting.*

Five minutes later, his reply came through.

Kaz: *Rude. My handwriting is poetry.*

Me: *Your "poetry" gave me a migraine.*

Kaz: *Miss you too, Erei, but go to bed.*

I smiled at the screen. Dumb, but honest.

As the week drew to a close, I looked around the dorm: pages scattered, laptops glowing, soft breathing from my friends sleeping nearby.

I was tired. Mentally, physically, emotionally.

But I was also weirdly content.

I had my girls.

I had my goals.

I had… a little bit of peace.

Chapter 22: When the Waters Rise

Finals arrived like a flood.

Not the neat kind, the storm kind. It was more like the moment God released the waters over the earth in Noah's time, and the ground didn't even get a chance to cry out before it was swallowed whole. That's what exam season felt like on campus.

It poured over everything.

Every classroom, every café, every hallway conversation became a frantic stream of half-remembered definitions and formulas. Students moved in a daze fueled by caffeine, adrenaline, and the eternal hope that the one thing they didn't study wouldn't be on the exam. Spoiler: it always was.

Andromeda, Amerei, and Mita had gone into full academic lockdown, joined occasionally by Odessa, who, though she lived off-campus, made a regular appearance in their study huddle with her neon highlighters and extra snacks.

And in the middle of this chaos, something strange happened.

Mita started praying.

Not just quietly in her room anymore.

Out loud.

In the middle of their study sessions.

It started subtly, barely audible whispers at first.

"Lord, help us focus."

"Give us peace."

"Remind us we're not alone."

But then she got bolder.

One night, mid-study, just after the clock struck midnight and the energy in the dorm had turned from "focused" to "existential crisis," Mita closed her textbook with a loud snap and said, "Can I pray?" her frustration leaking into her words

Amerei blinked. "Like… now? Out loud?"

"Yeah," Mita said simply, folding her hands.

And before anyone could object, she started.

Andromeda didn't look up from her notes. She wasn't against it, per se. Just not *into it.* Not a Jesus girl. Not a "God, take the wheel" type. The only people she'd known who claimed to follow Jesus were also the people who wore two faces and hid their claws behind Scripture. Hypocrites. Liars. Manipulators.

Except Mita.

To Andromeda, Mita was different.

However, she kept studying… at first.

Until she saw, out of the corner of her eye, **Amerei,** full-on, hands clasped, head bowed like she was born in Sunday school.

Andromeda stared.

"Really?" she mouthed.

Amerei closed her eyes and raised a finger to her lips, saying, '*shh.*'

Andromeda didn't fold her hands. Didn't bow her head. But she stopped highlighting. Stopped scanning flashcards. Just… paused.

Because if her friend was speaking to the heavens, the least she could do was not scribble about anatomic models while it happened.

It wasn't her faith.

It wasn't even respect for the God Mita was praying to.

It was something else.

Something like, *I might not believe what you believe, but I respect that you believe it, and if I love you, maybe I can hold space for what matters to you.*

She refused to call it an obligation. She wasn't that kind of girl.

She didn't get manipulated, not anymore. Didn't follow the crowd. Didn't fold to pressure.

If she stopped what she was doing, it wasn't because of Mita. It was because *her own conscience* bothered her. If the moment felt too sacred to interrupt, that was on *her, and no one demanding it of her.*

And honestly? She was kind of okay with that.

Amerei, on the other hand, found herself leaning into it.

Not the God part, at least, not *openly.*

But there was something in the way Mita prayed. Her voice changed, not just in tone, but in texture. Like she stepped into something bigger than the room, it was calming. Gentle. Steady in a way that no amount of peppermint tea or melatonin could be.

Amerei once whispered to her after a particularly intense group prayer, if you could call it that, "You know… if this digital marketing thing doesn't work out, you should do ASMR prayer recordings. That voice? Therapeutic."

At the time, Mita had laughed so hard she cried.

But it was true.

There was a peace that clung to the air after every prayer.

Even when the exams loomed, and the clock ticked faster than the information could be absorbed, even when group chats exploded with panic and professors dropped last-minute updates.

Even when their bodies were giving out before their minds did.

There was *peace.*

Odessa still came by in bursts; when exams had started, her off-campus commute cut into her time but not into her loyalty to her friends. She once brought everything from iced coffee to pre-torn notes. and sometimes even those stick-on under-eye patches to "reduce exam-induced puffiness."

Her energy was different. vibrant, loud, and magnetic, but she, too, quieted during the prayer moments.

She was not religious either. Just respectful.

"You know this is your fault," Amerei said one night.

Andromeda looked up. "What is?"

"These… these graphs. These organized thoughts. These unnecessarily straight lines. I've been infected."

"Good. You're welcome."

Amerei rolled her eyes. "I was fine living in academic chaos."

"You were also borderline failing."

"Touché."

The nights blurred together.

They'd go to sleep at 3 a.m., wake up at 8. Someone always brewed coffee. Someone always forgot to brush their hair. No one judged.

There were still Post-it notes on every surface. Motivational quotes. Dumb inside jokes. At one point, someone scribbled, *"Jesus take the grade"* on the fridge. No one said to take it down, but everyone laughed.

By the time exams actually started, they were exhausted.

But they were ready.

And not just academically.

They were *anchored*.

Mita prayed on the morning of every exam day. Sometimes over their coffee. Sometimes in the elevator. Sometimes while lacing her shoes.

She didn't care who saw.

"God," she whispered once, as they left for a final. "Just help us and bring back what we studied. Even the stuff we don't remember studying. Amen."

And they said Amen.

Even Andromeda. Quietly. Barely above a whisper.

They each walked into different exam halls, under different pressures, and answered different questions.

None of them knew their scores yet.

But they all knew this:

If they failed, they would have a meltdown

Chapter 23: We Survived. Barely. Let's Celebrate.

The moment finals ended, they all just… collapsed.

No poetic metaphor. No grand, soul-searching relief.

Just bodies, exhausted, running on academic fumes, dragging themselves to Mita and Amerei's shared dorm like zombies who hadn't devoured their next prey in a year. In other words, extremely fatigued.

Mita opened the door first, holding it dramatically like a flight attendant awaiting the boarding of passengers. "Welcome to the post-final haven," she said.

And then, one by one, they dropped.

Andromeda claimed the floor. Straight-up fell face-first into the carpet and didn't move.

Odessa curled into the couch like a cat, arm over her eyes.

Amerei went straight for the one-man couch and sprawled out like a queen who had just ended a reign of chaos.

Mita stood at the door, watching them all with a fond smile plastered across her face.

"We made it," she whispered to herself.

For about thirty seconds, no one spoke. Just the sound of soft breathing and the occasional "ow" from Andromeda, who realized carpet wasn't exactly chiropractor-approved.

Then Amerei, eyes half-closed, murmured, "Mita... say a prayer. Like... knock-us-out level prayer."

Mita laughed. "Seriously?"

"I'm not joking," Odessa added. "Like... ASMR meets divine intervention."

"Please," Andromeda said into the floor. "Put me in a coma. A holy coma."

Mita chuckled, slid down the wall adjacent to the door, and sat cross-legged on the floor opposite them.

"Alright, alright," she said, closing her eyes and taking a breath. "Let's pray."

And in her soft, sweet, now-famously soothing voice, she began.

"God... thank You for getting us through this week. Through these months. Through every mental breakdown, every group project gone wrong, every failed printer, and every late-night meltdown. Thank You for holding us when we were too tired to hold ourselves. Let this rest be deep. Let our hearts be light. And please let nobody dream about exam questions. In Jesus name, Amen."

"Amen," Amerei echoed, already half-asleep.

Ten minutes later, the room was dead silent.

They were *gone*.

Hours passed.

Sunlight turned to dusk.

Dusk faded into deep, quiet evening.

They eventually woke up slowly one by one, blinking into the soft glow of lamplight outside that flowed in through the windows.

"Wait... what time is it?" Odessa asked, hair a mess and voice still groggy.

"Like... 8," Mita said, checking her phone, accidentally blinding herself with the light from her phone screen.

"In the morning?"

"No. night."

"Perfect," Andromeda mumbled. "Let's ruin our sleep schedule some more."

So they ordered food, changed into even *baggier* clothes, and let the night roll on. Since they had left spare clothes here when they came over to study.

They watched crime documentaries until their brains felt fried again, then reverted to cartoons to 'cleanse the trauma,' as Amerei put it.

Sometime around midnight, someone said, "We should celebrate."

Mita blinked. "Like… now?"

"Not now…maybe tomorrow," Odessa grinned, but the exhaustion written on her brows was noticeable. "We just finished surviving the semester; let a girl breathe first, but that being said, we do deserve a party."

"Okay, okay," Andromeda said, sitting up. "Hear me out: first, we visit Reed. Then we do something fun. Like movies. Or chaos. Or both."

"Both," Amerei nodded. "Definitely both." They all had their own ideas for chaos for that day, but decided to lay them to rest for now.

The next day, they were still on campus, arms full of snacks, little decorations, and one big card for Reed that looked like four different art styles had fought for dominance, because that's what happens when four girls with different opinions make a handcrafted card.

They arrived at the hospital, energetic and loud with soft hearts.

Reed was still in his quiet world, eyes closed, chest rising and falling, but his presence still filled the room like sunshine.

Each girl took turns updating him on their semester.

Mita told him about her new viola skills thanks to Andromeda.

Andromeda confessed to the chaos of medicine and how she was "one lab kit away from burning the science wing down."

Amerei told him all about Merrick again, about the calligraphy club and 'her new ink-stained sibling,' Kaz.

Odessa ranted about group work and how she deserved a medal for surviving it.

Then they all played the same little guessing game from the first visit they did at the start of the term—"**What would Reed say?**" They laughed, cried, and left their chaos on the walls of that quiet room like graffiti made of joy.

That night?

They *turned up*.

Movie theater first—popcorn bigger than their heads, screaming at previews, judging trailers like professional critics.

Then the parking lot happened.

Odessa pulled out a random Bluetooth speaker from her tote bag and yelled, "Dance battle. Right here. Right now."

"I'm wearing Crocs," Mita protested.

"You're wearing *confidence*," Odessa declared, turning up the volume.

"I said Crocs, not pads," Mita retorted.

They danced. Horribly. Gleefully.

Then came impromptu karaoke, truth-or-dare lightning rounds, and a game where they tried to guess each other's secret crushes—which ended in gasps, threats, and near-tackles.

Security passed by once.

They waved politely at him, a subtle *'please don't tell us to leave.'*

He waved back.

Didn't even try to stop them.

When they returned to the dorm, they were breathless.

And full.

And weirdly peaceful.

Shoes kicked off. Hoodies tossed. Blankets claimed.

The girls took up every surface again in the living room of Mita and Amerei's shared dorm. The floor was littered with couch cushions dragged into makeshift nests; some even dragged blankets and extra pillows from each girl's room.

"I love you guys," Amerei said dramatically from under two blankets.

"We know," Andromeda replied, already halfway asleep.

"I'm sleeping in my jeans," Odessa groaned. "This is true exhaustion."

Mita smiled, pulling the blankets tighter around herself.

For the first time in months, the storm had passed.

Finals were over.

They had survived.

And before they all went home for winter break, before life scattered them to family homes and long trips and endless holidays—

They had this.

One weekend. One sleepover.

One final memory to tie the semester together like a perfectly chaotic bow.

Chapter 24: The Girl With Secrets and Silence

The lights in Mita and Amerei's dorm room were dim. A few string lights cast a soft golden hue over the space, flickering gently like stars. The floor was littered with blankets and pillows. Cartoons played on mute in the background, and forgotten bowls of popcorn sat untouched.

They were full. Not with food—but with sleep, survival, and silence.

Until Mita, curled up on a floor pillow in fuzzy socks and a hoodie two sizes too big, lifted her head from Andromeda's lap.

"I said this to Meda the other day, but I wanna say it again," she said, voice hushed but firm. "We know each other… but we really don't *know* each other. If you know what I mean."

The room stilled.

"What are some things y'all have been bottling up?" she asked, eyes wide but warm, looking at each of the girls. "No pressure. I just… I love you guys. And I don't want us secretly suffering in silence as I did."

She was met with silence again.

Then, Odessa rolled over, tugging the blanket off her head. "Okay, fine. Let's do this recovery meeting or whatever. Because y'all gonna need recovery after hearing my story."

Mita chuckled softly. "No judgment here, Dessa."

"I think mine's worse," Andromeda muttered.

"Mine's probably just weird," Amerei said.

But Odessa sat up, brushing popcorn crumbs off her tank top, her expression unreadable.

"Alright," she exhaled. "Here goes."

Odessa's Story

The air in the room changed. Heavier. Still. Like something sacred was being unboxed in the open.

"I don't have parents," Odessa started. "Well, not in the 'they died tragically' kind of way. My mom was a drug addict. My dad—he was an abuser."

Amerei blinked. "Wait… like emotionally or—?"

"Physically. And worse," Odessa cut in. "But here's the thing. He wasn't the typical alcoholic deadbeat. My dad was sober. Very sober. The kind of man the neighborhood called respectable. Active in the community. Always mowing the lawn on time. Always greeting neighbors. Always pretending."

She let out a bitter chuckle.

"Everyone thought my mom was the problem. The druggie. The one who'd disappear for days and forget the stove on. But what they didn't see was *why* she used."

Odessa's eyes glazed over. "He drove her to it."

Flashback

She was seven.

The living room reeked of bleach and burnt toast. Her mom was passed out on the couch again, arms limp, eyes sunken. And from the kitchen… moaning.

Not from pain.

Odessa remembered padding barefoot into the kitchen because she was hungry. She wanted cereal. But instead, she saw him.

Her dad. And some woman in a red dress.

Laughing. Half-dressed.

It doesn't take a genius to know what her dad was doing with that woman at that age.

When they both saw her, her dad looked annoyed, but the woman stood there, frozen. He asked her politely to leave, which was just like him, 'the perfect dad,' but when the woman left, her dad turned to her slowly, like a villain in a movie. Calm. Cold.

"You saw something you shouldn't have, little girl," he said.

Then the belt came out. It wasn't a regular-ass whooping; it went on until she passed out.

Present Day

"I never cried," Odessa said, voice dry. "Not then. Not when I was taken away. Not even when my mom stabbed him in the chest six times and collapsed that same night from an overdose."

Dead silence.

"I was nine. And by the end of the week, I was in foster care."

Mita's hand flew to her mouth. Andromeda had gone stone still. Amerei stared down at her lap, fists clenched.

"I spent a year in the system," Odessa continued, her voice lower now. "House to house. You learn to stop unpacking. To stop getting attached. One foster mom made me scrub toilets every day. Another foster dad tried to get handsy. I kicked him and ran."

She paused before continuing.

"But then… my now brother adopted me."

Flashback: The First Day

She remembered walking into the giant marble-floored mansion like a refugee.

The social worker was all smiles. "This is Noah," she had said. "He's 19. His parents died two years ago. He wanted a sister."

She'd looked up to see a tall, lanky guy with thick black hair, wearing a hoodie 2x his size, holding out a bag of gummy bears like it was gold.

"You want the blue ones? They're the best," he said.

She didn't speak.

He ruffled her hair. "Cool. You'll love your room."

And she did.

It was big. Soft bed. Warm lights. Shelves lined with books and stuffed animals. Clothes in her size. A little post-it on the mirror that read, *You're safe here. -N.*

Back in the Dorm Room

"I didn't know how to be safe," Odessa said, a sad smile on her lips. "But he taught me."

"I live lavishly now," she said, forcing a laugh. "Nice clothes, nice school, my brother's loaded. I act confident. People like confident girls, *right?*" Her voice sounded like she was sure, but there was a hint of uncertainty laced in her tone.

She gazed at everything in the room but them, seeming to find it difficult to look at them. "But really? I'm just a girl who watched her dad bleed out with my mom's overdosed corpse beside him. Who saw love in the most twisted way. Who flinches when men raise their voices?"

Tears slipped down her cheeks.

"And sometimes I wonder if I'm just putting designer bags over trauma. If I'm still the scared little girl in a hallway, listening to her mom screams as her dad beat the living crap out of her."

The room went silent before Mita broke the stillness.

She launched forward and wrapped Odessa in a hug, weeping.

"Dessa…" she whispered. "I had no idea."

Neither did Andromeda nor Amerei, until now; all they knew was the firecracker Odessa, who wore stilettos to morning class and flirted with waiters like it was a sport.

"I told you," Odessa sniffled. "You're all soft. And you were all gonna cry."

"And you were gonna break my heart," Andromeda said, wrapping her arms around them too.

"I'm just here, putting cars and money over my trauma…" Odessa sobbed, breaking down fully.

"You were surviving," Mita affirmed, "and you don't have to anymore. Not alone. We can't take back what happened already, but one thing is for certain: we are all here for you."

They all cried then. Together. A healing, kind of cry that someone finally knew her behind her mask of wealth.

"I should've gone last," Odessa joked through tears. "We're already emotionally wrecked, and we just started."

But they laughed; wet, broken, but together

This was recovery.

This was family.

Chapter 25: What We Don't Say

The room was still thick with Odessa's confession: its gravity, its sorrow, its sudden burst of dark truth shattering the assumption that anyone ever had it "together."

But then, Andromeda wiped her tears.

And when she looked up, her usual stone-cold eyes were bloodshot, glassy. Still sharp with the usual fire in them. But now cracked. Shattered even.

"I can say this now, I guess."

Everyone turned.

"You know how I'm snappy at guys? And anyone new?"

Odessa nodded, still sniffling. Amerei hugged a pillow tightly to herself. Mita sat up straighter, her eyes already glossing over again.

"Well…" Andromeda exhaled. "There's a reason for that."

She leaned back against the foot of the couch, her voice growing quieter, but steadier.

"I grew up in a family that looked perfect. Affluent. Gated compound in the hills. Christian flags in every living room. Bibles on the coffee tables that hadn't been touched only for display, never really read, unless someone from church was visiting."

"Everyone in the family lived in the compound: cousins, aunts,

uncles, grandparents. Think of it as a high-society town, curated and sealed in pride and control. *Reputation was everything, IS everything in fact.*"

"My siblings? All of them golden children. The eldest, a surgeon. Next in line is an architect. Fourth, a future engineer, but the baby wants to be an artist; if it were me, I would be disowned, but he is the youngest, the family's pride and joy, so he's spoiled like royalty. I'm the third. Middle child. People like to say the middle gets ignored. That wasn't my case. I got all the attention. All the pressure."

"My parents demanded perfection. I had private viola lessons by age five, as it would make me seem like a refined young lady. I also did martial arts by six. I was home schooled because, you know, private school wasn't enough. They wanted complete control of what went on in my head."

"If I failed, I didn't get grounded; I got bruises. If I made a friend who came from a family of lower status, they'd threaten their parents' businesses or livelihood, aka their source of income. I learned how to be excellent with a black eye."

She paused, swallowing. "They didn't love me. They wanted to *shape* me into something to show off. A trophy."

Odessa slowly reached for her hand. Andromeda let her.

"I asked once if I could do boxing. You know, something **I** wanted. They said it was too vulgar for a girl, that I had to be proper. That I was being groomed to be a *wife.* Not some fighter."

Mita muttered something under her breath. Andromeda smiled bitterly. "You'd think that's the worst of it. But no."

Her voice dropped.

"That same summer… I was eight. I woke up to something wet on my neck. And then the weight of someone: a heavy, disgusting weight on my body."

Her voice caught.

"My uncle. My dad's brother. Dry humping my leg while I was asleep.

I tried to scream, but his hand clamped down on my mouth. I was small. I couldn't move. I remember my hands pinned over my head. His belt buckle digging into my ribs. My heart beating out of my body."

A wincing sob escaped her lips as though she was that same helpless little girl that night.

"When he finished, he had whispered in my ear. 'No one will believe you, so don't even try.'"

The room was dead silent.

Mita was frozen in place, hand over her mouth. Odessa clutched her pillow tightly, and Andromeda pulled her knees to her chest like she was trying to hold herself together. Amerei had gone so still, she looked like she was carved from stone, except for the single tear rolling down her cheek.

Andromeda cleared her throat before continuing.

"I ran to my parents. I told them everything. I showed them the red line on my thigh. They said I got it from playing outside. And then my father beat me for 'lying' on his brother."

Flashback

The echo of the belt. The sting of it over already sore skin.

Her mother, standing in the doorway, silent. Not stopping it. Just watching.

"You'll not shame this family with those dirty lies!" her father roared. "Do you understand me?!"

Andromeda sobbed on the floor.

But the floor offered no mercy.

"He came back the next week. And the week after. Every other night. Until I stopped crying. Until I learned how to separate my mind from my body."

Amerei gasped-sobbed.

"I called the police once," she said softly. "Thought I was brave. They showed up. My parents had paid them off as an apology for my 'inconsideration,' saying I was an 'imaginative and moody' child with too much time on my hands."

A silence fell again.

"I got beaten for that too."

She wiped her nose roughly with her sleeve.

"I made up a story, said animals were coming in through the window while I slept. Asked for cameras to be installed. I thought maybe, *maybe* if they saw something, they'd believe me."

Mita whispered, "Oh no…"

"My uncle was in tech. Guess who installed the cameras?"

"Oh my God," Odessa breathed.

"He edited the footage. Cutting out those parts, it showed me sleeping peacefully all night. My parents reviewed it *with him*. And that was when they 'had enough of my lies', and I became the family liar."

"I became the black sheep. My father never looked at me the same. My mother just cried and told me, 'Why do you keep trying to ruin our family'?" Throughout all this, he was spending time with us because he and his wife had a huge argument so bad she kicked him out for half a year. My guess is she caught him watching something similar to what he has been doing to me.

"I started sleeping with furniture in front of the door and closed my window."

Flashback: Last Summer

It was the summer break after she had completed her first year; she went back home as her mom demanded it, as she always would, and if that didn't work, she would guilt-trip her. Now, here she was back on the retched piece of vast land belonging to her family, having a get-together. It was the family's outdoor banquet.

The compound was loud, music playing, laughter echoing. Everything was *perfect*.

But she remembers there was a moment when she blacked out, a huge gap in her memory. She remembers saying no to a drink and then feeling dizzy. Then nothing.

The next thing she remembered?

Her body. Raw.

Hair matted.

Sheets stained.

Two cousins laughing as they zipped up their pants.

No evidence. No video. No cameras this time.

Just… a hazy memory.

"I think they drugged me. Took turns. They said I acted like I was untouchable. That I needed to be 'reminded' who I really was."

Andromeda's voice cracked.

"So yeah. When I say I don't trust men? When I flinch at hugs? When I keep people at a distance, why I'm blunt? It's not because I'm mean. It's because the people who were supposed to protect me used me like a toy. Discarded me and declared my truths as lies. They didn't spare nor care for my emotions. So, I had to care for me. I was never taught how to be careful with other's emotions, as mine was never cared for."

By now, the room was wrecked.

Mita was sobbing into her sleeve. Amerei had curled into herself, shaking. Odessa stood up and walked into the kitchen.

They heard a drawer slam.

Then her voice: "Where's the damn knife?"

"Dessa—" Amerei jumped up, chasing after her.

"No. No! These monsters are walking free. Her parents, her own *blood*, **let** her be destroyed and then called her a liar?! And those cousins—"

"Odessa." Amerei grabbed her arm. "We get it. But this, this isn't the way."

Odessa fell to her knees, knife clattering on the tile, wailing hard into Amerei's chest.

Andromeda was still sitting there, expression blank, gaze empty as though she had dissociated from the situation. She felt wrung out.

Mita knelt beside her.

"Medie…" she whispered. "Why didn't you tell us?"

Andromeda looked at her. "Because no one ever listened. And the ones who did? Hurt me worse."

Odessa came back and knelt on her other side. "Well, I'm listening now. And if I ever see that uncle of yours… God help me."

Mita wiped her tears. "I'm sorry your parents failed you. But we won't."

Amerei crawled across the floor and joined the hug, shaking. "You're not alone anymore, Meda. Not ever again."

And for the first time in years, maybe her entire life, Andromeda let herself be held.

Chapter 26: The Silence Between Stories

The room was quiet now.

Not the kind of silence that suffocates—but the kind that settles in trying to recover.

The weight of Andromeda's story still hung heavy in the air, draping over their shoulders like a storm that had passed, leaving behind not destruction, but fragile stillness.

They didn't speak for a long time.

No one wanted to break the silence first.

Odessa had put the knife away, her hands trembling—not out of anger like before, but from frustration and hopelessness. She sat with her knees pulled to her chest, staring at the floor.

Amerei had moved to the couch, her eyes red and distant. She'd stopped crying, but her lips were still trembling every now and then, like her body hadn't caught up with her brain yet.

Mita had gone to the bathroom to get tissues. When she came back, she passed them around. No words. Just care.

And Andromeda?

She lay curled on the floor with her head now in Mita's lap, eyes closed but not asleep. Her mascara had smudged down her face. Her arms were crossed tightly across her stomach, like she was holding herself together.

No one dared move too fast. No one reached for snacks or turned back on the cartoons or suggested a distraction.

This wasn't a moment for forgetting.

This was a moment for *being*.

Just being. Together. Breathing.

"Hey," Odessa finally whispered, voice hoarse. "Meda?"

"Yeah?" Andromeda answered, her eyes still closed.

"I meant what I said. If I ever meet any of them…"

"I know."

"And I'll go full-on psycho if you say the word."

That made Andromeda smile. Just a little. "You already *are* full-on psycho."

"Facts," Amerei murmured from the couch.

"I hate that I can't fix it," Mita whispered. "That none of us can."

"You don't have to," Andromeda said. "You're here. That's already more than anyone else ever was."

The room exhaled.

A few minutes passed. Mita traced patterns in Andromeda's hair, absent-mindedly.

"Do you guys realize," Amerei said suddenly, "that we all met in college? Like… strangers. Different majors. Different rooms. Different backgrounds. And somehow, we ended up here. Like this."

Odessa let out a tired laugh. "Trauma-united girl gang."

"The trauma Avengers," Amerei added softly.

"Sad girl squad," Andromeda mumbled softly.

"I mean," Mita said, looking up at the ceiling, "I'm not saying the trauma is a *gift* or anything, nor that bonding over trauma is healthy or desired … but if this is what came out of it, us coming together, then maybe it wasn't all in vain."

No one said anything right away.

But they all nodded.

Mita eventually got up and brought water to everyone. She passed the bottle to Andromeda first, and then to the rest of the girls before getting back to her own spot.

They drank slowly. Sipped like people who were returning to themselves.

Outside, the hum of the rain became a soothing ambiance in the background.

Odessa reached over and took Andromeda's hand again.

Amerei rubbed her eyes, then her temples, sighing deeply as though it came from her bones.

"I don't want to go next," she said honestly.

"You don't have to," Mita replied gently.

"Yeah. No pressure," Odessa added. "This was… heavy."

"I know," Amerei said, sitting up straighter. "But…I think I *need* to say it."

Andromeda opened her eyes for the first time since she shared. "Only if you're ready."

"I'm getting there," Amerei nodded.

Mita placed a hand on Amerei's shoulder and squeezed.

"You can take your time."

And so they sat.

The rain fell.

And the healing continued.

In the silence.

In the stillness.

In the quiet before the next brave voice said, *"Okay… here's my story."*

Chapter 27: Gray Zones and Red Flags

"So… my story's simple," Amerei began, her voice light at first like she was trying to ease the weight in the room.

They'd gone quiet again, curled into their spots in the living room of the dorm. The TV, they decided to turn on, buzzed quietly in the background, forgotten, as the time ticked by slowly.

"I grew up with two parents, mom and dad. Nothing crazy. No insane plot twist. They were always working though, like always. But I respected that. Their hustle gave me and my sister a great life. Everything we needed and most of what we wanted."

She pulled her knees up and rested her chin on them.

"I didn't feel neglected, just… separate. Like, emotionally, I mean. But it made me and my sister really close. She's older, louder, always been the life of the party. Like, she's the type to make friends in an elevator, and I was her shadow. Her 'little one,' as she would call me."

The girls listened quietly. Amerei wasn't crying. She wasn't trembling. But her voice had that quiet type of emotion, like she'd lived in her own skin long enough to narrate her life without falling apart.

"When she went to college, I'd visit her sometimes. I was home-schooled, so my parents would hire one of her classmates to tutor me while I stayed at her off-campus apartment. They thought it was an educational experience for me to see what college entails before even going."

Odessa raised an eyebrow. "And was it?"

"Well…" Amerei smirked. "Educational, yes. Just not the way they thought. I got a firsthand tour of college life. Parties. Hookups. Hangovers. Freaky little clubs hosted by bored rich kids with too much money and too few morals."

Andromeda hummed. "Sounds familiar."

"I never did anything too wild, though. I always had a line I wouldn't cross. My sister gave me space to explore but kept an eye on me, hovering just enough to make sure I didn't drown in the mess and chaos."

Amerei's voice turned soft again.

"So yeah. My childhood wasn't traumatic. Just… exposed. Too early, maybe. But I had control. And I had my sister."

Mita smiled a little. "That's actually kind of beautiful, Ame. Not the part you were exposed to that stuff, but that you are close to your sister."

"It was. And that's why I think this next part's been hard to process."

A quiet pause came over the room.

Amerei fidgeted with the corner of the throw pillow in her lap. Then she looked up.

"You remember that weekend I spent at Merrick's place after midterms?"

The girls all nodded slowly.

"Yeah," Odessa said. "You were glowing when you came back."

"I know. It was good, most of it. We got to spend some time together, and I missed him so much. With him working full-time now and me in my sophomore year, our schedules clash a lot."

"So what happened?" Andromeda asked, impatiently,

Amerei hesitated.

"Well… I'd wake up to him already, you know… *inside* me two different times."

The room fell still.

"He never asked. Never woke me up first. I'd just feel it happening and… be in it."

The silence was loud in the room.

Amerei looked around at them. "Is that like… borderline rape?"

Andromeda was the first to answer. "Yes. Or at the very least, serious consent violation."

Odessa leaned forward, voice low. "That's not something you just *do* to someone in their sleep without prior consent."

Amerei swallowed. "I brought it up to him. Told him it made me feel weird. And you know what he said? He said it added some spice to our relationship. That it was 'fun' and we should be open to trying new things. He said it was more exciting that way."

Mita frowned. "Did you tell him clearly how it made you feel?"

"I told him I'd rather be asked first," Amerei said. "That I'm not comfortable with being unconscious during sex."

"And how'd he take that?" Odessa asked.

"He didn't blow up or anything. Just kinda brushed it off like it was a kink we needed to 'talk through' eventually. Like it was a couple's game night idea."

"That might be a kink. That could very well be a problem," Andromeda said bluntly. "Especially if he keeps doing it after you said no."

Amerei shifted uncomfortably. "He hasn't done it again, at least, not that I know of. But we haven't spent the night together since then, so…"

It was quiet for another moment, everyone thinking.

"But also," Amerei added, voice quieter now, "is it bad that… like… I didn't hate it? I mean, waking up to him wasn't terrifying. It was Merrick. My boyfriend. And part of me… kinda liked it?"

"No," Mita said gently. "It's not unusual to be confused. But liking something *after* it starts doesn't mean consent was given *before* it started, and that's not right."

Odessa nodded. "It's okay to feel mixed about it. But it's *not* okay that he didn't ask."

Andromeda crossed her arms. "Here's the deal. In relationships, trust is everything. If he doesn't even wait for you to wake up or if that's his thing, at least ask permission prior to; that's not trust, that's entitlement."

"I didn't want to make a big deal out of it," Amerei whispered. "We've been so good together. He's never done anything to hurt me before."

"But this *did* hurt you, Ame," Mita said. "Maybe not physically. Maybe not even immediately. But emotionally? Mentally? You're carrying it. That says enough, because if you weren't, we would be having this conversation."

Amerei stared at the floor, blinking slowly.

"I just… I guess I didn't think I'd be the one having to question stuff like this. We're in love. We've made plans. He's *Merrick* for crying out loud."

"Even good people mess up," Odessa said. "But when they love you, they care about how their actions make you feel."

"You're not overreacting," Andromeda added. "You're just reacting to something that crossed a line for you."

Mita reached for her hand. "I know we're gonna have different opinions on this topic. I don't support sex before marriage, and I would rather honestly tell you not to have premarital sex because you are disrespecting yourself and your body and opening yourself up to things that you don't know or understand, but I know you won't listen to me, but that doesn't mean I'm condemning you. I just want you to feel safe. Loved. Respected."

Amerei gave her a small, grateful smile.

"Thanks, M. That means a lot."

The mood shifted softly after that.

No explosions. No breakdowns. No pretending.

Amerei leaned her head on Odessa's shoulder.

"I don't know if I'm gonna bring it up again. I probably should. But I just… I need time."

"Take all the time you need," Andromeda soothed. "We're here."

"Always," Mita added.

Odessa wrapped an arm around her. "And if he ever crosses another line, say the word. I will throw hands and heels."

That got a small laugh from everyone.

Even Amerei.

And in the quiet that followed, they didn't feel broken. Or bitter.

Just human.

And healing.

Together.

Chapter 28: Grace is Greater Than the Guilt

The four girls sat huddled on the floor and the couch, wrapped in mismatched blankets, remnants of snacks surrounding them, still recovering from the two mind-blowing stories and one off-putting one that was previously told. Mita sat cross-legged on the floor, a pillow hugged to her chest. Her eyes were glassy, her heart racing, her hands slightly trembling. She'd heard all their stories: raw, painful, vulnerable, and now… it was her turn.

She cleared her throat.

"So my story isn't as traumatic as y'all's," she started quietly, "but it's still my story. And I think I've spent a lot of time pretending I didn't need to share it. But I do."

All eyes turned to her.

"I grew up in a small community. Mom and Dad were both present… technically. But Dad? He was rarely home. Always off on business, even during the holidays. I think it was when I was eight that I became aware of the fact that he doesn't come home for Christmas. He said it was work and how hectic it was, but after a while, I stopped believing that he would stay home ever. It was just how it was."

She gave a small, sad smile. "But last summer, he was actually home. And for the first time in forever, I didn't feel like I was a guest in his life. We got closer. And it felt… good. Like I wasn't invisible, like I wasn't an accessory to his life, and his job was his actual family."

"I'm an only child, but when my mom was pregnant, this other family moved in next door. Their parent is friends with mine. And he had two boys: Joshua and Ruach. Joshua's older, Ruach's just three months older than me. And they became my brothers. Not by blood, but by life."

She paused, eyes growing misty. "We did everything together. Prayed, played, did chores, celebrated birthdays. Joshua was the wise one, Ruach the sweet one. I was the chaos in the middle. But they loved me anyway."

Mita took a shaky breath. "But there was this kid in the community. A real troublemaker. Everyone told me to stay away from him. Joshua especially warned me, he said this boy had no boundaries, no morals. But I didn't listen."

She looked down, the shame of her past trying to claw its way into her mind. "I let curiosity get the better of me. I played with him one summer when I was bored and curious and wanted friends other than my brothers and dragged poor Ruach along. I blatantly ignored Joshua's warnings. And before I knew it, I wasn't just playing with fire, I *became* the fire."

The room stayed quiet.

"I joined the wrong crowd. Started acting out. Pranking kids, bullying without realizing it, because I thought it was fun, and having a good laugh. But… it hurt people, I was *hurting* people. And when Reed got stabbed last year, I thought, 'This— this is my punishment. This is God getting even with me for all the pain I caused others when I was younger.'"

Her voice cracked.

"I used to believe that every bad thing that happened to me was God paying me back."

Odessa's face softened. Amerei pulled her blanket tighter. Andromeda didn't blink.

"And then Rune happened," Mita continued. "I met him last year, as you guys know, we all did. He was Charismatic. Smooth. Charming. Funny etc. You name it, he had it . We were friends, then more than friends… and then we went on that trip. And yeah… we had sex. Not once. Not twice. A lot. And I told myself I loved him. That it wasn't that bad. That God would understand because Rune basically proposed ."

She wiped her tears, her voice growing smaller. "But I didn't even understand. what I was saying or thinking."

"I grew up believing in Jesus. I even started to really love Him right before I started college. But after what I did with Rune, I didn't even want to look at my Bible. I stopped going to the Christian club. Stopped praying. Because every time I tried, all I could hear in my head was, 'Hypocrite.' 'Fake.' 'You failed.'"

She let that sink in.

"I thought I'd lost God. That He was done with me."

Her eyes welled up again. "I cried myself to sleep so many nights, thinking I could never go back to Him because of what I did. And I started convincing myself that *my guilt* was *His anger.* That God hated me. That He had disowned me."

Amerei reached for her hand and held it tightly.

"But then… Ethan found me," she said, her lips breaking into a smile. "He saw me at a coffee shop one day and just… asked how I was. I couldn't even lie. I broke down right there in that seat."

She laughed softly through the tears. "He invited me back to Christian club. I didn't want to go. I didn't feel worthy. But I went anyway. And I will never forget what I heard that day. that I even saved it as my wallpaper"

She pulled her phone out and read aloud: ***"There is therefore now no condemnation for those who are in Christ Jesus." —Romans 8:1***

"If we confess our sins, He is faithful and just to forgive us our sins and to cleanse us from all unrighteousness." —1 John 1:9

"But God demonstrates His own love for us in this: While we were still sinners, Christ died for us." —Romans 5:8

"They weren't preaching shame," she whispered. "They were preaching *grace.* And I realized… I had been lying to myself. I thought I had to earn God's love back. But he never stopped loving me: he died to give me his love long before I was born, long before I could think to earn it. So, if he gave it to me long before I could try to earn it, then why would I waste time trying to earn a love I already had? So, since I already have his love, I live to show him I am grateful by not spitting on his kindness and living a life that makes him pleased, and pleasing him pleases me."

She looked up at the girls. "Jesus didn't die for the version of me or the version of any of you who had it all together. He died for the <u>me</u> **now**, the <u>me</u> **then,** and the <u>me</u> **ahead.** He went ahead, letting them brutally murder him for you all, knowing we would fail and still *choose* to love me, to love us anyway. And that guilt? That shame that I felt? It wasn't from God. That was the enemy, trying to keep me in chains that were never mine to begin with."

A silence fell over the group like a blanket, thick and sacred.

"I let my guilt convince me that God hated me," she said. "But guilt and shame don't come from God. Conviction does. And conviction leads you back to Jesus. Not away."

She swallowed, pressing her hand to her heart. "So I came back. And He welcomed me with open arms."

The room was still. Odessa wiped her eyes. Andromeda looked stunned. Amerei's lip trembled.

"I don't support sex before marriage," Mita said gently. "Not only because I want to be holy. But because I know how much it breaks *me.* I know how deep the consequences go when I tie my body and soul to someone who isn't my husband. I know how the enemy uses it to drown me in guilt and open doors spiritually to bring me down ASAP."

"But I'm not drowning anymore," she whispered. "I've been *rescued.* And *washed.* And God... oh, God has been so gentle with me."

Andromeda choked out a small sound, like a sob caught in her throat. Odessa buried her face in her sweater. Amerei leaned forward and hugged her tightly. None of them understood what a relationship with God was, but to them, Mita's story was heartbreakingly beautiful, and they were already bare of pouring their hearts out.

So they felt what Mita felt when she said she was welcomed home.

As a softened open heart is where God really starts working.

"I love you guys," Mita said, her voice hoarse. "And I didn't want to suffer in silence anymore, nor do I want any of you to."

"You're not suffering alone anymore," Amerei said, voice shaking.

"Yeah," Odessa added, sniffling. "You might've sinned, but you're not a hypocrite. You're *human.* And God clearly still has you wrapped in His arms."

Andromeda finally spoke. "I've seen a lot of fake Christians. And I can say you're not one of them. You actually… You actually *believe* this stuff."

"I do," Mita answered firmly. "And even when I didn't… *He still held me.*"

They sat in silence for a while, the kind of silence that heals. That sees. That holds.

Then Amerei, her face tear-stained, muttered, "Mita… you should really do an ASMR prayer channel. Your voice during prayer is like my substitute for melatonin."

They all burst into laughter, ugly, teary, beautiful laughter.

And for a moment, they weren't recovering from trauma.

They were resting in grace.

Chapter 29: One More Morning, One More Memory

Sunlight peeked through the half-drawn curtains of Mita and Amerei's dorm room, filtering across the floor where Odessa was draped like a blanket burrito and Andromeda lay flat on her back, one arm over her face.

Amerei stirred first, blinking at the warm light and the rhythmic sound of 'cooing'.

"Whose alarm was that?" she croaked.

No one answered.

It hadn't been an alarm. It had been a dove outside the window.

Mita sat up next, her bonnet askew and pillow crease carved across her cheek.

"I think I drooled in my sleep," she mumbled.

"That's gross," Andromeda said, her eyes still closed. "But I respect the honesty."

Odessa groaned from her corner. "Why does my back feel like it got hit by finals… again?"

They all laughed. A sleepy, slow, shared laugh that only comes when you've cried together the day before, and your brain hasn't fully loaded to start the day.

"Morning, munchkins," Amerei sang, stretching with a yawn.

"I can't believe we survived finals," Mita muttered, blinking as she stood and shuffled to the mini-fridge for juice boxes.

"You mean 'I can't believe we're still functioning humans,'" Andromeda replied, sitting up and grabbing a nearby sock like it was coffee.

After a round of half-asleep teeth brushing and pulling themselves together, the girls gathered in the living space with mugs of tea, mismatched slippers, and tangled hair.

"So, what's everyone doing for Christmas?" Odessa asked, curling her legs beneath her.

"I'm heading home," Mita said. "My mom's excited to have me. And my brothers are already planning some chaos. Ruach and Joshua haven't stopped texting."

"Family dinner?" Amerei asked.

"Yeah," Mita replied, grinning from ear to ear. "And Christmas Eve service at church. You're all invited, by the way."

"I'm going to my brother's," Odessa said. "I miss him. And he said he already bought me a ridiculous number of gifts. So I can safely say, we're going all out this year."

"I'd say I'm surprised," Andromeda muttered with a smile, "but that man seems like he buys you a pony every holiday."

"You're not wrong." Odessa smiled.

Amerei sipped her tea. "I'm splitting time. Christmas with my fam, then heading to Merrick's for the New Year. His Dad is out of town this year for business stuff for New Year's, and my sister is going out with her boyfriend for New Year's, so I told him I'd stay through New Year's."

Odessa raised her brow. "Oooooh. Spicy sleepover energy?"

"Crazy spice, the type to give you a pregnancy scare," Amerei grinned. "Promise."

Mita gave her a look.

"Okay, okay," she amended, laughing. "No promises, I'll behave… kinda."

Then all eyes turned to Andromeda, who quietly sipped her peppermint tea like it was armor, avoiding eye contact.

"And you, Meda?" Mita asked.

"I'm staying."

The room quieted.

"I'm not going back home," she said, voice steady. "I'm not ready. Not yet."

Odessa sat forward. "But you don't have to be alone, you know that, right? I have more than an extra room."

"Same," Mita added quickly. "My mom would *love* to meet you. My brothers would probably adopt you instantly."

"And I can sneak you into Merrick's house," Amerei offered. "Not even kidding. We could make it a fake third-wheel rom-com."

Andromeda smiled. Genuinely. Softly. Gratefully.

"I appreciate you guys, really. But I need this winter to just… breathe. Alone. Sit in silence. Maybe do some journaling. Maybe cry a little. Maybe dance in my room. I just… need the quiet."

The girls didn't push. They knew. Some healing needed solitude.

"But next year," Andromeda added, looking at each of them, "I'm staying with one of you. Not you, Ame, I'm not watching you and your boyfriend feed each other strawberries."

"Understandable," Amerei said. "Valid, even."

"Okay," Mita said softly. "We'll miss you, though."

"I'll miss you guys too."

The rest of the day was a mix of **board games, skincare face masks, and ridiculous soap operas**. They played UNO like it was war, Odessa cheated at Monopoly, and Mita made everyone try her grandma's avocado-honey mask recipe (which burned slightly, but no one said anything until they all wiped it off at once and screamed).

They laughed. They played charades. They turned on a drama where the main plot revolved around a stolen baby and an evil twin pretending to be the protagonist.

They didn't care how unrealistic it was, they ate it up like popcorn.

As evening settled, they laid on the floor again, backs sore but hearts full. The twinkle lights glowed gold above them.

"Promise me something," Mita whispered.

The girls turned toward her.

"No matter what next semester looks like… we stay us. We keep this."

"We will," Amerei said.

"Even if life gets messy," Odessa added.

"Especially then," Andromeda said quietly.

They reached for each other's hands and squeezed.

Tomorrow, they'd go their separate ways. To families. To cities. To quiet. To love.

But tonight?

They were home.

Right here.

With each other.

Chapter 30: Silence Doesn't Mean Empty

Andromeda POV

There's something about the sound of a radiator ticking in an empty dorm that makes you feel like you're the last living soul on Earth.

It's been... what, three days since the girls left? Mita had hugged me so tight and made me promise to text. Odessa left in a whirlwind of energy, glitter eyeliner, and way too many goodbye kisses blown through the air. And Amerei? She'd left with that love-struck look in her eye like she was walking straight into a Hallmark movie.

They're gone. And I'm here.

And you know what?

I don't mind.

At first, yeah, it was weird. Too quiet. Too still. I wasn't used to waking up without hearing Mita humming in the kitchen or Odessa blasting some playlist with more bass than lyrics. I even missed Amerei complaining about assignments while simultaneously acing all of them.

But there's something... kind of beautiful about silence.

The first couple of days, I didn't do much. I stayed in bed, ordered in food, watched crime documentaries, and replayed old K-dramas where every romantic lead either had amnesia or was secretly a chaebol's heir. I cried. I laughed. I screamed at the screen like a lunatic.

Then I started... talking to myself.

Out loud.

And listen, I don't mean the occasional mumble like, *"Ugh, where's my charger?"* or *"Why did I eat that last cookie?"* I mean full-blown **commentary**. Like I was filming a one-woman documentary on college life narrated by yours truly.

Sitting on the couch wrapped in a blanket, I stared at the ceiling. You know, come to think of it, I think this is Odessa's blanket. I am taking it; she won't miss it anyways.

"Day three of being left behind on campus. Still no sign of intelligent life. Only the echo of my own thoughts and the passive-aggressive flickering of the hallway lights."

I looked at the coffee table where I'd stacked my half-finished cup of tea and an empty ramen bowl.

"And here we see the remnants of a well-balanced college diet. The caffeine-fueled elixir of fake productivity and the sodium bomb of poor decision-making."

I stood, stretched, and began pacing my room like I was on some detective show in an interrogation room questioning a suspect who was a hard nut to crack.

Then the commentary continued, *"Now let's discuss Exhibit A: Professor Klein. An interesting specimen. Has the wardrobe of a man lost in the 1970s and the teaching enthusiasm of a wet sock. Still, his rants about global economic systems could rival Shakespeare in sheer drama. In a microbiology lab session"*

I stopped in front of the mirror, raised a brow at my own reflection.

"Next on the list, we have Zebedee. Or as I like to call him, 'Painter Boy Who Thinks Art Talks Back.' Kinda weird. But weird in a way that makes you want to ask him to paint your soul. That man makes awkward silence feel like an art form. Still haven't decided if he's harmless or a walking red flag dipped in acrylics."

I laughed out loud at myself. "My therapist is gonna love that one."

I threw on a hoodie, Mita's, actually, because I missed her scent; that would have sounded weird out loud.

You know, I could start a thrift store with all the girls' clothes that have somehow 'ended in my possession' by pure coincidence and not by me stealing them, of course not. I am a woman of integrity.

I made myself a cup of tea. Chamomile. It was like a cup of peaceful bliss.

Then I flopped back on the bed and sighed.

"This campus is mine now. My empire. My territory. The world belongs to me and my thrift store collection."

I grabbed my journal and flipped it open. Not to write, just to hold it. I like how the leather feels warm, lived in.

For the first time in a while, I wasn't chasing peace.

I *had* peace. probably

Well, it's not isolation, per se. Just… stillness. So that's a win regardless of how small.

Later that night, I sat by the window with fairy lights twinkling around me. The snow had just started to fall. It was soft and quiet, like the world was breathing slower.

And there I was, curled up with a blanket, sipping tea, whispering thoughts to myself like secrets meant for the stars.

"Who knew I'd be okay with being by myself?" I said aloud. "Not healed. Definitely not whole. But not having my own thoughts strangling me to the point of literal breathlessness. but being just…okay."

I suddenly thought of all the people I'd met since arriving here:

Mita. The soft voice that turns into steel when it comes to faith. She prays like she's having a coffee date with God Himself.

Odessa. A whole hurricane in designer jeans. Loud, funny, with a soul so scarred and strong it makes you want to fight for something. Anything.

Amerei. A puzzle. One minute, she's girl-next-door sweet, the next, she's snatching your phone to scroll through your texts like a CIA agent. That girl loves hard.

Then… there's me.

And for the first time, I don't mind being me. Even if I'm still figuring out what that actually means.

As I watched the lights from the streets of campus lit up the snowfall in isolated rays, and being present to behold its beauty was simply magnificent.

The next morning, I woke up late. Made pancakes. I burned half of them and ate them anyway, sitting on the kitchen floor in my Christmas socks. Laughed at my reflection in the oven door, played jazz too loudly, danced in the hallway, and talked to a plant I didn't know I owned.

I was alone, yes. But I wasn't lonely.
I was quiet, yes. But I wasn't empty.

Chapter 31: Paint, Pianos, and Unexpected Company

Andromeda POV

It was the next morning, and I was thriving.

Okay, *"thriving"* might be a strong word. I was existing. Which was enough.

I had my cartoons, my oversize mug of peppermint tea, and my usual running commentary with myself that had only grown more entertaining by the day. I lounged on the couch in a hoodie twice my size, which I'm pretty sure is Mita's again.....oops, and socks that had tiny avocados wearing Santa hats.

"Day five of solitary campus life," I said between bites of burnt toast, updating my commentary. *"Mood: stable. Vibes: questionable. Breakfast: underwhelming."*

I paused the show I was watching, a random anime about a cat detective, and sighed.

'*Maybe I should check out the music room.*'

The thought had come out of nowhere, but it felt right. The silence was starting to shift from peaceful to stale. And the music room had this... softness to it. A kind of soul that always pulls you back to it.

I threw on joggers and a black tee. My hair? A bun, a messy one at that.

Makeup? Not even a thought, right about now. Comfort was the goal. *"This is my winter break aesthetic,"* I told my reflection. *"Call it 'college burnout chic.'"* I threw on some gloves and a jacket before heading out.

The walk across campus was surprisingly nice. The air had a sharp chill to it, but not biting. Just enough to make you feel awake. Alive.

The arts building was still and silent—most of the doors locked, and the halls dimly lit. It was strange seeing this place not teeming with over-caffeinated creatives running late to critique sessions.

I headed straight for the music department. The hallway greeted me with that faint smell of polished wood and old sheet music.

When I opened the double doors to the music club room, I grinned.

It was empty.

Completely empty.

But full of instruments. And warmth. And memory, though few they may be.

"Maybe staying back for break *was* the best decision I've ever made," I whispered.

I walked over to the piano and flipped open the lid. There, sitting right where Mita and I had left them, were the dry erase markers.

I chuckled. "Guess it's time for a solo lesson."

I grabbed the black one and carefully wrote the letters on the keys: C, D, E, F, G, A, B, repeat.

It was messy. A little slanted. But it worked.

I pulled up a song tutorial online some moody ballad with "easy" in the title. (Spoiler: it was not easy.)

And I began to play...poorly.

"Okay, wow," I muttered. "That is *not* what that chord was supposed to sound like."

I tried again. My finger slipped. A note rang out like a dying bird. I winced.

I tried again. Missed a key. Tried again. Forgot which finger did what.

"Human being here," I said aloud to no one, rolling my eyes. "Not a machine. Let me make my mistakes in peace, brain, stop criticizing me."

After maybe thirty minutes of trying and failing to sound remotely decent, I gave up and sat there, staring at the keys like they'd betrayed me. Because they kinda did.

YouTube was kinder. It gave me five videos with "Piano Hacks for Beginners" in the title. One promised I'd play like Mozart in seven days. Bold. But I clicked anyway.

Halfway through the first video, I realized I needed to use the bathroom. Badly.

So, I went and did my business, and when I was finished, I wandered out, phone still in hand, the music echoing faintly in my ears as I walked down the now-familiar halls.

That's when I passed a corridor I had definitely been down before, but I hadn't paid much attention to. It stopped me in my tracks as I headed to the music room, making me take notice of it and remember what happened the last time I wandered down this path. It had doors on each side with gold plates bearing names; I guessed these were students' names and their studios. If you go to a school for rich kids, expect the unexpected. I know my family has money, but the rich never cease to surprise me. Having actual gold nameplates is a different level of 'My coffers are full.'

But this time, I noticed a familiar name on a gold plate on one of the doors.

"Zebedee Kefah."

I stopped.

"It rolls smoothly off the tongue," I said in my commentary with a smirk.

I knocked. Instinctively. Of course, there was no answer. It was winter break. People had lives. Families. Holiday traditions.

Not like me, who avoided home like the plague and was now narrating my own life like it was an indie film.

Still, I don't know why, but I tried the door.

It opened. *Why though?*

The scent hit me first: paint, turpentine, the faintest trace of old books and lavender. It was like stepping into a dream.

That was before I saw it.

A mini art gallery.

Framed canvases, paint-stained rags, sketchbooks stacked high, half-finished sculptures, and colors splashed across every surface like the aftermath of an emotional storm, though the splash zone was covered in some protective film to protect what lay beneath.

Zebedee might be a little… intense. But he was *talented*.

"Zebedee might be a lowkey stalker," I muttered aloud, stepping closer to a canvas, "but the man's got serious talent."

"Thank you for the compliment," came a voice from behind me, smooth and amused. "But you know, *you* being in *my* studio seems a little more stalkerish than me."

I froze.

My soul left my body for a full two seconds.

And that, dear diary, is when I knew:

This winter break was about to get way more complicated.

Chapter 32: Paint, Proximity, and Problematic Flirting

Andromeda POV

I froze.

No, really, I literally *froze*.

Not a cute "oops, you caught me staring" kind of freeze. No, I was standing dead still in the middle of someone's personal art cave, practically inhaling the smell of turpentine and oil paint, caught in a very obvious moment of *trespass-y curiosity*.

"Uh," I spluttered with all the grace of a malfunctioning dishwasher. "The door was… open?"

I knew how pathetic it sounded the second it left my lips.

Zebedee, Zeb, or whatever his name is, just grinned at me like an idiot, as though he were used to people sneaking around where they shouldn't be. "It's cool. You're an acquaintance. Feel free to drop by anytime."

"Thanks… I guess," I said, trying to play it cool but failing miserably. I shifted my gaze back to the nearest painting to avoid further eye contact.

The painting in front of me was bold and soft at the same time, like conflict and peace learning to hold hands. Layers on layers of color, and then lines, soft at the edges but focused, intentional. It felt loud and quiet. Like him.

"Beautiful, huh?" Zeb commented, stepping up beside me.

"Yeah, it is," I affirmed, surprising even myself with how honest it sounded.

"Thanks. That means a lot coming from someone like you."

I paused, one brow arching before I could stop it. "Someone like me? What's *that* supposed to mean?" I asked Incredulously,

Zeb didn't flinch. "Nothing bad. Just… from our very brief interactions, I can tell you don't mince your words. If you don't like something, you say it. If you *do* like it, you say it too. You don't really hold back, and I appreciate that. Artists like me, we need people around to give honest critiques. And compliments when due."

I blinked. Oh.

That was… actually a decent answer. I gave him a small nod and looked away like I wasn't thrown off by how well he read me. Not that I'd admit that out loud.

"So why are you here?" he asked suddenly.

I tilted my head. "Why are *you* here?" I argued.

"I asked first. You can't answer a question with a question."

"I just did though."

"That's not how communication works."

"Who says I want to communicate with *you*?" I retorted, smirking.

He opened his mouth. Paused. "Well—"

"Thought so," I said, walking past him toward a canvas like I hadn't just rendered him momentarily speechless.

There was a brief silence before I finally said, "I'm staying on campus for winter break. What about you?"

"Oh, sweet! Me too." His voice lit up like I'd just invited him to co-star in a buddy comedy. A weird part of me liked that he sounded… genuinely excited. Not performative. Just happy.

"Why are you so excited?" I asked flatly. "Happy your 'victim' is still within proximity of being stalked?"

"Maybe," he said, casually strolling toward me.

And okay, yeah, I took a step back, not because I was nervous, obviously.

But because I didn't know what kind of weird artsy thing he was about to pull. Yeah, let's go with that.

Then he walked *past* me. Go figure.

"Or maybe," he continued, picking up a canvas from a low shelf, "it's just easier to stalk you when you keep showing up in my orbit."

He held the canvas carefully, turning it toward me like a magician about to reveal the final trick.

The painting was… mesmerizing.

A man standing on water, arms open as the sun dipped behind him and the moon rose ahead. Between the two, suspended in the sky, was an arrow shaped like the recycling symbol, but it only appeared when Zeb tilted the canvas just right, catching the light. Otherwise, it was invisible. Hidden in plain sight.

"You hid the arrows using gloss variation?" I asked without thinking, stepping closer. "That's… subtle and Smart."

He raised a brow at me. "You know about layering and texture gloss?"

"I dabble," I muttered.

Zeb grinned. "You're full of surprises, you know that?"

"I know," I said, eyes still on the painting. "Most people just don't stick around long enough to find out." I didn't even question why I told him that. But it was the truth.

He didn't answer right away. Instead, he quietly placed the canvas back and gestured to the next piece, an abstract mix of reds and blacks with gold leaf slicing through like lightning.

"Okay, real talk," he said, voice softer now. "You seriously have a presence. Like… when you walk into a room, it shifts. You're like jazz music, but in human form."

I looked at him, deadpan. "That might be the cheesiest thing I've heard in my life."

He shrugged. "I stand by it."

"You really talk to your paintings like they're people?" I asked, changing the topic.

"Absolutely. I mean, why would you ever pour your whole heart into something and *not* treat it like it's alive?" He answered like it was a no-brainer.

I didn't have an answer to that. But I understood it more than I wanted to admit.

He turned toward his workstation, a messy wooden desk covered in paint tubes, charcoals, crumpled sketches, and a mug that said *"I Paint, Therefore I Am Colour"* in Comic Sans.

"What?" he asked, catching me staring at the mug.

"Nothing. Just, your taste in fonts is more criminal than your stalking."

"Hey, don't hate on Comic Sans," he said, in mock-offense. "It's a classic. and Underappreciated."

I let out a laugh before I could stop it. A real one.

And maybe it was the vibe of the room. Maybe it was the way his eyes crinkled when he smiled. Maybe it was the stupid mug. But for the first time in a long time, I felt light. Not just not heavy. But *light*.

"Do you want to paint something?" he asked suddenly.

I blinked. "Now?"

"Why not? I've got extra brushes. And a canvas. Or you can just sit here and roast my work for fun. I'd still call that quality time."

'Quality time?! This guy, I don't even know you sir?!'

I looked at the easel. Then at him.

And despite every instinct telling me to bolt, because people, connection, *openness*? Scary stuff. I sat down.

"Okay," I said. "But if it turns out awful, I'm blaming your weird energy."

"That's fair," he said, already grinning. *This boy loves to smile*

And just like that, I spent the rest of my afternoon painting next to a guy who talked to canvases, made too many bad puns, and maybe......just maybe, understood silence better than most.

And,

I kind of... liked it.

Chapter 33: Holy Paint, Coffee Walks, and Unexpected Peace

Andromeda POV

If you'd told me a month ago that I'd spend my entire Christmas break hanging out with a guy who talked to paintbrushes, prayed like it was breathing, and made me laugh harder than I had all semester? I'd have laughed in your face.

No, seriously, I would

And yet…

There I was.

Every day that passed, I found myself spending less time in the music room and more time in Zebedee's studio. It was weird at first, how natural it felt; how he made space without even trying. Like he wasn't just inviting me into his creative chaos, he was handing me a key and saying, "Yeah, this too can be yours."

He taught me brush techniques, how to blend with oils, how to make a sky look like it had depth without painting stars, and how not to completely ruin a canvas by using too much paint too fast. I messed up a lot. Like, *a lot*. But he never got frustrated.

"You have great instincts," he told me once, watching me smear color across a blank surface. "You just don't trust them yet."

I'd scoffed, but I knew he wasn't wrong.

When we weren't in the studio, we were out. At a tiny café on the edge of town that served overpriced hot chocolate with roasted marshmallows that stuck to your lip. Or a quiet Japanese restaurant where we ate in content silence and he ordered for us in flawless Japanese—*show-off.* Sometimes we'd walk through the park, watching people feed birds or ice skate in crooked circles, talking about nothing and everything.

It was… nice.

Okay, fine—it was *more* than nice. But I wasn't about to ruin it by thinking too hard.

What did surprise me, though, was how often Zeb prayed.

Before we ate, he'd bow his head and whisper under his breath. Before we started a new painting, same thing. Even before our walks, he'd just mutter a quick prayer under his breath. It wasn't dramatic or loud. It was soft. Quiet. Just… I would call it steady.

Like it was simply part of who he was.

I didn't ask at first. I didn't want to make it weird.

But one day, while we were sitting on the floor of his studio, eating cheap takeout and listening to some soft instrumental playlist, I finally blurted, "So you're one of those quiet Christians, huh?"

He laughed, mid-bite. "Quiet Christian?"

"Yeah, you whisper a prayer before, like, everything."

"I guess I do."

"I've only seen one other person like that," I muttered.

"Mita," he said, smiling.

My eyes narrowed. "Wait, how do you know—?"

"We're in the same Christian club," he said casually. "She talks about you guys all the time. You, Amerei, Ocessa. Calls you her answered prayer. Says you're all chaotic blessings who just don't know it yet."

I didn't even know what to say to that.

"You okay?" he asked.

I shrugged. "I just… didn't think you were that kind of Christian. You don't—" I paused, struggling for the words.

"Come off overly preachy?" he offered. "Holier-than-thou? Smug? Judgmental?"

"I wasn't gonna say all that, but… yeah. Kind of."

He nodded. "Fair. I know people like that too. I've been hurt by them too."

That made me glance up at him. "Really?"

"Yeah. But I had to learn that God isn't them. They're not the measuring stick for God's love either."

I stayed quiet. Let that sit.

"I don't expect people to believe like me, I want them to, I want them to live the life Jesus said we should Love like how he says we should, and live lovingly with each other just like how Jesus did," he continued. "I just want to live in a way that makes it hard not to see Jesus in me."

I blinked. Okay… that hit a little harder than I expected.

I didn't say anything, I mean, I didn't have anything to say. But for the first time in a long time, I didn't feel defensive about it. I wasn't rolling my eyes or internally shutting down to avoid the conversation. I was actually… listening.

Which was new.

Between art and weird theological moments, I still made time to visit Reed. Usually once a week. I'd bring snacks the nurses allowed, and I'd just sit by his side and talk about life.

"You wouldn't believe the winter I'm having," I told him once, leaning back in the hospital chair. "Zebedee's the name of an actual person, not a cartoon. And he prays before he paints. *Paint*, Reed."

He didn't respond—couldn't, obviously. But I liked to imagine he was listening.

"I'm starting to think people aren't always one-dimensional. That perhaps, just maybe, not every guy is out to—" I stopped myself. Took a breath.

"Anyway. Zeb's okay. The rest of the girls would like him. You'd like him too."

I squeezed his hand before leaving. "You'd better wake up soon. Or I'm gonna tell everyone you snore like a chainsaw."

By the time Christmas Eve rolled around, I found myself curled up on Zeb's studio couch, wearing one of his oversized flannels because I forgot to bring a jacket that day.

We didn't talk much that evening. We painted in silence, each working on our own canvas, the soft hum of Christmas jazz playing from the speaker in the corner. The lights were dim, golden, warm.

He didn't ask why I stayed on campus. And I didn't ask why he did either. But I think we both understood.

Some questions don't need to be asked or answered.

And maybe that's what I liked most about him.

He never tried to fix me. Never asked questions; neither he nor I was ready to sit quietly through those questions together. He just gave me space to be.

No pretending.

No masks.

Just… me.

Chapter 34: Christmas Roads and Unexpected Lessons

Andromeda POV

I'll admit, I never thought I'd be getting ready to go to church on Christmas morning. Not because my parents never made me, they did. In fact, it was expected. Mandatory. With a capital **M**.

But back home, Christmas service wasn't about baby Jesus. It was about appearances. Sitting in the front pew with the other chaebol daughters, smiling and bowing to elders, and answering the pastor when asked the same question over and over again about what I am grateful for even though he doesn't care, but nonetheless I answered with rehearsed gratitude about being "blessed with such a loving, God-fearing family." Lies in linen and lace.

But today, it wasn't like that. Zeb had invited me. No force, no passive-aggressive guilt trip, just a casual offer and room to say no. And I almost did, until I realized, for once, the choice was mine. Fully mine. I could attend church because *I* wanted to.

I picked something tasteful but sophisticated: high-waisted taupe trousers, a soft ivory blouse tucked in clean and smooth, a camel-toned wrap coat with gold-button detailing, and suede heels the color of burnt honey. My makeup was minimal but precise, and a swipe of rich berry lipstick to seal the OOTD.

As I dabbed the gloss, my phone buzzed.

Mom was the caller ID.

I stared at the screen, thumb hovering over the answer button. But something in me tensed. No. I already knew. If I answered, she'd say something cold or gaslight me to come home and say *'everyone is asking for me, especially since I am acting like I don't have a house or family to come home to, and people in the family's compound would think that there is something wrong in the family. It's Christmas, and I chose to stay at school, and people will question it and I would make them look bad, and the family will become a laughingstock, yada yada ya'* But I knew if I went along with my parents' scheme and manipulation, I'd lose this fragile, weird sense of peace I had today.

So, I hit *ignore* and walked out the door.

Zeb was already waiting by the parking lot, leaning against his car like some novel male lead brought to life. His car was an older model Honda coupe: matte black, classic trim, polished within an inch of its life. Not flashy. Just timeless.

And he, he looked like a page out of GQ. Charcoal Grey suit, crisp white shirt, slim black tie. The coat he wore was wool and layered effortlessly over his shoulders, his curls freshly trimmed and shaped.

Like, if someone wrote *"and then he turned around, stealing her breath away,"* they probably meant moments like this.

"Well, don't you look radiant, Meda," he complimented, looking me over, respectfully, unlike most guys. His eyes didn't linger where they shouldn't, no suggestive facial expression, no smirking. He just took me in. As though I were a painting he wanted to remember.

"You look handsome too," I replied, matching his calm. "Merry Christmas, Zeb."

His grin widened like he'd been waiting for that. "You finally said *Zeb*… it really is Christmas. Thank you, Jesus, you still do miracles, even on your birthday," he exclaimed, glancing toward the sky like he was having a moment with God himself.

I actually laughed. *This guy.*

"Merry Christmas, Meda," he said, this time softer. Warmer.

We decided to take separate cars since I planned to visit Reed after the service. He walked me to my car, opening my door for me, offering his hand to help me climb in, because heels were not for the weak. He'd started doing this more often, recently; I wasn't used to it at first, but now… I kind of liked it. Still, I always said *thank you.* Chivalry wasn't dead. It just drove a black coupe and knew how to button a suit.

I turned on the heater in my car and waited for him to head to his car, but his wouldn't turn over.

I saw him through his window, turning the key, but nothing. Again. Still nothing.

My phone buzzed. *Zeb Calling.*

I answered. "Passenger prince on Christmas?" I teased. "The Lord is good. Huh?"

He chuckled. "Shut up and unlock your car."

I did. He climbed in, buckled up, and flashed me a grin.

I called a mechanic on the way to church to come check out his car. I told them to look at the engine and maybe upgrade the interior too, since it needed some work. I particularly instructed them to use only parts from the car's original year, keep its vintage aesthetic, and touch it up a bit. I knew Zeb was attached to his car; he had gone on and on about that car once before, so it was obvious.

"Okay, Miss Flexxxxx," he joked, flexing his wrist like he was a rapper showing off new iced watches, after I had ended the call with the mechanic.

"Shut up, Zeb," I said, side-eyeing him. "How are you so okay with a *woman* fixing your car?"

"Why wouldn't I be?" he replied casually. "I appreciate it. I'll treat you to something nice next time."

I glanced at him, more curious than annoyed.

"Most guys I know, especially Christian ones, become antagonistic when a woman helps them. Like their manhood is melting if you even *dare* to assist. They say stuff about being the head and needing to provide. And crap like that." I explained, trying not to sound offended, but failed

"Well, yeah. Men are the head of the house and all. But the Bible also says we should *ask for help* when we need it. And accept it when it's offered with a genuine heart. Refusing help? Sitting in your problems out of ego? That's sin. That's pride." He cleared his throat before continuing, "I'm just saying. People think sin is just stealing or sleeping around. But pride? That one's sneaky. It tells you to suffer silently instead of asking for help. It tells you not to accept kindness because you didn't earn it. That's not strength; it's self-destruction."

Then he looked at me, his expression shifting just slightly serious and thoughtful.

"People think pride is just arrogance or needing to be above someone. But pride can also look like *fear of asking for help*. Like shame. Or silence. Pride wears a hundred different masks."

And then he dropped scripture like he'd been waiting his whole life to do it. "Proverbs 26:12— ***'You see a person who is wise in their own eyes? There's more hope for a fool than for them.'*** Pride makes you think you gotta do it all yourself because you may think you've *'got it'*, but you don't.

Look at Proverbs 18:12—***'Before a man's downfall, a person's heart is proud, but humility comes before honor.'*** If someone is too sure of themself and doesn't double-check because *'I know I got this; I am right,'* that very attitude will be the reason for his/her downfall. Pride blinds you. But if your heart is humble, if you seek sound advice, and if you accept trusted or sometimes entrusted help, relying on God, of course, you will be successful. It's not a matter of if you should humble yourself before God and humble your heart as well; it's a matter of when.

And Romans 12:16? ***'Live in harmony with each other. Don't be proud; instead, associate with the humble. Do not be wise in your own estimation.'***

I could go on."

"You studied for this for a while, didn't you?" I said, looking over at him, half grinning and half shocked.

He shrugged.

I didn't say anything. I didn't have to.

No one had ever told me that before. Not my church. Not my parents. Not even my therapists. That pride wasn't just about arrogance. That it could wear the face of fear, or survival, or silence.

Zeb started singing as we drove, loud and off-key, steering me out of my thoughts. I didn't know any of the songs; they were probably Christmas hymns or Christian radio hits, but his energy filled the car like sunlight.

He tapped the dashboard to the beat, his fingers drumming to rhythms only he knew. I rolled my eyes, but I didn't stop him.

Because why would I?

Chapter 35: A Christmas Kind of Peace

Andromeda POV

Zeb and I pulled into the church parking lot. He hopped out first, walked around, and opened my door for me like he always does. "You ready?" he asked as he opened the door, smiling.

"Not remotely," I muttered, stepping out and smoothing my coat. "Let's go before I change my mind."

The air was crisp, and the sun had that December shimmer to it, warm light but no warmth in the wind. We walked up the stone path to the entrance, and the second I stepped through those double glass doors, I was **swarmed**.

Not by bees. By people. **Smiling** people.

"Merry Christmas!"

"Hi there, welcome!"

"Are you Zeb's friend? You're beautiful, dear!"

"Happy Holidays!"

Everywhere I turned, I saw smiles, handshakes, cheerful nods, women in bright Christmas reds, and men in tailored suits with shiny shoes and polished wedding bands. Someone even tried to hand me a cookie.

I stood there, back straight, eyes wide. This… was a lot.

Zeb must've noticed my discomfort. He leaned over and said to the people talking to me, "Good morning, everyone. It's a full house today, huh? We'll go ahead and grab seats before they're all gone. See you in service."

Grateful, I let him lead me to the inner part of the church. He moved through the sea of people like he was Moses parting it, offering short greetings and polite "catch-you-laters" to everyone who tried to stop him for conversation.

"Thanks," I said once we were seated in the sanctuary, still catching my breath.

"No problem. Meet-and-greets are a lot for me too. For you, I imagine it felt like a job interview, a prom entrance, and a college tour all at once."

That got a chuckle out of me. He was right.

The sanctuary was beautiful. High ceilings with arched beams, soft warm lighting that felt like a glow-up filter for your soul. There was a nativity scene near the altar and rows upon rows of filled pews. People were buzzing with joy and warmth, evidence of their desire; they actually wanted to be here. The stage lights flicked on, and just like that, worship started.

I froze for a second. I wasn't sure what to do; should I clap or lean from side to side with the rhythm? At my family's church it was about sitting still and hearing the preacher. But then the first song hit, **Joy to the World,** I actually... knew it and started to vibe with it but not outwardly. And then *O Come; All Ye Faithful.* Something flickered in me. Because these songs were stored somewhere deep in my childhood, the good parts of it, dusty but still there. I wasn't singing loudly or lifting my hands like others around me, but my lips were moving. And I felt...happy.

And I couldn't even lie about it.

Then the pastor came up. A young-ish, well-spoken guy, with a smile so warm it couldn't be fake, standing behind the Rostrum looking like he knew what he was about, began his sermon. "Merry Christmas, everyone," he welcomed. "We thank God for giving us another year and for giving us His Son, Jesus."

"Today," he continued, "we're asking three questions: Who is Jesus? What did He do? And why did He come?"

He opened to John chapter 1.

"In the beginning was the Word, and the Word was with God, and the Word was God... The Word became flesh and dwelt among us."

I leaned forward a little. My brows furrowed. I'd heard these things before, but it seem more captivating coming for this pastor's mouth than the one back home.

The pastor kept going. "Jesus didn't begin in Bethlehem. He existed before Mary was even born. He stepped into our mess. Why? To give us life. Not just any life, **abundant** life."

"John 10:10," he said.

"I have come that they may have life, and have it more abundantly.'"

I blinked. Wait... what? How can you have life more abundantly?

I pulled my journal from my purse, the one I kept for doodles and cynical thoughts, and for some reason wrote:

John 10:10 – life more abundantly? Look into this later.

I wasn't taking notes because I was moved, obviously. It was just curiosity. For fact-checking. That's all.

The pastor flipped through a few more verses. Matthew 20:28, about Jesus coming to serve. Luke 4:18, about healing the broken. Isaiah 9:6 -**"For a child will be born for us..."** Stuff I'd heard, yeah, but never actually *listened to.*

"Jesus didn't come to start a religion," the pastor declared. "He came to reconcile us to the father. To bring us home."

I swallowed.

Not that it meant anything. But still.

Whenever the pastor said "turn to..." Zeb would lean his Bible slightly toward me. Not pushing it on me, but more in the sense of offering it if I wanted to follow along. And I'd read from his side. Because I didn't bring mine. Because I left everything from home behind, even the things that looked holy. Especially those.

Now, in this strange sanctuary next to a guy I barely knew, reading words I didn't fully understand... I felt as though a fresh wind was blowing over the mess of a well-oiled automation I called my life.

It was kinda beautiful.

Like, this day wasn't what I expected at all. I thought Christmas would feel hollow. Just another 25th. Instead, I was surrounded by people who believed in something. Who looked like they had hope. And even though I wasn't sure I wanted what they had… I didn't hate being here.

I might even have liked it.

When the service ended, Zeb turned to me and whispered, "So, how was your first Christmas service?"

This wasn't technically not my first Christmas service, but it was the first one that felt like 'CHRISTmas' so I'll count it as a first for me. So, I didn't answer right away, but when our eyes locked, the joy on his face was so genuine. So pure. Like nothing I'd ever seen back home. Back there, church was all posture and politics. Here, it was peace.

I smiled up at him. "You win."

He raised a brow. "Win what?"

"I don't know. Something. But you won it."

He grinned. "I'll take it."

Chapter 36: Deck the Halls

Andromeda POV

By the time the final "Merry Christmas!" was called out and the post-service crowd started to dissolve, I was ready to sprint out the door in my heels. Not that I didn't appreciate the sea of smiling strangers, but… how many cheerful handshakes and "You should come back next week!" conversations can one girl survive?

Zeb was a trooper, though. Guiding us through it like we were in some secret church maze. I just nodded politely and threw in a few half-smiles while he answered a flood of questions with the ease of someone who's done this more than once. Honestly, he could run for mayor and win.

"Back in one piece," he exhaled as we reached the parking lot.

"Barely," I said, digging for my keys like they were my escape ticket. "How do you not melt under all that human interaction?"

"Practice," he shrugged, flashing a grin. "Also, I may or may not be a crowd-pleasing extrovert. It's a burden," he mockingly lamented.

I rolled my eyes and unlocked the car. *'I don't know if he is bragging or complaining.'*

Once we were both inside, the heater kicked on, and the Christmas chill on my cheeks finally thawed. I tapped my fingers against the steering wheel, trying to figure out how to tell him that the date, if you could even call it that, wasn't over but needed a detour.

"Hey," I prompted, clearing my throat. "So... I kind of have plans."

"Oh," he said casually, already buckling up. "No worries. You want me to grab a cab back? Totally cool."

"No, no! It's not that," I said quickly, waving my hand. "I have to stop by the hospital. I'm visiting a friend, and it might take some time. I just didn't know if you were... cool with that?"

"Oh, ok, cool." He tilted his head, considering something for a moment before he continued. "You're not, like, sick or something and using 'the friend in the hospital' excuse, right?"

"What? No, no. Not me." I smiled at his concern for me. "I'm actually visiting a friend who's been in a coma for a while. It's kind of a thing I do."

Zeb's eyes softened, and he nodded. "You don't even have to ask. I'll wait. That's really cool of you, though. I was thinking maybe we could grab lunch after church, but we can do that after your visit. No rush."

A weird warmth spread across my chest at his kindness and patience. He didn't even flinch at the change in plans. Didn't make it about him or groan about changing plans. He just... went with it. Honestly, I wasn't used to that. Not from anyone. Well, except for the girls.

"Okay. Great," I agreed, starting the engine, not knowing what else to say.

He didn't even give me time to fall into some reflective silence, because the second my phone synced up with the car, he opened it and blasted the most **dramatic, joyful, full-volume** version of *Feliz Navidad* I had ever heard in my entire life.

I shot him a look. "Really?"

"Absolutely," he beamed. "It's tradition. Can't ride with me on Christmas and not scream sing."

"I'm driving. I could leave you on the side of the road if I wanted, you know."

"But you won't," he challenged, plastering on that grin that I have been taking a liking to a lot lately, making me smile in turn. "You like my company too much to do that."

The audacity. The nerve. The completely correct assumption of this man.

Before I could clap back, he started singing, badly. Like, unapologetically bad. He hit notes that didn't exist and added hand gestures and everything.

"I wanna wish you a Merry Christmaaaas…….."

He pointed at me dramatically. "……..*From the bottom of my heaaaart!*"

I cracked. I couldn't help it. I sang along. Full voice. Off-key. Terrible harmony. And we both laughed so hard between verses I thought I might crash the car.

We kept going, song after song. At one point, he tried to rap along to *Drummer Boy* and failed so miserably that I actually wheezed. It was ridiculous yet joyful, as the season seems to be. It was… kind of everything I didn't know I needed today.

We pulled into the hospital parking lot still laughing.

"Okay, passenger prince, you want to come up with me and meet my friend?" I asked, unbuckling.

He nodded, still singing.

"Ok passenger prince, let's go check in on a coma patient and ruin the mood."

Zeb smiled. "Or bring the Christmas spirit to the ICU. You never know."

And somehow, with him next to me, even the hospital didn't feel so heavy.

Chapter 37: The Stillness and the Spark

Hospitals always have a certain kind of silence.

Not the peaceful kind, no; it's the type that hums beneath the surface, a quiet that almost holds its breath. Like the walls remember every whispered prayer, every held hand, every "I'm sorry" ever spoken in those pale blue rooms.

And yet, when Andromeda walked in, head high, heels clicking softly down the corridor, it didn't feel heavy. She moved with such calm that I half-wondered if this place bent itself around her to let her in gently. Like it knew who she was coming to see.

We took the elevator to the third floor. She didn't say much. Just hummed under her breath while looking ahead. But I could see the slight press of her lips, the faint tension in her jaw. At first, I thought she was nervous, but that wasn't the case. Though I assume she was carrying something deep.

When we reached the room, she knocked softly even though there was no need.

"He doesn't talk," she said, turning to me with a small, ironic smile. "But I still think he deserves a warning."

I chuckled. "Sounds fair."

She opened the door, entering and holding it open for me to follow in behind her.

There he was, pale but peaceful. His chest rose and fell with mechanical rhythm. Tubes and wires connected to quiet machines beeped in the background, steady and sure.

"Hey, Reed," she announced, walking in like she'd done this a thousand times. "Merry Christmas. Hope you're enjoying the free room and board, you lucky punk."

I blinked. Wait—what? I didn't even get a chance to process before I was introduced.

"And this is Zebedee," she said, gesturing casually toward me. "My stalker turned holiday companion."

"Wow," I said, stepping forward with a small smile. "Nice to meet you, Reed. Big fan of yours, actually. I mean, any guy who can stay unconscious for a year and still have this girl coming back to check on him weekly? That's legendary status."

Andromeda laughed, fully and unfiltered. A sound that somehow filled up the entire room, chasing the stillness into the corners. It wasn't the first time I heard her laugh like that since I'd met her, but man, was it too rare; it still catches me off guard.

Reed didn't stir. But something about the way she looked at him, how her voice softened as she talked, how her fingers gently adjusted the blanket over his chest, I could tell he wasn't just a routine visit. He was important to her.

She pulled up the chair beside the bed and started talking to him about our day. Church. This surprise visit. My ridiculous singing. It should have been *our* ridiculous singing, but hey.

"He didn't hit a single right note, Reed. I'm serious. Not one."

"Exaggeration," I interjected, settling into the other chair. "She has selective hearing."

She glanced at me sideways. "Selective tone-deafness."

I grinned. Reed's mouth didn't move, but I imagined if he could speak, he'd be on my side.

For the next thirty minutes, I sat in the quiet warmth of something I wasn't expecting. Andromeda's voice. Her stories. Her little jabs at me. Her effortless comfort in this space.

She was different here. More open. Softer, maybe. Or maybe just more real.

When it was time to go, she brushed her hand along Reed's arm and whispered something only for him to hear. Then she turned off the lights and gently closed the door behind her.

We made it to the car, the silence following us for a moment before she turned on the heater, which was working overtime today.

Then, as we pulled out of the parking lot, she said, "You want to know what happened to him?"

I glanced over. "Only if you want to tell me."

She nodded, lips pressed tight, as if she was contemplating whether to tell him or not.

She went ahead and told me everything that happened

I exhaled slowly after she gave me the recount of events that led up to Reed's current situation. "Man."

"Yeah. She ran. Everyone talks about how brave Reed was, and he was. But she never even said thank you. Never visited. Not once."

There was something raw in her voice. Not bitterness. Not really. More like deep, unspoken grief mixed with frustration. The kind that doesn't know where to land, so it just hangs there.

"I didn't know him that well before all of it," she continued. "But after… I started visiting. I don't know why. Maybe guilt. Maybe I just needed something consistent. Maybe I wanted to remind myself that not all guys are…" She trailed off, clearing her throat.

"Like your family?" I asked gently.

She looked at me, surprised. "You really are an artist. You pay attention to the smallest details, don't you?" she said

I smiled faintly. "Not because of my artistic ability, but because of the Holy Spirit."

She leaned back into her seat, looking down the road as she steered the car. "He's the only guy I ever trusted before I met you."

It wasn't a grand declaration. She didn't say it with drama or expectation. Just truth.

I didn't reply with something cheesy or deep. I just let the moment be what it was.

A moment later,

"So," I said, nudging her lightly. "Lunch?"

Her face lit up a little, the shadows shrinking back. "Only if you promise not to sing again."

"No promises," I smirked. "But I do take bribes. Especially ones that involve dessert."

And just like that, we drove off into the afternoon, the air outside cold, but the space between us… warm.

Chapter 38: Christmas, Quiet and Kind

Andromeda POV

After we left the hospital, we went to get some food.

"I'm starving," I said, glancing at him as we headed to lunch.

He looked at me. "My goodness, Meda, where do you think we are going?" he drawled sarcastically, exasperated.

I snorted. "You're so dramatic."

"Says the girl who wore 7-inch heels to church like we were walking a Paris runway."

"I dress for the occasion." I retorted

"And what occasion is sitting in a parked car and eating greasy food like raccoons in a dumpster?"

"Christmas," I said proudly.

He laughed. Loudly. And unapologetically. I swear I saw a lady in another car at the stoplight jump.

We had hit up a local burger place Zeb vowed had "life-changing curly fries," and I'm not saying I found salvation in the seasoning, but I definitely felt close.

Instead of eating at the restaurant, we drove to a quiet little park nearby. I picked a spot under this massive old tree by the lot, where golden light filtered through the branches like something out of a Hallmark movie. We stayed in the car because, hello, it's December, and turned the seats to face each other a bit while we ate.

"Have you ever noticed how fries taste better when you're with someone who doesn't judge how much sauce you're using?" I asked, dipping mine in an *obscene* amount of ketchup.

"I'm literally using two sauces per bite right now. Judge not unrighteously lest ye be judged by the same measure, Meda," he quipped.

I chuckled, leaning my head against my seat, watching him carefully balance his burger like it was an art piece. "You're weird, Zeb."

"And you're just now realizing this? Tragic." He teased.

We joked about everything. Professors who clearly hated their job. Students who dressed like background characters in a low-budget fantasy film. Random inside jokes we somehow made in a span of an hour.

It was… easy with him this entire winter break.

I didn't have to be sharp. Or careful. Or quiet. I could just be.

After lunch, we drove back to campus, and somehow, don't ask me how, we ended up back in Zeb's studio. It felt like the obvious place to go. Familiar. Safe. The moment we stepped inside, that familiar scent of paint and pine-scented diffuser hit me, and I exhaled.

"Be right back," I told him, bolting to my dorm. About twenty minutes later, I was back with my laptop, a cozy blanket, and some hot cocoa packets I stole from my dorm living room. He lent me a hoodie and his shorts to change into, and I did just that, because I went to the dorm and, in a rush, grabbed the stuff I needed, only changing my shoes, and going back to the dorm again in this cold seemed far too unnecessary.

And that was the rest of our Christmas.

Movies. Blankets. Banter. Me watching him sketch random things when he got bored of whatever was on the screen. Him pretending not to notice when I stared too long at the way his eyes crinkled when he laughed. We didn't say much about it, but we didn't have to.

For once, I didn't feel like I was being dissected or judged or studied. I wasn't anyone's project or someone's next chess piece in a family game. I wasn't even the girl with the perfect grades or the sharp tongue or the baggage.

I was just Andromeda.

And Zeb made space for that without ever needing to say so.

Reed was still the only other guy I ever felt that way around. But now Zeb… well, maybe he didn't replace that space. But he carved out a new one. One just his own.

"I'm glad you stayed on campus," Zeb said around midnight, his voice quiet as he flipped to the next movie.

"Me too," I replied, laying my head on the cushion on the couch under a thick layer of blankets.

Once again, he didn't ask why. He didn't need to.

That was the best part.

Chapter 39: Fireworks, Friendship & A New Year

Andromeda POV

I was sitting cross-legged on the floor of Zeb's studio, charcoal in hand, drawing… something.

I wasn't really sure what. It wasn't a person, not exactly. It wasn't a tree, or a structure, or a landscape either. It was just… expression. That's what Zeb would call it.

"Drawing an expression, huh?" Zeb said from across the room, where he was reorganizing a shelf of paint jars. "Not practically definite."

"Not practically anything," I mumbled, tilting my head and smudging the lines that already didn't make sense. "It's just… something."

Zeb wandered over and stood behind me, looking down over my shoulder. "Looks like a very emotionally constipated jellyfish."

"Wow, thank you. I was going for divine agony wrapped in confusion, but sure—jellyfish works."

"I'm here to keep you humble, Meda," he teased.

I rolled my eyes and tossed the charcoal aside. "You're here because I let you be."

"You wound me," he feigned sorrow, clutching his chest like some hero in a tragic novel. "Anyway, speaking of divine agony and confusion, wanna watch fireworks tonight?"

I blinked up at him. "That's quite the segue," I muttered.

"There's this big window in the music room. Great view of the sky. Figured we could watch the fireworks from there." He shrugged like it was no big deal, but the hopeful twitch of his mouth gave him away.

"I'm down," I agreed. "Blankets, karaoke, movies after?"

He groaned. "You and movies."

"You and art. Let me live." I fired back

"Fine," he muttered, "but only if I get to pick one of the movies tonight."

I raised a brow. "Deal, if I get to veto any horror that features creepy dolls."

"You really think I'd waste movie night on creepy dolls?"

"You drew a painting of a Victorian porcelain doll with blood-red eyes last week."

"…Okay, fair. It was supposed to mean childhood with sadness, but it came out too demonic, so I threw it away. So fair," he said, shrugging.

We packed up and headed to my dorm. Normally, security would be buzzing around like caffeinated wasps, but New Year's Eve meant they were off-duty, making the building feel weirdly quiet. I used my dorm card to get in while Zeb lagged behind on the steps like a lost duck.

"Come on," I called, holding the door to the entrance of the building.

"I'll just wait here," he wavered,

"I'm not making trips." I declared,

"I'm fine down here," he assured,

"Zeb," I warned. "If you don't come up, I will drag you by your little sketchbook."

He blinked before running up to the door. "Okay, wow. Fine. You didn't have to threaten the sketchbook."

When we stepped into my room, he stopped in his tracks.

"This is… terrifyingly clean," he commented,

"I'm terrifyingly organized." I reminded.

Color-coded calendars. Labeled folders. My planner lay wide open on the desk where I left it. Everything was where it was supposed to be.

Honestly, it was kind of comforting to have someone other than the girls to notice.

He walked over to the bookshelf. "You alphabetize your novels?"

"Obviously." I drawled

"Of course you do," he whispered.

We gathered everything: laptop, blankets, my emergency snack stash, my tea bags, my phone charger, a string of fairy lights, because duuuh. Then we drove to the art building where his studio was because walking was suicide, not only in distance but also because it was freezing outside. After dropping off my stuff for tonight from my dorm in the studio. We headed off campus for a snack stop and grabbing takeout. His car was still getting its surprise makeover, aka, I was fixing everything while pretending I wasn't flexing. So we took my car. which Zeb offered to drive.

"Let me drive today," he said, jingling my keys like they were candy.

"I don't let people drive my car."

"I'm not people. I'm Zeb."

"That's exactly why I'm nervous."

He stuck his tongue out like a five-year-old. "C'mon, Meda. It's Christmas, part two. Be generous."

I relented.

We picked up a microwave and a toaster from the store too, because apparently, we were turning the studio into a second apartment. Honestly? I was even happy about it.

Once back at the studio, we loaded everything into the music room. It was empty, silent, and cold, but the perfect place to watch the sky explode with color. We set up blankets by the window, draped the fairy lights across the edge of the piano, and threw pillows everywhere like kids.

Zeb opened the takeout boxes and immediately started humming a tune I didn't know. "We should do a Disney karaoke round later," he said, out of nowhere.

"You assume I know Disney songs." I countered,

"You do," he debated.

"I hate that you're right." I relented.

We ate. We laughed. He told me a story about the time he accidentally dyed his mom's cat purple with paint water. I told him about the time I tricked a teacher into believing I was deaf for three weeks.

He watched me like I was the most fascinating creature on earth when I laughed. And I guess… I kind of watched him the same way. But I'd never admit that out loud. *Because who does that?*

At some point in the night, it wasn't us watching the movie, but the movie watching us. As the both of us were now admiring the expanse of the sky—well, I was; I don't know if he was spacing out or praying with his eyes open—but the sky was so incredible, beautiful in its place in the world. The dimness of the gray expanse was a contrast to the quiet in the room. The soft flicker of the fairy lights casting glows on the blankets was nothing short of the type of dream that is always disrupted by something in the real world when it is heading to its climax, never letting you know the end of a dream that was already rare to begin with.

"I'm really glad I didn't go home," I whispered, feeling his gaze. I looked over at him, and when our eyes met, it was as if he were staring through me and not at me. "Yeah?" he prompted.

"Yeah," I affirmed.

"Me too."

I looked away, not sure where this was headed, before adding. "Not like I had a warm family to return to…" I trailed off

"Well," he said, "you've got a warm friend now."

I smiled at his sentiment. I didn't say anything. Just leaned back on my elbows atop one of the many pillows and let the sky burn above us while the year closed its eyes.

Chapter 40: Spark, Spark, Boom

Amerei POV

PLAYLIST-Turn your lights down low Bob Marley Ft Lauryn Hill

Christmas with my family was… good. Surprisingly good.

No church, obviously. My family's agnostic, Christmas is less about "Baby Jesus" and more "Hey, we survived another year, let's eat overpriced cheese and argue over board games."

Which, to be fair, is a tradition I can get behind.

We didn't do the matching pajama thing because my mom said it was "cultish," but we did go full force on brunch. French toast, waffles, fruit platters, sparkling apple cider, *my dad thinks mimosas are "fake joy in a cup," so we go dry,* and homemade cinnamon rolls that we absolutely ruined the first batch of. We even had a gingerbread house contest; my sister and I won, obviously. Our house had a driveway. With a tiny car made of gummy worms.

It was loud, chaotic, and warm. And for once, I didn't have to think about school or projects or my GPA. Just family, laughter, and the occasional backhanded compliment from my aunt about how "college hasn't changed you much, still the little know-it-all."

Thanks, Aunt Bev. Love you too.

But now it was December 31st, and I was back at Merrick's. My favorite place to be when the world slows down and everything else fades.

The whole day had been oddly perfect. When I arrived that morning, his house was already in full "New Year's Prep" mode. Balloons. Fairy lights. A sign that read *"Goodbye 2025, Hello More Chaos."* Which I'm 100% sure he made just to mess with my obsession with "aesthetic decor."

"Merrick," I called as I walked in, eyes squinting at the glittery chaos, "What is this?"

"Welcome, love of my life," he answered from the backyard, "to the most chaotic neutral New Year's Eve you'll ever have."

I peeked outside to see him in sweatpants, a black long sleeve, arranging a fortress of fireworks.

"You bought your own fireworks?" I asked

"No," he said, after a dramatic pause, "I bought *our fireworks.*"

I dropped my overnight bag. "Merrick. You cannot be this cute before 10 a.m. It's illegal." I cooed,

"You knew what you signed up for," he teased, pulling me into a tight embrace.

We spent the entire day setting up the backyard. It was huge; his family estate was enormous. I picked a spot far from the house, helped him carry lawn chairs, blankets, a Bluetooth speaker, and the snack table he insisted on decorating with "snack-themed fortune scrolls." Don't ask. One of mine said, *"You will eat seven marshmallows before midnight."* And yes, I did.

"Okay, firework prince," I teased as we adjusted the chairs to face the perfect open stretch of sky, "tell me the plan."

He dusted his hands off and sat beside me. "The plan is simple. We sit here. We stuff our faces. We launch literal explosives into the sky and kiss when the year changes," he announced, sounding so proud of himself.

"Oh, wow. You're really on-brand for the holiday." I joked

"I've watched three Hallmark movies to prepare." He said, with all seriousness,

"You hate Hallmark movies." I rebutted,

"I'd watch ten if it meant I got to be cheesy with you," he said matter-of-factly.

"You already are cheesy with me." I noted

"And you love it," he replied

"Unfortunately, I do," I said, soaking up every moment.

We leaned back in our chairs, snuggled up under multiple blankets. It's a good thing he *thinks ahead, because* he brought a heated one.

Watching the sun dip behind the mountains on the horizon and glancing at the fireworks stacked nearby, some already lined up on a makeshift wooden launching board he had built earlier in the week, I released a contented sigh, thinking about how extremely thankful I am for moments like these.

"You did all this by yourself?" I asked, genuinely surprised at the setup and the planning that went into this.

He gave me a look. "No. Obviously, I had help. My assistant and my assistant's brother helped. But I planned it."

"Of course you did," I murmured, not knowing what I was expecting.

There was a quiet moment where we both just sat in silence, the kind that doesn't demand to be filled.

"Hey," he said suddenly, stealing my attention away from the sky. "Yeah?"

"You're still my favorite person, even in ugly socks," he commented, looking down at my feet

I looked down at my socks; one had Santa doing a headstand, and the other said, *'Jingle Babe.'*

"Okay, first of all, rude, and second of all, these socks are cute," I argued.

"I'm just saying, if I were a sock model scout, I would not sign you," he mocked

"You'd be a terrible scout." I retorted

We laughed at our stupidity, and then he kissed me on the cheek so sweetly I forgot I was annoyed. I sighed and rested my head on his shoulder.

Later, as the sky turned dusky and the world hushed for the countdown, he started setting up the first line of fireworks.

As the countdown ticked on through the Bluetooth speaker—10, 9, 8… —he reached out and laced our fingers together.

"Happy?" he asked.

"Yeah," I affirmed. "This was perfect."

"Want to do the honors?" he asked, handing me a lighter.

"I feel like this is not OSHA-approved." I wavered

"You're not OSHA. Light it," he mocked.

3... 2... 1...

We lit them together. And they went off—one by one, burst by burst—loud and bright and stunning. Greens and pink and glittering golds. We shouted and laughed and flinched like cowards when the big ones went off too close.

And when the final set exploded in a shower of sparks that lit up the whole sky in silver, I looked over and saw him already looking at me.

"What?" I asked.

"You're beautiful," he whispered in my ear

I rolled my eyes. "Sappy," I whispered back, flustered.

"Still true," he affirmed.

"Happy New Year!" He yelled over the last few that went off, pulling me to him. He held my face like he was about to win a trophy, leaning down, placing a longing kiss on my lips. The kiss was long and warm, with fireworks still going off behind us.

I kissed him back like we had all the time in the world.

When we finally pulled away, he whispered, "2026 better be ready for us."

"Or we'd better be ready for it." I added

Either way, I was glad I had him for the ride.

Chapter 41: Happy New year

Andromeda POV

The final moments of the year felt like golden syrup, slow and sweet. Zeb and I had finished our food, the takeout containers folded neatly beside us on the windowsill of the music room, where the last pinks and oranges of the setting sun spilled in through the towering panes of glass.

It was warm inside. Not just because of the mini space heater Zeb had wheeled in from his studio or the fuzzy blankets we'd laid out like a picnic, but warm in the sense of comfort: belly-deep, chest-wide, smile-tugging warmth. His laughter filled the space beside mine, bouncing off the keys of the piano and the polished strings of the harp as we took turns poking fun at each other's music skills.

"Okay, okay," Zeb said, adjusting the strap of the bass guitar over his shoulder. "Watch this. This is the note that changed the world."

He strummed a single vibrating note. It buzzed awkwardly, too flat to be taken seriously.

"Are you sure that wasn't the note that ended it?" I teased in between laughter, clutching my side.

"You wound me, Meda. I was honoring Beethoven's legacy," he lamented

"Beethoven would come back from the grave just to unplug that amp," I replied.

We kept score like it was a real show: Zeb as a contestant, me as the

185

judge, and then we'd switch. The cello was a disaster; Zeb knocked it over before even getting a note out. The harp? We both sat in front of it like we were trying to defuse a bomb.

"I think it's staring at me," Zeb whispered, eyes wide.

"It should be. You insulted its ancestor, the bass guitar." I laughed.

Even the triangle made an appearance. We both tried to outdo each other with the most dramatic single note.

"Ten out of ten for flair," I appraised as Zeb dropped into a deep bow after *one* chime.

"Thank you, thank you," he said, pretending to wipe a tear from his eye. "It's been an honor."

The day drifted gently toward night, and the sky outside turned to black velvet, scattered with the first sparks of celebratory light. Midnight was inching closer.

As we tidied the space a bit and nestled into the pile of blankets we had left on the floor earlier, a hush settled between us. We sat together near the window, shoulder to shoulder, watching the stars blink into life, chatting softly about everything and nothing. Our voices melted into the lull of the ticking clock and the distant pops of early fireworks.

Zeb leaned closer to glance at my phone, where the countdown app glowed faintly. Ten. Nine. Eight. He shifted beside me, and I noticed his hands fold together. He bowed his head.

He didn't speak. He just moved his lips in silent prayer, his head bowed with reverence. No performative gestures, just something quiet and personal, intimate. I watched him, a strange tug at my heart. That he would thank Jesus before speaking to anyone else at the start of a new year? That was… a singular charm.

While he prayed, I moved carefully to the side. I reached for the viola we'd ignored earlier, its glossy wood catching just a whisper of firework light from outside. I had connected my phone to the speaker previously. I lifted it to my shoulder, bow in hand, and without saying anything, began to play.

PLAYLIST- HOSANNA (HILLSONG) viola cover by ticaaadilly 0:16

The notes of "Hosanna" by Hillsong poured out, tentative at first, then stronger as my fingers remembered the old muscle memory from lessons long ago. It was the only Christian melody I knew by heart, but I knew enough to make it sing.

Zebedee's POV

The first note hit the air just as I lifted my head.

I turned instinctively, like something invisible had tugged me toward the doorway. And there she was.

Andromeda.

Bathed in soft light, part golden spill in the music room from the fairy light we'd set up, part flickering glow from the fireworks outside. For a second, she didn't look real. Her silhouette was all sharp edges and soft curves, the viola nestled perfectly between her shoulder and chin, like it had always belonged there. Her posture, effortless. Her brows drawn together in focus. Lips slightly parted. Eyes closed—not to perform, but to feel. To remember..

Then the bow moved again.

And everything in me went still.

The notes floated out, gentle and trembling at first, then stronger, and I could feel each note run throughout my body. "Hosanna." I knew it from the first bar. But I had never heard it like this. Not from a speaker, not in church, not in a chapel with lights and lyrics projected on walls.

This... was different.

Raw. Unfiltered. Holy.

I sat back slowly, almost afraid to breathe too loudly. Each note she played wove itself into the room: soft, aching, sacred. She wasn't performing. She wasn't trying to impress anyone. It was as if right before my eyes, she was letting go. Layer by layer, like the music was peeling something off her. Armor, maybe. Hurt. Pride. I don't know. But I felt it. Every note. Every breath between them. It was like watching someone pray without words.

Andromeda was… stunning.

Not just beautiful in the usual sense, though, God help me, she was that too. But it was the kind of beauty that didn't care to be seen. The kind that happened when someone forgot the world was watching. There was something luminous about the way she let herself be known without ever saying a single word.

It made me want to close my eyes too. To breathe in every note. To make something beautiful with my own hands. To worship in a way that was Holy Spirit-filled, to call to our Father in heaven.

I wanted to tell her.

That she had just given me one of the best gifts of my life.

That I could sit here all night, just watching her play, and that would be enough.

But I didn't want to interrupt her moment. Didn't want her to open her eyes and find out I'd been here, quietly unraveling under the weight of her music.

So I just watched, still and quiet, while she spoke with strings and silence and soul.

And I prayed again: softly, stupidly, desperately, that she would never stop.

So when the final note hovered in the silence, I simply clapped softly.

"That was… incredible."

Andromeda's POV

I lowered the viola slowly. I heard him clap before I opened my eyes.

"You tricked me," Zeb started, crossing his arms with an exaggerated pout. "You let me think you couldn't play."

I shrugged, amused. "I never said I couldn't play the viola. I said I couldn't play any of the other instruments."

Zeb narrowed his eyes like he was trying to decide whether to be offended or impressed. "Fine. You win. But you owe me another performance soon."

I smiled. "Happy New Year, Zeb."

"Happy New Year, Meda," he replied.

The hug we shared after that lingered a little longer than usual. Not awkward. Not forced. But warm. I felt safe in his arms.

When we pulled apart, I didn't comment on the way he stepped back slowly, like he was reluctant to let go. Which was weird because Zeb didn't do much physical contact, and neither did I, but I knew we had different reasons, though.

We packed up slowly, still wrapped in the newness of a new year. The fireworks continued to bloom in the sky as we lingered just a little longer, leaning against the glass like children watching a wonderland unfold.

After the fireworks were finished, we made our way to his studio, reheated the takeout we'd stashed earlier in the mini microwave we bought together, and grabbed some more blankets we had left there earlier.

Then, head back to the music club room.

We mirrored my laptop screen to the TV mounted on the wall in the club room and settled in under our blankets to resume the movie marathon, classic Hallmark ones we could both make fun of.

"This guy literally met her for one day and is already baking gingerbread houses with her family," Zeb groaned.

"Plot twist," I added. "She's a CIA agent undercover, and he's actually Santa."

He snorted.

I laughed.

Then he reached for the popcorn bowl and said, "New Year's resolution: never let Meda pick the movie again."

"And mine is to make you suffer through them," I replied, tossing a kernel at him.

We laughed until our cheeks hurt. And I thought, maybe this was the best start to a year I've had in a very, very long time.

Chapter 42: New Year blossoms

Amerei

The first few days of the new year were exactly what Amerei needed: slow, soft, and completely wrapped in Merrick's presence.

After the New Year's Eve fireworks, the kind that painted the night sky in brilliant colors and echoed with their laughter, Amerei had expected things to return to normal. She figured Merrick would go back to his usual whirlwind schedule of back-to-back meetings, long emails, and endless phone calls. But to her surprise, Merrick had other plans.

"We earned this break, Erei," he told her that first morning as he brought breakfast to her in bed. The tray held fluffy scrambled eggs, toast browned just the way she liked it, and a bowl of apple slices. He even remembered her favorite herbal tea, served in the floral mug she always teased him about.

"You're spoiling me," she murmured, still half-asleep, tugging the blanket up to her chin.

"I absolutely am," he smiled, settling beside her. "And I plan to keep doing it."

And he meant every word. The days that followed felt like they belonged to a storybook. Each moment was its own little vacation, a chapter filled with soft joy. They took long, lazy walks around the backyard, her hand tucked into the pocket of his hoodie while his other arm draped loosely around her shoulders. Sometimes they wandered without a goal; other times they ended up beneath the gazebo out back, legs tangled together despite the cold, their conversations drifting between the future, the past, and silly what-ifs.

Other times, they didn't talk at all. The silence was comfortable, a kind of language of its own.

One evening, Merrick pulled out his telescope and set it up on the back patio. Wrapped in a thick fleece blanket, Amerei leaned against him, pointing at constellations she could barely remember from high school astronomy.

"Tell me one of those stars looks like me," she teased that one time, squinting at the sky.

"Only one? That one right there," he had replied, pointing without hesitation. "The one making all the others jealous."

She rolled her eyes, grinning despite herself, heart warm and full.

Cooking together turned into a full-blown event. Or more accurately, Amerei attempted to cook while Merrick provided exaggerated commentary on her technique, or lack thereof.

"You're holding that knife like a toddler holding a crayon," he declared once, dodging a carrot chunk she tossed his way.

She chased him around the kitchen with a spatula, both of them laughing as old-school R&B played in the background. They danced in socks across the tiles, bumping into counters, stepping on each other's feet, but never stopping.

Merrick started taking Polaroids of their moments: her mid-chop with a goofy expression, him ducking behind a cupboard door to avoid flying vegetables, and her balancing a spoon on her nose. They pinned the snapshots to the fridge and corkboard until even the hallway looked like a scrapbook had come to life.

Afternoons were calm, filled with reading and soft touches. Amerei would curl into the armchair by the fireplace, a book open in her lap. Merrick would lie across the rug, head resting gently against her knees, eyes closed in contentment. Sometimes he asked her to read aloud because he said he liked the sound of her voice better than the one in his head.

One especially sunny afternoon, he surprised her with an indoor balcony picnic, as outside was too cold for that. Amerei wouldn't change the moment one bit when it was just them. A soft blanket, simple sandwiches, sparkling juice in wine glasses, and a playlist of their favorite songs from the past year were all done for her. They lay on the fake grass, watching clouds shift and reshape.

"That one looks like a bunny," Amerei pointed out.

"That's clearly a pirate ship," Merrick said flatly.

"No way. It even has floppy ears." she argued

"That's a sail, Ame. Do we need to get your eyes checked out?" He countered.

They debated for ten whole minutes before calling it a draw and collapsing into giggles.

Evenings became something special. Under oversized blankets, they lounged on the couch, binge-watching horror flicks, cringey rom-coms, and classic anime series. Merrick always made the popcorn with way too much butter, just how she liked it, and Amerei never failed to sneak more than her share. They took turns picking movies and roasting each plot.

One night, curled beneath the throw blanket, Amerei whispered, "This is nice, us having this time to just be together."

Merrick gently brushed her hair away from her face before he replied, "This is everything."

They didn't travel. They didn't host parties. They didn't flood social media with polished pictures or grand declarations. Yet somehow, the simplicity of their quiet time, how they laughed, how they held each other, and how present they both were made it unforgettable.

One morning, while Amerei stood at the bathroom mirror doing her skincare routine, she caught Merrick watching her from the doorway, leaning against the threshold.

"Why are you staring at me like that? " she asked, raising a brow.

He grinned, unbothered. "Just admiring my New Year's blessing."

She threw a washcloth at him, laughing as he caught it midair like it was some kind of prize.

As the second week of January crept closer, Amerei felt something she hadn't allowed herself to feel in a long time: hope. True, steady, unmistakable hope. She didn't know exactly what the year would bring. But with Merrick beside her, loving her in quiet, intentional, and honest ways, she couldn't help but believe that this year might be different. Maybe this year would be better than the last.

Chapter 43: First Day In Of The New Year

The first Sunday of the year came quicker than I thought. I should've been dreading it, but when Zeb asked if I wanted to come to church again, the hesitation I had the first time was…barely there. Maybe it was because he asked so casually, like it was just another stroll through the park. Or maybe it was because last time wasn't as bad as I expected. I really couldn't say, but I did say yes once again.

We met up in the dorm parking lot again, right under the winter-Grey sky. When he leaned against his car waiting for me, hands tucked into the pockets of his coat, his head tilted back toward the morning sun, I wasn't even surprised anymore by how good he looked. I guess I was getting used to Zeb looking like he walked out of one of those perfectly imperfect K-dramas: clean, neat, casual but polished. It was just…him.

"Morning, Meda," he greeted, flashing that easy grin that was getting more dangerous the more I saw it.

"Morning, Zeb," I replied, feeling a weird little flutter in my stomach.

We climbed into my car; he was driving this time. As soon as he started the engine, he tossed me a look and said, "Your turn. Pick a genre."

I scrolled through the playlist on the dashboard screen, teasing him with a few questionable choices before settling on a mellow indie pop mix. But to his total shock, and maybe mine too, I started singing along right off the bat.

Zeb let out a sharp laugh. "Meda! You have a voice! And here you were, making me do all the solo concerts."

I shoved his shoulder slightly, smirking. "Shut up, I did sing last time."

We laughed the whole drive there, singing way off-key at points, but it didn't matter. It felt…normal. Good. Easy.

When we arrived, Zeb pulled my car door open for me like he always did and held open the church doors, too. I offered him a quick "thanks," which earned a playful wink.

And then—boom. The flood of greetings hit us the second we stepped inside.

Even though this was technically my third time here, since I'd gone once more after Christmas, people still acted like I was some long-lost friend returning home. Warm hugs. Kind words. Excited squeals. Bright smiles everywhere. It was overwhelming, but not in a bad way this time. Maybe because Zeb stayed close by, gently excusing me from conversations when he noticed my eyes start to glaze over.

Some people tried to stop him, too, but he just nodded, gave brief responses, and kept steering us forward like he was on a mission every single time. By the time we finally made it into the sanctuary and sat down, we both exhaled like marathon runners crossing a finish line.

Praise and worship started first. I actually knew most of the songs this time and found myself singing along under my breath just like at the Christmas service. Announcements came next, then birthdays, anniversaries…and the offering. I surprised myself by reaching into my purse and dropping a folded bill into the basket. No pressure. No guilt. Just…wanting to give.

Then the sermon began.

"Today, we're talking about the love of God," the pastor announced from the Rostrum. "The real love of God. And how to recognize it in this world where fake love is everywhere."

He had the congregation open to **1 John 3:1-3**, and I followed along on the big screen:

"See what great love the Father has lavished on us, that we should be called children of God! And that is what we are! The reason the world doesn't know us is that it didn't know him. Dear friends, we are God's children now, and what we will be has not yet been revealed. We know that when he appears, we will be like him because we will see him as he is. And everyone who has hope in him purifies himself just as he is pure"

The pastor continued, voice strong but kind. "God's love isn't conditional. It's not based on our performance, our image, or our achievements. It's given freely, fully, even when we fail."

He flipped a few pages over and pointed to **1 John 3:11-24**:

"This is the message you heard from the beginning: We should love one another. For this is the message you have heard from the beginning: We should love one another, unlike Cain, who was of the evil one and murdered his brother. And why did he murder him? Because his deeds were evil, and his brother's were righteous. Do not be surprised, brothers and sisters, if the world hates you. We know that we have passed from death to life because we love our brothers and sisters. The one who does not love remains in death. Everyone who hates his brother or sister is a murderer, and you know that no murderer has eternal life residing in him. This is how we have come to know love: He laid down his life for us. We should also lay down our lives for our brothers and sisters. If anyone has this world's goods and sees a fellow believer in need but withholds compassion from him, how does God's love reside in him? Little children, let us not love in word or speech, but in action and in truth. This is how we will know that we belong to the truth and will reassure our hearts before him whenever our hearts condemn us, for God is greater than our hearts, and he knows all things. Dear friends, if our hearts don't condemn us, we have confidence before God and receive whatever we ask from him because we keep his commands and do what is pleasing in his sight. Now this is his command: that we believe in the name of his Son, Jesus Christ, and love one another as he commanded us. The one who keeps his commands remains in him, and he in him. And the way we know that he remains in

us is from the Spirit he has given us."

He explained how fake love is rooted in selfishness, control, and pride, but God's love, real love, was pure, sacrificial, and patient. He spoke about how people might say they love you but manipulate you, use you, and discard you when you don't meet their expectations. God's love doesn't work that way.

"God's love frees you," he said. "God's love calls you by name, not by performance. And real believers? Real followers of Christ? They'll reflect that love too."

I sat there, frozen. Every word felt like it was peeling something back inside me.

For the first time, I realized… my parents' *love*, the constant pressure, the conditional approval, and the public image they demanded I uphold? It wasn't the same love this man was talking about. It wasn't the love of God. Maybe it never was.

And somehow, that hurt. And somehow, it also made me feel a little less crazy.

When church ended, the hugs and handshakes started up again, but Zeb once again played my social bodyguard, guiding us gently out toward the car.

"You good?" he asked once we climbed in.

I nodded, swallowing a lump I didn't even realize was there. "Yeah… just…a lot to think about."

He didn't push. He just smiled and said, "Wanna head to see Reed?"

"Yeah," I breathed. "Let's go."

We drove to the hospital, singing lightly to whatever was playing on the radio. At the hospital, Zeb followed me up without hesitation. This was his third time meeting Reed now, and it showed; he greeted the nurses, smiled kindly, and walked into the room like he belonged there.

"Hey Reed," I said as I sat down beside the bed. "Guess who's back? Your stalker and her backup dancer."

Zeb chuckled. "Man, I keep telling her, I'm the victim here. She won't leave me alone."

I laughed, and for a second, it was easy to pretend everything was normal.

We chatted about the new year, school starting up again soon, and random little things. I updated Reed about Zeb and me hanging out over Christmas, about my slowly growing tolerance for social greetings at church, and about how, despite myself, I actually liked singing at the top of my lungs in the car.

After the visit, we headed out and picked up lunch, grabbing takeout burgers and milkshakes before heading back.

"Thanks for letting me tag along today," I said.

"Thanks for being a good third wheel," he teased.

He laughed, flashing a grin that made the whole dreary afternoon look a little brighter.

After dropping me off at the dorm, Zeb said he had a quick run to make and left. I quickly changed into comfy clothes, grabbed my laptop and extra blanket, and drove back to the art building, back to Zeb's studio, because I am not walking across such a huge campus in this weather when I have a car. Ninety percent of the time now, we were there anyway. His studio was practically a mini-apartment, complete with a small bathroom, a microwave, and a fridge.

Props to attending a rich kid's school, I guess.

When I arrived, Zeb wasn't there, so I punched in the code. I drop my things on the couch and head to the corner of the room. I started sketching something at his desk, music playing softly in the background. I threw my blanket over the couch and switched the heater on. Zeb had run to his place to change and grab some stuff, so I had some quiet time in his studio.

And for the first time,

My mind wasn't on Netflix or homework.

It was still on the message from this morning.

The real love of God.

The fake love of the world.

The difference.

The freedom.

And for once…I wanted to understand it for myself.

Chapter 44: Black and White vs First Time Seeing Colours

Andromeda POV

PLAYLIST - COME JESUS COME BY CECE WINANS

Zebedee had come back a while ago, but I hadn't even noticed.

I just sat there at his desk, staring blankly at the sketch I was supposed to be working on, my pencil untouched in my hand. The faint scratching of Zeb's pencil against paper filled the studio, soft and steady against the quiet.

Then the dull roll of his chair broke the silence.

A second later, I heard his footsteps getting closer.

"You okay, Meda?" Zeb asked softly, his voice full of concern.

I blinked a few times, trying to swallow the lump forming in my throat. "I-I'm… fine," I lied, which was dumb, because I wasn't even convincing myself, let alone him.

Zeb crouched beside the desk in front of me, elbows resting loosely against his knees. Not too close. Not too far. Just there.

Waiting.

His eyes searched mine carefully, patient and calm, never forcing.

And somehow, that made it worse.

And before I knew it, the words were spilling out.

"I don't even know what's wrong with me exactly," I admitted shakily. "It's just... my parents." I tried to clear my throat. "My parents, they call themselves Christian. Always have. They were always at church. Always hosting Sunday dinners with the pastor and the board and... all that."

I laughed, but it sounded empty even to my own ears. "But the expectations, Zeb—" I paused, trying to collect myself.

The memories, the pieces of the puzzle, were being placed together right now:

The times when the dictatorship mentality of my father and the way our family worships image over actual feeling—it was suffocating growing up like that.

I roughly swiped at my tear before continuing, frustrated with everything and nothing at the same time.

"My house never felt... loving." My throat tightened painfully. "Everything was about image. About perfection. About obedience." I shook my head slowly. "My dad especially, it was always his way or nothing. Every conversation felt like being evaluated instead of heard."

Zeb stayed silent.

"The older I got, the more I started associating Christianity with that version of them." I looked down at my trembling hands. "Cold. Performative. Brutal behind closed doors." My voice cracked. "And I remember thinking, if that's what faith makes people become, then I wanted no part of it."

The tears came before I could stop them; no amount of swiping could stop them.

"Then I met Mita," I whispered. "And she confused me because she was genuinely kind. Not

fake kind. Real kind." I sniffed weakly. "But I still convinced myself she was just an exception."

I laughed quietly through my tears.

"Then I met you."

That made my chest ache even worse.

"You're patient. You listen. You don't make people feel small just to feel powerful." My voice wavered. "And I kept trying to explain it away too. Like maybe you were another exception."

I shook my head.

"But then today happened. The sermon. The people at church remembering me. Welcoming

me." I pressed a hand against my chest like it physically hurt. "Nobody wanted anything from me, Zeb. Nobody cared about my last name or what I looked like or whether I sounded

impressive enough."

A sob escaped me.

"And now I don't know what to do with that."

The tears spilled harder now, hot against my cheeks.

"Because what if I was wrong?" I choked out. "What if I spent years believing a lie just because it came from the people who were supposed to love me?"

I tried to swallow the lump in my throat

"Was it—was it because it hurt too much to question it that I never did my own research like I always do with everything else?"

I wrapped my arms around myself tightly.

"I research everything," I whispered brokenly. "Everything. I always need facts. Proof.

Understanding." My breathing turned uneven. "But I never questioned this. I just accepted what they showed me and built my whole perception around it."

The realization hit me all over again.

I shook my head, sobbing now, unable to stop it. " I believed what they showed me. I let the lie fester. I let it shape me. I led myself away from the one thing I needed most… **love**."

I sobbed even harder; I was so angry at myself

"And because of that, I convinced myself love was something controlling. Something painful." My voice cracked apart. "Something you survived instead of something that made you feel safe."

Before I could stop myself from falling apart completely, Zeb stood and pulled me into his arms.

No hesitation.

No overthinking.

Just instinct.

And that nearly broke me worse.

Because physical touch was usually such a careful boundary for him. Me too, honestly. But he didn't seem worried about that right now. He just held me tightly, grounding me while I cried against his shoulder.

"And see?" I whispered through sobs. "Even this. You saw me hurting and your first instinct was to comfort me." I clenched weakly at the fabric of his hoodie. "That's love, right? Not whatever my parents were trying to pass off as love?"

Zeb's arms tightened slightly around me.

"It hurts," I admitted, my voice raw. "The one thing I ever wanted was for them to see me. To hear me. To love me not because I was some model daughter but because I was…me. But they couldn't. They wouldn't."

I drew in a ragged breath. "Instead, they tried to mold me into something they could parade around. And when I didn't fit exactly into that mold, they… they chipped pieces away to 'refine me' until I didn't even recognize myself anymore." I muttered, my words finally sinking in.

I pulled back just enough to see his face, his gaze steady, kind, never judging.

The words still settled heavily between us.

For a moment, neither of us spoke.

Then I laughed weakly through my tears, embarrassed by how hard I was spiraling.

"I spent years telling myself I didn't need anybody," I muttered. "Didn't need God. Didn't need love. Because every version of it I knew just took pieces out of me."

But then I felt my expression softened despite myself.

I engulf myself in his embrace once more, resting my head on his shoulder.

"And then I got friends."

Zeb let out the faintest huff of amusement against my hair.

"Odessa with her terrifying 'I'll fight everybody in this room' energy," I sniffed.

That earned a quiet chuckle from him.

"And Amerei," I continued, my voice wobbling again, "my lovable fluffball. Always smiling and who genuinely hugs people like her heart physically cannot contain affection."

Zeb laughed harder at that one, trying and failing to suppress it.

"And Mita," I said, voice softening. "Witty, sweet, sarcastic sometimes, but a born fighter. She believes so deeply even when life gives her every reason not to sometimes."

I sniffed again before pulling back to look up at him once again

"And then there's you," I whispered quietly. "You never push. You never perform kindness just to hold it over people later." My throat tightened again. "You just stay."

"And me?" I spat, tears burning. "I'm the broken one. The shattered one. The aftermath of everything life can crush. The bottom of the barrel, draped in fine clothing and expensive brands, masking what I actually am. A chip off the old, cracked block my parents built."

I was not shattered.

Just tired.

Tired of carrying versions of myself built for other people.

My knees weakened slightly, and Zeb steadied me immediately without a word.

He didn't interrupt.

Didn't preach.

Didn't try to solve me.

He just stayed there holding me while the weight of everything finally collapsed out into the open.

And somehow, that quiet kind of presence meant more to me than any sermon ever could.

Chapter 45: The Shifting Of The Tides

Andromeda POV

I stayed curled against Zeb while my crying slowly dissolved into shaky breaths and quiet

hiccups.

He didn't rush me, didn't shift away, or start talking to fill the silence.

He simply stayed there beside me, one arm steady around my shoulders while I tried to pull myself back together

After a long while, his hand brushed gently over the back of my hair.

"You ready for what I have to say?" he asked softly, voice close to my ear.

I nodded against his chest, still not trusting my voice.

Zeb leaned back just enough to look at me properly. His expression was calm, but there was something deeply emotional sitting behind his eyes too.

"Meda," he said carefully, "I'm really sorry your parents failed to show you what God's love actually looks like."

The ache in my chest deepened instantly.

"But listen to me for a second, and I want you to hear me clearly, okay?" he continued gently. "You were never abandoned by God. You felt unseen by your family. Hurt. Forgotten maybe." His thumb brushed lightly against my knuckles. "But God never turned His back on you."

More tears burned behind my eyes immediately.

"But," he said softly, "the question is, do you want to accept His love now? Not out of being forced, but you of your own accord." He asked

The question settled heavily between us.

I hesitated; fear twisted together with something else inside me. Something fragile and aching and hopeful all at once.

"I don't know if I'm ready," I admitted quietly. "And what if He doesn't want me after all this time?" My voice cracked. "After all the times I pushed Him away?" He would really want me, of all people?" I asked

A small smile pulled at Zeb's mouth, soft and understanding.

"Med," he said, his voice low and sure, "none of us are ever ready for God's love. **None of us.**" he shook his head slightly. "There's no such thing as the 'right time' or 'perfect time' to accept his love. Young or old, broken or proud, it doesn't matter. The best time to accept His love is the moment it's offered. Whether by someone who loves him and loves you or by Him Himself knocking on your heart."

His voice stayed steady and warm.

"That's kind of the whole point."

He cupped my hands between his.

" Meda… none of us deserve it," he assured, voice thick with emotion. "Not one of us." His

eyes held mine firmly.

"He doesn't love us because we're worthy. He loves us because He *IS* love itself. All He asks is that we love Him back with everything we have. Even if it's broken pieces. He can work with broken pieces."

Something in me cracked open at that.

Not violently.

Quietly.

Like a locked door finally giving way.

"There's no checklist. No 'get your life together first.' No 'prove yourself worthy.' The invitation is open right now. No barriers. No conditions. Just love."

A tear slid down my cheek.

"The invitation is open now, Meda. Exactly as you are."

I looked down at our joined hands, trembling.

Then finally whispered:

"What do I do?"

The panic hit almost immediately afterward.

"Do I need to call a pastor or—or get baptized again or something?" I asked quickly. "What if I do it wrong?"

Zeb laughed softly under his breath, not mocking me. Just warm.

"You're okay," he soothed gently. "There are no complicated traditional proceedings. No complicated ritual. Let's just pray, okay? Repeat after me."

His fingers squeezed mine reassuringly.

"We can just pray."

My heartbeat thudded hard against my ribs.

"Okay," I whispered.

Zeb spoke slowly, giving me time to follow.

"Lord Jesus… I accept You as my Lord and Savior.

I repeated the words shakily after him.

I believe You came down as a man to walk the earth, to show us the truth, how to live, and how to love.

My throat tightened as I spoke.

I believe You died on the cross for my sins, and rose again three days later, and conquered death.

Tears blurred my vision again.

I believe that salvation is a gift I cannot earn, but one You freely give.

Something in my chest started aching differently now.
   Softer.

Thank You for making a way for me to come before the Father boldly.

My voice cracked harder there.

I believe You are the Way, the Truth, and the Life.

The tears kept falling steadily down my face.

You are the Light of the world, and now, You live in me.

Help me to walk in obedience, in both trials and blessings.

Not my will, but Yours be done in my life.

And finally:

In Jesus' Name I pray. Amen.[3]

Silence settled over the room afterward.

For a second, nothing happened.

I just sat there breathing unevenly, staring down at our hands while tears slipped quietly down my cheeks. Thinking about this huge decision I made.

Then suddenly it hit me.

Not dramatically.

Not like lightning.

More like a wave finally breaking after holding itself back too long.

I bent forward with a sob, pressing my hands against my face.

But this crying felt different.

Lighter.

Almost overwhelming in the opposite direction.

I started sobbing uncontrollably because my heart felt lighter than it ever had before, flooded with something so big, so pure, I couldn't even name it.

"Zeb," I laughed through tears helplessly, "I don't even know why I'm crying this hard."

Another breathless laugh escaped me.

"I just— I feel…" My chest tightened painfully again. "I feel okay."

The words shocked me the second they left my mouth.

Okay.

Not fixed.

Not magically healed.

But lighter.

Like something crushing had loosened its grip around my ribs.

"Zeb, what's happening to me? I feel something, this calmness, its weird, I can't even explain it!" I muttered through tears.

Zeb smiled at me with so much tenderness it almost made me cry harder..

"That's the Spirit of God, Meda," he whispered. "That's His love. That's the Holy Spirit filling you. That's God meeting you where you are. Just breathe. Accept it. Thank Him. Worship Him, however it comes naturally," he instructed

I clutched his hands tighter without thinking.

The room suddenly felt so small and sacred all at once.

The dim studio lights.

The stars outside the windows.

The sound of our uneven breathing.

I wept. I smiled. I laughed. I worshiped without knowing I was doing it, murmuring I whispered thank you over and over without realizing I was saying it aloud.

Thank You.

Thank You.

Thank You.

Zeb bowed his head too, emotional himself now, tears bright in his own eyes though he stayed quiet about it.

When the storm of emotions finally began to settle, I felt raw and new, like a fresh page. With a tear-stained face and a swollen heart I have never felt so refreshed in such a state,

Zeb grabbed his Bible, flipping through worn pages until he found what he was looking for.

"I want to show you something," he said before clearing his throat, voice still thick with emotion.

He opened to **1 Corinthians 13**, reading it aloud, slowly:

"Love is patient, love is kind.

It does not envy, it does not boast, it is not proud.

It does not dishonor others, it is not self-seeking, it is not easily angered, it keeps no record of wrongs.

Love does not delight in evil but rejoices with the truth.

It always protects, always trusts, always hopes, always perseveres.

Love never fails."

His voice stayed low and steady as he read through 1 Corinthians 13.

When he finished reading, he looked up at me.

"This is what love is supposed to look like, Meda," he said quietly. "This is the love God gives. "Not manipulation. Not performance. Not constantly proving your worth. Not perfection. Not power plays. This," he explained, pointing to the words on the page.

I hugged my knees closer to my chest, tears gathering again, softer this time.

"And one more thing," Zeb said, flipping back a few more pages. "Remember? You wrote this down?" He smiled gently, tapping the verse with his finger.

John 10:10. *I can't believe he saw that*

"The thief comes only to steal and kill and destroy; I have come that they may have life, and have it to the full."

He met my gaze and said firmly, "God doesn't want to steal your joy or chain you down, Meda. He came to give you life. Full, abundant life. Not a fake version. The real thing. He wants you to actually live it, but in a way that is beneficial to you long term,' he explained

I couldn't even speak past the lump in my throat.

I just nodded.

For the first time in years, I didn't feel like I was surviving a performance.

I wasn't trying to become smaller.

Quieter.

More acceptable.

Neither was I trying to be bigger than I felt
I was just sitting there exactly as I was.
And somehow still loved anyway.

After Zeb closed his Bible, he just stayed there, by my side sitting cross-legged across from me, the small lamp in the studio casting a golden circle around us like we were sealed in some sacred little world.

Neither of us spoke for a while, but the silence wasn't heavy.

It was wonderful.

Outside, the sky had turned completely black, stars scattered across it like tiny pinpricks of light.

Inside, the air buzzed faintly with a peace I didn't know how to explain. Not the kind you pretend to have when you fake a smile and say you're fine. No, this was the kind of peace that reached down into your bones and told you you were finally safe.

Safe enough to just *be*.

Zeb was the first to move, stretching his legs out and leaning back on his hands with a low, content sigh.

I mirrored him, lying back on the big, overstuffed pillow I'd dragged from his couch earlier.

"You wanna sketch for a bit?" he asked, voice casual but warm, like offering a favorite blanket.

I smiled faintly.

"Yeah."

He slid his sketchbook over and fished a second one out from the messy shelf nearby.

He handed it to me with a pencil tucked neatly in the spiral.

"No rules," he warned lightly. "But please abandon whatever artistic crime scene you were creating earlier."

I let out a startled laugh.

"Wow. So supportive. Keep this up, and I might just draw a stick figure crying and label it 'Meda at 9 PM.'"

He grinned. "Hey, honest art is the best art," he joked.

And somehow, sitting there shoulder to shoulder while we sketched badly and talked about absolutely nothing important felt healing too.

Sometimes he'd hum a random song under his breath. Sometimes I'd giggle at how absolutely terrible my sketches were turning out.

When I peeked over, I saw he was sketching something soft and dreamlike, clouds maybe, or a wave curling against the sky. His lines were sure, flowing.

I felt no need to make mine perfect though.

Tonight wasn't about being perfect.

It was about being *free.*

At some point, Zeb dropped his pencil and leaned his head back against the wall, sighing up at the ceiling.

"Good night, huh?" he murmured lazily.

"The best," I whispered back, tracing lazy circles on the edge of my sketchbook.

The weight of today's event catching up to me.

We stayed like that for a long time.

No rush to speak.

No need to fill the space.

The heater hummed low. The stars blinked outside the big window. The clock ticked in the corner.

I didn't know what tomorrow would hold: our art sessions, family calls, messy life.

But right here, right now, I had peace. I had God. I had a friend who saw me.

Eventually, the night started to blur at the edges.

At some point my pencil slipped from my hand entirely, exhaustion finally catching up to me. My head leaned to the side before I even realized it, brushing lightly against Zeb's shoulder.

He chuckled low in his chest.

"Tired, Meda?"

"Mmm,"

I felt him shift slightly, pulling one of the oversize blankets over us. He kept as much of a respectful distance, but the warmth was still there, the steady presence of someone who wasn't trying to fix me, just willing to stay.

The soft sound of the heater filled the space.

The stars outside blinked like quiet sentries, watching over us.

Zeb didn't say anything else.

He just adjusted the pillow behind my head carefully so my neck wouldn't cramp and leaned his own head back against the wall.

For the first time in what felt like forever, I wasn't terrified of sleep.

I wasn't as afraid of my own mind or the past clawing its way forward.

Not so much.

I was safe here.

Under God's eyes.

Besides a friend who didn't demand a polished version of me.

As my eyes drifted shut, I barely heard Zeb whisper softly into the quiet room:

"Thank you, Lord. For tonight. For her. For peace......"

It was the last thing I heard before slipping into the gentlest sleep I'd had in years.

Chapter 46: One Is Never Prepared For The Unexpected

Amerei POV

It was our last two days together before I had to head back to campus.

Back to group chats, late-night studying, and the endless buzz of life with the girls.

Merrick and I had been soaking up every moment: long walks, movie marathons, and late mornings tangled up in each other. We both knew once Wednesday came, it would be another stretch of missed calls and scheduling around school and his business meetings.

So maybe that's why tonight felt heavier.

Fuller.

Like we were both aware of how little time was left.

I was in the kitchen, determined to make us lunch myself, no fancy chef today, no takeout. Just me, a borrowed apron, and a surprisingly complicated sandwich recipe I found online.

I heard his footsteps before I saw him.

A second later, Merrick leaned against the counter beside me, arms crossed, looking like something out of a daydream.

"Ame," he stared, voice low but steady, "So, there's something I have been meaning to talk about in terms of my preference, or, as some would put it, my liking." He paused before coming up to me and tucking loose strands of hair behind my ear. "Not many people I have entertained seem interested in it and have disliked it even, but as you are now my girlfriend, I know it is best to let you know that part of me." The silence that followed caused me to look up from where I was clumsily slicing tomatoes, arching an eyebrow without thinking. *Where was this going?*

"I want to involve you in everything I do," he continued, softer now, "because you're important to me. I love you."

The words warmed my chest, melting away the worried feeling that was bubbling in my chest. A thousand snarky replies flashed through my mind.

Instead, I just wiped my hands on a dish towel and smiled a little.

"Merrick," I started, turning fully to him, trying to ensure my next words convey my sincerity. "I want to know *every* part of you. I love you too," I confessed, my heart pounding a little harder than my voice let on.

Merrick's smile rewarded me with the satisfaction that I needed to know he felt my honesty; he wrapped me into a warm, comforting embrace and placed a soft, lingering kiss on my forehead in that way that still made my knees wobble a little. He pulled away to look down at me, not saying anything, before releasing me completely, and he walked off toward the living room, leaving the air in the kitchen still buzzing from the moment we just had.

I stood there for a moment longer, tomatoes forgotten, feeling the weight of his words settle in.

He wanted me to see all of him: the polished parts, the messy parts, even the ones he isn't confident in.

And I wasn't scared of that.

I was ready.

Third-person Pov

That evening had been so intimate, so sweet.

Merrick had cooked them dinner, poured them wine, played her favorite songs softly in the background. They had curled up under a blanket on the couch, talking about nothing and everything, laughing at stupid jokes, feeling the weight of their coming separation hang heavier with each passing hour.

Amerei had eventually dozed off, the comfort of the night and the wine tugging her into sleep. She barely remembered Merrick lifting her up and carrying her to bed, just the warmth of his arms and the scent of his cologne in the haze of her dreams.

But when she woke up again, something felt off.

She stirred groggily, blinking in the dim light of the room.

A faint, familiar sound, of a zip? Maybe fabric moving, brushed at the edge of her awareness. Then she saw Merrick, undressing at the foot of the bed.

"You should have woken me up if you wanted to do something," she murmured, her voice thick with sleep.

Merrick glanced over his shoulder at her, a crooked smile tugging at his mouth.

"Now, where's the fun in that?" he purred.

Amerei blinked, confused.

"What... what's that supposed to mean?"

"You remember when I said I wanted to show you my other side?" Merrick muttered, his tone light, almost playful.

He nodded toward her, and that's when she saw it.

Her hands were **tied** to the headboard. She immediately glanced down at her feet out of reflex

Her ankles were also **bound** to the foot of the bed.

Spread out like a starfish.

The cold shock that rushed through her veins was instant and violent.

Panic clawed at her chest.

"Merrick, what—?!" she started, trying to pull at the ties, but they didn't budge.

He chuckled softly, as if this were a game.

"I thought you might enjoy this. Don't worry, you'll be fine," he cooed.

"But you didn't even ask me!" she snapped, her voice rising in pitch, a tremble threading through it.

"You said you trusted me," he countered casually, as if that explained everything.

"And it's more exciting this way… when you don't see it coming," he chirped

Amerei stared at him in disbelief.

"*What?*" She whispered-yelled, her pitch raised, voice cracking under her emotions.

This wasn't intimacy.

This wasn't trust.

This wasn't the man she loved.

This was something else, something wrong.

A pit opened up in her stomach.

She wanted to scream. She wanted to cry. She wanted to break free.

Chapter 47: I Thought I Knew You

At first, she tried.

Tried to convince herself this was just another one of Merrick's ideas, something he thought would be exciting if she would open herself to it, something she should be open to because he was her boyfriend. Because he **loved** her.

Right?

She obeyed his quiet, firm commands even though her skin crawled with discomfort.

She squeezed her eyes shut, willing herself to relax, to make this be okay.

She told herself it would be over soon.

But then he grew rougher.

His movements became harsher, losing any trace of gentleness.

Pain flared everywhere where it wasn't supposed to, even at her wrists and ankles, where the ties cut into her skin.

"Merrick, stop," Amerei whispered, her voice cracking.

He didn't.

"Merrick," she pleaded again, louder, fear now threading her voice. "Stop."

Still, he kept going, faster, harder, crueler.

As if he couldn't even hear her.

Pain lanced through her body, making her flinch instinctively.

She winced, tears springing into her eyes.

"Stop, Merrick," she commanded, her voice breaking.

Nothing.

No slowing down, no hesitation.

"Merrick, STOP!" she shouted, yanking at the restraints, feeling the sting of skin tearing, wrists burning raw.

But there was no mercy.

Only his hands, his weight, his force.

"It hurts!" she sobbed. "Merrick, please, stop—it HURTS!"

She screamed, loud and sharp, but the sound only seemed to fuel him.

His body crushed into hers, and she swore she could feel something tearing deep inside.

Hot, sharp pain bloomed in her hips, her thighs, every part of her.

Amerei's mind fractured.

The room spun.

The world blurred.

And finally, she stopped screaming.

There was no point.

He wasn't listening.

He didn't care.

The man she loved, the man she trusted with every fragile, bruised part of her heart, was gone.

Replaced by someone who caused her pain and did nothing.

Someone who heard her begging and kept hurting her anyway.

She lay there, body pinned under his weight, hands tied, sobbing uncontrollably, wishing she could vanish, wishing she could be anywhere but here.

Wishing she had never trusted him.

Hatred curdled in her chest, bitter, raw hatred.

Not just toward him.

Toward herself, too, for staying silent.

For thinking love meant sacrificing her voice.

For thinking love looked anything like this.

But most of all, she realized something brutal and devastating:

The man she loved didn't see her as someone to protect.

He saw her as something to take.

Chapter 48: Discarding Boundaries How far Is Too Far

Amerei

After he was finished, Amerei barely noticed when Merrick shifted back into the version of him she used to know: the loving, the gentle, doting boyfriend.

It was so sudden, so sharp of a change, it left her mind spinning.

One second, he had been cruel.

The next, he was gentle again.

He wiped her skin carefully with a warm cloth, humming under his breath like this was routine.

Like nothing terrible had happened between them. His movements were slow, almost tender.

He kissed her wrists afterward, right over the angry red marks left behind by the restraints.

Then her ankles, still bound.

Soft apologies brushed against her skin.

Little endearments.

As if affection could erase what he had done.

Amerei lay completely still beneath him, her body rigid against the mattress, her heart hammering painfully inside her chest.

Her mind couldn't keep up with the whiplash of it.

Was this the real Merrick?

The attentive boyfriend now wrapping ointment around her raw skin with careful hands?

Or the monster who had ignored her cries a few moments ago?

The questions twisted violently inside her chest.

No matter how she tried to rationalize it, one truth finally settled heavily into place.

This was not love.

It wasn't rough passion. It wasn't miscommunication.

This was **rape**.

The word hit harder now that she allowed herself to think it.

No more sugarcoating it.

No more lying to herself.

He had heard her cry.

He hadn't cared. He hadn't stopped.

He had **taken whatever he wanted**.

She blinked rapidly, trying to force back her tears as Merrick held a glass of water to her lips, coaxing her to drink. She drank greedily as her throat burned from screaming, staring only at the rim of the glass because she couldn't bear to look at him.

Anything to avoid meeting his gaze.

Afterward, he set the cup aside.

But he still didn't untie her.

Instead, he climbed back into bed beside her and pulled her against his chest.

Talking softly.

Petting her hair.

Acting like they were simply winding down after an ordinary night together.

His fingers traced absent circles along her arm.

Amerei flinched before forcing herself still.

Obey.

Stay calm.

~~Smile if you have to.~~

Do whatever keeps him predictable.

Fear pressed against her ribs so hard it hurt to breathe.

She wanted to scream. To fight. To claw her way out of the room.

But she couldn't risk it.

Merrick was bigger than her.

Stronger.

And there were guards stationed inside and outside the estate at all hours.

No one was coming to save her;

If she panicked now and ran, she would be fooling herself, making the situation less safe

So she swallowed every ounce of terror and stayed quiet.

She needed to survive.

She needed to see her friends again, Mita, Odessa, and Meda, to **get out of here and never look back**.

"I can't wait for you to see what I planned for tomorrow," Merrick murmured against her hair.

A chill crawled through her instantly.

Not from cold.

From dread.

Something inside her finally cracked open enough to see him clearly.

Maybe the sweet version of Merrick had never really existed.

Or maybe that was the worst part.

Maybe he was a terrible mix of both.

Tender when it benefited him.

Cruel when it didn't.

Amerei stared blankly toward the ceiling, numbness slowly replacing panic.

She had loved a monster.

And now she was trapped with him.

Amerei POV

I didn't know what time it was when I finally stirred.

The gray lights of the sky filtered weakly through the curtains were the only indication of the time of day.

The only covering I had was the blanket Merrick had tossed over me the night before.

My phone was downstairs.

Dead, most likely.

Out of reach. ~~Out of help~~.

The unsettling feeling of being helpless stirred in my stomach, but I fought the feeling, trying to numb myself because panicking and being emotional would do the opposite of what I want.

I lay there, minutes blurring into hours.

Merrick came and went throughout the day as though nothing had changed, bringing food upstairs with an easy smile that made my skin crawl.

Breakfast.

Then lunch.

I barely touched it. I had no appetite. Not for food. Not for conversation.

He'd try to have casual conversations, but I would tell him, 'I'm tired' or 'you wore me out last night.'

He would just smile calmly, with a subtle hint of arrogance, like he was proud of himself.

Like yesterday hadn't happened.

.

I must have fallen asleep again because when I woke up, the room had already darkened. I was still exhausted from the nightmare that was yesterday.

My body felt heavy.

Bruised.

Hollowed out from the inside, emotionally, physically, and mentally drained.

At some point I drifted off again.

I woke up for the third time, suddenly to the weight of someone on top of me.

Not Merrick.

Someone else.

Panic exploded through me so violently, pressing down on my lungs, stealing my breath, like ice water.

I opened my mouth to scream, but before I could make a sound, I felt lips press against my ankle.

Amerei froze.

The room was dimmer now, shadows stretching across the walls, making everything feel distorted and unreal.

I couldn't see their face clearly as the room had grown dark by the mid-evening light.

But to the side of the room, I heard a voice.

Merrick's voice.

"Relax, Ame," he coaxed like this was something normal, something casual.

"These are my friends."

The Chill.

The fear.

The adrenaline that ran through my body all at once was so strong, it felt painful to just lay there

"This was the surprise."

The smile in his voice made her stomach turn.

"You like it?"

I turned my head in the barely lit shadows to look a him.

It took a sec for my brain to fully register his face.

Also giving my heart the time to do the most vile thing, trying to find the man I fell in love with in the face of this monster, but as I stared at him, the only thing that I saw was my own horror.

Bile rose to the back of my throat. This wasn't real. This couldn't be real.

"Merrick…" I tried, my voice shaking, trying so hard to keep it calm, reasonable, and as non-threatening as possible. "What the heck is this? Yesterday, and now this? I don't even know these people."

But he only watched me.

Smiling.

Calm.

As though I was overreacting to something harmless.

I tried again, speaking carefully now, the same way someone might speak to a dangerous

animal.

"You don't even know if I'm okay with this," I whispered, practically begging. "I don't know these people."

Nothing changed in his expression.

Not guilt.

Not hesitation.

Nothing.

Fear clawed higher inside her chest.

"You're really okay with strangers touching your girlfriend like this?" I asked, weakly grasping for anything that might reach him, thinking he would react to a damsel-in-distress act.

But he only leaned back and watched.

Watched as their hands touched me.

Watched as I quietly cried.

Watched as I wept quietly, helpless to move or fight back.

And he…

He enjoyed it.

So much that he joined them. Laughing. Participating.

And worst of all—

Merrick kissed these men.

They kissed him back.

Some twisted part of me registered it.

Not only was he a rapist, but he was also a liar.

He had kept even this.

Who he was

And what he liked, hidden from me.

The realization numbed somewhere inside me completely.

But none of that mattered now.

The only thing that mattered was surviving.

At some point, laughter filled the room.

Low voices.

Movement.

The sound blurred together until it stopped sounding human at all.

I turned my face to the wall, trying to disappear into the darkness.

Trying to forget where I am

Trying to leave my body behind.

Nothing felt real anymore.

Not this room.

Not Merrick.

Not herself.

At some point, my body, my mind, gave up.

I don't remember anything else.

I passed out.

Chapter 49: When God gives You doors You Open Them

Amerei POV

When I woke up again, I was exhausted.

Tired.

Sore.

I blinked against the weak sunlight pouring through the window, my body aching from places I didn't even want to think about.

Frustrated, I pulled weakly at my wrists and realized with a jolt that they were free.

No more binds. No more fog clouding my mind.

I looked down to the end of the bed.

My feet were free too.

I sat up immediately, ignoring the sharp stab of pain between my legs and the dull throb in my ankles.

I looked around the room, my heart hammering against my ribs.

He wasn't here.

On the bedside table, I spotted something: my phone, plugged into the charger.

God, finally.

I lunged for it, hands trembling so badly I could barely unlock the screen.

I was just about to call someone, **anyone**, when the door burst open.

Merrick stood there, leaning against the threshold, smiling as if nothing had happened.

"Hey… what are you doing? Calling the cops on me, Ame?" he asked, his voice light as he joked, but something sharp hid underneath it.

'So, he was not oblivious to the fact that he committed a crime these past two days.'

I froze. My mind raced.

Quick. Think.

I forced a smile onto my face. "No, sweetheart. I was just calling Odessa and Mita. Remember? I told you we were planning to meet up today to hang out."

His smile widened, and he exhaled like a kid reassured that Santa was still real.

"Oh, right. Yeah," he chirped

He walked over before sitting on the bed. "Can't you stay longer, though? School doesn't even start 'til next Monday. Why don't you stay till Friday and hang out with them over the weekend?" He whined like a child, pressing a kiss to my temple as he wrapped his arms around me.

I used to find that cute, but now

I swallowed the bile rising in my throat and leaned into it. *Pretend. Be happy*

"I wish I could," I cooed softly, keeping my voice breezy, "but you know how it is. As soon as school starts, it's crazy. Especially in the spring semester. You remember how it is."

He pouted but nodded reluctantly. "Yeahhh," he sighed, finally releasing me.

"Go shower, freshen up, and come downstairs. I made breakfast." He ruffled my hair. "And I had the maid pack your stuff… but I still wish you'd stay," he added, trying to persuade me to stay.

"Thanks, Merrick," I said, smiling so sweetly I almost fooled myself.

I slid out of bed, leaving him there, wincing at the ache between my thighs, and limped toward the bathroom.

Every. *Step* Hurt.

"You're beautiful like that," Merrick called after me, voice full of something that made my skin crawl.

I froze for a moment, not knowing how to respond, but I didn't turn around.

Instead, I kept moving, locking the bathroom door behind me, not trusting him not to come in on me and continue what he did yesterday.

I scrubbed my body raw under the hot water, trying to rinse away what no soap could touch.

I could wash my skin… But how did you wash your heart? Your soul?

When I finally came out, I forced myself to get dressed quickly. As Merrick was still in the room watching me get dressed.

Jeans. Hoodie. Sneakers. Something that was not easy to take off.

As I finished, a sick thought crossed my mind.

I turned, staring at Merrick.

"Merrick… the people you invited last night… they wore protection, right?" I asked, forcing my voice to stay casual.

He blinked lazily, like I was asking what time dinner was.

"Hmm? Oh yeah," he said as though he was coming out of a daze, "They did. I made sure."

He smiled, charming and horrible all at once.

"Why would I do something so horrible to the love of my life?"

So he would let others have their way with me, without my consent, but getting pregnant by them was worse. The sick bastard."

I nodded slowly, getting ready, then I grabbed my phone

I pretended like I got a text from Mita by making the text notification come on to my phone.

"Merrick," I said sweetly, "something came up with Mita. I have to go now, okay?"

He cocked his head, studying me like he could smell the fear.

"Feels like you're running," he said so casually, like he was talking about the weather. It scared the crap out of me.

I laughed—bright, airy, practiced.

"Nooo, baby. Just busy," I said, walking up to him, cupping his face gently, pressing a kiss to his cheek the way I always did.

He relaxed under my touch.

"Okay. Let me call Cain to drive you," he said easily.

"Sure, baby," I agreed, my heart hammering against my ribs.

Just keep playing your part, Amerei. You're almost free.

In the car, I chatted with Cain, the driver, as if nothing was wrong.

I kept the conversation light, cheerful, joking when appropriate.

I knew Merrick's people always reported back to him.

When we pulled onto campus, I waved goodbye like normal.

Walked calmly up the steps.

Took the elevator to my floor.

Never once looked back.

Not until my dorm door was closed. Locked. Blinds drawn tight. Only then did I let myself breathe. And then—

I broke.

Tears burst out of me, raw and violent.

I collapsed to the floor, sobbing uncontrollably, throwing anything my hands could reach.

Books. Pillows. Lamps.

I didn't care.

No one was around to hear me scream.

Most of the students hadn't returned yet.

And thank God for that.

Because I needed to fall apart.

Needed to scream and break and rage.

And I did.

Until there was nothing left but silence and shaking and the terrifying knowledge that nothing would ever be the same again.

Chapter 50: What does One Do After

Amerei

My hands trembled as I sat on the edge of my bed, the phone slipping once, twice, almost crashing to the floor.

Breathe, Amerei. Breathe.

I opened the '*serious*' group chat.

I typed quickly, my thumbs moving so fast I could barely control them, because if I didn't do it fast, if I thought too long, I would talk myself out of it.

Amerei:

Hey guys, I'm back on campus. Can you come over? Please? I really need all of you right now

I sent it.

No re-reading. No second-guessing.

And then, because I was scared the weight of my words would crush me if I didn't do something else—

And before they could reply in that group chat, I dropped another message into the **main group chat** too, the one where we normally only spam memes and funny updates.

Amerei:

Hey... I'm here. Need you guys. ASAP.

Short.

Vague.

Safe.

I didn't want to scare them.

Didn't want them to panic.

Didn't even know how to explain it if they came running with questions.

Within seconds, replies flooded in:

Meda:

I'll be over soon. Just grabbing my keys.

Mita:

10 minutes out! Hold on, Ame!

Odessa:

3 minutes away. Don't move. I'm flying up those stairs.

I clutched my phone to my chest, squeezing it against my heart like it could somehow hold me together.

I glanced around my room,the wreckage of my breakdown still everywhere.

Pillows thrown. Books scattered. One of my lamps tilted on its side, its shade broken.

It looked exactly like I felt.

A shattered mess.

I sat there waiting, heart pounding louder than any knock could ever be.

I heard the front door to the dorm room open, then footsteps. Then,

Three knocks came, quick and sharp on my room door.

I barely made it to the door before Odessa nearly threw herself into the room.

Mita rushed in right behind her, dropping her bag at the door.

Meda not even two steps later, breathless like she sprinted the whole way.

And then—

They froze.

All three of them.

Their eyes darted from me, standing there in oversize sweats, arms wrapped tight around myself—

to the wreckage behind me.

To the way I was trembling. The red rims of my eyes. The swollen, cracked lips. The way I couldn't quite meet their gaze. Their faces shifted immediately.

From confusion—

To worry—

To horror.

No words.

No gasping.

No asking questions.

Just… silence.

And in that silence, the dam inside me cracked a little more. I opened my mouth to speak, but nothing came out. Only a broken sound that wasn't even a word.

And that was enough. Because in the next second, they all moved at once.

Odessa rushed forward first, wrapping her arms around me like she could shield me from the whole world.

Mita was right there, one hand on my back, rubbing slow circles.

Meda pressed her forehead gently to mine.

No questions. No pressure. Just them. Holding me.

Holding all the shattered pieces, I couldn't carry anymore.

They helped me sit down on the bed carefully and gently, treating me like I might break into pieces if they even breathed too hard.

I curled up, pulling my knees to my chest, staring at my trembling hands.

The room was too quiet, like it was holding its breath with me.

Finally, I broke it.

My voice cracked, barely above a whisper.

"I need to tell you… everything."

Odessa, sitting cross-legged in front of me, nodded firmly.

"We're right here."

Mita reached for my hand, squeezing it gently.

Meda grabbed a pillow off the floor, hugging it tight to her chest, her eyes never leaving me.

I took a shaky breath.

before beginning,

"I spent New Year's with Merrick." I swallowed hard. "It was good at first. Sweet. Perfect, even. He was… he was the Merrick I thought I loved."

They all stayed silent, patient.

"But two nights ago… he changed." I looked down at my wrist, still faintly bruised, and flinched. "I woke up tied to the bed," I said, my voice creaking slightly. "Hands. Ankles. Bound. And he…" I couldn't even say it at first. Mita leaned closer, her hand now rubbing slow, steady circles on my back. "He, he said he wanted to show me his 'other side.' And I thought… I thought he meant being freaky or something stupid. I tried to laugh it off, tried to trust him. But then he—"

The words caught in my throat. I had to force them out. "He hurt me," I said, my voice void of emotion "I told him to stop. Over and over and over. But he didn't. He just… kept going."

I heard the sharp intake of breath from Odessa. "He raped you," Meda confirmed, fury vibrating in each word. I nodded, silent tears slipping down my cheeks. "And that wasn't even the worst part," I croaked. "The next day… he…"

I shook my head, bile rising in my throat for the millionth time. "He brought two strangers. Men I'd never seen before. He let them; he let them touch me. Hurt me. Violate me. While he watched. While he—" I broke off, gagging on the words. Mita pressed a water bottle into my hands. I didn't even remember her grabbing it.

"You don't have to say it if you can't," she whispered, voice shaking.

But I needed them to know. Because if I held it in, it would eat me alive.

"He joined them," I hissed. "He…k-kissed them. Kissed me. Like it was normal. Like it was some twisted, disgusting party."

I wiped my face with the back of my hand.

"I blacked out. I don't remember when. Maybe my mind just... couldn't take anymore." I breathed.

The room was dead silent.

For a moment, all I heard was my own breathing. Shaky. Shattered.

Then—

"That sick, twisted bastard—" Odessa burst out, standing up so fast the chair behind her crashed over.

Her fists were clenched so tight her knuckles went white.

"I'll kill him," she spat, pacing the messy room. "I will literally kill him. I don't care. I'll drive back to his house right now."

"Odessa—" Mita said sharply, but her voice cracked too.

Mita was crying.

Soft, silent tears running down her face as she pressed her hand to her mouth.

Meda was just sitting there, frozen, like she didn't know whether to scream or cry.

I gave them a small, broken laugh. It sounded wrong coming out of me.

"Funny thing is...I don't even know who I'm mad at more. Him. Myself. My stupid, stupid self for trusting him." I spat, pulling on my hair

"Don't you dare," Meda said fiercely, moving to sit right beside me, grabbing my wrist,

She looked at the bruises, then squeezed her eyes shut before opening them again, looking at me.

She grabbed my chin and made me look at her.

"Don't you dare blame yourself for this, Ame. **He** chose to hurt you. You didn't ask for this. You didn't cause this." She grilled.

"But I stayed," I whispered. "I stayed after the first night. I smiled and kissed him and—"

"Because you were scared," Mita soothed, her voice thick with emotion. "Because you were trying to survive. Because you thought maybe, maybe if you kept it together, you could get away safely. I am sure of it; anyone smart would do the same."

"You did the best you could," Odessa added, seeming calmer now, crouching beside the bed, her hands gripping my knee tightly. "You survived. That's what matters."

"And you're safe now," Meda said. "You're here. With us."

I broke down again, ugly sobs wracking my body.

Mita pulled me into her arms, rocking me gently like I was a little girl again.

Meda wrapped her arms around both of us.

Odessa leaned in too, their warmth surrounding me completely.

We sat like that for a long time.

No one caring that tears soaked shirts and shoulders. No one caring that we were a tangled mess of limbs and heartbreak.

I believed in that moment that I wasn't alone.

I believed I would survive this.

Maybe not today. Maybe not tomorrow.

Probably someday.

Because I had them.

And they weren't going to let me drown.

Chapter 51: Audacity Should Have Limits

Amerei POV

I stared at my phone like it might bite me.

The message on the screen was painfully simple.

Merrick XO: Hey Ame, you settled in okay?

My stomach twisted so violently I thought I might throw up.

And worse—

I had already replied earlier.

Like everything was normal.

Like he hadn't—

It hasn't been 24 hours since it happened.

I shut the thought down before it could drag me under again.

My hands trembled as I passed the phone to the girls so they could read the conversation

themselves.

Odessa's face twisted with disgust. "Girl, you cannot keep doing this."

"I know," I whispered. "But what am I supposed to do? If I suddenly disappear on him, what if he snaps? What if he sends people after me?" My throat tightened painfully. He's…he's connected, Dessa. His family has ties everywhere. You saw what happened with Reed and how those snobby rich people are like."

"Reed's situation is completely separate!" Odessa snapped, "And we are also rich and snobby." Odessa argued fiercely, like a wildfire ready to burn the world down for me.

But I shook my head, biting my lip until I almost tasted blood.
   I was so frustrated with myself.
   Merrick.
   With what he is putting me through.
   With everything.

"No, it's not, Dessa. With *these* rich kids, *everything* is connected; *everyone is connected.* You have no idea." I complained
   The room fell quiet for a moment.

Mita reached over and took my hand gently.
   "Then tell us everything," she said softly. "Anything you remember. Anything strange. There must be something; he must have some secret, some dirt. Men like him don't operate in a vacuum."
   "You might not be able to get rape charges to stick to him.'" Meda's voice came from the corner. "You'd be seen as just another ex, another girl victimizing yourself to make money off the heir to the Hughes Corp. His parents will not stand for it and sit idly by; he will come up with something, and even if you do get the charges to stick, it won't be for long. Money is like oxygen to guys like him. I know guys like that back home."

That silence, everyone in the room leaving us deep in our own thoughts
   "So Amerei," Meda continued, "I would urge you to think deeply and as far back as you can."

I swallowed hard.
   Fragments of old memories began surfacing one after another.

"When I used to go with him to dinners or business events…" I hesitated. "I heard things. Saw things."

The girls stayed silent, listening carefully.

"Merrick knew the family connected to the guy who stabbed Reed," I continued quietly. "And they weren't good people. I remember overhearing conversations once at a summer party. Stuff about bribes. Money changing hands. Deals nobody talked about openly."

A chill ran through me as the memories sharpened.

"At the time, I thought it was just rich *rich* people business stuff," I admitted. "Private meetings. Networking. It's mostly gossip, but now…"

Now it looked different.

Now it felt ugly.

"No," Mita said firmly. "Don't do that to yourself."

But guilt still clawed at me anyway.

Meda leaned forward slightly, her expression serious.

"Since we know that his family really has that kind of influence, then we have to be smart," she said carefully.

"People with money know how to bury problems. Especially ones involving their kids."

The reality of that settled heavily in the room.

"Mita exhaled slowly. "I've heard rumors too," she admitted. "About donors controlling things behind the scenes at school. Students getting away with horrible stuff because their parents fund more than half the campus."

"But rumors aren't enough," Meca added. "Not legally."

My phone buzzed again.

The sound nearly made me jump out of my skin.

Another message.

Merrick XO:

You didn't text me when you got back. Are you ignoring me

I showed the girls again.

They all leaned in.

Their faces twisted into a mix of rage, disgust, and annoyance. "He's testing you." Odessa's expression darkened

"It seems more like he's checking whether he still has control," Meda interjected

Mita's face tightened with worry. "You need to be careful how you respond."

I nodded shakily and typed with stiff fingers.

Me:

Sorry, I forgot. And yeah, I'm settled in thanks for checking in on me :)

The typing bubble appeared almost instantly.

Merrick XO:

Ok. Get some rest. Love you.

My chest tightened.

The girls watched me as I stared at the screen.

Slowly, mechanically, I typed back: *'Love you too.'*

The words tasted poisonous.

The girls watched me in horror.

"You can't keep pretending forever," Meda said gently.

"I know."

But how?

How do you break up with a boy who smiles while he chains you to a bed?

Who hurts you and then kisses your forehead like he's proud of himself?

Who pretends to love you with the same hands he used to destroy you?

Someone who acts loving one second and terrifying the next?

How do you do it when fear wrapped itself around my ribs every time I thought about ending things?

"I'm scared," I admitted, voice breaking. "I don't know what he's capable of if I push him."

"I'm scared," I admitted finally, my voice cracking. "I don't know what he'll do if I try to leave." Mita squeezed my hand harder. "You're not doing this alone."

"You're not gonna take one more step without us," Odessa insisted, her voice like steel. "Not anymore."

Meda nodded. "If he even tries anything, we deal with it together."

"If he even *breathes* wrong, we'll make sure you're protected," Odessa added

Something inside me cracked then—not from fear this time, but from the overwhelming weight of being believed.

Being protected.

"Thank you," I whispered.

"Always."

Sitting here with them, I realized how badly Merrick had twisted my understanding of trust and love.

The mood in the room shifted- from brokenness to fierce determination.

Odessa grabbed her laptop off the nightstand, flipping it open with a clack.

"We need a plan," she commanded, her voice razor-sharp. "And I mean a real plan. Not just 'block his number and hope he gets bored.'"

I wiped at my eyes quickly. "Where do we even start?"

"Documentation," Odessa answered immediately. "Everything."

I frowned weakly.

"Texts. Calls. Photos of injuries. Dates. Locations," she listed while typing quickly. "Anything you remember, write it down while it's fresh. Even memories- and we're gonna write down everything, you too, Amerei, everything you can remember while *it's still fresh.* Dates, times, places. It all matters."

"A rape kit too," Mita added carefully.

The words made my stomach twist, but I nodded.

"And we save copies in multiple places," Mita chimed in, nodding to herself. "On the cloud. On a flash drive. In an email draft. If he finds out somehow and tries to erase something, you'll still have a backup."

I swallowed thickly.

"Second," Andromeda stated, "we have to protect your immediate environment."

"What do you mean?" I asked my brain, lagging, trying to process what everyone is saying all at once.

Meda crossed her arms thoughtfully.

"And you stop being alone."

"What?"

Mita leaned forward, her eyes burning with intensity. "You can't let him catch you off guard. No walking alone across campus. No random late-night texts to meet him anywhere. Always have one of us nearby. Always."

"We'll take shifts if we have to," Meda ordered.

They all nodded as though they had all decided this the minute they walked through the door.

"And third…" Odessa hesitated, tapping her fingers against the keyboard.

"We collect leverage."

"Leverage?" I asked, heart pounding, thinking of possibilities, "We do have a lot of witnesses, his security detail, and CCTV in his house." I smiled, but then relief quickly wore off, "but the guards won't be in my favor, and the CCTV can and will be tampered with. They can pay off the cops and say I am just seeking money off the rich. This is bigger than us, just like you said before."

I glance over at Odessa, dread pooling in my stomach at the menacing smile splayed across her face. "If Merrick's family plays dirty, we can, did you forget whose sister I am. If we can get evidence, like proof of shady deals, bribery, or anything shady you mentioned, we have something to hold over his head. Insurance. Something that says: 'Back off, or we expose you.'" she hissed

The idea made my stomach churn.

Playing that game… going *that* deep… it terrified me.

But wasn't that what survival looked like now?

"How do we even actually find something like that?" I asked.

"We'll figure it out; I'll call my brother," Odessa promised. "But first, we keep you safe. That's the priority."

I nodded, tears blurring my vision again.

"I feel so stupid," I choked out. I croaked, my throat dry, thinking back on everything and how it has become what it is now. "I can't believe it's come to this. "I loved him. I trusted him—"

"Don't," Mita said sharply, cutting me off. Her hand found mine again, squeezing hard. "This is not your fault," she comforted, voice trembling with anger.

"You trusted someone you loved. That's not stupidity. That's *humanity*." Meda added

"You are not to blame for what he did to you," Odessa hissed. "Never. Not even for a second."

Their words wrapped around me like armor, patching up the cracks Merrick had tried to shatter me with.

I nodded, even though I didn't fully believe it yet. Perhaps I would, eventually.

"And remember," Mita said, her voice gentling, "you are *not* alone anymore. You never were. You have us."

The flood of gratitude that hit me almost knocked the breath from my chest.

They meant it.

Every word. Every fierce, protective promise.

I wiped my eyes again and took a deep, shaky breath.

"Okay," I said finally. "Let's do this."

And just like that, surrounded by the strongest, fiercest women I knew, I finally stopped feeling like a victim.

I started feeling like a fighter.

Chapter 52: Putting Words Into Action

Amerei POV

The room was still heavy with the weight of everything that had been said when Odessa stood up, wiping her face with the sleeve of her sweatshirt.

"I'm calling my brother," she said firmly, pulling out her phone. "Right now."

"Odessa—" I started, worried, but she cut me off with a hand to stop me.

"You said yourself: this is bigger than us. We're not handling this alone. When we have perfectly good resources in our back pockets," she insisted

She stepped outside into the living room; we could hear her pacing as she spoke into her phone. The conversation was quick and intense and filled with low murmurs we couldn't quite make out from my room. After about ten minutes, Odessa reentered, closing the door softly behind her like we were keeping a secret from the rest of the empty dorm room, as everyone was already in my room.

"Okay," she said, looking at all of us. "It's handled."

"Handled?" Mita echoed, confused.

"Yeah. My brother's taking over. He's already pulling in his contacts. He said he'll handle everything from a legal and corporate side, from investigating to gathering evidence to setting up protective measures. He even said he's getting a few undercover guards to keep eyes on us, *especially* you, Ame."

I stared at her, stunned.

"Guards?" I repeated dumbly.

"Yeah," Odessa said, her voice softening. "You won't even know they're there. They'll blend in like students, maintenance staff, or whatever. But they'll be close. Always."

"And we just… go back to normal?" I asked, feeling like I was balancing on a tightrope stretched too thin.

Odessa nodded. "He said for us to relax, go to class, live our lives, and to not give Merrick any clue that you're upset or against him, as you are already doing. Just don't meet up with him; make up an excuse like what you did before. y'all's schedules were always packed to begin with, making it hard to see each other anyway. Basically, you're keeping up what you were doing before, but this time you are not actually making time for him, but keep the texts going as per usual and do what you normally do. He'll update us if necessary. And when the time is right, we'll bring Merrick down properly. Legally. Publicly."

I pressed a hand to my chest, feeling my heart hammering against my ribs.

I let out a breath I didn't know I'd been holding.

"Thank you," I whispered.

"You don't have to thank me," Odessa said. "You're my best friend. Ride or die, right?"

Mita and Meda nodded fiercely beside her.

That night, we didn't talk anymore about Merrick. We didn't talk about trauma or plans or fear.

We just… *lived.*

I picked the first movie. I chose something light, ridiculous, and so laughably cheesy that we couldn't help but snort and giggle our way through it.

At first, the girls were tense, their smiles a little too forced, their laughter a little *too* loud, and their eyes darting toward me every few minutes like they were checking if I was about to break.

I noticed.

Of course, I noticed.

When the credits rolled on the first movie and Meda reached to pick the next one, I spoke up.

"You guys…" I said, setting down my half-empty mug of hot cocoa. "I know you're worried. I get it. But don't worry… I'll get through this; I just need time to make it happen. They say time is the doctor to all wounds." I joked, trying to lighten the air.

They all were still looking at me: Mita, Odessa, and Meda, their faces open, waiting.

"What happened…" I began slowly, feeling the words claw their way up from my chest, "was horrible. Beyond horrible. And I know it's gonna affect me. I'm not naive."

I swallowed hard.

"But if I sit and think about it too much, if I let it consume me… I'm scared I'll fall into a hole I won't be able to crawl out of." I confessed

Mita's lip trembled.

Meda's hands twisted the edge of the blanket.

Odessa blinked hard as though she was keeping back tears.

"So," I said, voice shaking, "I want to put a bandage over it. For now. Just until justice is served, until it's safe. Then I'll go to therapy. I'll heal properly. But right now… I need to keep my head. I need to stay functional. If I don't…" I trailed off, the unspoken ending heavy in the air

'I might not survive it.' I thought, keeping that last bit to myself.

I remain silent, not wanting to say the truth, as that would worry them, and not wanting to lie to their faces and say I would be ok.

Mita got up from her spot, crossed the room, and sat beside me. She pulled me into her arms and held me tight; no words were needed. Meda piled in next, and then Odessa, until we were one tangled, messy heap of limbs and blanket and fierce, unbreakable love.

"Okay," Odessa whispered into my hair. "We'll follow your lead."

"Yeah," Meda said. "Whatever you need."

"And we'll keep an eye on everything," Mita added. "You won't have to carry it alone."

Tears burned my eyes again, realizing how much these beautiful souls meant to me and how much I meant to them.

These were tears of *thankfulness.*

We untangled ourselves eventually, wiping eyes and laughing awkwardly, and dove into the next movie marathon.

We made jokes. We roasted the bad acting. We quoted the cheesiest lines dramatically. We stuffed our faces with popcorn, Doritos, and sour gummy worms.

At one point, Odessa even dared Meda to re-enact a cringey romantic confession scene, and we all practically rolled off the couch from laughing so hard.

For a few precious hours, we let ourselves be just that—girls *who were young and alive and free.*

Even if the world outside was dangerous.

Even if shadows lurked.

Even if wounds still bled silently beneath the surface.

We had each other.

Chapter 53: What's New With You

The next morning, the girls decided to meet up at their favorite café just a few blocks off campus, the cozy little spot they used to sneak away to between classes or after a stressful exam. The place hadn't changed: fairy lights still hung from the ceiling of the dimly lit space like lazy constellations, the scent of fresh croissants and brewed coffee wrapped around them like a warm hug.

They claimed their usual corner booth, squishing into the plush velvet seats, tossing their coats aside. Each of them ordered their favorite drink — Mita with her chamomile tea, Odessa with an iced caramel latte because *"I don't care if it's winter, I live for iced coffee"*, Amerei with her overly sweet peppermint hot chocolate, and Andromeda with her classic caramel latte.

There was a slow, content silence as they all sipped and just *breathed* in the peace of being back together.

It was Mita who broke it first, eyes gleaming with excitement.

"Okay, full winter break debrief. No one gets to skip," she beamed, clapping her hands together like a teacher at roll call.

"Yeah!" Amerei chimed in. "Spill the tea, guys, I want all the details."

"You first," Odessa insisted, pointing at Mita with a teasing grin.

Mita laughed lightly, the sound bright and genuine. "Okay, fine…. Christmas was really sweet this year. I stayed with my parents, and my brothers, Joshua and Ruach, were here this year. We spent a lot of time together, you know, family dinners, game nights, that kind of thing. But we also went to church a lot. Like… a lot."

The girls chuckled.

Mita's eyes softened, her voice growing more tender. "Honestly? It was different these last two years. It wasn't just routine. I felt… closer to Jesus. After everything that happened this semester, I just needed that reminder that no matter how messy life gets, I'm still **His.**"

The others smiled, feeling the sincerity roll off her in waves.

"And!" Mita added, perking up, "My mom made her famous gingerbread cookies! I brought some back for you guys, so you're welcome."

The table cheered, and Mita laughed, promising to pass them out later.

"Alright, my turn!" Odessa chimed in, flipping her hair dramatically. "You already know how I roll; I hit the malls like a madwoman. My brother and I basically did a shopping tour of the city."

She reached under the table and pulled out a large tote bag that had been hidden beside her seat.

"And because I love you losers," she smirked, "I brought you presents."

Squeals and excited gasps filled the booth.

First, she handed Mita a delicate silver bracelet with a tiny music note charm, something simple but thoughtful.

Mita's face lit up. "Oh my gosh, Dessa, it's beautiful!" she gushed, immediately clasping it onto her wrist.

Then she tossed a package to Amerei, who ripped it open to reveal a sparkly, rose gold makeup bag packed with mini lip glosses, face masks, and scrunchies.

"I figured you needed something girly since you're always stealing my stuff at the sleepovers," Odessa teased.

Amerei laughed, hugging the bag like it was pure treasure. "You know me too well."

Finally, Odessa handed Andromeda a slim, neatly wrapped box. When Andromeda opened it, she found four beautiful leather journals, dark green with gold corner protectors, and a smooth, heavy pen tucked inside.

"They are not planners or anything; you have a lot of those already,"

Odessa said casually, "but I figured… for your thoughts, you might need more journals. Or whatever you want to use them for."

Andromeda blinked, a lump rising in her throat unexpectedly. "Thanks, Dessa" she whispered, genuinely touched.

"Okay, my turn!" Amerei said, grinning. "Christmas was chill. Just me, my parents, and my sister. No church or anything, you know how we are. But we did this big movie marathon after dinner. And then board games, which turned into chaos because my dad *always* cheats."

They laughed.

"And New Year's…" Amerei's smile faltered a little, but she recovered quickly. "You guys know what went down after."

The table fell respectfully quiet for a beat, the unspoken support heavy between them.

Then they all looked at Andromeda, waiting for her to say something.

Then Odessa leaned forward, her smirk back in place. "Alright, *your* turn, Meda."

"Yeah," Amerei said eagerly, leaning forward. "Spill."

"Come on," Mita added. "Was it boring without us?"

Andromeda, sipping her latte, just smiled smugly out the window.

She waited long enough for them to squirm a little, then finally turned to face them, her smile growing.

"Actually," she began, setting her cup down, "no. It wasn't boring at all."

The girls leaned in, practically vibrating with anticipation.

Andromeda launched into the story, her voice light but vivid, telling them about how she first bumped into Zebedee in the art studio after everyone had left for winter break. How at first, it was awkward and random, but then, somehow, they were cool with each other. How they became… friends.

Real friends.

The kind of friends who talked about everything and nothing.

The kind who could sit in silence without it being weird.

She told them about the spontaneous church invite on Christmas Day.

How she debated for hours but eventually decided to go.

How she went back again the following Sunday. And the next.

"And then," she said, fiddling with the edges of her cup, "on first Sunday, after church… after a bit of pondering… I gave my life to Christ."

The table went dead silent.

Mita's eyes instantly welled up with tears, and without warning, she launched herself across the booth and hugged Andromeda so tightly she almost knocked her latte over.

"Oh my goodness, congratulations! I'm so, so happy for you!" Mita cried, beaming through her tears.

Amerei wiped her eye quickly and scoffed teasingly. "Well, cheers to more sleep for me. More melatonin. Meda, when you sleep over, pray loudly like Mita, ok?"

Andromeda laughed, slapping Amerei's arm playfully while still holding Mita.

Odessa shook her head, grinning widely. "Wow. I mean, you were technically 'born into it,' but you never really *believed* before. I'm happy for you though. What changed?"

The table leaned in, holding their breath.

Andromeda took a deep breath, her fingers tightening around her cup.

"I guess… I spent so long rejecting the fake version of Christianity I grew up with," she said quietly. "My parents… they cared about appearances. About rules. About reputation. But love? Real love? Grace? That wasn't something I saw."

She paused, her voice cracking slightly. "But then I met Mita. And even though I didn't get it at the time, she lived differently. And then Zeb… He didn't preach at me. He didn't push me. He just… lived it. Honestly and quietly, which was the realest thing I've ever witnessed."

The girls sat in stunned, emotional silence.

"And when I went to church," Andromeda continued, "I saw it again. Joy in people's eyes. Kindness in their actions. People actually caring. And I realized… I wasn't running from God. I was running from a lie someone told me about Him and blamed Him." She swallowed thickly. "When Zeb prayed with me on that first Sunday evening… I just broke. Everything I'd buried inside for so long, the anger, the hurt, the loneliness… It shattered. And for the first time, something real took its place." Her voice dropped to a whisper.

"Love."

There wasn't a dry eye at the table.

Mita grabbed her hand again, squeezing hard. "You have no idea," she whispered, "how proud I am of you. How proud *He* is of you," she reassured.

Amerei swiped at her eyes. "I mean, I'm not religious or anything, but… Meda, I'm seriously proud of you too. I am happy you found something that makes you happy. "

Odessa leaned back, tossing a napkin at Andromeda's head to lighten the mood. "Typical. You go and have a whole movie plot moment without us." she teased.

Andromeda laughed, wiping her eyes, her heart full.

For the first time in forever, she wasn't pretending.

She wasn't lost.

She wasn't afraid.

She was found.

And she was home.

Chapter 54: Right Before The Routine

As the days rolled into the weekend, the girls spent practically every waking hour together, making the most of their last stretch of freedom before school picked up again. It was like the calm before the storm, but this time, they felt more prepared.

First on their list: visiting Reed.

They piled into Odessa's car, the atmosphere buzzing with a chirpy energy. The hospital halls were more welcoming, the sterile white walls no longer closing in like they used to, as this path was now a memory, of the hallway that led to a good friend of theirs. Reed's condition was steadily improving. His brain activity was increasing every day, and though he hadn't yet woken up, the doctors said he was out of the critical uncertainty zone. It was no longer a question of *if* he'd wake up, just *when*.

The moment Mita heard the good news from the doctors, she rushed to call Reed's family, her voice trembling with tears of joy as she shared the update. The relief in their voices on the other end of the line was overwhelming.

They stayed by Reed's bedside for a while, talking to him, as they now believed he could hear them.

"I swear, Reed," Odessa said dramatically, perched at the edge of the chair, "if you don't wake up soon, you're gonna miss the best group karaoke session we're planning," she said, poking his arm.

Amerei giggled, reaching out to squeeze Reed's hand gently. "You'd better get your VIP pass ready, man. We're gonna blow your eardrums out with our phenomenal singing," she teased

Andromeda just smiled quietly, setting a small origami crane on his bedside table, something Zeb had taught her to make in the art studio once.

"One step at a time," Mita whispered, brushing a stray hair from Reed's forehead. Everyone was always attentive to Reed when they visited. Odessa would occasionally straighten his clothes or bedding, and Meda would always tuck his sheet when they left, and Amerei would give him massages, as the nurse had done sometime when they visited and told them it's good for circulation, so Amerei naturally took up the job whenever they visited.

They vowed to themselves, this is something Reed can never find out, how pampered he was when he wakes up, or they won't hear the end of it.

Later that afternoon, craving fresh air and lighter hearts, they scrapped their karaoke plans and made their way to the skating rink at the park. The ice gleamed under the winter sun, smooth and inviting. Laughter echoed off the trees as kids zipped across the ice and music blared from speakers at the side of the ring.

It didn't take long before they rented their skates, bundled up in their scarves and gloves, and hit the ice, some more gracefully than others.

"Somebody call the ambulance in advance!" Odessa shouted, arms pinwheeling as she barely avoided crashing into a rail.

"You're doing amazing, sweetie," Andromeda deadpanned, gliding by with surprising grace.

"Show-off!" Odessa pouted, slipping again.

Meanwhile, Amerei and Mita clung to each other, shrieking and laughing as they attempted to skate without looking like newborn giraffes.

"I thought you said you used to Rollerblade!" Mita accused, laughing so hard she could barely keep upright.

"I *did!*" Amerei wailed. "When I was *ten!*"

They spent hours there, hearts light, faces flushed from the cold and laughter. Afterwards, they all climbed back into Odessa's car, heater blasting, sharing hot chocolates they had got delivered, and playing charades with exaggerated dramatics. Amerei's impression of a squirrel hoarding nuts had everyone crying with laughter, while Mita's terrible British accent during her "Sherlock Holmes" round left them breathless.

It was perfect. Messy. Loud. Chaotic.

But perfect.

For a little while, none of them were thinking about Merrick, or hospitals, or everything they had survived. They were just *friends,* living and breathing, stealing moments of peace.

But the weekend couldn't last forever.

Monday came, and with it, the campus woke up from its winter hibernation.

Students flooded back over the weekend, hauling luggage, laughing, and shouting greetings.

The once ghost-town campus was buzzing again—skateboards on sidewalks, the low thrum of music pouring from dorm windows, and the smell of coffee wafting from every open café.

And just like that, life moved forward.

Classes resumed, lecture halls filled, professors returned, and the rhythm of academic chaos thundered back into their lives.

But this time, the girls knew one thing for sure:

Whatever storms were coming, they had each other.

Chapter 55: Back Into Routine

Andromeda POV

The first week of classes moved like a storm cloud at first, loud, fast, and demanding, but surprisingly, I didn't drown.

I showed up.

Planner in hand, with my color-coded tabs glowing like tiny trophies.

Old me would've obsessed over every tiny detail. The new me, or at least, *the trying-to-be-new* me, still struggled not to let perfectionism drive everything I did.

It wasn't easy.

It was like learning how to breathe differently after a lifetime of doing it wrong.

But I figured one step at a time was better than none.

When Friday rolled around, Mita caught me outside one of the lecture halls with that determined glint in her eye. "You're coming with me tonight," she said, linking her arm through mine before I could protest.

"Where?" I asked, even though I already had a guess.

"Christian club. Don't chicken out, Meda. New leaf, remember?" She grinned up at me, her voice light but firm.

"Fine," I sighed, playfully dramatic, tossing my scarf over my shoulder. "Lead the way, O Wise One."

I walked confidently with Mita towards the direction of the club, into this new chapter, a new path for my life, and honestly? I *was* nervous.

Not because I didn't want to go, but because… this was real now. Turning over a new page with Jesus as the main character of my story—not just a footnote, a name attached to my twisted family, or a name I muttered in vain when things got bad.

So when we entered the club room, I was fully expecting some super formal, sit-up-straight, hymn-singing kind of thing.

Instead…

I walked into cozy chaos. Beanbags. People sprawled on the floor. Laughter. Soft guitar music strumming lazily from a speaker.

It felt more like a giant sleepover than anything else.

And I liked it. It was far more preferred than my initial expectations.

I was still looking around when I heard it, my name

"Meda!"

My head whipped around instinctively, searching.

At first, nothing, just a sea of faces, some familiar from campus, some not.

Then I spotted it.

A hand, waving like it was trying to flag down an airplane from the far corner.

Zeb.

Big grin in a casual hoodie. Sitting cross-legged on the floor, I couldn't help but smile and wave back.

Before I could move, Mita leaned over, smirking.

"So *that's* the Zeb you're always talking about," she whispered, her voice full of mischief.

"I don't *always* talk about him," I hissed, feeling heat creep up my neck.

"Uh-huh. Sure. And the sky's not blue," she teased, nudging me with her shoulder. "He's a sweetheart, Meda. Good eye, girl."

"Stop," I muttered, feeling slightly panicked. "We're just friends."

Mita raised both her eyebrows like she didn't believe me for a second. "Mhm. Whatever you say. Now go sit with him."

"No! I came with you," I said, half hoping she'd offer me a graceful out.

"Go," she ordered, already peeling off toward a group of girls across the room, leaving me there.

With no backup plan, I sighed and made my way over to Zeb.

"Hey," I greeted, stuffing my hands in my jacket pockets.

"Hey, stranger," he said, eyes crinkling at the corners. "I was starting to think you were wanted by the cops, the way you busted out of the studio like your life depended on it."

I snorted. "I *did* have to make a quick getaway, but it wasn't your fault. Emergency friend situation." I explained

He immediately sobered, sitting up straighter. "Is everything okay now? You good?"

"Yeah," I said, feeling warmth bloom at how genuinely he looked at me. "All good. Just had to be there for someone important."

"I'm glad," he smiled. "Though you deserve to have people who show up for you just as you do for them, you know." I ducked my head a little at that, weirdly shy.

"Yeah, well. I'm thankful for the friends I have; I can safely assume they would show up for me as well." We grinned at each other, an easy silence falling between us. I can never get over the fact of how easy it is with him, like breathing.

Before we could dive back into our conversation, a tall girl with curly hair bounced up to the front of the room.

"Hey, hey! Settle down, you goofballs," she called out with a laugh. "I'm Ruth, your semi-official club president/club mom for the semester. If you don't know me yet, you will. I have no concept of personal space or indoor voices."

The room erupted in chuckles, seeming to agree as everyone shuffled into looser circles.

Some pulled beanbags closer, others sprawled lazily, and a few just plopped down with thuds like tired puppies.

I found myself pulling my knees up to my chest, glancing sideways at Zeb, who stretched out next to me like a lazy cat on his stomach.

"You ready for tonight?" he teased under his breath, looking up at me from where he lay on the floor.

"As ready as I'll ever be," I whispered back, trying not to smile too wide.

He nudged my foot gently with his arm.

"Don't worry. No initiation rituals necessary. Unless you count awkward icebreaker games." He joked

I rolled my eyes, laughing quietly.

Ruth finally kicked off the night with a prayer and a welcome, and I found myself leaning in, not just with my body, but with my heart.

Maybe this wasn't going to be so scary after all.

Chapter 56: The Lifting Of The Veil

Andromeda POV

Ruth pulled out a Bible that looked about two seconds away from falling apart, flipping dramatically through the pages until she found her spot.

"Okay, tonight's gonna be a chill night," she began, pushing her sleeves up to her elbows. "I want us to talk about starting fresh, new year, new beginnings, that kind of thing."

I tucked my chin on my knees, half-listening, half-wondering what it would feel like to really have an actual fresh start.

Not just running from old stuff or slapping new paint over cracks.

A real one.

"As cheesy as it sounds," Ruth continued, grinning, "the Bible is *full* of people who got restarts. Big, messy, ridiculous restarts. And guess what? God was still all in with them."

Someone from across the room commented, "Peter was the blueprint for second chances."

Everyone laughed knowingly, including Zeb.

Ruth nodded. "Exactly. Peter messed up so badly that he denied knowing Jesus three times. **Three. Times.** If Twitter existed back then, it would've been **#Cancelled** situation. But Jesus still called him the rock on which the church would be built," she explained,

I blinked.

I've heard the story before.

Ruth flipped her Bible open wider, balancing it on her knee like she was about to deliver some top-class information.

"Okay," she said, brushing strands of hair out of her face. "We will start with something that's easy to miss if you're not looking for it: fake gospel. False truth. We're gonna dig deep, and I'm warning you now, it's going to get a little heavy. But it's real, and it's necessary."

I shifted slightly on the beanbag I sat on, hugging my knees closer. Zeb nudged my legs gently, a small, encouraging tap.

"We'll be mainly focusing on the entire chapter of 1 John 3 and 4," Ruth continued. " Galatians 1:6-10, and the entire book of Jude."

She paused dramatically. "And to make it even clearer, we're going back to Genesis 40 — and focusing especially on verse 8."

A few people murmured "okay" and flipped open their Bibles or tapped open their apps. I found myself leaning in, genuinely curious.

Ruth smiled warmly. "Let's start with 1 John 3."

She began reading, voice steady:

"See what great love the Father has lavished on us, that we should be called children of God! And that is what we are! The reason the world does not know us is that it did not know him."

She paused. "First point: receiving and accepting God's love makes us His children. Not religion. Not effort. But Love."

She continued:

"Dear friends, now we are children of God, and what we will be has not yet been made known. But we know that when Christ appears, we shall be like him, for we shall see him as he is. All who have this hope in him purify themselves, just as he is pure." She took a breath,

"Having hope in Jesus changes how we live, how we operate, how we navigate, what we agree to, how we explain things, do things, interpret things," Ruth explained. "If we're looking forward to Him and have hope and faith in Christ, our lives should show the difference as we purify ourselves to be as pure as he was by trying to live a life similar to His in terms of His character."

She read on, her voice steady:

"Everyone who sins breaks the law; in fact, sin is lawlessness. But you know that he appeared so that he might take away our sins. And in him is no sin. No one who lives in him keeps on <u>willing</u> sinning. Anyone who continues to <u>willfully</u> sin has neither seen him nor known him."

The room was dead silent.

"This doesn't mean you'll be perfect, as a matter of fact, the popular verse in Romans 3 in verse 23 reminds us of that *For all have sinned and fallen short of the glory of God,*" Ruth reminded gently. "It means we all have and unfortunately *will* mess up, but we shouldn't let it stop our pursuit of attaining a righteous and Godly character; when we live to obey God, our heart continually changes. You fight sin. You don't live in it like it's your home. The next verse is not as popular as verse 23, as it continues, *'They are justified freely by his grace through the redemption that is in Christ Jesus'.* It all comes back to Christ and our faith in him to rectify our wrongs through him, that's the restart I am talking about, that is how we do it."

She went further:

"Dear children, do not let anyone lead you astray. The one who does what is right is righteous, just as he is righteous. The one who does what is sinful is of the devil, because the devil has been sinning from the beginning. The reason the Son of God appeared was to destroy the devil's work. No one who is born of God will continue to sin, because God's seed remains in them; they cannot go on sinning, because they have been born of God."

I scribbled as fast as I could, in a journal I happened to carry with me that day.

Ruth went on "This is how we know who the children of God are and who the children of the devil are: Anyone who does not do what is right, who don't actively, consciously purse righteousness is not God's child, nor is anyone who does not love their brother and sister aka people around them, people on the street, people at your school, people in your home town, even your family both immediate and extended."

She looked around the room at all our faces before continuing. "God draws a line when it comes to his children and their love, their heart posture. Their willingness to fight to do what's right. They don't stay in hate, selfishness, sin. They aim to be just like their *Abba father.*"

She flipped pages in her Bible quickly, creating a sort of windmill effect with the pages.

"The rest of the chapter? It's all about love. Real love."

She read:

"For this is the message you heard from the beginning: We should love one another. Do not be like Cain, who belonged to the evil one and murdered his brother. And why did he murder him? Because his own actions were evil and his brother's were righteous. Especially, when he was so envious of Abel."

Ruth sighed. "The world hates **Real** righteousness. <u>**Be ready for that**</u>."

She read on,

"We know that we have passed from death to life, because we love each other. Anyone who does not love remains in death. Anyone who hates a brother or sister is a murderer, and you know that no murderer has eternal life residing in him." she read.

"This can be explained as John 14:6 says *"I am the way, the truth, and the life. No man comes to the father except through me,"* and **1 John 4:8**: *"Whoever does not love does not know God, because God is love".* *1 John 4:16: "And so we know and rely on the love God has for us. God is love. Whoever lives in love lives in God, and God in them."* These verses explain why John would say we passed from death to life because of love, because God is love, and love is in us; we have life because he is life. But we will soon get into those verses." she further explained

"Matthew 5:21-22 explains, *"You're familiar with the command to the* ancients, *'Do not murder.' I'm telling you that anyone who is so much as angry with a brother or sister is guilty of murder. Carelessly call a brother 'idiot!' and you just might find yourself hauled into court. Thoughtlessly yell 'stupid!' at a sister, and you are on the brink of hellfire. The simple moral fact is that words kill."* She paused, "Hate isn't just strong feelings. It's the absence of love. Indifference. Contempt. Jesus explained that, similar to how adultery begins in the heart, so does harboring hate in your heart for someone is murder in God's eyes, and both will face judgment. Not saying people won't hurt you and your feelings; we live in a cruel world, but those negative feelings, no matter how valid they are in a moment, give them to God by asking him to take the burden of it, and he will." she took a moment to look around at everyone before she moved on.

" *This is how we've come to understand and experience love: Christ sacrificed his life for us. This is why we ought to live sacrificially for our fellow believers, and not just be out for ourselves.- 1 John 3:16."*

My throat tightened. That was love. Not just words of promise. Not sentiment. Action.

Ruth continued reading:

"If anyone has material possessions and sees a brother or sister in need but has no pity on them, how can the love of God be in that person? Dear children, let us not love with words or speech but with actions and in truth."

She smiled softly. "Love is active. Real. Tangible and Intangible."

'She flipped to another page:

"And this is his command: to believe in the name of his Son, Jesus Christ, and to love one another as he commanded us."

Ruth looked up, engaging the group. "Pretty blunt, right? God calls us His children because He loves us, but our actions, especially our love for others, show whether we're truly walking with Him or not."

I felt something tighten in my chest at these words and how they were just so well put together. They weren't fancy words; they had no loopholes. Just truth.

"Now," Ruth continued, flipping a page, "let's move to 1 John 4. This whole chapter talks about testing the spirits. About how to tell if a message comes from God or from somewhere… else."

She picked up her Bible right before placing it back on her knees, tying her hair into a messy ponytail before she began read again, her eagerness evident as she picked up her bible again:

"Dear friends, do not believe every spirit, but test the spirits to see whether they are from God, because many false prophets have gone out into the world."

She glanced around the room, letting it settle.

"And I need you to hear me when I say this: **Not everyone who speaks about God _speaks for God_**. Some people twist it: his words, his teaching even his way of live while he was here on earth, just a little, enough to make it sound good, taking scripture out of context to please the ears of the congregation, pat people on their backs, tell them that 'you doing good' to keep them coming back, withholding the truth of the word of God, and the is very dangerous, it's deadly because they are risking people's eternity for large assembly and following. After all, people love to hear 'good news' and not **"*the good news*"**. Even if they do sprinkle in some truth, the whole thing becomes poisonous, and it's still not **_the truth,_**" she emphasized

Zeb nodded next to me, solemn.

"Fake gospel isn't just wrong," Ruth said firmly. "It's dangerous. Because it leads people away from Jesus, not toward Him. Even if the message is 'only a little off', _it's still off_."

I scribbled into my notebook, trying to catch every word.

She moved on to Galatians 1:6-10.

"I am astonished that you are so quickly deserting the one who called you to live in the grace of Christ and are turning to a different gospel, not that there is another gospel, but there are some who are troubling you and want to distort the gospel of Christ. But even if we or an angel from heaven should preach to you a gospel contrary to what I have preached to you, let them be under God's curse!" she read

Pausing, Ruth looked around the room, seemingly checking whether everyone was understanding where they were in the message and our understanding. Seemingly pleased with what she saw on our faces, she continued,

" Verse 9 repeats that anyone who should rearrange the gospel should have a curse placed on them. People would say, 'Why is a person claiming to be a follower of a forgiving God curse them instead of forgiving them?' Well, forgiving someone doesn't mean they will stop doing what they needed forgiveness for. That's why, as Christians, we repent, which means to **turn away from** the wrong we committed. It's not only saying 'I am sorry' but also to stop doing what we apologized for, but back to the matter at hand, *why not forgive the false teacher?* As I said, forgiveness doesn't stop them, and your forgiving doesn't always affect the other person more than it does you. I am not saying you should take matters into your own hands, we *know* what the bible says about that."

A few voices in the room echoed *'Vengeance is mine, says the Lord'*, that's a popular verse .

This verse brought up a memory when my mother would use that exact verse as an excuse whenever I wanted to get even with someone back home, because it would look good on the family, but when she or dad did it cooperatively, it was fine.

"Exactly," Ruth agreed, "so Paul was a forgiving man, but he was also very strict, and when you spread lies about the one thing that can help everything ever created, choosing lead them to destruction, the naive souls, the people who need the truth, will be caught up in a wonderful story that can't help them. So Paul didn't go looking for these people, but instead declared a curse on them, which can be lifted or even withheld if God's will doesn't align with Paul's and if they repent, but it will definitely hinder their progress in spreading lies to unsuspecting souls." she paused "The verse that follows is on a wall back in my living room to remind me of who I am. The 10th verse sums up the hypocritical and false gospel and prosperity preaching by saying, *'For am I now trying to persuade people or God? Or am I striving to please people? If I were trying to please people, I would*

not be a servant of Christ. I will leave that there for you all to sink in."

Ruth pointed at the verse like it was burning hot. "Paul's like, 'What are you doing my guy?' There's only one gospel. Only one Good News. Anything else is a counterfeit. Stop trying to make yourself look good. Stop telling people 'you're a good person, so you're all set for judgment day. Keep up the good works.'" she spat

Her voice softened just a little. "It's easy to get caught up in messages that sound good. 'Follow your heart.' 'Your truth is your truth.' 'Live your truth'. 'God just wants you happy no matter what.' But that's not Scripture, because John 14:6 has a lot to say about **TRUTH**."

I found myself biting my lip. Those were all things I'd heard, even believed, for most of my life, now crumbling like the mock-up walls of fortitude I built around my life.

Ruth flipped dramatically through her Bible again, landing in Jude.

"Now on to Jude, the whole book is short. But don't let that fool you into skimming over the words quickly. The author of the book gave a fierce warning. Jude warns about people sneaking into the church, using grace as an excuse to sin."

She read:

"For certain individuals whose condemnation was written about long ago have secretly slipped in among you. They are ungodly people, who pervert the grace of our God into a license for immorality and deny Jesus Christ our only Sovereign and Lord."

She shook her head sadly. "Fake teachers don't always announce themselves. They sneak around. They whisper. They tell you what your itching ears want to hear," she pronounced each word as though she was trying to physically engrave it into our minds,

The whole room was dead silent now, hanging onto every word.

"That's why," Ruth continued, flipping again, "2 Peter 2 is important."

She read slowly:

"But there were also false prophets among the people, just as there will be false teachers among you. They will secretly introduce destructive

heresies, even denying the sovereign Lord who bought them, bringing swift destruction on themselves."

She looked up, straight into the group.

"This is not a matter of *if*. But a situation of <u>When</u>. False teachers **will** come. False truth **will** come. That's why you have to know the real thing, know the Word of God for <u>yourself</u>, and not let anyone tell you what is written when you haven't read it for yourself. **Scripture must be tested in its entirety, considering not only individual verses but also the timeline, context, setting, laws, and culture of the time**. It is essential to go before the Lord Jesus Christ personally for clarity, whether you are confused or believe you understand. Just because we think we understand does not mean it is true biblical knowledge, as we may be holding onto previous misconceptions that have shaped our perception of the Word of God. " she pause causing everyone include myself to be on the edge of my anticipation, "we are intelligent and as intelligent beings, we possess the capacity to find meaning even in confusion, yet human intellect does not always align with God's law and truth. So guys, consistently bring your study into prayer and the secret place, seeking the Lord in your quiet time.

Ruth smiled gently. "And remember Genesis 40? Joseph was in prison, right? Two guys had dreams. They asked Joseph for the meaning. And Joseph said…"

She opened her Bible, flipping to her desired page

"Do not interpretations belong to God? Tell me your dreams."

She closed the Bible softly. "Joseph didn't claim he had the answers. He pointed them right back to God. Always. The true gospel always points you back to Jesus. Not to a pastor. Not to a feeling. Not to some experience. **But only To Jesus."**

I stared down at my notebook, heart pounding.

The truth wasn't supposed to be flashy. It wasn't supposed to feel good every second. It was supposed to be *Him*. Only Him.

And somehow, right there, surrounded by bean bags, and pungent coffee smells, and a slightly broken AC unit humming overhead, I felt more "home" than I ever had in my life.

Chapter 57: New Leaf

Andromeda POV

After Ruth finished teaching and people started filtering out of the club room, I packed my things slowly, still turning over everything she said in my head.

My notebook was crowded with scribbles, underlines, and question marks.

But mostly?

Hope.

Which still felt strange to admit.

I slipped my bag over my shoulder just as Mita called out behind me.

"So, you remember Ethan and Zyran, right?"

I turned and smiled politely when I recognized them. "Yeah. Nice seeing you guys again."

"You too," Ethan replied easily.

"Oh—and there's someone else I want you to meet." He waved someone over. "This is my

friend Anika. Anika, this is Andromeda. I feel like you two would get along."

A girl with bright purple hair and an even brighter smile walked over quickly and hugged me before I fully processed what was happening.

I stiffened for half a second out of surprise before awkwardly patting her back.

Apparently, hugs were normal here, the new hello.

"Nice to meet you," I said once we pulled apart.

"You too," she replied warmly.

"I see you already know Zeb," Zyran added with a knowing grin.

"Yeah, we know each other," Zeb answered casually as he stepped beside me.

Like standing next to me was the most natural thing in the world.

"Cool," Zyran said. "So, everyone heading home?"

"Actually, Andromeda and I already have plans," Zeb answered before I could say anything.

I blinked.

Plans?

But I nodded along anyway like I knew exactly what he meant.

Mita immediately stretched out an exaggerated "Ohhh," while giving me a teasing look that said, '*I see you.*' I gave her a look, saying, '*Be blind.*'

"Well then, we'll catch you later." Ethan said, starting to make his way to the exit with Anika and the others.

After a few more goodbyes, it was just Zeb and me left in the gradually emptying room..

"You got everything?" Zeb asked, adjusting the strap of his backpack.

I nodded. "Yeah."

"You got everything?" he asked, adjusting his backpack strap.

"Yeah."

We stepped outside into the cold night air together.

"So," he said, glancing sideways at me with a slight grin, "how do you feel about late-night

food?"

I nodded almost immediately. "Very positively."

"Good answer." He unlocked his car with a click. "Also, I can't thank you enough for helping me out with my car, so I figured it's only right we take mine this time and buy food. Your car's been our trusty ride all winter break; it deserves a day off."

I huffed out a quiet laugh as he walked around and opened the passenger door for me.

Then he paused.

"Actually..." He scratched the back of his neck. "How much do I owe you for fixing it up?"

I muttered under my breath, "My ring," kicking a pebble across the pavement and immediately cringing at the absurdity of the joke and at myself for even thinking it.

"What?" Zeb looked over, confused. "How much?"

"Nothing," I said quickly, louder this time. "You owe me absolutely nothing, Zeb."

He frowned, not buying it for a second. "Come on, at least tell me how much so I can do something equal to repay you if you won't take cash."

I sighed dramatically. "Zeb, listen. Your time with me over winter break, your friendship, your prayers... that was worth more than anything money could buy. Seriously. Your debt's paid, my dude."

"That was nothing," he muttered, finally opening the passenger door for me.

I looked at him firmly before getting into the car. "It was everything I needed."

That finally made him go quiet.

We spent most of the drive lightly bickering about nonsense until we picked up takeout and ended up parked at a small overlook with the city lights stretched out below us.

"I wanted to do this tonight," Zeb admitted while unwrapping his sandwich, "because once school fully starts again and your friends are around all the time, we probably won't get as much time together as we did over break."

I swallowed my food thoughtfully before answering.

"We could make it a tradition, though. After Christian club on Fridays, we go eat somewhere."

"Our thing?" he asked.

I nodded. "Yeah. Our thing."

His grin widened almost immediately. "I actually really like that idea."

The next hour passed easily.

We ate, laughed, complained about professors, mocked terrible campus Wi-Fi, and debated why every classroom was somehow either Antarctica or the Sahara Desert.

Being around Zeb always felt easy.

Natural.

Safe.

Afterward, he drove me back to the dorm and parked near the entrance.

"Thanks, Zeb," I said while gathering my bag.

"Anytime, Meda," he replied with a smile warm enough to cut through the cold night air.

I said goodbye and headed upstairs.

The moment I stepped into my dorm room, I shut the door behind me, kicked off my shoes, and dropped my bag onto the floor.

Then I sat on my bed and closed my eyes.

I folded my hands and whispered a prayer, one that flowed out of me naturally now:

"Thank You, Lord, for today. Thank You for Your Word, Your love, and the people You've

placed in my life. Thank You for peace. Thank You for laughter. Thank You for Zeb, for Mita, for all of them. Please let me sleep well tonight. In Jesus' name, amen. "

When I crawled into bed, pulling the blanket up to my chin, I fell asleep with a small smile still resting on my face.

And for the first time in a very long time, peace reached me before the memories did.

Chapter 58: Favorite Routine

Amerei POV

I said it before, and I'll say it again. The second semester of my second year came rushing in harder than I expected, like a tidal wave of numbers, case studies, economic theories, and financial projections. Being an economics major wasn't easy. Honestly, no major really was.

But mine felt like a never-ending mountain climb, and every lecture was another steep step upward.

Monday through Thursday, my days were packed with classes that demanded precision, attention, and an ability to think ten steps ahead. School just started back up; I don't think it should be like this. Corporate Finance, Advanced Investment Strategies, Quantitative Methods, just hearing the course names was enough to make someone cry, but somehow, I kept showing up.

I kept showing up even though my brain felt heavy… even though my heart felt heavier.

Because if I slowed down, even for a second, I'd have to think about it.

Think about *him.*

Think about *what they did.*

Think about *how broken and humiliated and violated* I really was.

And I couldn't afford that right now.

If I cracked open that door even a little bit, I knew what would come spilling out: despair so deep and dark that I wouldn't be able to climb out.

So I kept pushing it into the farthest corner of my mind.

Ignoring it.

Pretending like it was some distant nightmare that would fade if I just… worked harder.

My last thread of sanity was my family, my parents and my sister texting and checking in on me, completely clueless about what happened, and my friends, my beautiful friends, were anchoring me to life itself.

I clung to them, even when they didn't realize how much I needed them.

When Thursday finally rolled around, I was almost desperate for the distraction.

I missed my calligraphy club. We didn't have one last week, but now I am so ready.

I missed the soothing feeling of ink sliding across paper.

I missed the peaceful hum of creativity filling the room.

And, if I were being honest…

I missed Kaz even more.

Kazuya, Kaz, my partner-in-crime at the club, the one person who could make me laugh without trying too hard, who made the world feel a little less sharp-edged and a little more bearable.

I dressed a little quicker that day. Grabbed my bag a little faster because, for the first time all week, there was something, someone, I was actually looking forward to.

The walk to the calligraphy club felt lighter than anything I'd felt in weeks. My heart was still heavy in its quiet, broken places, but today—today, there was a small piece of it that fluttered among the rubble with something close to hope.

I adjusted the strap of my bag before pushing open the familiar double doors of the arts building.

When I stepped into the club room, a wave of warmth hit me harder than I expected. The familiar scent of paper, ink, and old wood flooded my senses. It was weird how even smells could feel like a hug, how a familiar place could provide a sense of safety.

The soft chatter of people setting up, the low scrape of chairs being moved, the shuffle of paper and brush kits being unwrapped, it was everything I didn't know I'd missed that much until now.

And standing right in the middle of it, waving like he owned the place, was the club leader — Mr. Reyes.

I blinked.

I hadn't realized how much I actually missed *him* too.

The way he always wore slightly mismatched socks, his dad-joke level of puns about ink spills, and his surprisingly serious lectures about brushstroke techniques.

He grinned when he spotted me, giving me a big thumbs-up. I smiled back, relaxing the tension in my muscles.

But then—

"KAZ!"

I don't even know if I said it aloud or screamed it in my head, but my body moved on instinct.

I ran across the room and practically slammed into him, wrapping my arms around him in a bear hug so fierce he stumbled back a step.

"EREI—I can't breathe!" Kaz gasped out, but he was laughing and squeezing me just as tightly.

I buried my face in his hoodie for a second, breathing in the familiar smell of soap and pen ink.

God, I missed this.

Missed *him.*

Finally, I pulled back, and he was grinning so wide it almost split his face in two.

"I see someone missed me," Kaz teased, cocking an eyebrow.

"Shut up," I said, rolling my eyes and shoving his arm. He laughed and shoved me back lightly.

It was easy.

It was simple.

It was safe.

Exactly what I needed.

We grabbed our aprons off the hook, they were washed but I guess the staff couldn't get out Kaz's handiwork out of it over the break, cause mine was still stained with last semester's ink wars.

Putting them on we headed to our usual seats.

Mr. Reyes clapped his hands, gathering everyone's attention.

"Today," he announced, dramatically pulling out a giant scroll, "we're going traditional. Chinese characters. Historical scripts. Powerful stuff. And as usual, Respect the ink!" He finished, his tone final.

The whole room cheered, excited for the evening events.

I actually found myself cheering along with the others, genuinely laughing, for the first time in what felt like forever.

We spread out our supplies, Kaz helping me adjust my paper when he noticed my corners curling up.

"You're hopeless," he muttered under his breath, grinning.

"You love my hopelessness," I shot back.

"I tolerate it," he shot back mock-serious, sticking out his tongue at me.

I grabbed a brush and dipped it into the thick, dark ink, my heart racing slightly with excitement.

The characters were complicated, intricate, so different from the sleek Japanese scripts we last practiced.

But I didn't even care if I messed up.

I finally felt excited about something that was not blatantly used to forget *that* day.

I felt Alive, normal even.

Kaz and I, as usual, couldn't stay serious for long.

He kept sneaking little dots of ink onto my apron when I wasn't looking, so I retaliated by "accidentally" flicking a big splash of ink onto his hand.

"EREI!" he gasped, holding his hand up like it was a mortal wound.

"Oh, please," I laughed. "It makes you look tougher. Very warrior-esque."

He laughed, and the sound was so easy, so good, it made my chest ache a little, in a good way.

When the club ended, Mr. Reyes told us we could hang out and practice more if we wanted, so naturally, Kaz and I took it as a photo-op opportunity.

We snapped pictures of our "masterpieces", aka, very questionable Chinese characters, and exaggerated our poses like we were ancient calligraphy masters.

I did a fake solemn bow, pretending to present my scroll to a pretend emperor.

Kaz threw his head back dramatically, fake-sobbing over a smudge on his "perfect" character.

We took one final picture together, him holding up a paper that said "Besties in Ink" in messy English letters and me flashing a peace sign behind his head.

I looked at the photo afterward and felt a weird, warm bubble of happiness inside me.

I wasn't okay.

Not really.

Not fully.

But right now, sitting here with ink-stained hands, laughing with Kaz, feeling the glow of friendship in my chest,

Maybe… I would be…….. someday soon.

Chapter 59: A Friend Who Cares

Amerei POV

The crisp air hit my skin, running up my spine, causing goosebumps the second we stepped outside the building. It was cooler than I expected, the faint smell of winter still lingering in the air even though spring was technically creeping in.

Kaz slung his backpack over one shoulder, walking lazily beside me, hands jammed deep in the pockets of his hoodie.

"You still have ink on your nose, by the way," he said casually, nudging me with his elbow.

"Seriously?!" I shrieked, wiping my face.

He burst out laughing. "Nah, just wanted to see you panic."

I smacked his arm as hard as I could, and he had the nerve to pretend to stumble.

"You're evil," I laugh, shaking my head.

The weird thing about Kaz was, here and now, walking with him, laughing with him, it felt like the huge invisible weight had lifted off my shoulders, even if only for this little while we are together.

I wasn't thinking about *him* anymore.

I wasn't thinking about what had been done to me.

I wasn't trapped in my own head.

I was just... here, free from the shackles of my thoughts.

I watched as Kaz kicked a pebble down the sidewalk before giving me a sideways glance.

"So, uh, Erei," he started, using that nickname that always somehow made my heart feel lighter, "you doing anything this weekend?"

I shook my head. "Nah. Just planning to get a little work done, chill out, maybe rewatch old anime I don't remember the ending to."

"Perfect," he said, grinning.

"Perfect for what?" I asked, narrowing my eyes.

"Perfect for *lunch*," he said dramatically, throwing both his hands in the air. "You, me, and some food. No ink. No brushes. No club leader judging my terrible technique."

I laughed. "You're not that bad. You're just… I would say creatively reckless."

"Creatively reckless. I like that," Kaz muttered.

"Okay, Saturday?" he offered, out of the blue, looking hopeful in the most awkward, adorable way possible.

I tilted my head, my index finger tapping my chin, pretending to think about it just to mess with him. "Saturday works. But only if you promise to stop trying to sabotage my work with your 'accidental' ink spills." I said, trying my best to give him my meanest glare.

"No promises," he said seriously, holding out a pinky, trying to seal a deal with me that was unfavorable for me.

I hooked my pinky with his nonetheless, without even thinking about it.

The simplest gesture, but it meant something.

When we reached the fork in the sidewalk, the way to the dorms split from the way back to the parking lot, Kaz slowed down.

"Get to your dorm safe, Erei," he said, his voice softer now.

I smiled up at him. "I will. And Kaz?"

"Yeah?" he said, his full focus on me.

"Thanks… for today. For everything," I said, voice low.

His grin softened into something real, something warm.

"Anytime," he said simply, and with a wave, he turned and jogged off down the path to the parking lot.

I stood there for a second, just watching him go, feeling the goofy warmth inside my chest spread wider.

No darkness.

No bad memories.

Just this moment.

Just me and a goofy idiot who made ink stains feel like trophies and laughter feel like a second chance.

I turned toward the path to the dorms, feeling like I could breathe again with the chill of the late winter season wrapping around me like an embrace from the world that hadn't forgotten me.

Chapter 60: Friday Nights and Ink-Stained Friendships

Friday came in quietly, just how I liked it. The second semester of my economics major wasn't playing around: tough lectures, weekly assignments stacking like pancakes, and long nights glued to spreadsheets. It was intense, but not the kind of intense that drowned out the noise in my head. If anything, it added to it.

Mita had her Christian club after classes, so the dorm was mine for the night. I tossed my shoes off the second I got through the door and face-planted into the couch, my bag hitting the floor somewhere behind me with a dull thud. I just lay there, hoping the cushions could swallow me whole.

I reached for my phone, looking for something, anything, to distract me. A meme, a post from Odessa, even a random ad would do.

But there it was.

Merrick.

His name lit up the top of my screen like a warning sign. My stomach twisted so hard it made me sit up. I stared at the unopened messages sitting there like ghosts waiting to be acknowledged.

Merrick XO: "Hey babe, just checking in. Hope everything's good. I know things have been hectic, but you are always on my mind."

Merrick XO: "Sorry I haven't been calling. Work's intense. Hope you're not upset. Love you."

Merrick XO: "I miss you. Really, I do. Hope you're doing great back on campus. Can't wait to hear your voice. Love you always."

Reading each word aloud made my throat burn. How can someone do something so cruel to someone they claim to love and go on, existing in that said person's circle, acting like he didn't do the most vile thing known to mankind?

As promised, Odessa's brother, Noah, sent undercover guards to protect me. There are more than I expected. I saw a few in passing; I knew who was who because they used a code communicated to us in person when Noah visited campus once, but there were more guards posted here than I have yet to meet, according to the number Noah said he'd dispatched. So I was safe, but these guards don't and can't protect me from the thing I most want:

1. saving me from myself
2. and having to text Merrick back.

But I was too proud to ask for help even when they offered. I have to clue in why I am so hard-headed about putting up this *"I am a big girl, and I'm not a fragile glass ready to shatter"* mask when I was exactly that—glass, ready to shatter. At any sudden force, someone just needed to say the right thing, and I would go off the edge, so here I was.

Hands visibly shaking as I forced myself to reply to his messages, every letter typed feeling like a betrayal to my own sanity. But I had to. He couldn't allow him to suspect anything.

Me: "That's okay, Merrick. I know things are getting busy on both ends. Semester's picking up here, too. I'm not upset."

Me: "Love you too."

The second I hit send, nausea twisted in my gut. I threw my phone across the living room like it burned my hands. It hit the carpet and slid under the coffee table.

I leaned back and let my head rest against the couch cushion, breathing in slow, shaky breaths. My chest felt too tight, like my ribs were closing in on my lungs. I wanted to scream. I wanted to cry. I wanted to do something, anything, but what could I do? So I just sat there, eyes wide, frozen in place, clueless of what to do now.

If I let myself spiral, if I really think about what happened in those two days, I wouldn't be able to come back; I wouldn't be sane.

So I didn't. I grabbed the remote and put on an Avengers marathon. Something loud. Something heroic. Something to numb the pain, other than the liquid death that causes a hangover and that would worsen my hangover.

It worked.

Kind of.

Until it didn't.

Until I started seeing flashes again, the things I couldn't say out loud. The *fear*. The *confusion*. The *pain*.

I reached for my phone like it was a lifeline.

Me: *Hey you free?*

Kaz: *Heading home, what's up?*

Me: *Wanna call? I'm bored.*

Kaz: *Sure.*

I didn't hesitate. I FaceTimed him instantly.

He picked up on the first ring, and the sight of his goofy face filled my screen.

"Hey, butt-head," I greeted, my voice a little steadier than I felt.

Kaz tilted his head. "Erei, that's not very nice, especially when your camera angle makes you look like a duck."

I gasped, laughing. "Wow. Rude. I'm adorable, and you know it."

"If ducks are adorable, sure," he teased with a smirk.

"You're lucky I like you."

"I *am*" he said, dramatically clutching his chest as he walked into his building. "Blessed and highly favored."

We kept the call going while he unlocked his apartment, gave me a brief tour of his very sad-looking fridge: leftover rice, expired almond milk, and three different jars of jam, before he collapsed onto his bed.

"Bachelor life at its finest," I commented.

"It's called minimalism," he defended.

I rolled my eyes. "It's called survival on fumes."

When he ducked into the bathroom for a shower, he muted the call and left me in his room, looking at the view of his ceiling through my screen. I didn't hang up. Just lay there on the couch, phone propped against a cushion, observing the details the architect put into his ceiling and even taking particular notice of his ceiling fan through my screen. It was calming in a way I hadn't expected. It was like peering into someone else's world just for a second.

He came back, hoodie on, hair damp, and dropped onto his bed.

"So," I prompted, "what'd you do for Christmas?"

He grinned. "Same as always. Dinner with the fam, midnight service, arguing with my mom about whether fake snow is tacky…"

I blinked. "You go to church?"

"Yup. And on campus when I can too."

"Wait. You're Christian?"

"Yeah? You didn't know?"

"You never said."

"That's a no-brainer, plus you never asked. What? Do you want me to have a megaphone and walk around campus saying, "I'm Christian", "

I looked at him, really looked. "I think a shirt would work better," I teased, earning an eye roll from him. "I just thought you were, I don't know… some Mr. nice guy."

"Thanks. I'll take that; at least I am nice." he spat mockingly

The silence that followed was surprisingly comfortable.

We kept chatting, mostly nonsense. We laughed about our ink war during the calligraphy club. He even accused me of turning his apron into a Jackson Pollock original, but I call it art. He called it a mess. We both agree to disagree that it was a masterpiece.

Eventually, I was wrapped in a blanket, eyes heavy, in my room, phone still in my hand.

"You still awake?" he asked.

"Barely."

"You want me to hang up?"

"No. Keep talking. Your voice makes good white noise."

"Wow. I've been downgraded to background ambiance."

I chuckled, eyes fluttering closed, trying my best to conceal a yawn. "Better than a duck."

"Touché."

I was barely awake before he could say anything else.

"Goodnight, Erei. Sweet dreams" was the last thing I remembered before falling asleep.

His voice.

Safe. Peaceful. A small island in the storm.

Chapter 61: Saturday Lunch and Soft Places

Amerei POV

Saturday rolled in gently, like honey warming on a stove-top: slow, golden, and sweet. Sunlight crept between the curtains, painting soft patterns across my dorm floor. For once, I didn't wake up choking on dread or dragging myself out of a nightmare; it was the kind of morning where you blink a few times and realize your mind isn't screaming. And that in itself was a miracle.

I sat up slowly, wrapped in my blanket like a burrito, and stared through the open doors of both mine and Mita's to see her room, unoccupied. She had Music Club plans today, which meant I had the space to myself again, well, until lunch. My phone chimed beside me.

Kaz: "Lunch still on, Duck Queen?"

Me: "Only if you're paying. Background noise"

Kaz: "You drive a Benz and *you* want *me* to pay?"

Me: "And *you* drive an *Aston Martin*. Plus, you owe me for emotional labor. I'm underpaid and emotionally overworked."

Kaz: "Fine. But I'm picking the place."

Me: "If it's tacos again, I'm throwing you in a koi pond."

Kaz: "Blasphemy. It's sushi."

Me: "Acceptable. You live another day."

I actually laughed. Like, real, chest-shaking, eyes-crinkling laughter. I forgot how good that felt. Sometimes, when I revert to those memories, I forgot what it was like to want to laugh at something dumb instead of crying over something real. Kaz was one of the people in my life who just had this way of making the world feel a little less… sharp.

I got dressed for lunch when the time rolled around in a soft beige turtleneck and my favorite high-waisted jeans. No dramatic glam today, just eyeliner, mascara, a swipe of gloss, and a half-up hairdo. I looked like me, the version of me that existed before everything got twisted and stained.

That alone felt like a victory.

I left the dorm and took the elevator to the ground floor, exited the dorm building through the revolving door, and headed to the parking lot.

Kaz was already waiting when I arrived. Leaning on his car with a bubble tea in hand, he looked like trouble and warmth wrapped in one human being.

"There she is," he said, pushing himself off the hood with a grin. "Miss Inkblot herself."

I rolled my eyes. "You're *never* letting that go, are you?"

"Not unless you invent a worse nickname." he argued,

I gasped, feigning offense. "How delightful."

He held the door open for me, mock-bowing. "After you, Duchess of Duck Faces." I rolled my eyes, so done with this guy. We peeled out of the parking lot and headed to our destination of the day.

We got a window seat at this cozy little sushi bar tucked between a bookstore and an overpriced juice shop. Inside, the ambiance was warm: wood-paneled walls, dim lights, soft, slow Japanese music in the background. The kind of place you could get lost in without meaning to.

Kaz ordered miso soup and a rainbow roll. I got tempura shrimp and salmon sashimi. When the waiter left, we settled into the kind of conversation that only comes when you trust the other person won't twist your words.

A little too dark there Amerei

I cleared my throat

"So," I began, raising a brow as I sipped my tea, "Did your fridge ever recover from the apocalypse?"

He groaned. "I'm still in therapy. That rice developed a soul and had the audacity to judge me, as if I was the one who told it to become a cloud of bacteria."

"I bet it left you a note when it died." I teased

"It said, *'Clean me, coward.'*" he cried

I laughed so hard I snorted, which only made him laugh harder.

"You're ridiculous." I choked

He tilted his head. "You laugh like that more often now," he noted.

That froze me for a second. Chopsticks suspended mid-air.

"Do I?" I asked,

He nodded. "Yeah. You're lighter. Well, not always. But… it's coming back."

I didn't have a reply for that. Not one that made sense. I didn't think he would pick up on my behavior after I tried my best to hide it so well. So I just smiled, eyes stinging a little, and went back to my shrimp. That tiny, casual observation meant more than he probably knew.

After we ate, we walked it through the park, passing the ice rink with kids in neon skating gear. Couples strolled hand-in-hand. A golden retriever wearing a plaid scarf barked at a balloon. The air was crisp but not biting like on Thursday.

We settled on a park bench with two bubble teas—mine taro, his mango.

"Okay," Kaz said. "Top three fonts that deserve to be banned," he challenged.

"Easy. Comic Sans, Curlz MT, and that one with dripping blood. What's it called...?" I trialed off,

"Chiller," he answered.

"Yes! Literal war crime." I chirped, "What about you?"

He leaned back, smug. "Papyrus. Times New Roman *bolded*. And Wingdings."

I choked. "Wingdings? That's bold slander."

"Name one valid use for Wingdings. I'll wait," he argued

I gave it a second to think about it, but came up with nothing. "Okay, fair."

We kept going. About fonts. Favorite sandwiches. Which Marvel Universe would we be in. He swore I was an X-Men universe girly with Black Widow tendencies. I told him he was an Earth 616 with the chaotic energy of Tobey Maguire's Spider-Man Universe.

Our conversation slowly trickled into a peaceful, quiet calm as we took in the scenery before us. Then, out of nowhere, he said, "You're stronger than you give yourself credit for," sipping his tea thoughtfully.

I was taken aback for a couple of seconds, trying to process what he said and how to respond. How do you even respond to something like that?

I just let his words linger in the air, like gentle, glowing fairy lights.

By the time he dropped me off at the dorm entrance, the sky had turned a soft, watercolor purple and gray.

He smiled at me before I got out, wishing me a good night. Today was perfect enough to make me forget the last couple of weeks.

When I got back to the dorm, I dropped onto the couch, exhausted but at peace. Then my phone buzzed.

Kaz: "Thanks for today. You made it fun."

I reread it twice before replying:

Me: "You too, Kaz."

Maybe I was still trying to heal. Maybe I was still broken inside. Maybe the mask I wore around Kazuya wasn't as convincing as I thought. But sitting here in my warm dorm room, bubble tea still in hand and laughter still in my throat, I knew one thing:

I was going to be okay.

And that was enough for now.

Chapter 62: Strings and Smiles

Andromeda POV

There was something comforting about routine. Something healing, even. When the week rolled around and I found I had a free day, there was no question about where I'd spend it. I grabbed my viola case, slipped into my usual "casual chic" outfit, and headed to the music room to meet Mita like we used to in the semester before.

Some traditions were worth keeping.

Mita was already there when I walked in, perched at the edge of a bench like she was ready to tackle a concert hall performance. I couldn't help but smile. "Eager much?" I taunted as I approached her.

"Ready to finally play something other than scales on the piano?" she shot back with a grin, adjusting her hair tie. "Today, I will *try* not to sound like a dying goat. Promise," she said, shifting the conversation back to today's lesson.

"High standards," I drawled, setting my case down and pulling out the viola. "Let's get you there."

Last time, we'd focused on how to hold the instrument properly: where to place her chin, how to position her fingers, the angle of the bow, and simple notes. This time, we moved on to Open strings. Slow, careful strokes. I did a little music theory lesson to explain what she was hearing me play. I would demonstrate and explain, and she would return the demonstration.

One thing I liked about Mita as my student was that she always had a way of picking up on details with this quiet determination that made her very easy to teach.

"I promise, if I get this melody right, I'm going to start a band and name it *Mita and the Misnotes*," she muttered, drawing her bow across the A string.

I laughed. "I'm not joining unless I get top billing."

"You can be lead misnote," she negotiated, so seriously I almost took her up on that offer.

We were halfway through "Twinkle Twinkle Little Star," or her version of it, which honestly sounded more like a haunted music box, when I saw a familiar silhouette past the door.

Zeb.

I saw the flash of curls first, then his black hoodie and sketchbook tucked under one arm as he walked past the doorway with purpose. He hadn't seen me. Or maybe he had. I wasn't sure.

"Give me a sec," I told Mita before hurrying for the hallway.

I jogged out of the room and spotted him at the end of the corridor.

I ran after him. "Zeb!" I called out.

He turned, flashing a small smile. "Hey, Meda."

"Hey," I breathe, catching up to him and catching my breath. "You gonna be... in the studio... tomorrow?" I took a breath. "I was thinking of dropping by."

"Yeah, I'll be there," he said, shifting his sketchbook under his arm. "So..... see you there."

Before I could say anything else, he gave me a quick nod and kept walking, disappearing around the corner. I guessed he was busy, so I didn't take it personally, but I stayed there a bit longer than I needed to, watching him around the corner, his silhouette grow smaller as he took his steps.

"Okay," I mumbled to myself, letting out a breath, my running thoughts seeming to calm

As soon as I returned to the entrance of the club room, I saw Mita standing at the door with her arms crossed with the most obnoxiously amused grin I'd seen on her all day.

"Chasing Romeo down now, huh, Juliet?" she teased, leaning against the doorframe like she'd been waiting her whole life for this moment. "Oh, how the roles are reversed."

I gave her a flat look. "Mita."

"Don't 'Mita' me. You basically sprinted," she argued, gesturing down the corridor behind me.

"I did not sprint," I shot back, brushing past her. "It was a brisk walk," I defend, raising my chin, like I was trying to lift my confidence in the same manner, while trying to bury my embarrassment as far back in my mind as I could

"*With purpose*," she added airily with a slightly higher pitch than usual, which meant she was insinuating.

I turn to dissuade her annoying thoughts, only to see her still smirking as she picked up the viola.

"Keep talking and I'll teach you nothing but scales for the next hour." I threatened

"Threats?" She gasped in mock horror. "From Juliet herself?"

"I'm serious, Misnote." I hissed

She laughed and dropped onto the bench, bow in hand, ready to pick up where we left off. "Fine, fine. Teach me, oh string master," she relented

The evening light filtered in through the tall windows as more club members started trickling in: chatter rising, instruments tuning, laughter echoing. The club was coming alive.

And for the nth time since that day after New Year's, I didn't feel like I was holding my breath.

Mita was finally producing notes that actually sounded like part of a melody. I was laughing again. Zeb was still Zeb, just a few corridors away.

And maybe I wasn't saying it aloud, but things, life, felt like it was slowly falling into a rhythm that was better than before.

Chapter 63: Paint, Prayer, and Peace

Andromeda POV

The sun was barely peeking through the clouds when I cracked my eyes open. It was the kind of gentle morning where nothing felt rushed, and the dorm was so quiet, I could hear the hum of the radiator against the wall, just like when it was winter break.

I stretched, yawned, and rolled over to sit on the edge of my bed. Then, without thinking too hard about it, I whispered a prayer.

"God... thank you for continuously waking me up. Thanks for yesterday for keeping me under your wings of love and protection. I don't know what today holds, but I trust you to direct it, guide me, and protect me, cover me in my comings and goings of today. I give my day to you, and let me keep on the path you have for me, continually growing into the person you made me to be, to let your will be done through me here on earth as it is in heaven, to help me show up. And be grateful. And maybe, I don't know... have a little fun? In Jesus name, Amen."

I reached for my phone to open the Bible app and read a chapter or maybe two, which reminds me I need to get a Bible.

After my quiet time in the word, I sent Zeb a quick message.

Me: "Hey, I'm up and getting ready to head over :)"

No reply yet, but that wasn't unusual. He was either asleep, deep in a sketch, or already elbows-deep in paint. I hopped in the shower, scrubbing off the last remnants of sleep and conditioning the heck out of my hair because, let's be real, painting days were still selfie days, and humidity was never on my side.

I dressed comfortably—baggy straight jeans and a cream sleeveless turtleneck shirt with a trench coat that I was 97% sure I had once again stolen from Mita over winter break. Outside might not be freezing, but it was still uncomfortably cold. I tied my hair up in a high bun, pulled my tote bag over my shoulder, and just as I was sliding into my sneakers, my phone buzzed.

Zeb: "Ok cool, see you then!"

I smiled at my phone a little more than I meant to, locked the door behind me, and headed out.

The walk across campus was chilly but peaceful. Students were out and about now that classes had kicked into full swing, but the art building still felt like this tucked-away pocket of quiet. I had no classes scheduled for today, and neither did Zeb, nor was he going to church today, so I guess it's a free day for us to chill together.

When I reached the door to Zeb's studio, I knocked out of habit even though I knew the door code, and he wouldn't care if I just slipped inside.

It still smelled like paint and that specific brand of male scent: cologne, soap, and something slightly woodsy.

I glanced around and smiled.

Some of my stuff was still here from winter break —my sketchbook, technically his, in its corner, a hoodie (not Mita's this time) tossed over the back of a chair, and the travel mug I'd left during one of our late-night movie marathons. I even spotted my crumpled blanket folded neatly in the corner by the window. There were also a few of his hoodies and mines, all folded and stacked neatly together on a shelf with such meticulous care that it kind of made my heart ache just a bit.

Most people might've thought it was weird to have their stuff mixed with another person's. But to me?

It felt like… being a part of someone's everyday life.

"Hey, Meda! You're early," Zeb called out, waving from where he was standing in front of a large canvas blocking this view of the door and me, with a brush in hand, splatters of blue on his forearm.

"Yeah," I said, grinning. "Had no class today, so I figured I'd head straight over."

I walked to the apron rack, grabbed my usual one. It had faint paint stains and a smear of clay from a day we tried pottery on a whim, and tied it around my waist as I walked over to him, rounding the canvas standing behind him.

"What are you working on?" I asked, tilting my head at the canvas. It was still abstract—brushstrokes forming something I couldn't yet recognize.

I could see the corner of his lip quirked up in a smirk, but he didn't take his eyes off his work. "Assignment piece."

"What's the theme?" I quizzed

He glanced sideways at me, voice dropping into a secretive whisper. "That's a secret. I want you to figure it out when I'm done."

That's when I noticed his damp hair and the clean scent of soap coming from him, just taken a shower not too long ago. I pushed that unnecessary observation aside, but then he turned, causing our eyes to meet, so I quickly answered, "Whoa, okay. Very mysterious of you, Zebedee."

"It's called artistic integrity, Andromeda," he replied, in mock seriousness, rolling his eye, turning back to his work.

I let a soft 'tsk' and wandered over to the corner cabinet, where we kept shared supplies (his supplies). I pulled out the sketchbook he'd given me during winter break and flopped down at the big table near the window.

The light from the window was soft and cool, perfect for sketching.

We didn't talk much after that. But it wasn't awkward.

He painted. I sketched. Quiet Christian R&B played from a small speaker in the corner. Only the occasional tapping of his brush in the water cup or the light scratch of my pencil filled the room. It wasn't what I'd expected, honestly. I thought we'd talk more, laugh more, maybe snack on something unhealthy, and debate movies again. But this? This quiet? It felt… almost perfect.

His presence was the kind that didn't demand anything from me; I could just exist.

Now and then, I'd glance up and see the way he tilted his head as he painted, or how he struck a pose when he was concentrating, even though I could only see his back profile; it was like reading a book that you weren't interested in, but you can't put down. There was something steady about him. Not perfect. Just… steady.

Time passed quietly whenever I was in his company.

A while later, I felt it, before I acknowledged it—eyes. I didn't even have to look up.

"You're gonna bore a hole into my face," I said, feeling his stare on me.

"Last I checked, Superman doesn't hang out in art studios," Zeb quipped, now sitting in front of me.

I smirked, eyes still on my sketch. "What are you doing?"

"Taking a break," he said. "And admiring your progress."

I turned my sketchbook around so he could see my work better. He leaned in, taking in the work I had composed on the sheet of paper.

He took a moment to analyze every inch of what was stretched across the page. Taking in every time depth and maybe even my perspective, I could never tell with this man, "Good job, Meda. You're getting better at this," he praised.

"I know, right?" I said with a grin, proud of the growing detail in my lines.

There was a pause, which was growing slightly tense by the second.

The kind that feels ripe with something unsaid, maybe, it was just me, as I did have something I had left unsaid.

"Zebedee," I started.

"Oh, we're back to Zebedee now?" he teased.

I chuckled, "Zeb, I've been meaning to ask…" I paused, trying to get my words together without making it sound like some weird interview, taking a breath and continuing, "I've noticed you're really strict about physical touch/closeness. Is that, like, a Christian thing I should know about or a personal boundary?"

Zeb leaned back in his chair, fingers tapping the edge of the table thoughtfully. His brows furrowed in thought.

"It's actually both," he began. "Not every Christian is exactly the same, but a lot of us take and should take physical boundaries seriously, like wise for other things that can also lead us into temptation." He clarified.

"There's a passage in *1 Corinthians,* I believe, and it really shaped my views," he said as he went to grab his Bible from the shelf behind him and opened it, and turning to the correct page to find the scripture before, reading aloud:

"'All things are lawful for me,' but not all things are helpful. 'All things are lawful for me,' but I will not be dominated by anything. Food is meant for the stomach and the stomach for food' and God will destroy both one and the other. The body is not meant for sexual immorality, but for the Lord, and the Lord for the body...

Do you not know that your bodies are members of Christ? Shall I then take the members of Christ and make them members of a prostitute? Never!

Or do you not know that he who is joined to a prostitute becomes one body with her? For, as it is written, 'The two will become one flesh.'

But he who is joined to the Lord becomes one spirit with him.

Flee from sexual immorality. Every other sin a person commits is outside the body, but the sexually immoral person sins against his own body.

Or do you not know that your body is a temple of the Holy Spirit within you, whom you have from God? You are not your own, for you were bought with a price. So glorify God in your body." (1 Corinthians 6:12–20, ESV)

He let the words settle before speaking again.

"I know it sounds intense, but when you think about how sacred our bodies are and how culture just tosses sex around like it's fast food...it's crazy and it's dangerous. Lust doesn't start with sex—it starts with glances, then prolonged looks, with proximity, with compromise."

I sat still, taking it all in.

"That's why," he continued, "I draw clear lines. Because if I don't, the enemy won't waste time to tempt me with the same things that have been plaguing me, and one moment of weakness is all the enemy needs to open a can of worms spiritually, having me in warfare that could have been avoided if I remained diligent and grounded in what I believe and in God." he elucidated.

He flipped again, landing on a page, and read:

"Now Joseph was handsome in form and appearance. And after a time his master's wife cast her eyes on Joseph and said, 'Lie with me.'

But he refused and said, '...How then can I do this great wickedness and sin against God?'

...She spoke to Joseph day after day, but he would not listen to her, to lie beside her or to be with her. But one day... she caught him by his garment, saying, 'Lie with me.' But he left his garment in her hand and fled and got out of the house." (Genesis 39:6– 15)

"Joseph *ran*," Zeb said. "He literally fled. Because sometimes running is wisdom, not cowardice. And Jesus took it even further—"

He flipped one more time,

"You have heard that it was said, 'You shall not commit adultery.'

But I say to you that everyone who looks at a woman with lustful intent has already committed adultery with her in his heart.

If your right eye causes you to sin, tear it out and throw it away. For it is better that you lose one of your members than that your whole body be thrown into hell.

And if your right hand causes you to sin, cut it off and throw it away." (Matthew 5:27– 30.)

"Jesus didn't mean literally dismember yourself," he explained, probably noticing my slightly horrified expression. "But he meant to *cut off <u>whatever</u>* leads you to sin. Protect your spirit like your life depends on it—<u>because it does</u>."

I swallowed the lump, trying to process everything he said .

"Wow," I breathed after a minute.

"That's... a lot. But it makes sense. It really does." I don't even know what to say when someone just drops bars on your lap

Zeb smiled gently. "I knew you already had strong boundaries before Christ. But now you get to *build* on those, with Him as the foundation."

I reached for my phone. "Can you repeat all the verses? I want to write them down properly in my journal later."

He nodded and listed them again slowly as I typed.

—**1 Corinthians 6:12–20**

—**Genesis 39:6–15**

—**Matthew 5:27–30**

The quiet became calming again. Not silent, but soothing.

I looked over at him, deeply moved, not just by the wisdom but by how much he cared to live it.

"Thanks," I said softly.

Zeb just gave me a small nod drawing me in with his warm eyes.

That little conversation became a full-on Bible study.

Sitting there with our sketchbooks and his Bible open, two people who couldn't be more different on the surface, now bound by something deeper.

God had a funny way of making soft places out of art studios.

Chapter 64: The Quiet Hurt

Amerei POV

It was Sunday. The kind that just… drags.

Gray sky. Gray thoughts. No classes. No Kaz. No movie plans. Just me alone in the dorm with too much time and a mind that refused to shut up.

Mita was gone. Odessa was probably off on another school trip to some TV company. And

Andromeda… I didn't know. She was better than the rest of us at bottling things up. Probably fine. Probably not. But at least she had Zeb.

I had silence.

And silence, it turns out, is painfully loud when you've lived through something that should have broken you.

The curtains stayed drawn. Not because I wanted the room cozy, but because sunlight felt wrong now. Too warm. Too clean. Too pure for someone like me to soak in.

So I moved from my bed to the living room and curled up on the couch with a blanket wrapped around me, some action anime for the third time this week.

I barely processed any of it.

I couldn't tell you who was fighting or what the plot even was anymore.

I just need something, anything, loud enough to drown out the replay of memories too vivid for comfort in my head.

But my brain doesn't do quiet.

And it definitely didn't *forget*.

The memories always started small.
   Merrick's voice.
   His hands.
   The wine glass.
   The way his smile changed into something sharp and unfamiliar after his supposed 'surprise' before I realized what he actually meant.

The way he watched everything unfold like he was proud of it. Like he planned it.

Even the sound of a zipper made my stomach twist now.

I stared down at my hands resting in my lap. Soft pink polish. Perfectly manicured.
   The same hands that once held his.
   I wanted to peel the polish off. I wanted to scream, I need to throw something.
   Revulsion climbed up my throat so suddenly I had to stand.

Before I fully realized what I was doing, I was already standing in the kitchen barefoot against cold tile, staring into the open cutlery drawer.

The knife I picked up was small. Barely sharp. A simple paring knife.
   Still dangerous enough.

I pressed the edge lightly against my wrist.

Just thinking.
  Just breathing.

Just wondering what it would feel like to stop carrying all of this around inside me.

I wasn't going to do it.
  Not really.

But I also couldn't completely convince myself to put the knife down.

So I paced.
  Back and forth across the kitchen floor while the blade hovered against my skin.
  My thoughts wouldn't stop.

I'm damaged now.

Nobody's ever going to want me after this.

I let them do that to me.

The pressure against my wrist increased slightly.
  No one can ever love someone like me,

My skin pinkened.
  I only burden everyone around me, my friends; they are probably annoyed with me secretly

It stung, but I didn't stop the voices.
  Kaz wouldn't even look at me the same if he knew.

A tiny bead of blood surfaced.

Merrick just sat there and watched. Like I didn't matter; maybe I don't; maybe he didn't love me.

And the worst part?

I loved him enough to trust him.

I stopped pacing long enough to squeeze my eyes shut.

No.

My parents loved me.

My friends loved me.

They were trying.

And I was still here.

Another shallow press broke the skin before I finally pulled the knife away with a sharp breath.

I can do this. I can get through this. Merrick is the villain; he is the one who hurt me. And I am the victim.

I'm the victim here.

Not him.

Not me. Not the other way around...

Yes, of course, I can get through this. I have to

I winced, more from guilt than pain.

This wasn't me

This isn't who I am.

This isn't who I was before Merrick.

But somewhere deep down, a terrifying thought kept whispering:

Maybe this is who he turned me into.

And what scared me more than anything? It helped.

Not in a healing way. Not in a *hopeful* way either. But in a "this gives me something to feel besides shame.

Besides disgust" kind of way.

And that terrified me.

I couldn't tell anyone.

Not Mita. Not Odessa. Not even Kaz. Especially not Kaz.

They'd look at me differently. Or worse—they'd worry.

And I couldn't handle either of those things right now.

So I cleaned the knife. Wiped the tiny wounds. Wrapped it up and pulled down my sleeve. And breathed.

By tonight, Mita would come back and pray out loud like she always did, and I'd pretend

Everything was normal.

Tomorrow, I'd wear long sleeves. Smile when people talked to me. Go to class. Laugh at a dumb joke. Maybe sit with Kaz and complain about fonts over lunch, as nothing had changed. No one would know.

No one *could* know.

Because if they did… they'd make me stop. And I wasn't sure if I was ready to stop yet.

But maybe one day. Maybe soon.

But not now.

Right now, I just needed to survive.

Chapter 65: Surviving on Splinters

Amerei POV

Classes picked up with a vengeance in the coming weeks: assignments, deadlines, readings, and discussions. Everyone around me was groaning about midterms creeping in and how school felt like it started a few weeks ago, and now we are in the middle of the term, yada yada ya, but me? I welcomed the chaos with open arms. Let the workload bury me alive. Let the pressure swallow me whole.

Because busy meant my kind of quiet.

And quiet, real quiet, meant thinking. And thinking meant remembering. And remembering meant I was back there again, reliving everything back at that house.

Thursdays with Kaz were still my lifeline. The soft brush of ink on paper. His dumb jokes. Our quiet but not-so-quiet banter. Our hands stained black with ink and comfort.

Those hours were mine. The only time I felt like I was still *me.*

But the worst part of every week are the texts.

Merrick never stopped texting.

Merrick XO: "Still thinking about you. Hope you're not mad. Work is crazy. I'll make it up to you."

Merrick XO: "You're not ignoring me, right? I miss you."

Every message made my skin crawl, bile rising at the back of my throat, but I had to respond to keep up this charade. So, I'd respond like I always did:

Me: "It's okay, I understand. School is busy too."
Me: "Miss you too. So much!"

The lies dripped from my fingers like poison. I hated typing them. I hated reading his name. I hated that my phone still lit up with his words like they had a right to be in my life.

And every time I hit send, I would press my nails into my palms and count slowly.

One. Two. Three. Four……

And if that didn't work, I'd go to the drawer; each time the knife would be sharper than the last because the damage, the pain, wouldn't be enough.

I had to find a new spot. Always a new spot. Somewhere no one could see. Somewhere I could cover with sleeves or jeans, or makeup. Something small. Controlled. Quiet.

Just enough sting to feel. Just enough pain to reset.

And the worst part?

It always worked.

It worked just long enough for me to go to class. To smile at Kaz. To wave at Mita. To function overall.

And then it would wear off. And I'd need it again.

Sometimes I would sit on the floor of the bathroom, staring at my reflection in the tiles, and think about him.

How he laughed with his friends that night, like it was all a game.

How he watched. How he didn't stop them. How he joined in.

And I stopped screaming after a while because what was the point? He wasn't listening. None of them were.

I remember wondering if I'd die that first time or even that last night.

Now I wonder if I had died and never really came back to life.

He's out there, still walking in tailored suits, sipping vintage wine, smiling for cameras. Still free. Still beautiful. Still powerful. While I'm here, trying to remember how to breathe without bleeding.

Existing like he didn't just crush someone's world.

And there are moments when the cloud of darkness over my life isn't just sadness. It's rage.

But I've thought about it, carrying out my own justice, thought about going to his house. Using the same knife I use to hurt myself to end him. Making it look like an accident, like a robbery. Something clean and quick. Some poetic reversal of power. Hah!

I imagine the look on his face when he sees me. The girl he thought he broke, standing with fire in her eyes and vengeance in her hands.

But I couldn't do it; I couldn't go over there. I couldn't die or even go to prison

I have a sister, a family, and my girls. Odessa. Mita. Meda.

I have Kaz.

I have a list of names in my heart who make this unbearable world slightly more bearable. Who reminds me that the best revenge isn't death or prison? It's healing. It's thriving. It's living so loudly that your abuser hears your joy and can't un-hear it.

So I didn't kill him. I didn't grab that knife. I didn't go over to his house. I didn't seek ut my own justice.

But I do hate him. I hate what he did. I hate who I became. I hate that sometimes I see his face in my dreams and still feel like it's my fault.

And I hate that the thing that helps me survive, even if only for a few hours, is the thing that proves I'm still bleeding on the inside.

Chapter 66: The Quiet Between Pages

Amerei POV

There was a rhythm to it now.

Wake up. Coffee. Study. Cut. Breathe. Repeat.

My life, ever since returning to campus, had become a carefully curated performance.

The only way to muffle that screaming was to keep going. Keep working. Keep pushing.

My days were full of numbers and projections. Balance sheets and case studies. Group projects and professors who thought a heavy workload equaled brilliance. Good. Let them pile it on. Let them drown me in assignments.

Let. Me. Forget.

But even distraction has its limits.

Some nights, when the walls of my dorm room felt like they were pressing in, I'd stand by the bathroom mirror and stare at myself. Not at my face. Not my hair. But I'd lift my sleeve and trace the faint scars or fresh ones that were tattooed to my skin like the trauma in my heart, assessing the damage and where else to make new ones if I had to. Just enough to bring a sting. Just enough to reset the spiral.

And always in hidden places, of course.

No one has found out. Not Mita. Not Odessa. Not Andromeda. I was too good at pretending. Too good at smiling just enough. Laughing at the right moments. keeping everything firmly sealed like heavy-duty tape and mascara.

But it was getting harder.

I still had to answer Merrick. I had to play the part. His texts came like clockwork:

Merrick XO: "Hey, sorry things are crazy here. Thinking of you."

Merrick XO: "Hope you miss me as much as I do. I love you."

Merrick XO: "Miss you. You still love me, right?"

And every time, I replied like a puppet:

"Of course."

"Totally understand. Love you too."

It felt like barbed wire sliding down my throat.

I hated him.

I hated how he took something from me and walked away like it was nothing. I hated that I was the one bleeding, the one hiding, the one stitching myself together just to function.

I knew why I was doing it. Why I *had* to do it, but...

I am sick of doing it every single time!

He raped ME!

They raped ME!

And somehow, *I'm* the one who has to fake a smile?!

There were nights I would look at the knife in our dorm kitchen and think about pressing it deeper. Not just for a sting and definitely not for a scratch.

For an escape.

But then Mita would start praying all of a sudden, like she knew what I was thinking.

I knew; she knew I listened. But I don't think she knew I listened every night like clockwork. Every night, when the lights went off, I'd lie still and wait for her voice.

"Dear Lord... thank you for today. Thank you for peace. Watch over Amerei.

Whatever she's carrying, please carry it with her…."

I'd cry silently into my pillow,

Those simple words reopening a cup overflowing with pain and torment.

She didn't know her words kept me breathing, that her little prayers were the lifeline keeping me from ending it all.

Maybe she didn't need to.

That Thursday, I nearly didn't go to calligraphy club. But I couldn't miss it. Kaz was there, and for three hours every week,

I got to forget about my problems.

I got to laugh with genuine humor.

I got to breathe deeply and fully.

He had no idea how much he helped just by being present. Just by being his ridiculous, bright, safe self.

But the second I walked into the dorm building by myself after our post-club walk, it started again.

The thoughts. The ache. The itch to feel that familiar sting.

But I couldn't do it every time I wanted because that would cause lasting pain and scars, and I can't hide pain that well… so they would find out!

But they can't.

I won't allow it!

So I kept studying. Kept pushing harder. Stayed up later. Worked longer. Typed faster.

Because I couldn't let myself stop.

Because stopping meant thinking.

And thinking meant remembering.

And remembering?

That could actually kill me.

Chapter 67: Peace in the Chaos

Midterms crept in quietly, no dramatic thunderstorm or brewing panic in the halls—just the steady, inevitable march of test dates and assignment deadlines. For once, Amerei didn't feel the usual dread that came with them.

She hadn't gone to the calligraphy club in a bit, not because she didn't miss it, she did, but because her time had been swallowed up by textbooks, flashcards, and color-coded notes. The truth was, drowning in coursework gave her a break from drowning in memories. The long hours in the library meant fewer hours in her head. And honestly, she liked the silence that came with productivity.

The exam she just came out of? Easier than she expected. Maybe it was all the late nights and early mornings paying off. Or maybe, for once, life had decided to throw her a bone. She stepped out of the exam hall without the usual knots in her stomach. She even smiled a little when she passed the other students, muttering about how hard it was.

Still, the relief was paper-thin.

She hadn't stopped cutting, not entirely. The frequency had lessened, barely though. When her mind went too quiet, when her room got too still, when the air felt too heavy, the blade was still there.

At night, after the world settled and the campus dimmed, she lay in bed and listened. Across the hall, Mita's voice would rise in prayer. Gentle.

Faithful. Predictable. She never missed a night, and Amerei never failed to listen in.

Mita's soothing voice was the only thing that helped her fall asleep.

Not because she believed in what Mita believed, but because hearing someone speak to a God so earnestly somehow made her feel… a little less abandoned. She didn't know how to explain it; it didn't make sense to her. She didn't even understand why it was so calming. But for now, it will have to do.

Chapter 68: Thursday's Unspoken Ache

Amerei POV

The week after midterms blurred like watercolor left in the rain.

Everyone around me was dragging their feet, groaning over grades and projects, but I moved through it with the kind of calm that only a psycho or 'someone who wanted to forget that her boyfriend raped her and let his friends join in with him' can give.

I wasn't excited for classes, but they kept my focus.

Monday, Tuesday, and Wednesday slipped by, marked by caffeine stains on my planner and aching hands from writing too much.

I hadn't gone to the club for a while now.

Barely even saw Mita or Meda, in the daytime, much less Odessa, except for their texts in the group chat.

We all had our worlds to hold up.

Mita, with her scripture studies, music rehearsals, and classes.

Meda drowning in science and labs.

Odessa somewhere between internships and hustling.

We loved each other deeply, but outside of our girl-nights, we lived in separate orbits.

Thursdays, though… those were mine. Mine and Kazuya's.

Kazuya was the kind of solid that didn't demand anything but presence. I didn't have to lie to him because he never asked for explanations. He just made room for me.

So when Thursday came, I was buzzing a little. Nervous and excited. About the one constant thing that highlights my week. I walked into the liberal arts building, making my way to the calligraphy club room early for once, practically grinning.

Pushing the door to the room, only to find it locked. Locked?!

"What?" I muttered under my breath. "Why is it locked? Am I early?"

I pulled out my phone and skipped past Merrick's name, lighting up my screen. I didn't want to see what he said. It was always some variation of "Hope you're okay," "Miss you," and "Love you," and all I could think was liar. Monster. Pretender. Rapist.

I opened Kaz's contact instead.

Me: "Hey, why is the club room locked? Where are you btw? Is it canceled?"

Kaz: "Yeah, he texted earlier this week. It's cancelled."

Me: "Oh."

I stared at that short word for a while, disappointment and dread washing over me, my fingers shakily hovering over the screen, not knowing what to say after hearing the one thing I had been looking forward to was cancelled!

Kaz: "You still there?"

Me: "Yeah."

Kaz: "Stay there. I'm coming."

I didn't know what to say to that, so I didn't reply. I just waited, leaning against the wall, letting the wind brush past my face, attempting to push away the heavy wave of panic trying to drown me.

Six minutes later, Kaz jogged into view, hoodie pulled up halfway, looking like he actually ran.

"Hey," he smiled, a little out of breath. "Wanna use this free time to hang out?" he asked, hands on his hips, still trying to catch his breath

"Yeah, sure," I said. I didn't care where we went. As long as it wasn't back into my thoughts.

He led the way, our words meandering between trivial chatter and deeper topics, until we reached one of the school's parking lots.

At his car, he pulled the passenger door open, allowing me to climb in. The moment I sat, pain ripped through my thigh like fire. My body trembled, my jaw locked tight—I could almost feel my not-so-recent wounds reopening, tears pooling, threatening to fall. The denim bit into my flesh mercilessly, as these wounds were deeper, and I cursed myself for not choosing looser bottoms. My vision blurred for a second, but I refused to give in. No gasp. No whimper. Just air forced through my nose, shaky but controlled, and a smile stitched across my face when we made eye contact when he closed my door, before rounding the car to his side, settling in, and starting the car

He didn't realize something was wrong. Great, perfect.

"We're going on an adventure," he announced.

"Do I get a hint?" I prompted

"Nope. You just have to trust me."

And I did.

Even if I couldn't trust myself right now, I could trust him.

Chapter 69: A Get Away

Amerei POV

The wind was stronger up here, not aggressive—just steady gusts, wrapping around me like invisible silk, rocking me off my heels if I didn't have proper support; carrying the scent of salt and seaweed and something wild I couldn't name.

I stood near the edge of the escarpment, the palisade railing running along the border intruding but not obscuring the elaborate scenery, making my heart thump either in nervousness from the height of the cliff or with excitement. I didn't know, nor did I care to figure out, which one was correct because it's been so long since I had such a surge of energy in months.

Watching the waves crash against the cliff in a wild, freeing rhythm below me shook loose the heavy weight of my dark thoughts, accompanied by the wind, filling my lungs with salty air. In that moment, the world softens, and a deep, steady inhale carries my hardened heart back to life beneath the endless sky.

I turned around, my cheeks stinging a little from the chill of the sea breeze, to see Kaz at the car, arms full with a blanket and a basket and that same easy grin that makes my scared heart do strange things in my chest.

He looked so proud of himself.

So, he planned this.

"You had this planned out, didn't you?" I quizzed, jogging toward him, the wind catching my words and sending them flying like paper cranes.

Kaz looked at me like he'd just won a game. "Yeah. Ever since the club got canceled. I figured… you wouldn't say no to a good view and food you didn't have to cook." he said with a cocky grin,

He really does look so pleased with himself.

"Thanks, Kaz." I smiled up at him

"You're welcome, Erei." he nodded as he set the stuff down

God, I'd missed the way he said my name. Like it was an inside joke. Like it had its own gravity. Together we picked a spot to lay out the blanket—on a small hill with a clear view of the lighthouse and the edge of the world. The evening wind tugged at the edges of the blanket, so Kaz pinned the corners down with some smooth stones from the path nearby. The basket was placed right in the center, like it were the crown jewel.

"Hey," I chirped, pointing to the lighthouse, "do you think we can go up?"

"Totally," he agreed. "Though who's going to guard our royal feast?"

I grinned. "The seagulls."

Laughing, he took my hand, and we made our way toward the lighthouse steps.

They. Were. Endless.

"Why didn't you tell me we were hiking up the Eiffel Tower?" I gasped after the first spiral.

"Oh please, Miss I-Did-CrossFit-One-Summer," he hassled, clearly struggling too. "You're the one who said you ran track in high school."

"That was three years ago, and also I faked a cramp halfway through every meet." I spat

"Wait—you faked cramps?" he gasped.

"Of course I did. I only joined for the jacket." I grinned.

When we finally reached the top of the lighthouse, we were both breathless and dramatically leaning against opposite sides of the threshold, trying to catch our breath, which slightly burned the back of my throat with the sudden draft in the air being so high up in the tail of winter, and fruitlessly attempting to distract ourselves from our aching muscles, we looked out at the view before us.

And everything stopped.

The ocean stretched out like a living canvas, its waves shimmering gold as the sun dipped low on the horizon. Behind us, the city stood hushed, bathed in a gentle, amber glow, as if holding its breath, as if it didn't want to disturb the expanse above. And the sky—painted in strokes of red, orange, and soft lavender—looked like it had been brushed with oil pastels, each hue melting into the next in a slow, surreal cascade. I hadn't seen anything like it. I hadn't let myself look in a long time.

Click.

I turned sharply to find Kaz snapping a photo of me, camera in hand, that I completely overlooked all this time.

"Hey- I wasn't ready! Where did you even spawn that camera from? Did you have it with you all this time?!" I interrogated

He shrugged, waiting while I fixed my hair. "I'm not surprised; you have the observation skills of a door," he stated.

I struck a mock model pose.

"Okay, now," I said, completely ignoring his comment

He took a dozen more, switching angles, teasing me about my "model face," then we took turns capturing the view. I got one of him squinting into the sun like a hero in a coming-of-age film, and he got a super awkward one of me blinking because my hair got in my eyes. It was a wonderful time. These were days I envisioned when I thought about coming to college, but after that night, I believed it would never come to pass, but here we are.

When we descended the stairs and found our way back to the blanket, the sky had deepened. Everything had gone quiet. The wind whispered now, gentler. The food was simple—fruit, sandwiches, and lemon soda—but it was perfect. We ate, stretched out, and talked about nothing. And for a little while, I forgot.

I forgot that I was broken.

Until he broke the silence.

"Erei… are you okay?" His voice was soft, causing me to take a minute to hear and process what he had said. "Like, not surface-level, okay. I mean, really."

I stilled.

He continued, slower this time. "I saw you wince when you got in the car earlier. Then when you stepped out… I saw the small streaks of blood on your jeans. They were in lines, Erei. <u>Neat lines</u>. And… I've seen you lately. Around campus. You look… lost."

I didn't speak.

He wasn't done.

"And not like the 'I-forgot-where-my-class-is' lost. Like… like you don't even know where *you* are. And the light in your eyes… It's not there like it used to be. I didn't want to push, but when I saw the blood, I… I couldn't not say something."

The silence that followed felt like glass. Fragile. Too loud.

And then I broke.

A breath escaped me—long, shaky, ragged. I felt the tears come as my vision began to blur. Hot and unrelenting, slipping down the sides of my face as I stared at the sky and tried not to scream.

The weight I'd been carrying cracked open so easily, like whatever I had been doing to suppress it was in vain, spilling into the quiet of the dusk.

Kaz didn't say anything.

He didn't touch me.

He just... *stayed by my side,* letting the silence be my confession.

When I could finally speak, I did.

"It doesn't stop," I whispered. "The noise in my head. The memories. Him. It's like it's burned into me. And when I can't take it, I cut, and then I can breathe for a second. Just a second." I breathed, my voice breaking.

Kaz's hand hovered over mine. He didn't take it until I turned my palm up and invited him in.

"Every day I walk around and pretend I'm fine because I can't bear the thought of being someone else's burden. Everyone's carrying something already. I don't want to be... *more.*" I sobbed, a heavy lump forming at the back of my throat, making it hard to breathe properly.

"You're not more," Kaz assured quietly. "You're human. And you're hurting."

He turned to me fully, eyes dark and wet with unshed tears.

"And you're *not* a burden. You never were." He asserted firmly.

We sat in silence as the stars came out, scattered like promises over the water.

"I don't know how to get better," I admitted.

"You don't have to know," he said. "You just have to let us help you try," he begged.

I looked at him. Really looked at him.

Is it ok for me to let someone *see* me? And I wonder if I should let him see *more* of me?

Chapter 70: Under the surface

Amerei POV

PLAYLIST- CONTROL BY ZOE WEES

The sky above the lighthouse had turned soft gold, stretching into streaks of burnt orange and dusky pink. I lay back on the blanket beside Kaz, the sea breeze tugging at my sleeves, trying to convince me to breathe.

But even here, in this beautiful place, the storm inside me wouldn't quiet down.

I'd thought I could hide it—bury it under laughter, under assignments, under the way he smiled when I joked about fonts or bubble tea. But the silence between us now, the chill of the sea breeze against my skin, the quiet steadiness of Kaz just *being* here… it cracked my chest open.

"I didn't want to overstep," he muttered softly, "but I care about you. And when I saw that today, I knew I had to say something."

The second round of tears came before I could stop them.

The dam broke.

"Why does it look like everyone is getting their life together, but when I thought I was getting mine together, the floor was kicked out from under me?" My voice cracked, my throat burning as the words tumbled out. *"I came to college not wanting it to be too eventful with little to no drama. I just wanted peace. Like everyone else seems to have. Especially Mita and Meda. You probably don't even know them. But they went through their own crap, and somehow they found*

God or something, and now they have peace. And you—" I turned to look at him, sobbing. *"You have peace too. What do you guys have that I don't? What's so wrong with me?!"* I screamed

Kaz didn't interrupt. He didn't look away. He just… watched me, listening.

"Everyone seems to have it figured out, at least a little. I've never had anything. I'm not even a people person. Outside of my small group of friends, I can't socialize, I can't meet people, I can't even find a decent boyfriend—" my voice broke, *"and don't even get me started on God. I don't even know what I believe."*

I wiped my face furiously. *"I've been eavesdropping on Mita's nightly prayers—"* I laughed bitterly, *"she prays to a Jesus I don't even believe in, and somehow, I still fall asleep to her voice like it's the only anchor I have. What the heck am I even doing? I don't know anything, and I hate everything!"* I cried out, pulling out my roots.

Not being able to just watch me hurt, Kaz pulled me into a hug—no hesitation, no question—just his arms around me like scaffolding, holding me up while I fell apart.

"You wanna hear it so bad, Kaz?" I choked out into his shoulder. *"I hate him. I hate myself. I hate what I've become because of him."*

I squeezed my eyes shut. *"I cut myself, Kaz. Because I don't know what else to do to forget. My head is always remembering. Always reminding. It's the only thing that works, even for a second. That day... the first day I did it... it was the day I'd decided to end my life. I was ready. But then... I thought about my friends. About you. And I didn't do it. **I didn't.**"*

My shoulders shook violently, and then I realized it wasn't my shoulders; I wasn't the only one crying.

I felt his head fall onto my shoulders, then the sensation of wet fabric on my shoulder.

Kaz was shaking.

I pulled away quickly, alarmed. *"Hey, hey—I'm sorry. I didn't mean to make you cry. I don't hate you, Kaz. I hate the situation, I hate him, not you, I'm sorry."* I panicked

He looked up at me, and my heart broke again for a different reason.

His face was red, his eyes glassy. His lips, trembling slightly

"Don't apologize Erei, *it's not that,*" he whispered, voice barely steady. "*It's just... I didn't know you tried to... I didn't know you were that close to-.*" he voice broke off.

He pulled me back into his arms. I collapsed into him, crying harder than I had in months.

"I'm sorry, Kaz. I'm so sorry." I wailed

"Don't be," he cried. *"You were hurting. But I'm so glad you didn't go through with it. I'm so glad you're still here,"* he hugged me tighter.

We stayed like that for I have no clue how long, holding each other until our sobs calmed into slightly ragged breaths and sniffles.

After a moment, he asked gently, *"Did you break up with the idiot who's still bothering you?"*

"No... and yes," I said weakly.

He blinked. *"Wait, what? You haven't broken up with him?! After everything he did to you?! You almost—"* He stopped himself.

"Sorry, that came out too harsh. But... why haven't you? Do you still love him?" he finished in a quieter voice.

"No. Heck no," I spat immediately, my voice firm even through the tears.

"Then... I don't understand," he said, confusion washed over his features.

So I told him.

Everything.

What Merrick did to me.

What he let happen.

What he said afterward.

What I felt.

What I still feel.

I didn't spare the emotions, but I didn't go into graphic details. I just… told the truth.

When I finished, Kaz sat there, his jaw clenched, his hands trembling slightly in my grasp.

Then, without a word, he pulled me into a hug so tight, so warm, that I thought I might fall apart all over again.

He kissed the top of my head so gently, protectively, before whispering something I couldn't hear, but I felt his care.

Then he slowly pulled away and stood up.

"I'm gonna use the bathroom for a sec," he said, his voice calm, but I could see it. The storm building behind his eyes, the anger and tension in his retreating back.

I didn't stop him.

I knew he needed a moment; I did too.

I stayed there on the blanket, staring at the horizon, the sea stretching out beneath the night sky. My tears had slowed, but my heart still ached.

But… I didn't feel alone in it.

Chapter 71: Under the Stars

Amerei POV

The sky had fallen into an even deeper navy by the time Kaz returned from the lighthouse. I was still lying on my back, eyes tracing the now-silver constellations above us. The grass rustled gently beside the blanket, the sound of the ocean waves crashing softly in the background like the heartbeat of the earth. The cold wasn't biting anymore, as earlier in the evening at the top of the lighthouse, but a cool caress against my skin, and the blanket now felt like a shell—a thin barrier between me and the world.

I heard his footsteps before I saw him.

"Oh, you're back," I said quietly, not moving from my spot.

"Yeah," he replied, settling down beside me again as we both looked up into the expanse, letting the silence coat us in something surprisingly soft.

The stars blinked in the distance, far and unreachable.

I used to wish I were a star, burning brightly millions of miles away.

"God really is amazing to create all of this," Kaz said suddenly, his voice reverent and thoughtful.

I turned my head to look at him. Taking in his profile, he had this look of calm, peacefulness, even.

"Kaz… you believe in a God, right?" I prompted

"Yes," he replied without hesitation.

"And your God is Jesus, right? The nice one? The all-good God who came down to die and help us get into heaven?" I prompted again

"Yup. That's the one," he replied once more with no hesitation.

I rolled over to lie on my side, facing him. "If your God, if there's a God—is the one who's the all-loving, all-good Jesus—then why do bad things happen to good people?" I asked

He turned his head, meeting my gaze. "Well… that's a very good question."

I didn't speak and allowed him to continue.

"To answer that question, we have to go back to the start of time. In the beginning, God created heaven and earth—Genesis 1, verse 1. Everyone who has read the Bible knows by exact order how the earth was created and on what day, what came about. But the Bible also reveals, though scattered across different books, what happened in heaven.

Out of the tens of thousands of angels, assuming there were more, only three are named in the Bible: Gabriel, the messenger. Michael, the captain and warrior. And Lucifer, who was in charge of worship and music.

Lucifer was beautiful, majestic. He was adorned in precious stones, a book in the Bible named after its author, called Ezekiel, in chapter 28 verses 11–19 paints this. But even with all that, he grew proud. He wanted to be more than just adored. He wanted to *be* God. Isaiah 14:12–15 tells us that he said, '*I will ascend to heaven, I will raise my throne above the stars of God… I will make myself like the Most High.*'

That's where evil and sin began, not in the famous Garden of Eden," he paused, seeming to gather his thoughts, I guess?

"But no one can be better than God. I mean, look around. No one can do what He does—what we take years to create, He created that and more in six days.

Lucifer envied Him. Hated that he couldn't be greater. He rallied a third of the angels to rebel with him. But Michael and the faithful angels fought back, and Lucifer and his followers were cast down—Luke 10:18 says, '*I saw Satan fall like lightning from heaven.'*

And that's where evil began to exist <u>outside</u> of heaven.

God created man in His image. Gave Adam and Eve everything in Eden, with only one command in Genesis 2:15–17: don't eat from the tree of the knowledge of good and evil.

But the devil entered the garden disguised as a serpent; he came as something that was supposed to be in the Garden; he came as an animal so Adam nor Eve would not question his presence and doubt, as he was supposedly 'placed there by God', same as the rest of the animals. In Genesis 3:1–7, he twisted God's words and introduced doubt. Adam and Eve, untainted by deceit, fell into his trap. That's when sin entered the world by Lucifer **through** man, this is when the first fracture formed between God and man.

Since then, the enemy has manipulated people time and time again. He infiltrates culture, politics, and minds. 2 Corinthians 11:14–15 says he masquerades as an angel of light. He doesn't come with horns and fire. He comes soft. <u>Familiar.</u>

He comes through validation and twisted truths." he stopped, seeming to make that one land, and it kinda did... I think.

"Amerei, he intentionally created this image of being dark, mean, ugly, and scary, with obvious cruelty,

<u>But how does the bible describe him?</u>

<u>How does his creator describe him?</u>

The being who handcrafted him,

God, describes him as the complete opposite, but Lucifer molded himself to be everything he portrays to the media and the world: wicked, cruel, a monster physically and emotionally...

lies.

They are all lies because he is the father of lies, as Jesus puts it.

And with this plan, he, Lucifer, paints 'the devil' into a nasty image; he fools people into thinking *when you think of 'the devil', think big, mean, dark, and ugly,* but when he comes, he comes

AS HOW THE BIBLE DESCRIBES HIM, AS AN ANGEL OF LIGHT,

aka when he comes as the beautiful Lucifer, and no one bats an eye because the devil they are looking for is big, ugly, and scary.

His name is Lucifer Morningstar, which literally means bearer of light and also morning star, obviously, we just identify him as Satan and the Devil; those names are just adjectives used to describe his corruptive nature. But at the end of the day, he is not ugly and not dark and mean; when he wants to manipulate you, he is beautiful, caring, and kind. In fact,

he is your biggest cheerleader to take on something you want but can't actually manage and if or when you fall, he is the first to degrade you but when he degrades you, he does it disguising himself in people around you or even your own thoughts. So when you get up to try again, to do that same thing again or perhaps something else, you would not distrust 'his encouragement or discouragement' that's camouflaged as your very own confidence or judgment as well as the people you call 'friends or family'. Why? Because they were there for you the first time and 'meant well.' " he explained

"Think about a manipulator. They do not seem harmful to you if the manipulation is directed to you, and when things go wrong, they direct the blame off them and onto people around you and even onto you, the victim, but never themselves, and they do good things for you and give you things you want and and brainwash you saying *'no one else will do this for you'* or *'no one else can love you like I do because of this or because of that, so be grateful'* and when they do cross lines and you want to leave its not easy because they go back to giving you *'all you ever wanted'*, creating a tug-of-war bond, a kind of on and off thing, and when or if you do go off the rails, because of the mindset they implanted in your head, you are quick to blame yourself and people around you. Sounds like a toxic relationship, right?

Because that is exactly what it is."

I blinked, staring at him, processing it all.

"He doesn't just want to hurt us, Amerei. He wants us confused. Disconnected. **Alone.** Why do you think when people are depressed, they always seem stuck in their own heads, stranded inside their own thoughts, whether they choose it or not?" Because his voice is loudest when we are by ourselves. He whispers lies to make us question God; with those lies, he raises up generations to do his bidding, which includes harming everyone around them physically, spiritually, mentally, emotionally, psychologically, financially, politically, etc., as they were led to believe that since they were hurt, everyone should be, or if they have an opinion, no one should disagree, and anyone who disrupts their peace should feel their wrath, which comes back to when I say he, Lucifer, comes as someone who validates your feelings, even the stupid or even cruel ones, as he himself is cruel and stupid. It has been done time and time again over the years since creation. This results in doubts, violent unbelievers, and threats against believers, hypocrisy in the church, and so much more, and all of my example after based on Christians who should know better. Now, imagine the carnage of those who don't. A big example of this was in the Bible, where Jesus himself confronted the people in John 8:44, where Jesus says, *'You belong to your father, the devil, and you want to carry out your father's desires. He was a murderer from the beginning and does not stand in truth because there is no truth in him.'* That's where hate, greed, envy, and all the horror in the world began—with him, Lucifer." he finished.

"But if all that's true," I whispered, "why doesn't God just kill him? Is He too kind? Why let *us* suffer?" I asked, genuinely baffled, by such depth of kindness where God would be apparently stupid.

Kaz sighed, rubbing his hands together before speaking gently. "God will. Revelation 20:10 says the devil and his angels will be thrown into the lake of fire, tormented day and night forever. But not yet.

Why not now? You might ask

Because God is waiting. He wants us to choose Him. To love Him back freely. That's why we were given free will.

Forced love isn't love.

It's slavery.

And yeah… that means evil still exists, because people still choose it. And if God wiped out every evil person right now… most of us wouldn't survive. Romans 3:23 says, 'All have sinned and fall short of the glory of God.'

He doesn't want to destroy us. He wants to redeem us. But we have to choose that." He explained

I was silent for a long time.

No one had ever explained it to me like that.

Not a sermon, not that I ever listened to one before,

not a parent, they weren't home enough, nor did they themselves believe,

not a youth leader, not one I ever even stepped on soil dedicated to any God.

But this wasn't some overly simplified 'everything happens for a reason' talk. Like I would hear in some arguments, this was just a well-explained answer. The full story.

"You're saying… even what happened to me… that was *him*? That was evil at work?" I asked to try to put this all into a logical bracket for me to grasp.

Kaz's voice dropped, serious and steady. "Yes. What Merrick did was evil. It came from a place of sin, manipulation, and darkness. And God grieves that with you. He didn't want that for you. But He can still bring healing, redemption, purpose, *hope*—if you let Him."

I blinked rapidly as tears welled again, goose bumps rising up my body.

"And if I don't believe in any of this yet?" I asked, still unsure

Kaz looked over at me. "Then I'll keep reminding you of the truth until you do. I'll be here. I'll fight alongside you. You don't have to believe it all tonight. But I believe God hasn't given up on you, so I won't either." he smiled

I pressed my lips together as my throat clenched, trying not to cry again.

The stars above were the same stars I'd seen all my life—but this time, they didn't feel so far.

Chapter 72: Familiar Laughter and Unexpected Truths

Amerei POV

I had asked him to stop by a store before we head back, but the time Kaz pulled up to the store, the streetlights were casting golden halos on the quiet pavement. Most shops had already closed, but one small local bookstore still had its lights on, a welcome glow through.

"Thanks for stopping," I said, unbuckling my seatbelt.

"Of course," he replied. "You need to stop anywhere else?"

I shook my head. "Just this. I need to quickly grab a book so I can write what you told me and stop ignoring this before I forget."

He gave me a small nod, "I'll wait out here."

I darted inside the small convenience store, grabbed the first journal that didn't scream glitter or gothic poetry, paid, and returned within minutes.

As we pulled up to the entrance of the dormitory, he turned to me.

"Text me when you get in,"

"I will. Thanks again, Kaz." I smiled before getting off.

I didn't wait for him to pull off. My heart was already ahead of me, racing me back to the dorm.

When I walked in, the living room was warm with the glow of the TV screen, laughter bubbling softly from the couch. And there they were, Andromeda and Mita, curled into their usual comfort spots, snacks half-eaten between them, reruns of *Brooklyn Nine-Nine* playing like it was any other weekend night.

"Where have you been, missy?" Mita called out, grinning at me with a playful squint.

I kicked off my shoes. "Out with Kaz."

"We know," Meda said without looking up, munching on popcorn.

I raised an eyebrow. "Oh, well, that's great; why bother asking then?" I grumbled, plopping down dramatically on the couch beside them.

"Because we're nosy," Mita said matter-of-factly.

With a groan, I stretched across both their laps, tossing my journal onto the coffee table and sighing like the weight of the whole week had just slipped off my shoulders. "Wait a minute," I said, my brain finally clicked in. "How do you even know I was with Kaz? And, more importantly, how do you *know* Kaz?"

"Oh, honey…" Meda smirked.

"We're all in the Christian club," Mita said with a shrug as though I should have known this already. "He came to us last week, actually, worried about you. Said, 'Something felt off with you.' "Mita explained

"He even asked our permission to take you out earlier this week when he found out the calligraphy club was canceled," Meda added with a mischievous grin, poking me in the stomach.

I groaned and covered my face with both hands, sinking deeper into Meda's lap like her belly fat would swallow me whole. "I *literally* told him about you guys and said, 'You probably *don't even know each other.*'" I mumbled.

Embarrassment was an understatement to my current predicament. But thinking about it now, he didn't say he didn't know the girls; in fact, he didn't even say anything about that. Then again, hearing that someone was raped and almost committed suicide seems more pressing than clarifying someone's acquaintance with another.

Mita burst out laughing. "Girl, we've known each other for a while now."

"Ugh. This is *so* embarrassing." I cried

"That's on you," Meda said, her voice vibrating through my cheek as I burrowed into her belly. "Maybe do a little more digging next time before assuming, mmhm?"

I heard Mita snort.

"You're *not* helping, Mita," I groaned.

"What'd I do?" she said, blinking innocently.

"You didn't *tell* me!" I lamented.

"Then it wouldn't be a surprise now, would it?" she replied, smug.

We all dissolved into laughter, my body relaxing in the safe familiarity of my girls, my family.

And then the laughter faded, quieted by the gentle hum of the TV and the unspoken truths still lingering in my chest.

"Um... guys," I started softly. "Kazuya shared something with me tonight. And I wanted your thoughts on it. It's kinda... up your alley." I began

They both turned their eyes to me, nodding for me to continue.

I told them about what Kaz said—about God, about the story of Lucifer and free will, about how evil came into the world and why it remains. I didn't sugarcoat it. I used his words, his examples, and every bit of that long, intense explanation that had cracked open something in me.

When I finished, they were quiet. And then Mita was the first to speak.

"That... that's actually really accurate. He explained it really well."

"Yeah," Meda said thoughtfully. "He didn't just skim over things or use churchy clichés. That was a whole *lesson, and it's accurate too.*"

"And that whole thing about the devil being close to us, using what we trust… it checks out," Mita added. "It's biblical, and honestly—it explains a lot, even I needed to hear right now."

I blinked. "So… wait. It's not just a story? You're saying all of it's… true?" I questioned

"Yeah," Meda said. "And if you want, we can help you look into it more. Research it together, study it properly."

I smiled. Meda's love for research before telling me to just dive headfirst into their belief made me feel like I didn't have to rush into this whole thing. I could ask questions and still belong.

"Maybe this Jesus thing has a little truth to it, I guess," I muttered.

"Mmhmmm," Mita hummed gently.

There was a beat of silence. And then Mita sat up straighter. "Wait. Did you tell Kaz about Merrick?"

I nodded slowly. "Yeah. I told him everything. He… he even cried. Like, *really* cried. And then he gave me space, but I think it was an excuse also to give him time to cool off. I mean… the entire situation was just… a lot."

I didn't have to say more. They already knew what "a lot" meant.

We spent the rest of the night curled up together. Meda decided to sleep over, even though her room was literally upstairs. Mita laid her head on Meda's shoulder. And I remained on Meda's lap.

Right here in this dorm in this moment, I felt at peace.

And it didn't come from ignoring the pain but from knowing I didn't have to hold it alone anymore.

Chapter 73: A Step into Something New

Amerei POV

Friday was loud.

Not in the screaming, music-blasting kind of way—but in the weight-of-the-world-on-your-back, everyone-wants-something-from-you kind of way. I was barely keeping up. Classes back-to-back. Group work meetings. Leading projects I didn't sign up to lead. I didn't ask to be the one people relied on. That title just always sticks to me, and I was too tired to peel it off.

By the time I got back to my dorm, I felt like a deflated balloon.

My backpack hit the floor with a thud, and I collapsed onto the bed. I didn't even kick my shoes off. I think I blinked once, maybe twice, and then I was out. Just… gone.

When I opened my eyes again, the room was dim. The outside sky dipped into evening hues of burnt orange and magenta. I'd slept for maybe two hours, but it felt like I hadn't slept at all. My body felt heavy and uneasy, my stomach unsettled—not with butterflies, but with flies.

I dragged myself to the bathroom and washed my face in cold water. Still didn't help.

When I stepped out, still wearing the same jeans and sweater from earlier, my eyes fell on the journal I'd bought last night. I hadn't any memory of how it got onto the bedside table, but there it was, perched like it had something to say.

I picked it up. Sat on the edge of my bed. Grabbed a pen. The words spilled out of me.

Everything Kaz had told me about God, about Lucifer, about the world, about good and evil—it all poured onto the pages. His voice rang in my head. I wasn't sure if I believed it. Not yet. But I still wanted to write it.

And then... I felt it.

A tug.

I can't explain it. But it was just this quiet, firm nudge saying,

Go outside.

Not a scream. Not panic. Just...

Go.

So I did. I packed the journal, a pencil case, and my phone, and I left.

Three minutes later, I was walking aimlessly across campus, still wondering what I was even doing. I didn't have a destination in mind, I was just walking. That's when my phone buzzed.

Mita: Hey short notice, but you wanna come to the Christian club tonight?

I stopped walking.

Then another DM:

Meda: Remember when we said we'd research to find the truth? I believe coming to the Christian club tonight would be a good start, and then we can dive in more when we get back.

I stood there in the breeze, unsure. I didn't know if I was ready for this. I wasn't sure I believed in anything yet.

But then my fingers moved anyway.

Me: Where is the place?

Meda: Student union, downstairs, room 412.

I exhaled, knowing there was no point in turning back now.

I went ahead and made my way to the location.

I hadn't used my maps for direction, not this time. Just went off instinct and a vague memory of the campus map that I barely ever glanced at. Somehow, against all odds and my notoriously terrible sense of direction, I ended up near the student union building. The place glowed with warm, welcoming sunlight. Students gathered in little groups by tables and gazebos, laughing and chatting.

Then someone passed by me, walking in the same direction. A guy. Tall, soft curls. A calm energy about him. I needed directions, and I guessed he was a good bet, I guess.

"Um, hello, do you-" I said after doing a small sprint to catch up to him.

He took out his earbuds, turned, and smiled down at me. "Oh, hi. You're Andromeda's friend, right?"

My brain did a double-take. "How… how did you know….?"

"That you're one of Meda's friends? She shows me all the pictures on her phone of you guys any chance she gets," he said.

He held out his hand. "Zebedee."

"Amerei," I said, shaking it.

Oh, so this is Zeb. You go, girl.

We walked side by side toward the building.

"On your way to the club?" he asked.

"Yeah. I was going to ask you for directions, actually."

"Great. Let's hurry before they start."

He jogged ahead. Show-off, he knows his strides are far longer than mine.

I speed-walked to catch up. But that was not really a possible feat, as I am not that athletic to even move any faster than I am now, without breathing like I had just run a marathon by the time I entered the club

Inside, the room buzzed with life. Beanbags, folding chairs, floor cushions. People clustered in small groups, laughing, chatting like this was just a Friday hangout and not, you know, a *Christian* thing.

Then I saw them then.

"Merei!" Mita called out. She sat with Meda and Kaz, and someone else I vaguely recognized but couldn't place.

"I am so happy you came," Kaz said, standing up.

"Mita and Meda invited me," I said, eyeing him up and down in mock indignation. "And you, however, didn't. How rude."

He held up his hands. "I didn't want to rush you. I figured I'd invite you next week."

"Mm-hmm, sure…" I drawled

"I was, really."

Kaz and I bickered like siblings until a woman stepped into the room, immediately gaining the full attention of her audience. She had this presence about her; she exuded a specific type of confidence. It wasn't loud, but not subtle either.

"Hi, everyone," she began. "For all newcomers, my name is Ruth, and I will be leading today's teaching. Let's settle down and get started."

I took my seat, clutching the journal in my lap, slightly nervous.

Being here, in this space, seemed like an important step, a very big one.

I didn't know what I believed yet. I didn't know if I even wanted to be here.

But I was here, for now.

Chapter 74: Truth and Deception

Amerei POV

Ruth stood at the front of the room and called us to attention. She didn't yell. She didn't even raise her voice. But the room listened.

"OK, everyone," she said with a small smile. "Tonight, we're going to talk about truth, deception, and the righteousness of God. Let's go ahead and turn to 2 John. It's only one chapter, but it's loaded, and every line matters."

Kaz handed me a Bible. *Of course, he brought two.*

That guy always thought ahead.

I flipped to 2 John with much effort in finding it, thankful for Kaz's help.

Ruth began reading,

2 John (NIV)

1 The elder,

To the lady chosen by God and to her children, whom I love in the truth and not I only, but also all who know the truth

2 because of the truth, which lives in us and will be with us forever:

3 Grace, mercy and peace from God the Father and from Jesus Christ, the Father's Son, will be with us in truth and love.

4 It has given me great joy to find some of your children walking in the truth, just as the Father commanded us.

5 And now, dear lady, I am not writing you a new command but one we have had from the beginning. I ask that we love one another.

6 And this is love: that we walk in obedience to his commands. As you have heard from the beginning, his command is that you walk in love.

7 I say this because many deceivers, who do not acknowledge Jesus Christ as coming in the flesh, have gone out into the world. Any such person is the deceiver and the antichrist.

8 Watch out that you do not lose what we have worked for, but that you may be rewarded fully.

9 Anyone who runs ahead and does not continue in the teaching of Christ does not have God; whoever continues in the teaching has both the Father and the Son.

10 If anyone comes to you and does not bring this teaching, do not take them into your house or welcome them.

11 Anyone who welcomes them shares in their wicked work.

12 I have much to write to you, but I do not want to use paper and ink. Instead, I hope to visit you and talk with you face to face, so that our joy may be complete.

13 The children of your sister, who is chosen by God, send their greetings.

When she finished reading, Ruth looked up.

"So, let's break this down."

"In verses 1-3, do you notice the word 'truth' popping up already?" she asked.

A few people nodded. Someone called out, "Four times."

"Exactly. That's intentional. John is laying the foundation: love and truth always go hand in hand. Can't have one without the other. And this woman he's writing to, 'the elect lady,' may have been an actual mom or a leader of a church. Either way, he's reminding her that what they share isn't fluff, novelty, a story, or a fairytale. It's rooted in something eternal."

As she kept reading, Ruth explained each piece as if it were a doorway. We were walking through one verse at a time, and with every step, I felt like I was understanding something I'd never had the patience or humility to learn before.

I've never heard someone unpack words like that. She talked about how truth isn't just being honest; it's Jesus. That real love isn't just hugs and hearts; it's obedience. Being kind doesn't mean you let just anyone speak into your life, especially if they're speaking against the truth.

"In verse 6," she said, "we see that love is action. It's walking in God's commandments. It's more than emotion. It's choosing what's right, even when it costs you."

I shifted in my seat.

"She's good," Kaz whispered beside me.

"Yeah," I whispered back. "She really is."

Ruth kept going. When she got to verses 7 through 11, she didn't sugarcoat anything. She explained that the antichrist wasn't just some end-times figure in a movie. It was anyone who denies the truth about Jesus.

"Many deceivers have gone out into the world... such a one is the deceiver and the antichrist."

Honestly. That word, 'antichrist,' does sound like it came straight out of a horror movie.

But Ruth didn't skip a beat.

"Now, before you imagine some apocalyptic villain in a red cape, let's get clear. This verse isn't talking about *a* person per se. It's saying that **ANYONE** who denies the truth about Jesus, **ANYONE** who spreads lies about who He is and what He did, is already against Him. And that kind of deception doesn't always look evil. Sometimes it looks polished. Nice. Familiar even. It's backed with half-truths and sometimes its scriptures taken out of context. And if we, as the body of Christ, or individuals who just don't know and/or are unbelieving, will become susceptible, an easy target, not difficult to turn from truth and be deceived with lies that have logic but are voided of truth, real truth, voided of *Jesus*," she elucidated.

"That is why we should not be lazy with our knowledge and wisdom; we should not be lazy to read his word, because if we do become lazy with the knowledge and wisdom the Lord has provided through his word, people will take advantage of it and manipulate and trick you with logical reasoning or appeal to your emotions, which 9.99 times out of 10 drives people to make drastic decisions that they wouldn't do if they were in God's presence and discerning. That's why we should find out the truth, not our own truth but the truth backed with facts, witnesses, proven results, and the Bible has just that; **Jesus is that**," Ruth explained.

That... hit. Harder than I expected. I thought about how many lies I'd believed. About myself. About others. About what love was supposed to look like.

Meda raised her hand. "How do you know what's true then? How do you know what's real?"

"Great question," Ruth smiled. "Jesus said *He* is the truth. That's in John 14:6. So anything that doesn't match who He is: His character, His teachings, His love, the life He lived—that is a red flag."

"Truth matters," she emphasized. "A lot of people today are spiritual. A lot of people believe in some vague higher power. But truth, real truth, is Jesus. And if someone is teaching anything else, we don't entertain it. We don't invite it into our lives."

There goes my tea being clocked again and also tipped over.

Maybe because I've spent so long pretending I was fine, entertaining every voice but God's. I'd nodded along with things that sounded good, even when they didn't feel true, and even that brought me nowhere, to the point of confusion, where I didn't even want to care about this stuff anymore.

"Now let's go into 1 John 4, about testing the spirits and knowing God through love. But tonight, I want you to ask yourself:

Am I walking in truth? Or am I tolerating a lie because it's easier?"

I sat back. My heart was still. For the first time in... I don't even know how long.

And I didn't have the answers. But maybe now I was finally asking the right questions.

Chapter 75: A Love Worth Testing

Amerei POV

The room remained unmoving as Ruth stood at the front of the room, Bible in hand, voice calm yet commanding. I was trying to follow along, though my eyes were heavy from the long day, but something about the way she read the text made it hard to look away. So I came up with a decision.

So we're gonna blame Ms. Ruth for messing up my sleep schedule and completely ignore the fact that I have the will to literally get up and walk out, but it would be too embarrassing, so I will stay

"Alright, I know that was a lot, but," she said, scanning the room, gauging how well we were holding up. Nodding, seeming pleased with their nonverbal feedback, she continued. "Let's go to 1 John chapter 4. We're going to walk through it together, as I had already done a teaching on this. I want us to revisit it, verse by verse."

I leaned forward a little, the thin pages of the Bible crackling as I finally found the place after checking the table of contents. I looked beside me to see Kaz, already looking at me, with a small encouraging smile.

"Verse 1," Ruth began, her voice slow, like she was letting each word drop and settle into our hearts.

'Beloved, do not believe every spirit, but test the spirits, whether they are of God; because many false prophets have gone out into the world.'

"John is telling us here, don't trust everything you hear just because it sounds spiritual," she explained. "Not every voice that says 'God told me' is from God. You test it. Like a jeweler checks if a diamond is real, we test messages and spirits through God's Word."

That caught my attention. I'd been tested by school. Pushed by peers. Pressured by expectations. And I'd failed more than once at trusting the wrong people. But what did it mean to *test* something to see if it was from God?

She continued.
 'By this you know the Spirit of God: Every spirit that confesses that Jesus Christ has come in the flesh is of God...' (v.2)
 "So that's the first test," Ruth said. "Do they believe that Jesus came in the flesh—fully God, fully man? That's non-negotiable."
 I scribbled that down in my new journal.

'Jesus came in the flesh. Fully God. Fully man.

...and every spirit that does not confess that Jesus Christ has come in the flesh is not of God.' (v.3)

"This is the spirit of the Antichrist," she continued. "Strong language, right? But John's drawing a line. It's either truth or it's deception. There's no in-between."

My chest felt tight again. I didn't know if I completely believed yet—but something in me whispered *knowing how to tell the difference between truths and lies mattered more than I wanted to admit. Like that part at least was important, not because it made sense, but even now, I don't even know what makes sense.*
 Ruth went on.

'You are of God, little children, and have overcome them, because He who is in you is greater than he who is in the world.' (v.4)

That one. That verse.

Ruth paused. "That's one to hold onto when you feel surrounded by darkness. Greater is He who is in you. If you're in Christ, then whatever mess the world throws at you. You will be able to overcome, but only if you believe and have faith in Jesus."

Kaz gave me a little nudge again. I didn't even look at him, just smiled faintly, grateful for the gesture.

'They are of the world. Therefore they speak as of the world, and the world hears them.' (v.5)

"Basically," Ruth said, "don't be surprised when people love what's trending but hate the truth. The world celebrates what agrees with it. But truth doesn't change just because it's unpopular."

That hit harder than expected. I thought of Merrick, of how easily lies can wear suits and smile and hold your hand while stabbing your soul. He was anything but truth, and everyone celebrated him.

Ruth didn't slow down.

'We are of God. He who knows God hears us; he who is not of God does not hear us. By this we know the spirit of truth and the spirit of error.' (v.6)

"So you see?" she said, pacing a little now, energized by her teaching. "Truth and error have voices. And if you're walking with God, your spirit will start to recognize the difference. It's a gift from God called Discernment."

And then came the shift in tone.

'Beloved, let us love one another, for love is of God; and everyone who loves is born of God and knows God.' (v.7)

That soft part of my heart that still believed in love, the real kind, perked up its ears.

I guess my heart isn't completely dead after all.

'The one who does not love does not know God, for God is love.' (v.8)

"I have said this before, and I'll say it once again: love isn't just something God does. It's who He is," Ruth smiled, her tone softer now. "So if someone claims to know God, but they walk in hatred or manipulation or abuse, they're lying. That's not God."

I swallowed. Hard.

Verse after verse came, unfolding something both sharp and soft.

'In this the love of God was manifested toward us, that God has sent His only begotten Son into the world, that we might live through Him.' (v.9)

'In this is love, not that we loved God, but that He loved us and sent His Son to be the propitiation for our sins.' (v.10)

"Real love isn't about you climbing up to God," Ruth said. "It's Him coming down to you, because you couldn't save yourself."

That was new. That was… different.

She kept going.

'Beloved, if God so loved us, we also ought to love one another.' (v.11)

That made sense. But it scared me. Because how could I ever love like that? Especially after what he did. How do I open my heart up, knowing it could be trampled upon once more?

'No one has seen God at any time[1]. If we love one another, God abides in us, and His love has been perfected in us.' (v.12)

'By this we know that we abide in Him, and He in us, because He has given us of His Spirit.' (v.13)

It all felt like a soft wave, washing over the rough edges that life had cut out in me.

Verse 18 finally did me in.

'There is no fear in love; but perfect love casts out fear, because fear involves torment. But he who fears has not been made perfect in love.'

I felt like someone had taken a flashlight and aimed it right at my soul.

Fear. That was what I lived in. Constantly. Even before what happened.

But if there was such a thing as perfect love, and it could live inside me, maybe fear didn't have to.

By the time Ruth read the final verse—

'And this commandment we have from Him: that he who loves God must love his brother also.' (v.21)

—I was holding back tears. It felt like my entire life had just been one big ole lie.

When the study concluded, the room buzzed with soft conversation and the sound of shuffling feet.

I sat still with unshed tears, staring at my journal.

And I wrote:

If this love is real... I want to know it. Not secondhandly. Not as a theory, but for me, for myself, because Amerei deserves that.

Because if God's love was powerful enough to cast out fear...

I was ready to ask it to cast out mine.

By the end, I had underlined most of the chapter. My little notebook, my brand new one that I made kaz stop so I could buy yesterday, was already filled with scribbles and thoughts I didn't know I had space for.

When Ruth closed with a prayer, I didn't bow my head. I stared at the page. Because I was still stuck in a place where I had no immediate direction, I was lost in this oblivion of nothingness. I don't even know how to explain it, but as my mind, actions, words, and thoughts were stuck in a thick space of fog.

I wasn't sure if I was ready to accept.

I wasn't ready to call myself a believer. Not yet. But I wasn't rolling my eyes at the thought either.

As people continued to pack up and chat again, I stayed still, running my finger over a single phrase I'd highlighted.

"Walk in truth and love."

Maybe that was a start.

Maybe it was time to stop running and start asking real questions.

Chapter 76: Walks, Whispers, and Barbie Nights

Amerei POV

I stood up and gave a little stretch, arms over my head, feeling the mild ache from sitting so long.

Mita found me quickly, linking her arm through mine with a quiet smile.

"You okay?" she asked.

"Yeah. I think I'm more than okay," I said, glancing over at Kaz, who was now talking with Zeb and Andromeda near the chairs. Before turning back to Mita, giving her a smile to reassure her that I was indeed fine.

Eventually, the group of us naturally were clustered at the door: me, Mita, Meda, Kaz, Zeb, Anika, Ethan, and Zyran—laughing at some comment Zyran made about the iced tea tasting like "regret and lemon-scented floor cleaner."

When we stepped out of the student union building into the night air, everything felt softer somehow. The stars peeked out in a velvety sky, and a breeze gently swept across the campus walkways.

"I'm walking Anika to her car, so I'll catch y'all later," Ethan said, gently touching her arm to guide her path as she nodded as the two veered off in another direction.

"Night, guys!" Anika called.

Zyran gave a lazy two-finger salute and wandered toward the boys' dorms with a slight swagger. "Y'all don't do anything I wouldn't do," he smirked.

"You say that like your bar is high," Mita called after him.

He threw a wink over his shoulder. "It's higher than my grades, and that's sayin' something."

We all laughed, and just like that, the group thinned.

Zeb and Meda veered off down the arts building path, talking in hush-hush tones, Meda's soft laugh trailing behind them like wind-chimes.

Which left me and Kaz, walking side by side back toward the dorms, because Mita went ahead with Zyran.

"So," he said after a few beats, "how was your day before the club?"

"Busy. I had a full schedule of classes, back-to-back. My brain is basically oatmeal right now. You?"

"Same," he empathized. "Group projects are chaos and a nightmare rolled into one big burrito. I swear one of my teammates thinks memes are a research method."

I laughed. "Please, no."

"I wish I was kidding."

We walked a little more in silence, comfortable and calm.

"By the way," Kaz said, tilting his head toward me, "if you had any questions about the study or anything Ruth went through tonight, you can totally call me later."

I looked up at him. "You're seriously offering to get another hour of me blabbering after you already endured last night?"

"I enjoy your blabbering."

I raised an eyebrow, fighting a smile. "Dangerous words."

"I stand by them."

I nudged his shoulder. "Okay, then. I'll take you up on that. But only if we balance it out with something like—your insane hot takes on fonts or ice cream flavors."

"Deal. Oh, and also… are you free tomorrow?" he asked, a little more carefully now.

I blinked. "Um. I think so, yeah."

"Wanna hang? We could do a little study session, knock out the last of your assignments, and maybe finish the day with Bible study. If you're up for it."

I hesitated.

"Yeah. I'd like that."

He smiled. A soft, real one. "Cool. It's a date."

"Not a date-date." I said before I could think of a reasonable reply

"Of course not," he said, clearly amused.

We reached the entrance to the dorm building.

Kaz rubbed the back of his neck. "Alright, then. Goodnight, Erei."

"Night, Kaz."

He waited until I stepped inside, then turned and headed in the direction we had just come

.

When I made it up to the dorm, I pushed open the door and saw Mita sitting cross-legged on the couch, still in her clothes from earlier, the TV remote in hand.

She looked up and grinned. "Up for a Barbie movie marathon?"

I dropped my bag with a dramatic sigh and flopped onto the couch, laying my head across both her lap and the pillow beside her.

"I'll order the food," I offered.

"Look at you contributing to society."

"I'm the real MVP," I muttered, my eyes closed as I exhaled a long, content breath.

Mita started flipping through the options. "We doing classic Barbie or the cinematic masterpieces like *Princess and the Pauper*?"

"Please," I drawled. "I'm not a barbarian. Start with *Fairytopia* or we're not friends."

I ordered the food while she queued up the movie. The room glowed pink as the opening credits played. I didn't move from her lap, and she didn't ask me to.

Sometime between the second movie and the arrival of spring rolls and boba tea, Meda texted to say she was crashing with Zeb at the studio—*strictly to work on his canvas,* she emphasized with about ten eye-roll emojis.

We didn't judge. Not tonight. Tonight was for soft things. Safe things.

The kind of night where laughter was easy and food was comforting and the ache in your chest wasn't so loud. A night where healing didn't feel impossible.

And as Barbie gave a dramatic speech about friendship and destiny, I let myself believe, even if only for a moment, that I might be okay.

Chapter 77: Lines of Light and Laughter

After Bible study, in the evening air outside the student union, Andromeda and Zeb peeled away from the group as the others laughed their way across the quad under warm lamplight.

Zeb held the door to the arts building open for her, and they made their way up the stairs and through the silent halls until they reached his studio tucked near the back—a haven of creativity that always smelled like turpentine, paint, and sandalwood.

Andromeda dropped her bag by the couch and pulled up the sleeves of her silk blouse as she glanced around the room.

They settled onto the floor with their backs against the couch, talking through the teaching they'd just heard. Zeb was thoughtful as always, drawing lines from Scripture into real life, and Andromeda listened—half pondering, half enjoying the mellow cadence of his voice.

But then his phone buzzed; glancing at it, he paused with brows furrowed, and his face contorted into a quiet, horrified expression.

"What's wrong?" Andromeda asked, instantly alert.

Zeb blinked as if she pulled him back to reality. "I… I have an assignment due by 6 a.m."

She blinked. "And you're just now remembering this?"

"I didn't know! I swear. It wasn't on my calendar—I think my professor updated the portal late."

He ran a hand through his hair, pacing once before dropping into his desk chair.

Andromeda sat there waiting for him to tell her what the assignment was about, but lost her patience. " Zeb, what is the assignment about?"

"It's a video project. We're supposed to capture the creation of an abstract representation of a real human and their emotions. The catch is… it has to be based on a live model. Filmed. Start to finish."

He got up and began pacing again.

Andromeda stared at him like he was missing the obvious because to her, he was. "…..hello? What am I, chopped liver? I can model for you. Just draw me."

Zeb blinked. "What?" It took him some time to understand what she said

"Are you sure? I mean, I'd need to film parts of it—not, like, a full feature or anything. Just a time-lapse. Are you comfortable with that?"

Her eyes narrowed, playful. "Zebedee. I'm literally offering to help you not fail. Yes. I'm okay with being recorded, clear?

He chuckled. "Crystal clear."

With that, they got to work. Zebedee adjusted the lighting setup while Andromeda tied her hair up and adjusted her top. The camera was positioned on a tripod and angled to capture the whole room with a wide focus, in order to capture the mood of the space.

"Could you hand me my phone before we start?" she asked.

He passed it to her, and she shot off a quick text to the group chat.

Andromeda: Hey, girls. I'm at Zeb's studio helping with a last-minute art project, and he has to film it for class.

Andromeda: It is purely just work, so don't even go there.

She handed him the phone back. "Okay. Fire it up."

Zeb pressed record and turned toward his easel.

He envisioned a diptych. In the first panel, he wanted to capture Meda in her quiet, impenetrable facial expressions and body language—best described as 'still and assertive'—the kind of stillness that feels like a reinforced wall of glass: reflective, unreadable, and beautiful in its distance. It's tinted, but if you come close enough, you can see at least a bit of what's inside. The wall—the glass—is hardened; if you try to hit it with blunt force, the weapon you use will ricochet, in turn, causing you harm. But if you take the time to understand the different parts, you can use a hammer and chisel, carefully chipping away her facade. Only then can you discover the different layers, understand how they are made, and appreciate the effort, though not necessarily endorse it.

And when you reach the innermost layer, allow the creator of the wall to break it themselves. That's how I would describe Meda. It's the expression she wears when she retreats inward, signaling depth but denying access, an elegance that unnerves, even manipulates some, but that's how he felt when he tried to describe the first day of meeting her up to now.

The second panel would be the unveiling: her guard down, her smile blooming wide and real, the kind that lights from the eyes and spills warmth across her whole face. That rare moment of unfiltered joy, where the soul peeks through and the distance dissolves. Two sides of her spirit in conversation: mystery and openness, shadow and light.

Then he began the first piece.

He didn't want to think about anything, to rationalize anything, or to make anything perfect; he just wanted to replicate what he saw onto the canvas for 100% accuracy, authenticity, and genuineness.

He moved in silence, occasionally lifting his head to study her, then ducking down to fill the canvas with angular shapes and smears of expressive color. The air was still except for the scratch of pencil, the soft swish of paint on canvas, and the low hum of the space heater.

Then, phase two.

Zeb stood up and glanced over at her.

He knew he couldn't ask her to relax—real moments couldn't be summoned like that. So instead, he started talking. Not about the painting, but about their time together during winter break.

"Remember the snowball that hit you in the face? The one you tried to catch?" he said, grinning.

She groaned, but her lips twitched. "I was *helping* you build that fort and *You* betrayed me."

"That fort was doomed the moment you started adding a skylight to it," he teased.

She laughed, and then it began, her shoulders loosening, eyes flickering with mischief. And he kept going.

He reminded her of the late-night walks, how she hummed to herself without realizing it. The way she got misty-eyed over cinnamon rolls in that sleepy café with the fogged-up windows. The inside jokes, the quiet confessions they shared, the endless movie nights, and even her stick people, which she used to draw when she just started to draw.

He didn't need to say, '*Relax for me.*' Instead, he brought her back to the warmth of those moments and let her sink into them until she wasn't posing anymore—she was just there.

That's when it happened. Her smile unfolded naturally, slow and real, reaching all the way to her eyes. That was the moment he'd been waiting for. The brush paused midair because now, she wasn't just a subject. She was the memory. The softness of a beautiful of the story.

"What?"

He grinned. "Nothing"

He continued recounting ridiculous moments from their winter break— the time she'd slipped on ice and tried to make it look cool, the "frozen pizza masterpiece" night, and the impromptu game of paintbrush sword-fighting.

Andromeda groaned between giggles. "You're such a dork."

"Correct. But I'm your dork for the next hour," he said, brushing bright strokes into the canvas while she giggled at her own stories.

She added one, recounting the time Odessa mistook hot sauce for strawberry jam and nearly lit her own tongue on fire. They both erupted into laughter.

Andromeda didn't even notice the camera anymore, and Zeb worked with a kind of intensity, evidently showing that this was his passion, or maybe she was. He wasn't just painting her image; he was painting her. Her layers. Her contrast. Her light.

After nearly 8 hours, he clicked the camera off and stretched.

"All done. Well, mostly. Just a few finishing touches left," he said with a tired but satisfied smile. "You, on the other hand, it's really late, and I don't feel comfortable with you walking back tonight. Plus, I'm too tired to walk or drive you back. You cool with that?"

She nodded.

"So go ahead and blow up the mattress for me and take the bed. It's in the room in the cupboard to your left. I need to get this done."

She did just that, but instead of taking the bed and blowing up the mattress for him, she dragged it close to the couch and took it for herself, flopping onto it with a soft sigh, watching him work.

She didn't want to be in the room with the door between them, see wanted to see him, and the couch could unfold into a bed, which was even more comfortable than this mattress, so it was a win-win for both of them.

There was always a kind of glow about him when he was painting—subtle, but unmistakable. Like something inside him brightened the longer he was lost in the strokes and colors. *This must really be his passion,* she thought.

Silence settled around them, save for the quiet sound of Zeb's brush moving across the canvas. She guessed it lasted about three minutes—just him, the paints, and the focus in his eyes.

Then she broke it, deadpan.

"Now feed me. You made me emote for two hours."

Zeb chuckled. "I'll order Chinese. You earned it."

She grinned from her place on the mattress. "And don't forget dumplings this time."

He shot her a playful salute. "Yes, ma'am."

Andromeda watched him move across the studio, surrounded by canvases and color, and smiled quietly to herself. She liked this world of his. Most of all, she liked that he let her be part of it.

Chapter 78: The Guarded and The Revealing

Andromeda POV

The sun filtered softly through the tall windows of Zeb's studio, cutting through the leftover quiet of the early morning. Golden rays fell across the hardwood floor in sleepy stripes, and I blinked against the glow as I turned on my side. The air smelled like dry paint and eucalyptus soap—the familiar scent of him.

I'd fallen asleep still dressed in the same trousers and sleeveless turtleneck shirt from yesterday. I couldn't remember the moment sleep claimed me, somewhere between eating the final bite of the takeout and Zeb saying he was almost done with his final strokes, muttering something about checking the footage before morning. He stayed up way longer than me, working under the loud hum of his studio lights.

I sat up slowly, stretching out my arms, then looked over at the mattress.

Zeb was curled up with one arm behind his head, the other across his chest. His sketchbook rested closed on the floor beside him. Even in sleep, he looked like art. That same quiet intensity lingered in the corners of his features: the high slope of his cheekbones catching the soft light, the way his lashes fell over his cheeks in a delicate fan. His brows were relaxed, finally. He always wore his thoughts too loud on his face, but now there was peace there. His lips were parted just slightly, like he was mid-breath, mid-thought. Still thinking, even in sleep. That man never stops.

Wait, did I fall asleep on the mattress?! How did I get here?

Then I look over at Zeb once more, putting the piece together…. *this beautiful man.*

I stared too long. Way too long.

Quickly, I blinked myself out of it and turned away, standing slowly and tiptoeing across the studio floor. The canvases were still up on their easels, turned deliberately away from the rest of the room. My curiosity burned in my chest.

Last night had been such a rush of lighting, cameras, and posing. I tried to recount the events; by the time we were done, we'd barely spoken. I'd ordered food, he kept painting, and then… I crashed.

Now, I was alone with the result of it all.

I padded over and came around the easels.

And froze.

Taken aback by what I saw

These weren't just paintings. They were stories that I couldn't explain, but I'm sure an experienced artist could. But I knew these were amazing.

One canvas, titled at the bottom of the easel, said *The Guarded.* In the piece, I was captured in deep blues, grays, and bruised plums. My expression was calm, unreadable. My pose—sitting upright, eyes to the side, lips tight—was familiar, even to me. But Zeb had abstracted everything. My jawline was suggested with a sweep of shadow; my eyes were geometric fragments. Sharp angles whispered things no photograph ever could. I looked like a locked vault.

That was the point, wasn't it?

Next to it, the second canvas glowed with warmth. *The Revealing.* Soft oranges, golden yellows, rich cream tones swirled through the form of a girl laughing. Me. Except the me in this painting was… for lack of better words, alive. Hair messy and untamed, face lit with uninhibited joy, one hand thrown back. It was like he'd caught the exact second before the world had a chance to weigh me down again. The strings of orange mixed with gold began at my eye and circled my face in a tight circumferential spiral wrapping around the entirety of my face, then loosened as the spiral moved down my frame in a blurred effect. It was beautiful.

Both paintings together, side by side, looked like a mirror and a dream.

I felt something press behind my eyes. Well, I never…

He saw me

Maybe more than I saw myself.

A notification chimed in on my phone, catching me off guard.

My throat tightened with emotion as I reached for my phone.

Amerei: Meet. Now. Please. Emergency.

Then I grabbed my coat, slipped my shoes on, and left before he could wake up.

Chapter 79: Tension in the Air

Amerei POV

Knock, knock, knock.

I blinked slowly at the ceiling, brain still wrapped in the fuzzy veil of sleep. Groggy, still halfway in a dream I couldn't remember.

Another knock.

This time, I stirred, a groan escaped as I rolled onto my side. I attempted to stand, only to get tangled in the blanket like a fish caught in a net and tumble right off the bed with an ungraceful thud. "Ow."

Knock, knock, knock.

"Mita," I mumbled, eyes half-closed as I tried to shake off the cobwebs in my mind.

But then I heard the front door open. Mita's voice, muffled by the distance, talking to someone. I laid back down, sighing in relief. At least someone had the strength to answer the door at this hour in the morning. Last night had been long and emotionally heavy in ways I couldn't put into words.

I'd forgotten to call Kaz. I groaned inwardly. Another mental note to apologize later.

I heard her footsteps coming toward me. Then the door creaked open, and

Mita's head popped through.

"Good morning, Ame," she said far too cheerfully for this hour. Then her face turned serious. "So… we have a problem. The dorm manager wants to speak with you, now."

That sobered me faster than any cup of coffee ever could. "Huh? What?"

"I don't know either, but I'm coming with you," she added, already closing the door.

No questions. No hesitation.

I showered, dressed, and let her help brush the knots out of my half-wet curls while we made our way across campus to the Housing Administrative building. It was still early—sunlight and too bright. Everyone was in a weekend daze.

The moment we reached the dorm office, someone ushered us straight into the office like we were guests at a pre-scheduled appointment.

Or suspects.

The worker knocked before we heard a *'come in'* before they turned and left us there.

Was she that strict? Did I do something wrong?

That thought turned my stomach with knots bigger than those still in my damp hair.

Behind the desk sat a woman with sharp features, short cropped gray hair that curled perfectly at the ends, glasses low on her nose, and the kind of no-nonsense energy that made you want to sit up straighter.

"Good morning, girls. You must be Amerei Galanis, and I'm guessing, you are her roommate, Mitalmim Aziz?"

"Yes, ma'am," we chorused.

"Please. Have a seat." Her voice was polite, but clipped.

"I'm Mrs. Spencer, the manager of the female dormitory wing. Let's get straight to the point, if you don't mind."

I swallowed, trying to dislodge the lump formed in the back of my throat.

"I know you and Mr. Hughes are in a relationship, and I'm aware his family are long-standing donors and honorary alumni of this noble and accredited institution. But that being said, Ms. Galanis, I can't give you two leeways to do as much as you like here. If I did, it would cause an uproar with the rest of the student body. Therefore, yesterday's incident? We'd like this not to happen again."

Wait. What?

I froze; just hearing his name made my insides hurl. My fingers curled into fists in my lap. Mita's hand found mine under the table, squeezing gently.

"I… I'm sorry, ma'am?" Mita leaned forward. "I don't think we understand what's going on. What exactly is the issue?"

Mrs. Spencer sighed, folding her hands together on the desk. "Ms. Galanis, I've turned a blind eye to you staying out and not returning to the dorm. You've never caused any trouble before. Your academic record is outstanding. But last night was too far. Bringing a male guest into the female dorms during the semester is against policy. I can overlook certain things, but this…"

"Wait—what?!" Mita and I said at the same time.

"I didn't— I never brought anyone in," I said, my voice cracking slightly. My hands began to shake.

Mrs. Spencer didn't argue. She just turned to her computer and clicked a few keys before turning the monitor to face us.

CCTV Footage played.

There I was. Entering the dorm building after class, and then the footage cut to me entering my room from the hallway. Then another cut in the video.

"About 30 minutes later," Mrs. Spencer said.

A staff member accepting cash from Merrick. And him walking through the same doors, slipping through without signing in. The timestamp— indeed, thirty minutes after I came in.

My stomach dropped. My breathing hitched.

The screen changed to the hallway outside our dorm room. Merrick typed my room code and walked inside. Alone. Like he belonged there. Like it was his right. How does he even know our room code?

I felt sick. Wanting to dry heave, I was barely holding myself together.

My hands were fists now, but trembling ones. Mita, like the angel she is, shifted and placed her hand gently on my knee, grounding me. I didn't realize how badly my legs were shaking until she did.

More footage.

Me. Leaving two hours later, in my clothes for Bible study.

Then Merrick. Ten minutes after me.

But when he exited the dorm building, he didn't go the same direction as me.

Mrs. Spencer paused the footage. On him.

Something glinted near his jacket. Something in his hand. It caught in the light just enough to make out—

I stood up abruptly.

"I'm sorry," I gasped.

I didn't wait for permission. I just bolted. Out of the office. Down the hall.

My fingers fumbled for my phone, unlocking it with a shaking thumb. I opened the group chat.

Me: "Meet. Now. Please. Emergency."

Mita caught up with me halfway down the hall. "It's okay," she whispered. "We'll figure it out."

Her voice was steady, even as I felt like my world was slipping through the cracks beneath me. I didn't know what Merrick had planned. I didn't know what he *didn't* plan. But I knew this—it was getting worse.

And I needed help.

Now.

Chapter 80: I Just Needed to Breathe

Amerei POV

When we got back to the dorm, I still felt underwater.

Everything around me moved in real time while I lagged somewhere behind it—half-seeing, half-hearing, soaked in confusion, fear, and anger all at once.

I sat on the edge of my bed while Mita hovered nearby saying something I couldn't fully process. Her voice sounded muffled beneath the ringing in my ears.

My head bowed low, elbows on knees.

I just sat there.

Yesterday kept replaying in my head on a loop.

I remembered coming back after classes completely exhausted. I didn't even bother changing before collapsing into bed.

Then I woke up with that feeling again.

That horrible crawling discomfort beneath my skin.

The kind that makes you want to scrub your soul clean, not just your body.

I'd gone to wash up, hoping it would help.

It didn't.

Afterward, I grabbed my journal—the new one I bought after the lighthouse trip Kaz and I took together—and tried writing for a while.

Mostly about the things Kaz had told me.

About good and evil, about God and the devil.

Why is the world so broken.

Then came that feeling again.

That pull.

I couldn't explain it properly, but suddenly I needed to leave the dorm.

Immediately.

Not panic exactly. Just urgency.

Get out. Now.

Before I could overthink it, I grabbed my phone, my journal, and my pencil case and walked out.

Then Meda and Mita texted me.

The timing still felt impossible.

Too precise.

Too deliberate.

After the meeting with Mrs. Spencer, I told the others everything.

The footage.

The office.

My fears.

Every detail.

After that, we tore through the dorm searching for anything Merrick could've planted—cameras, microphones, trackers. None of us trusted the room anymore.

Mita called Odessa, and Odessa immediately contacted her brother. He said he'd send a female security professional to sweep the dorm properly just in case.

We had to think carefully about everything now.

Even trying to protect ourselves felt dangerous.

That's how far this had gone.

We didn't want to risk Merrick picking up on anything and assuming the worst.

As Mita pointed out, Mrs. Spencer had practically begged us to caution Merrick about his actions moving forward.

The school didn't want problems with his family.

They were scared of the Hughes. I knew all along.

And now, I am scared of him.

Later, Odessa's brother FaceTimed us. His voice stayed calm, but there was urgency underneath it.

"We've got movement," he said. "I won't go into details yet for your safety, but the company's being pressured right now. Strategically. Not enough to make them panic—just enough to distract them. When they get comfortable again, that's when everything gets exposed publicly."

His confidence should've reassured me.

Instead, I just felt exhausted.

Completely drained..

A few minutes into the conversation, my mind started drifting away from it entirely. From the room. From reality.

By the time the call ended, I could barely breathe inside my own skin.

"I want to be alone for a little," I said quietly.

That was immediately met with protests.

"No."

"Amerei, that's not a good idea."

"At least let one of us come with you."

But I insisted. "I'm not leaving the building. I just need to walk."

Eventually, they gave in.

So I left the room and wandered through the dorm halls like a ghost.

The urge to cut was still there.

Sharp.

Persistent.

But the girls were nearby, and somehow that alone stopped me from acting on it.

So instead, I forced myself to keep walking.

To go on a mini sightseeing venture in the building.

The building looked exactly the same as always, but nothing felt normal anymore. Every echoing footstep made me tense. Every sound behind a closed door made my chest tighten.

Still, I kept moving.

One step.

Then another.

Telling myself I could get through the next minute.

Then the next.

Eventually, I pulled out my phone.

Me: "Hey… can we meet up right now? Are you free?"

Kaz: "Yeah. Where are you?"

Me: "On dorm."

Kaz: "Okay. I'm leaving now."

I didn't say anything back. I just stared at the wall in front of me and slowly slid down against the one behind me, to the floor, back pressed to the cool plaster, pulling my knees to my chest.

I clutched my journal to my chest.

And for the first time,

I prayed. Not out loud.

Not some grand gesture.

Just me.

Whispering to God.

"God... I'm still iffy about all of this. I'm not gonna lie and pretend otherwise. But your

Existence is starting to make sense to me, and right now I need help like yesterday. I feel like maybe you were the reason I left the dorm yesterday. It can't just be a coincidence. So please...protect me. Keep Merrick far away from me. Distract him. Make me invisible to him. Let him stop loving me—or whatever that was—but please keep him away from me. And please... let justice come." My voice cracked as tears blurred my vision. **"In Jesus' name... Amen."**

The whisper disappeared into the empty hallway.

Then another thought hit me.

It was Saturday.

Mita and Meda missed music club because of me. Odessa probably should've been at work.

But instead they stayed.

Stayed for me.

And all I could think about earlier was how trapped I felt because they wouldn't leave me alone long enough to hurt myself.

The guilt sat heavy in my chest.

So I stayed there quietly, thinking about the prayer.

Waiting.

Hoping God heard me.

Not expecting some huge miracle.

Just peace.

Even a little bit of it.

A few minutes later, my phone buzzed.

"Kaz," I breathed.

And then I ran.

I didn't care who saw me crying.

Didn't care that tears blurred my vision or that I looked completely wrecked.

I just ran.

I didn't want explanations.

Didn't want advice.

Didn't want logic.

I just wanted him.

His hug.

His comfort.

His soft eyes that never demanded anything from me.

His gentle voice that somehow always met me exactly where I was.

I just wanted his presence.

I wanted Kaz.

And when I finally reached him, I collapsed into his arms like something inside me had been running toward that moment long before my body caught up.

He held me immediately.

No questions.

No hesitation.

Just warmth.

And for the first time in what felt like forever—

I felt *safe*.

Chapter 81: Return to the Lighthouse

PLAYLIST- WHAT A MIRACLE FEELS LIKE BY TAUREN WELLS

Amerei POV

As he opened the door for me after our hug, he got in,

"Drive. Drive far," I said the moment he shut the car door behind him, my voice barely above a whisper. "Back to the lighthouse."

Kaz didn't ask any questions. He didn't even blink. Just gave a short nod, shifted gears, and we pulled away from the dorm. The soft hum of his tires melted into the even softer gospel playlist he always had rolling low in the background. It felt like the only sound brave enough to ride with my silence.

I stared out the window the entire time, my mind a blur, the city thinning behind us like smoke. Every mile away from campus felt like air returning to my lungs. I didn't know why the lighthouse had become my place, but it had. Maybe because it was the last place I remembered feeling truly safe. Maybe because it was mine and Kaz's.

When we got there, neither of us made a move to get out. He cut the engine, and we sat in stillness for a few moments.

Then I turned toward him and collapsed into his arms.

I cried. Like ugly, full-body crying—the kind that made your ribcage hurt. Kaz didn't try to stop me. He didn't speak. He just held me, arms wrapped tightly around me like he was holding my very soul in place.

And when I finally calmed down, I looked up at him, knowing my eyes were red and puffy, my body still shaking. "I'm sorry," I said, looking at how my tears soaked his shirt, and my snot was running down my nose, and some on his shirt.

He passed me a box of tissues. "You never have to apologize for being human," he soothed, brushing hair from my face with fingers, tucking it back in place as gently as a whispered lullaby so it wouldn't get in the way of my snot.

I laughed, just a little. "You're perfect, you know that?"

He shook his head. "Not even close."

"Then maybe you're just perfect for me."

What the heck just came out of my mouth? Am I forgetting my situation?

I chuckled to brush it off as a joke.

"Okay, okay—enough about me crying over my demons. Let's do Bible study. Oh, and teach me how to pray. Like, properly." I said, trying desperately to change the topic, not giving him any room to address the crap that came out of my mouth.

He raised a brow. "How do you know that I even brought a Bible?"

"Are you kidding me right now? You always bring a Bible. Probably more than one. Don't think I don't notice your backpack is basically half library."

He laughed, reaching into the backseat, handing me one. "Alright then, Miss Observant. Let's start with 1 Timothy 2:4."

We flipped there together. His voice was calm, steady.

***"[God] who wants everyone to be saved and to come to the knowledge of the truth."* 1 Timothy 2:4**

"Okay, so let's break this down," he said. "It says God *wants* everyone to be saved. That means He's not picking favorites. He wants you, me, even the worst of us—He wants *all* of us. The hard part is that not everyone ***wants Him.***"

"That's kinda sad," I whispered.

"Yeah. But it also means you're *not* disqualified," Kaz said, looking at me with so much warmth I had to glance away. "No matter what's happened to you or what you've done. He still wants you to know Him."

I nodded slowly. "Okay... I like that."

"Alright," he said, flipping pages. "Next one. Matthew 7:21–23."

"Not everyone who says to me, 'Lord, Lord,' will enter the kingdom of heaven, but only the one who does the will of my Father who is in heaven. Many will say to me on that day, 'Lord, Lord, did we not prophesy in your name, drive out demons in your name and do many miracles in your name' Then I will tell them plainly, 'I never knew you. Away from me, you evildoers!'"

"That one sounds... scary," I said honestly.

"It is," he admitted. "But it's also a wake-up call. You can wear the title, go to church, post Bible quotes—but if it doesn't come from a real relationship, a real heart change, Jesus is saying... 'I never *knew* you.' because they never took the time to know him. They just know of him and what he could do, that's it. They won't be accepted into heaven by their work and what they did, nor by their accomplishments, nor by their qualifications. Only by salvation, which is the only admission into Heaven," he paused. "It is understandable why people believe that all their works and accomplishments will get them there, by them being a 'good person,' because in this world, to get a job, you have to have these requirements, some more specific than others.

You need experience for almost everything, whether it's getting into college, earning a promotion, securing a loan, opening a bank account, or being accepted into organizations, even charitable ones. Everywhere you turn, there are requirements to be met. This pattern starts early in life: for children, the word *requirements* is simply replaced with the *expectations* and the main could be of their parents.

It has been carved into our minds from youth, molded into us a mindset I like to call **'the checkbox mentality'**, which is understandable, God knows that, but He is telling you that, *that's not who I am*, because this checkbox mentality is not authentic, it's not genuine, and it's definitely not intimacy. That is why when God speaks of the Earth and the Heavens, he makes a huge separation, even though he created Earth, because the mindset and the lifestyle that we created, adopted, and continued to build on to further complicate our lives unnecessarily are in complete opposition to how heaven is, so they can never and will never be the same." Kaz explained, turning further in to face me.

"That's why God calls us to be set apart, and that's why the bible calls us a new creation in him in, I believe, 2 Corinthians 5:17, because we interact with this world differently. That's why he said our qualifications don't get us into heaven. He is basically saying in Matthew 7, 'If you thought that works is the way into heaven, then you never got to know me or what I did on the cross, you just heard *about* me and what I can do.'

For example, it is known that knowing someone on camera is different from getting to know them off camera. Though Jesus would be the same on and off camera, they just saw miracles and how powerful his name is; but, what about knowing what his likes, his dislikes, his favorite color, his favorite food, his hobbies, his personality, what makes him laugh, or what is his favorite joke, nothing; they know nothing of the sort. But they wanted Jesus the powerful and the Jesus who gets you into heaven.

People are using Jesus like a free admission ticket into heaven, thinking they're his +1s

I think many people misunderstand Revelation 20:12–13, where it says our works will be judged. The "works" being spoken of are not just outward actions, but the posture of your heart. It's about why you did what you did; whether you helped, gave, or served out of genuine love, obedience, and alignment with God's will for your life.

Where was your heart in those moments? What was its true intention? Our actions can sometimes appear kind, and even body language can be trained to look genuine, but the heart never lies, and that's what God judges. We may stumble, sin, or fall short, but what matters is whether our hearts desire repentance, whether we grieve over sin, and whether we truly long to follow Him.

Some people can hide their lies well without any outward 'telltale', but our hearts always reveal the truth. And the incredible thing is, only God can fully know and read a person's heart. Not a doctor, therapist, friend, or even a parent, only God.

What he looks for is a heart marked by love, grace, mercy, humility, and surrender. Real humility opens the way to heaven. And while these gifts come from God, it's up to us to accept them freely in our will through the choices we make with our hearts."

"So it's not about being religious," I sought, "it's about actually *knowing* Him?"

"Yes," Kaz replied. "Doing what He says. Loving people. Seeking His truth. Not just… looking good on the outside."

I bit my lip. "So… like Merrick's family? The whole 'we go to church, we're donors, but secretly we're awful' kinda thing?"

He nodded gravely. "Exactly like that."

I sighed. "Okay. Hit me with the big one."

He grinned, "Ummm, 1 Timothy 4. Let's read this whole chapter."

We read it together, verse by verse. Then Kaz broke it down.

"Now the Spirit expressly says that in later times some will depart from the faith by devoting themselves to deceitful spirits and teachings of demons…"

"Basically," Kaz began, "it's warning us: people are going to start mixing lies with truth. Even in churches. Even in families. They'll water down the truth or twist it just enough that it *sounds* right, but it's deadly. ummm" He paused before continuing

"…through the insincerity of liars whose consciences are seared…"

"Seared conscience," he pointed, "means they can't feel conviction anymore. They don't flinch when they do wrong. That's dangerous. It's how abusers sleep at night. They've numbed themselves to right and wrong."

I felt that. Deep in my bones.

We kept going.

"Have nothing to do with irreverent, silly myths. Rather train yourself for godliness..."

"Train yourself," he emphasized. "Like an athlete. You don't just *get* strong—you train. Little by little. Reading. Praying. Asking God questions and being patient in waiting on his reply, and trusted people in the faith with sound teaching **that lines up with scripture in context**. Like what you're doing right now."

I smiled at that.

"...Set an example for the believers in speech, in conduct, in love, in faith, in purity..."

"That," he said, tapping the page, "is the standard. Not just preaching to others. *Living it.*"

I nodded again, slowly. "So... Jesus isn't about perfection. He's about transformation. About trying. Growing."

"Exactly," he said with a soft smile, seeming proud of me.

"And prayer?" I asked.

Kaz leaned back against the seat, seeming to look out the windshield. "There's no script. Just honesty. Like... telling God exactly what's on your heart. Thank Him. Ask Him stuff. Apologize when you do wrong and try your best to not let there be a repeat of the act, just as you would to a friend you care about. Praise Him. Or just... talk. But cover your prayers in 'Jesus' name,' similar to how his blood covers our sins."

"I think I did that earlier," I admitted. "I was desperate. I asked Him to keep Merrick away from me... to help justice win."

He nodded. "That counts. He heard you."

"Even though I'm not... official yet?"

"He loves you just the same."

I felt my throat tighten again. Not from grief this time, but from relief.

"Want to try praying again now?" he asked gently.

I nodded.

And there, in the quiet stillness of our safe place in his car , I bowed my head and prayed out loud. Hesitant. Nervous. Raw. But it was honest.

And when I was done, he just whispered, "Amen."

We sat together like that for a while, watching the water. The sun peeked through the clouds just a little, lighting the sea like it was made of silver.

Maybe, I thought, *this is what a miracle feels like.*

Chapter 82: A Breakthrough in the Hallway

Amerei POV

When I got back to the dorm, I thanked Kaz again for the day. There weren't enough words in the English language to explain what it meant to me: his presence, his patience, his heart. I smiled to myself as I stepped out of the car, waving goodbye as the door shut with a gentle thud. My fingers still tingled from where they had brushed his during the Bible study.

I rode the elevator up, and just as I reached my floor, my phone buzzed.

Merrick XO: *Who was that guy you just got out of the car with?*

I paused, dread flooding my body. I didn't reply. I couldn't. I just forced one foot in front of the other, bracing myself against the wall toward my dorm room, unlocking the door with my keycard in a daze.

Was he watching me?

Buzz.

Another message came in.

Merrick XO: *I came to visit you. You were sleeping, so I wanted to surprise you since we've both been busy. And you're cheating on me? Me—Merrick Hughes? I should've known you were no better than my ex.*

Buzz.

Merrick XO: *I wanted to talk about what happened after New Year's. You seemed kinda off about it, and I was giving you space—but now you've proven* *who you really are. I need a break, Ame.*

I stopped in the midway of opening my door. The words on my screen blurred through tears, but they weren't the usual kind. These were tears of **relief**. My legs gave out beneath me. Right there, in the quiet of the hallway, I dropped to the floor, clutching the phone to my chest.

My prayer.

God answered.

He heard me. That feeble, hesitant prayer I whispered *"Let Merrick lose interest. Let him fall out of love. Just keep him away from me."*

And He did.

It was not what I expected, but it was an answered prayer, nonetheless.

I cried harder. Not out of fear. Not out of heartbreak. Out of sheer disbelief and happiness that God **listened**.

The door burst open behind me, and I heard voices.

"Amerei? What happened?"

"Is it Merrick? Did Kaz do something?!"

"Are you okay?!"

A chorus of concern swelled around me, arms lifting me gently from the cold hallway floor. I was still clutching my phone when I looked up at their worried faces.

And then, for some reason, the first thing out of my mouth was, "Kaz told you, didn't he?" I half-laughed through the tears streaming down my cheeks.

The tension in the air eased slightly. Meda and Mita exchanged glances, relief washing over their features. Odessa came closer, kneeling before me, glancing at my phone that I was clutching toward my chest.

"What's going on?" she asked.

"Read the messages," I whispered, pushing the phone to the group of them

They huddled together, scrolling through the texts. The room filled with stunned silence, then—

"Are you kidding me?!"

"Oh my gosh—this is it."

"He's actually letting go!"

"Thank you, Jesus!"

They screamed, jumped, and some even cried. Mita wrapped me in the warmest hug I've felt in weeks.

"I knew it," she whispered into my hair. "God always delivers."

"I can't believe it," I said. "I mean…I *can*, but—"

"It's happening," Meda cut in. "This is the beginning of your freedom."

"I'm ordering food!" Odessa shouted from the kitchen. "This calls for celebration!"

"Movie and girl night!" Mita said, already pulling her laptop toward the TV.

Odessa, 'ever the composed one,' went into the bathroom to call her brother with the update; bits and pieces of their conversations seeped through the door.

I just sat there on the floor for a moment, looking up at the ceiling. But really, I wasn't looking at the ceiling. I was looking **through** it—**up**. My vision blurred again with tears, but this time, they didn't sting.

"Thank You," I whispered. "Thank You for hearing me. For answering. For proving me wrong in all the best ways."

Mita and Meda joined me in that silent moment, heads bowed. We didn't even have to speak. They were thanking Him too.

That night, I was **light**. So light, it felt like I was flying.

The rest of the weekend bloomed in golden moments. First we change the codes on the door. Then we watched movies, TMI over takeout, and fell asleep in a tangle of blankets and laughter. No fear, no masks. Just girls being girls. And girls being Free.

By Monday, I was back to routine: classes, group presentations, oral prep. But everything felt easier. Lighter. I felt like **me** again, only stronger. Not perfect, but healing.

And this time, I wasn't walking alone.

Chapter 83: The Symphony of Stillness

Andromeda POV

The week rolled by like a soft tide—no harsh waves, just a steady rhythm. And for the first time in what felt like months, my soul was breathing.

Amerei was safe. Not completely healed, not untouched by what happened, but safe. Safer than she'd been in a long time. I didn't realize how much weight I'd been carrying on my chest until I felt it lift.

Classes had picked up, especially my labs. The weeks after midterms were brutal. Lab reports were stacked like forgotten mail, and I was practically living in my white coat. I'd rush from lecture to the hospital and back again, my notes practically tattooed on my arm, caffeine in my veins. But I wasn't spiraling like last semester. My perfectionism wasn't dictating my worth. I was doing well, but not because I needed to be perfect—because I wanted to learn. That shift in mindset? That was God. No other explanation.

I didn't have as much time for myself as I wanted, and my hours with Zeb were limited to scattered texts, late-night study breaks, and passing waves on the quad. Still, even those moments were bright spots in my day. On Wednesday, he texted me:

Zeb: "GUESS WHO GOT TOP 3 IN THE EXHIBITION ENTRY!!! 👀🔥"

Me: "No way!! That's amazing, Zeb!! WHICH PLACE?"

Zeb: "They won't tell me yet They're announcing this Friday at the awards thing. I'm screaming on the inside."

Me: "I'M SCREAMING ON THE OUTSIDE. You're gonna win. I'm declaring it in Jesus name. ◼︎✨"

Zeb: "Please keep praying. I'm gonna cry if I don't at least place 2nd "

Me: "I'm already drafting my 'Congrats, you artistic king' text in case you win "

Zeb: "I'd cry for real if you sent that."

I smiled so hard at my phone that Mita asked if I was watching cat videos again.

But beyond school and friendships, God had been showing me something deeper in my quiet moments with Him. I always thought I needed big worship nights or loud declarations to feel close to Him. But this week? It was the stillness. My walks to class. The early mornings with my journal open and my tea going cold. The five-minute windows between back-to-back lectures where I'd pause, breathe, and say, "Thank You."

I was learning to make space for God not just on Sundays or Friday nights at Christian Club, but in my anatomy notes, in my messy handwriting during morphology lab, even in my exhaustion. And that... that was changing everything.

I found myself praying more intentionally. Not out of guilt. Out of desire.

Sometimes it was just a whisper:

"Help me focus."

"Thank You for peace."

"Please keep Amerei steady."

Speaking of Amerei, our friendship had shifted too, grown deeper. She'd come into my room some evenings and ask me how I prayed. Not once or twice. Nearly every day.

"I know there's no 'right' way," she'd say, "but like... how do you start?"

I'd smile, set down my laptop, and share what I knew.

We talked about

Adoration—just telling God how amazing He is, not that God needs compliments, but do it with a genuine heart.

Confession—being real and honest not only about our sin but also about our desires as well.

Thanksgiving—listing the biggest and even the smallest joys and explaining that the smallest joys are important to remind ourselves of and how praying about them helps with our gratitude and adoration toward Jesus.

And then **supplication**—asking for small and big things, trusting, hoping.

"I mostly just talk to Him like I would if He were sitting on my bed," I said one night.

"I talk to Him like He's invisible air," she replied, snorting. "But yeah… I think He listens."

"He does," I said, and I believed it more than ever.

She'd leave my room after those talks a little lighter. Not healed. But healing, that was enough. It was my job to pray for her, not fix her.

And through it all, the days turned to weeks. The rhythm of faith wasn't easy. There were still hard days, draining classes, lab deadlines. But there was also quality. Depth. Richness.

Before, my life had been shiny on the outside but hollow at the core. Now it had layers. Academics. Music. God.

One night, I sent Zeb a message out of the blue. I had just finished a devotional on Psalm 42, and I needed someone to share it with.

Me: "My soul is downcast, but I will yet praise Him. Psalm 42:5. I love how David always ends with hope."

Zeb: "He wrestles, but he always worships. That's what I'm learning."

Me: "Same. That hope? It's like oxygen; I NEED IT ASAP!!"

Zeb: "God really be giving CPR when we're spiritually flatlining lol"

Me: "Stop but yes."

Zeb: "I'm proud of you, Meda."

Me: "For what?"

Zeb: "For seeking Him. For growing. For being light to others."

Me: "That's you too, Zeb. You're that for me."

There was a pause. Then his next text came.

Zeb: "You wanna come to the art room after my award thing Friday? Thought we could do a thank-you sketch session."

Me: "I'd love that."

Chapter 84: Becoming the Doer

PLAYLIST: ONLY U BY AARON COLE X TERRIAN

Amerei POV

It was a quiet morning. I hadn't heard from Merrick in a while, not that I was expecting to, or wanting to. Odessa's brother was still working on dismantling his little empire, brick by brick.

And me?

I was just trying to pass macroeconomics without combusting.

Classes were still a pain, but at least I had routine.

- Journal in the morning.
- Lecture.
- Pray with Mita if I see her in the dorm before we head out for class.
- Catch Odessa between her five million internships.
- And maybe scribble some Bible notes during lunch when I can.
- AND get prayer lessons for Meda

Prayer was still tricky. I'd never felt like I was doing it "right," even when my friends said there wasn't a right way. It felt like trying to talk to someone I couldn't see or hear, and I didn't want to sound stupid. But Mita gave me tips. Kaz did, too. Meda even sent me a screenshot of a prayer outline she found in some Christian blog she follows now. I was surrounded, gently, by people who weren't trying to change me but were just inviting me into something more.

Kazuya was still my Thursday joy. Calligraphy club hadn't lost its charm, and neither had he. Our walks back to my dorm had unintentionally become my favorite part of the week.

Like last Thursday:

"You know," Kaz had said, nudging my shoulder as we strolled under the streetlamps, "your brush stroke is getting better. You almost spelled 'eternal' without it looking like 'eggplant.'"

"Almost? Wow. Thanks for the wild confidence boost, Kaz."

"I'm just here to keep you humble."

"Humble is overrated," I shot back. "I think pride builds character. Just ask any cat."

"It doesn't, trust me" He laughed. "I bet if I challenged you to write Psalm 23 in cursive kanji, you'd start foaming at the mouth."

"I already have. That's why I avoid mirrors."

We kept walking, playful jabs tossed between us like frisbees in a windstorm. He never pushed. Never asked more than I could give. But he listened. And for someone like me, that was everything.

The Christian club had also, surprisingly, become one of my favorite places. It wasn't preachy. It wasn't stuffy. It was people. Laughing, studying, asking real questions. Messy, curious, honest. Like me.

This week, Ruth stood in front of the circle of bean bags and scattered chairs with her Bible open and eyes bright.

"Alright, fam. Today's teaching: 'Becoming the Doer,'" she said, flipping pages. "We're going to dive into James 1:22-24."

I opened my Bible slowly, still new to this whole page-flipping thing. Kaz sat beside me, already there. *Show off.*

"Let's read it together," Ruth continued.

'But be doers of the word, and not hearers only, deceiving yourselves. For if anyone is a hearer of the word and not a doer, he is like a man observing his natural face in a mirror; for he observes himself, goes away, and immediately forgets what kind of man he was.'

Ruth leaned forward.

"Okay, let's break this down like we're five."

I smiled. These were my favorite parts.

"So, imagine you look in the mirror, right? You see jam on your chin. Clear as day. But instead of wiping it off, you walk away, acting like you're clean. That's what it's like to hear what God says—like, love your neighbor, be honest, forgive—and then do the total opposite."

She paused. "We can't just be *informed*. We've got to be *transformed*. It's not about perfection. It's about application."

I scribbled fast in my journal. That made sense.

Then she flipped to 1 Peter 5. "Now this chapter—it's for the ones feeling overwhelmed."

She read aloud:

'Cast all your anxiety on Him because He cares for you.' (verse 7)

"This verse right here is a warm blanket," she pointed out. "God doesn't expect you to carry everything. Not your trauma, your pressure, your shame, your fears, none of it. If He said 'cast it,' He meant *throw it with force*. Not set it gently. Not half-surrender it. **THROW IT.**"

"And most importantly, leave it there. Many times we as believers carry our problems to God to set them down, but when we finish talking to him about it and asking for help, we take it right back up and continue through life with the same burdens he told us to leave to him. STOP THAT." Ruth said

"How can you leave them there and not pick it up?" someone asked,

"Great question, Christina." Ruth acknowledged. Any time that over-whelming thought comes, you can outwardly say that 'I gave this to God, and he is handling it' and say to God, 'This is a thought coming to me; please take it.' Distract yourselves with something else, a hobby, going outside, having talks and walks, or even going on a run with God. Meet up with people in your community or church family because it helps, but Most of all, Worship and read the word of God, trust me."

My chest swelled. I looked sideways. Kaz had his eyes closed, just listening. Absorbing. I wanted to ask if he really believed that—that you could just hand over your pain.

Then came 1 John. The entire chapter.

Ruth took her time.

"Let recap a chapter," she said

'Beloved, do not believe every spirit, but test the spirits, whether they are of God...' **(1 John 4:1)**

"This," she said, pointing to the page, "is how you don't get duped. You have to test what you hear. Is it loving? Is it aligned with Scripture? Does it reflect Jesus?"

'He who does not love does not know God, for God is love.' **(1 John 4:8)**

Ruth let that one sit in the air.

"Y'all, it's not complicated. No love = no God. Period. But real love? It's patient. It's kind. It shows up. It tells the truth."

I looked down at my lap. That hit something in me. Something still healing. Something still raw.

'There is no fear in love; but perfect love casts out fear...' **(1 John 4:18)**

"God's love doesn't manipulate you. Doesn't scare you into obedience. It casts out fear, pushes it out, similar to how light drives out darkness."

That reminder that there is still peace. That breath of something deeper.

Something true.

After the session ended, we walked back in a group—Mita, Meda, Kaz,

Zebedee, Anika, Zyran, Ethan. A *ragtag fellowship of thinkers, fighters, and questioners.* At the student union exit, Zebedee and Meda veered off together, chatting softly. Ethan walked Anika to her car as usual. Mita and Zyran were already ahead.

Kaz and I trailed behind.

"Any questions from tonight?" he asked.

"Not much," I said. "But my brain needs to defrag."

He chuckled. "Fair. You free tomorrow?"

"Yeah."

"Wanna do what we did last week?"

"I'm in."

"Up for The Chronicles of Narnia?" Mita asked as soon as I came through the door.

I grinned. "I'll order the food."

And that night, while Mita and I were 45 mins in, Meda came in, I opened the blanket, and she curled in right beside me

When we finished our movie night, I volunteered to pray before bed this.

"Okay... Jesus... I'm starting to understand this whole thing............. But thanks. For this. For them. For now. For everything......"

Chapter 85: The Weight of Joy

The campus was alive with spring's breath, branches budding, sun filtering through new leaves, laughter echoing from the dorm courtyards. It was the kind of warmth Amerei hadn't expected to feel by the end of the semester.

Finals were approaching fast, and the atmosphere was equal parts stressed and electric. But unlike the girl who had dragged herself through midterms on the brink of falling apart, Amerei had changed.

No, she hadn't just changed.

She had *healed*.

Not completely. Not perfectly. But truthfully. And that made all the difference.

Her schedule was still full: group projects, financial analysis reviews, flashcards, and caffeine-fueled nights, but now, she studied with peace in her chest instead of dread. There were no new wounds. Just faded ones, wrapped in grace. The spiral of pain she'd once felt caught in had been interrupted by friendship, by truth, and quietly, by Jesus.

Her journal pages were now filled with more prayers than pain. Her favorite pen no longer bled her shame into ink. Instead, she recorded scripture verses, half-formed prayers, and quiet revelations she never expected to understand—let alone live out.

Merrick had blocked her.

The text came two weeks before finals. Short. Final.

Merrick XO: *"I think we both need space. I wish you the best."*
Then silence.

And oh, what a *beautiful* silence it was.

She remembered staring at the screen, waiting for dread, for anger, for the familiar terror to rise.

But instead, tears welled for a different reason. Relief.

She had prayed—truly prayed—and God *answered once again*. She hadn't needed to fight. Hadn't needed to expose herself. He just… disappeared. No more manipulation. No more control. No more lies. No more text messages.

The girls had screamed when they heard. Odessa cried. Mita thanked God. Meda said it was the loudest "Thank You, Jesus" she'd ever whispered during lab.

And Kaz? He'd hugged her with such quiet gentleness, it almost shattered her.

That weekend, they went out together—all of them. A final break before finals. They dressed up, ate too much dessert, and took too many blurry selfies. Amerei wore white. Mita joked that it matched her new beginning.

Kaz stuck close, not too close, but close enough to notice when she needed water, when she needed space, or just someone to stand beside her in the noise.

They hadn't labeled anything. And that was okay. Amerei wasn't sure she wanted to. Not yet.

She liked the way they *were*. Gentle. Safe. Full of laughter and shared silence and inside jokes from their Thursday calligraphy club. She loved his ability to make her feel seen without being exposed, held without being caged.

When they walked back that night, shoes in hand and glitter from Mita's dress trailing on the sidewalk, Kaz quietly said, "You're really glowing, Erei."

She looked at him and smiled, not with her mouth, but with her whole soul.

"I feel… free," she said.

And she meant it.

Her relationship with God wasn't perfect. But it was real. Every question, every doubt, every whisper of prayer… she was learning that God didn't ask for performance. He just wanted her heart.

She was praying more. Asking more. Trusting more. Slowly, but surely, she was rebuilding a life with Christ at the center.

Sometimes she'd cry during worship, even if she didn't know why. Sometimes she'd sit in silence with a verse for hours. Sometimes she'd write "God, I don't know what to say" in her journal and still feel Him near anyway.

She had peace now. *Real peace.* The kind she used to think was fake. The kind that Meda and Mita used to talk about, and she'd scoff at under her breath.

And what she didn't have? She was learning to cast onto God, especially her fear about how her family would react.

She hadn't told them yet.

She didn't know how to explain what had happened to her, what had been done to her, and what God had *done for her.*

But she didn't need to have all the words right now.

She would pray. She would live differently. And maybe one day, they'd see the light in her and follow it back to its source for themselves.

Until then, she had her people.

She had Mita, who prayed out loud so she could fall asleep… joke of course

She had Meda, who researched verses with her like it was for a final exam.

She had Odessa, who made her laugh in the middle of breakdowns.

And she had Kaz, who showed up even when she didn't ask him to.

But most of all, she had Christ.

And that was more than enough.

As finals approached, she still had stress. Still had long nights. But now, her heart didn't carry it alone.

Every weight she carried had been replaced with something new.

Hope.

Hope that didn't deny the darkness she came from but declared, loudly, that she didn't belong there anymore.

Amerei stood outside in line for the room of her first final exam, heart racing, fingers wrapped around her favorite pen. She took a breath, looked up at the sky, and whispered, "Thank You."

Then she stepped forward, showed her ID before entering the examination room, and took her seat.

She was not alone in this life.

Not anymore.

Chapter 86: The Unshakable Ground

The halls of the hospital buzzed softly with the kind of steady rhythm Andromeda had grown used to: nurses murmuring reports, machines beeping in carefully spaced intervals, and the click of her loafers against linoleum floors. It was a tempo she had come to match: calm, quick, and relentless.

Her final clinical visit of the semester was wrapping up.

She carried her clipboard with ease now, her once-neatly pressed scrubs slightly wrinkled from hours of movement, her hair pinned up with strands falling loose—but she wore them like a badge of honor of the *three G's*. Growth. Grit. God's grace. Well, four G's, but who's counting?

She had survived a semester that tried to stretch her until she broke, but never quite succeeded.

Walking into the patient's room for the last time that day with the doctor she was shadowing, she greeted them with a warm, gentle smile, just as she had learned to do: "Hi, I'm Med student Tursyn . I'll be with Doctor Hills to observe."

The patient, a child no older than eight, smiled back. The little girl's fingers gripped a faded stuffed rabbit, and despite the IV taped to her arm, she had that same hope in her eyes Meda had seen in so many others. Children had a strange way of trusting: fully, openly, even in pain.

It reminded her of how Jesus told his followers to come like a child.

She had always admired that, but now she understood it better. There was power in surrender. In trusting the One who knew more, saw more, and held more than she ever could.

Later, after her rounds ended and charts were filed, Andromeda stepped outside into the crisp air, the sun setting in a splash of pink and fire. Her phone buzzed with a text from Zeb:

Zeb: "How's my favorite almost-doctor?"

Meda: "Scrubbed and done. Time for finals."

Zeb: "You got this. God's already ahead of you."

She smiled at that. Putting her phone away and making her way to her car, she knew that's what peace felt like now. Not an absence of chaos, but the presence of God *in* the chaos.

The weeks leading to finals had been a whirlwind. Her planner, still color-coded, was filled with scribbled Bible verses alongside study blocks and deadlines. Psalm 46:5 had become her anchor:

"God is within her, she will not fall; God will help her at the break of day."

She wrote it on post-it notes and stuck it on her bathroom mirror, inside her laptop case, and on the inside of her phone case. It wasn't superstition. It was a reminder: she didn't walk alone.

Not anymore.

She remembered how far she'd come.

The Andromeda who used to measure her worth by grades and performance, who used to bury every emotion under piles of textbooks—she still existed. But she was being transformed. Day by day.

And it all began with a quiet winter break, a boy with soft eyes and paint-stained hands, and a Savior she had ignored most of her life.

Now? She wasn't ignoring Him. She was leaning in.

The quiet time she carved out each morning between labs and lectures was no longer a checkbox. It was fuel, a drive to go on. She prayed before study sessions. Asked for discernment before exams. Worshiped softly while highlighting textbooks. She even helped Amerei learn how to pray.

They were all growing. Together.

Mita's faith became her support. Zeb's gentle questions stretched her thinking. And Amerei's journey to healing deepened her own trust that God really *does* rescue.

Andromeda wasn't perfect. But she was rooted.

As she made her way back to her dorm that evening, the buzz of students talking about finals filled the air like static. Some worried. Some overconfident. Andromeda?

She was ready.

Not because she had it all together.

But because she knew the One who held her future.

Her backpack felt lighter that night. Her heart did too. She passed the mirror in the lobby and caught a glimpse of herself. Same girl. Transformed spirit.

One full of truth.

Full of life.

Full of Jesus.

She entered her room, dropped her bag, and pulled out her Bible. With a soft breath and steady hands, she whispered, *"I trust You, Lord. Reveal to your servant what you want to be said. Silence every demonic voice, desires and thoughts, and in the name of Jesus, I silence my own flesh-led thoughts, desires, and feelings. Only the Holy Spirit speaks to me. Let your voice, Lord, be the only thing I hear, in Jesus' name, amen.*

Then she opened the Word and began.

<h1 style="text-align:center">Letters From Main character</h1>

Letter from Amerei to the Reader:

Hi, beauties.

I don't know how you found your way here, to my story, but if you've made it this far, thank you. For listening. For sitting with me through the darkest parts. For not looking away when I shattered.

There were days I didn't think I'd make it. Nights where silence was louder than any scream, and all I could feel was brokenness pressing in from every side. I thought pain was all there would ever be. I thought maybe if I just disappeared, it would stop hurting.

But then, light, Jesus found his way into my broken heart and made it whole.

Through my friends. Through kindness I didn't think I deserved. Through laughter, and honest conversations, and someone just sitting beside me, saying, "I see you, I hear you, and I'm not leaving." And strangely, even through the prayers I didn't understand, the ones I secretly listened to every night. The ones that made my thoughts start to whisper, maybe there's more than this, *helped in this transformation.*

And now? I'm still healing. I still cry. I still flinch when certain memories knock on the door. But I also smile. I laugh. I journal. I pray. I hope.

I have not arrived to where the Lord has taken me. But I'm walking, one step at a time, toward a new life. Toward peace. Toward God.

So if you're reading this and you're hurting… if you've been silent, or scared, or scarred… I want you to know something:

You are not ruined.

You are not your trauma.

You are not alone.

And there is a God who sees every invisible wound, every tear you never let fall, every tear left unshed, every scream you swallowed, and He's not disgusted by you. He's not disappointed in you. Jesus near. Closer than you know.

Because Matthew 5:4 says, ***"blessed are those who mourn, for they will be comforted."***

You don't have to have it all figured out. You don't even have to be sure of anything yet.

Just breathe. Just survive. And when you're ready, whisper *help*. That's enough and he will come running.

With all my love,

—Amerei Galanis

Letter from Andromeda to the Reader:

Hey everyone.

Hope you are all doing well.

This is my letter to you, and I hope you see my heart in it and you'll be encouraged by it.

I used to think life was something you could control, hence why my school work was all: color-code, plan, fix, and perfect.

I believed that if I worked hard enough, did everything right, kept everything neat… I'd earn peace. Maybe even a bit of happiness and self-satisfaction.

But I got neither of those, safe to say that there wasn't any ounce of peace in my life. It was all a performance. And it never loved me back.

This journey, one you've just read, was the unlearning of that lie. It was the unraveling of the idea that I had to hold it all together. That I had to be my own savior. That faith was a weakness instead of an anchor.

It was uncomfortable to change that part of me. I won't lie. Letting go of the idea that I had to earn love, even God's love, was terrifying, becauseifIcan'tearnitthatmeantIhad nothingtogivenothingtoofferandifIha dnothingtoofferIwasinadequateandIdon'tlikebeinginadequatebecausebei nginadquateisnotbetterthanbeingnothing. But in that letting go, I found something stronger than striving.

I found Jesus.

Not the abstract idea of Him. Not the cold religion I'd filed away with my childhood memories. I found the Jesus who sat beside me in a quiet art studio. Who heard every whispered fear and unanswered question. Who saw me and said, *I want you as you are, not as who you pretend to be.*

If you're like me, analytical, guarded, logical, fact-driven, I get it. Trust doesn't come easy. Maybe even belief in something you can't see feels hard. But I promise, it's worth exploring. Not for the rules. Not for appearances. But because the truth, cause the real truth, is more freeing than any success or perfection could ever be.

So to you, wherever you are in your story, I want you to hear this from someone who was there too:

You are not too complicated for God.

You are not too late. You're not too skeptical. You're not too far.

Ask questions. Wrestle. Doubt if you have to. But don't close the door. Because on the other side of that wrestle is a love more steady than the ground under your feet.

I'm praying you find what I found.

With grace,

—Andromeda "Meda" Tursyn

<h1 style="text-align:center">Author's Message</h1>

Every single person, no matter how clean they look on the outside, has a past. A lifestyle. A mindset. A heart that, at some point, was far from God.

Some carry it quietly. Some wear it openly. But all of us, everyone, fall short. And yet, none of us are beyond the reach of Jesus Christ.

You are not too far gone.

Salvation isn't a reward for the perfect. It's not earned by checking religious boxes or pretending to have it all together. It is a *gift*. Free. Unshakable. Blood-bought.

What is salvation?

It is rescue. It is deliverance from the judgment we deserve because of sin and entrance into eternal life with God through Jesus.

Salvation means this:

Jesus, the Son of God/ God the Son, came to this world fully God and fully man. He lived without sin, died on a cross to take the punishment we deserved, and rose again, defeating death so we could be reconciled to God. Through *Him alone*, we gain forgiveness, peace, mercy, and the unbreakable promise of life after death.

The Bible says in **Romans 10:9**:

"If you declare with your mouth, 'Jesus is Lord,' and believe in your heart that God raised Him from the dead, you will be saved."

It's that simple. But it's also that real.

And His love? It's not fickle or earned. It's **agape,** the Greek word for unconditional, self-sacrificing love. The kind of love that lays down everything for you… even when you're running in the opposite direction.

You don't need to clean yourself up before coming to God. Come broken. Come confused. Come tired. Just come. He meets you exactly where you are and loves you too much to leave you there.

If you've ever wondered if your past disqualifies you, it *doesn't.*

If you've ever felt like you'll never be "good enough," you're right. *That's why Jesus came.*

This book wasn't written to push religion. It was written to tell the truth: **There is a way out. There is a way home. And His name is Jesus.**

— *The Author*

Author's Encouragement

Are You Ready?

If something stirred in your heart as you read...

If you've felt the weight of shame, confusion, guilt, or emptiness...

If you've been searching for peace, for answers, for something real—

Know this: Jesus is not far. He is near. And He is calling you.

You don't need a perfect past.

You don't need a religious résumé.

You only need a willing heart that says: "I'm ready to surrender. I want to be made new."

If that's you, you can begin your walk with Jesus right now.

A Simple Prayer to Begin with God:

Lord Jesus,

I believe You are the Son of God.

I believe You died on the cross for my sins and rose again to give me new life.

I know I've sinned, and I need Your forgiveness.

Today, I turn from my old life and give You my heart.

Be my Savior. Be my Lord.

I trust You.

Teach me how to walk with You, day by day.
Thank You for loving me before I ever loved You.
In Jesus' name, amen.

Now What?

If you prayed that sincerely, *you belong to Jesus now.*
You've just stepped into a relationship that will never be taken from you.
Your next steps?

- **Tell someone you can trust.** Don't walk this out alone.
- **Get a Bible.** Start with the book of John. It's where Jesus speaks clearly and personally.
- **Find a church.** Not a perfect one, but a place where the truth of the Bible is taught and Jesus is loved.
- **Pray.** Talk to God like you would a trusted friend. He hears every word.

And most of all...

Don't stop.

You will grow. You will stumble. You will get back up again.
God is not looking for perfection. He's looking for your heart.
And now, He's holding it in His hands.

If this chapter became *your new beginning*, I'm celebrating with you.
Welcome home.

You are not alone anymore. You never were.

— *The Author*

Thank you all to all who have reached this far in the book, and I hope you were encouraged by these stories and will remain on this journey with me.

First, I would love to take a moment to honor my father, my best friend and Savior, Jesus Christ, for helping me along this journey, encouraging me, and giving me the gift of writing books, even though this was not even a prior passion of mine. I want to show my appreciation to Jesus Christ, as this series is a Spirit-led series, making him the main author of these books. I want to give you Jesus all the glory, all the praise, and all the honor for being the best Father God, not only to me but to all his children. Hallelujah to the most God, Alpha and Omega, the beginning and the end. Our soon-coming King.

I would also love to thank my family for encouraging me on this path and keeping me joyful, and their continuous support along the way, in every step, for believing and trusting God on this path he has for me. Thank you, God, for my parents, and I thank my entire family for their love and support through the hard time in my life whlist writing these books.

I also want to give a huge thanks to two of my street team members, Christina and Shelby, for being amazing members of my team and loyal associates. They are supportive and up for help anytime, and any author would be blessed to have them on their team. But I also want to shout out all my street team members of the Journey of the Heart Street team. And if you want to join, send me a DM on Instagram @samantha_joth

To Lumi, my editor, thank you for stepping into this story with care, precision, and a gentleness that matched the weight of what these pages carry. You saw what I was trying to say and helped me say it better. That is a gift not everyone has. I am grateful it found its way to this book.

Thank you to everyone who helped and participated in the making of the book and my series thus far.

Book 3 TEASER CHAPTER

Odessa

I was halfway through a DIY facial, sipping iced coffee in one hand, picking at the homemade face mask checking if was dry with the other to see if I could remove it to apply my cleanser all while listening to a true crime podcast in the background—peak moment, if you ask me—it really was that was until someone decide to interrupt it. The buzzing from my phone was so loud and sudden that I almost spilled my coffee because I had placed it on the new side table Noah had gotten me at the end of last semester, while I was away in my off-campus apartment. He said it was a '*congratulations, you made it through hell and back*' gift. I don't know whether to be grateful that he was happy I passed my classes or to question whether he thinks school was so bad it felt like hell. It was, don't get me wrong, but I was still second-guessing his reasoning. The buzzing on my phone continued, its screen lighting up to show a caller ID for an *unknown number*. I almost ignored it. Almost.

But something in me—intuition, boredom, divine intervention? Whatever you want to call it—said *pick up*.

"Hello?" I said it cautiously, but crisply enough to ward off the potential scammer.

There was a pause on the other side of the line before a voice, soft but slightly rushed, rang through the other end. "Hello, is this Odessa?"

"Yes, it is," I said, sitting up straighter, concerned as to why this stranger knew my name and I didn't know theirs, nor did I recognize their voice.

"Hi sweetie, it's Reed's mom. I hope I didn't catch you at a bad time. I was trying to reach Mita, but her phone seems to be off. She gave me a few other numbers to call—said that they belong to the rest of the friend group, so I'm giving you a ring."

I blinked. Reed's mom? Giving me *a ring* on a random Wednesday? *Why—?*

"I just wanted to tell you… Reed is awake."

Silence.

Not because the line cut out—because my brain did, because when she told me who she was, I was preparing myself for the worst, even though the doctors did say there were improvements in his condition.

"He's awake," she repeated, her voice warm now, trembling just a bit, hardly able to contain her joy even over the phone. "He woke up this morning. He's sleeping now, but one of the first things he did was ask about you girls. About all of you."

My mouth was open but empty. My heart had jumped into my throat. I was still trying to process what was said two conversations ago.

"I know it's your summer break, and you girls might have your plans," she went on, "but I was thinking of letting it be a surprise for all of you girls when you get back; however, Reed needs to help." That had me raising a brow because what help could Reed need that I could give? He was at a hospital, where all the help he needed was provided by professionals trained to do just that.

Reed's mom went on, "He's been planning something with the nurses for when you all come. But I thought—maybe Mita at first, but since she is unavailable by phone, as are the others, perhaps you could help pull it off. I know the nurses adore him because he is the little miracle patient, and they would do it for him, but they are already busy enough as it is, so I wanted to ask, hoping one of you was willing to record it for him. I just… I thought it would be best if one of you knew at least." I heard the uncertainty in her voice, making me want to reach out to her and give her a big hug.

She was just a mother, both happy to see her son awake again and wanting to give him everything he wanted, but at the same time not wanting to inconvenience anyone in the process.

She is just as sweet as Mita had described her

"Thank you," I said, voice low, hoping she would hear my sincerity through the phone.

I fully convince myself that I did indeed hear a sigh of relief on the other end, "Sorry to just drop that on you and leave, but I'm in a bit of a rush. But we'll stay in touch, alright? Bye for now."

Click.

Just like that, the line went dead.

And I was still frozen over the fact that Reed was awake.

I was still in my room. Still wearing my fluffy robe. Still with exfoliant drying unevenly on one cheek. Still planning for a smooth, slow summer as I had *earned* it.

Well. Apparently, life had *other* plans.

I sat back on my bed, blinked at the ceiling, then whispered the only logical thing that came to mind:

"Well… damn."

Because really—what else do you say when someone calls to tell you your friend who's been in a coma for almost three years just *woke up* like it's a casual weather update?

I tossed my phone onto the duvet, stood up, and began pacing, because pacing helped. It always helped. But even my runway-length bedroom couldn't contain the swirl of thoughts spinning behind my lashes.

What was I supposed to do now?

Mita was off the grid—again—probably in one of her "prayer caves" or whatever she called them, plus she was hosting both Andromeda and Amerei for the summer break, and if she is off the grid, so were they. Apparently, none of them were too eager to go home this year.

Shocker.

Andromeda's case? That was an Obvious. Her family practically handed out pressure and trauma like party favors. Amerei, on the other hand, didn't say it directly, but I could tell. Home wasn't home anymore. Not since the whole faith thing.

Her parents are agnostic, and so was she until she had gone full undercover faith trooper mode over the past semester. Cross necklace and everything. Respect. But… yikes.

So instead of confrontation, she camped out at Mita's. Church, peace, purpose. The Holy Trinity of Girl Summer, apparently.

And me?

I stayed home. Not because I didn't love my girls, but because I had an *internship* to snag this summer. A Resume to be made gold. Professional networking to dominate and expand said network. To build professional relationships and cultivate those contacts before fully tackling the industry, all that and more is on my bucket list this summer. They are all functionally identical, but be that as it may, future Odessa will thank me for this. Besides, someone had to keep the power suits warm and the iced lattes flowing.

I wasn't exactly *church club material.*

I had other things to think about.

Especially now that Reed was awake.

Reed.

The same Reed who made us laugh so hard we couldn't breathe. Who carried Mita's snacks like they were sacred cargo. Who once convinced me to try pineapple on pizza just to "expand my worldview." The Reed who laid unmoving in a hospital bed for three years.

He was awake.

Asking for *us.*

This was going to be a wild year for sure, I can feel it.

And something told me—it was only just beginning.

Notes

CHAPTER 75: A LOVE WORTH TESTING

1   No one has seen God the Father, but we have seen God the son which is Jesus Christ. And inside of believers dwells God the Spirit, which is called the Holy Spirit; they are three in one. JESUS is the word of God the Father, and the holy spirit is the characteristics of God the Father, not the same, but still three in one.